GREAT TALES
AND POEMS OF
EDGAR ALLAN POE

Edgar Allan Poe

Supplementary materials written by Charles Brower
Series edited by Cynthia Brantley Johnson

SIMON & SCHUSTER PAPERBACKS
NEW YORK LONDON TORONTO SYDNEY

Simon & Schuster Paperbacks
A Division of Simon & Schuster, Inc.
1230 Avenue of the Americas
New York, NY 10020

Supplementary materials copyright © 2007 by Simon & Schuster, Inc.

This Simon & Schuster paperback edition June 2009

SIMON & SCHUSTER PAPERBACKS and colophon are registered trademarks of Simon & Schuster, Inc.

For information regarding special discounts for bulk purchases, please contact Simon & Schuster Special Sales at 1-866-506-1949 or business@simonandschuster.com.

The Simon & Schuster Speakers Bureau can bring authors to your live event. For more information or to book an event, contact the Simon & Schuster Speakers Bureau at 1-866-248-3049 or visit our website at www.simonspeakers.com.

Cover illustration by Marco Ventura
Cover design by Jeanne M. Lee

Manufactured in the United States of America

12 11 10 9 8 7 6 5 4

ISBN 978-1-4165-3476-1

Contents

TALES

POEMS

CONTENTS

Introduction

Great Tales and Poems of Edgar Allan Poe: Dreams Within a Dream

Edgar Allan Poe died penniless and largely unappreciated, and in America he was mostly ignored for the latter half of the nineteenth century. But popular culture has been good to Poe; his stories and poems have been adapted into movies, inspired whole genres of novels, and been quoted and parodied in countless television shows and paperback thrillers. Once he was considered an eccentric minor figure, a genius who was constitutionally unable to achieve real success. But modern readers of detective stories, gothic and horror novels, and science fiction consider Poe a pioneer. The annual awards for excellence given by the Mystery Writers of America, the Edgars, are named after Poe in recognition of his central importance in creating the first ratiocinative (i.e., methodical and logical) detective, C. Auguste Dupin.

Poe's prose work in particular was written to capture the attention of a mass audience, at a time when there was great competition from other magazine journalists. His lurid imagination certainly made him stand out. Never one to moralize, unlike most of the writers of the day, Poe was interested solely in the aesthetic experience. He wrote about two sides of the life of the mind: the mind deranged by guilt, desire, or loss; and the rational mind that can impose order on a seemingly incomprehensible world. Although today Poe is treasured mostly by lovers of his gothic sensibility, he also had a sly sense of humor and a penchant for put-ons that remind us not to take even his most morbid writing completely seriously.

The Life and Work of Edgar Allan Poe

Edgar Allan Poe was born in Boston on January 19, 1809, into a family of actors. His father, David Poe, disappeared from his life before Poe was old enough to remember him, and his mother, Elizabeth, died shortly before Edgar's third birthday. Edgar; his older brother, Henry; and his sister, Rosalie, were taken in by different families. Edgar was raised in Richmond, Virginia, in the home of John Allan, a local merchant, and his wife, who had no children of their own. When Allan moved his family to England in 1815 in order to expand his mercantile business, Edgar attended several boarding schools during the five-year stay. Allan's British business endeavor ultimately failed, and the family returned to Richmond in 1820.

Despite the family's financial straits, Poe received the best education available in Richmond. He was a prizewinning scholar and an athlete, successful in school if not exactly popular. He attended school with the sons of some of the most prestigious families in Virginia, but his status as an orphan and the ward of John Allan, who never formally adopted Edgar, separated him from his peers, at least in his own mind. In 1826, at age seventeen, Poe entered the University of Virginia to study ancient and modern languages. When he racked up several thousand dollars in gambling and other debts during that first year at school—the result of his determination to present himself as a young man of means—his relationship with his foster father, already strained, reached the breaking point. Allan refused to send Poe back to the university in the spring, and Poe left the house, writing to Allan, "My determination is at length taken . . . to find some place in this wide world, where I will be treated— not as *you* have treated me." After complaining of what he considered to be his second-class status in the Allan household, Poe closed the letter with a request for money to get him started in Boston. In April 1827, he headed north on his own. It is unknown to historians whether or not he had assistance in this venture from Allan.

By the end of May that same year, Poe had enlisted in the army under an assumed name. He had also published his first book of poetry, *Tamerlane and Other Poems*, which he signed "By a Bostonian." In the army he trained as part of an artillery battery; over a period of eighteen months he was stationed in Boston Harbor, at Fort Moultrie on Sullivan's Island in South Carolina (the setting for his story "The Gold-Bug"), and at Fortress Monroe in Virginia. Poe rose to the rank of sergeant major but was dissatisfied with army life. In letters he sought the help of John Allan in arranging a discharge rather than serving his full five-year term of enlistment, in order to enter West Point. While waiting to enter the academy, he published a second collection of poems, *Al Aaraaf, Tamerlane, and Minor Poems,* in December 1829.

Also in 1829, Poe went to Baltimore to visit the branch of his family that his brother, Henry, had been living with: his grandmother, his aunt Maria Clemm, and her children, Henry and Virginia. His career at West Point turned out to be short-lived; another financial dispute with his foster father led to a renewed, more or less complete estrangement between the two, and Poe resolved to get himself court-martialed by disobeying regulations. He was formally discharged from military service in March 1831. While awaiting dismissal he prepared another volume of verse, *Poems by Edgar A. Poe. Second Edition,* for publication, drumming up subscriptions among his fellow cadets to pay for the book.

Poe returned to Baltimore to live with his grandmother and the Clemms in the spring of 1831. Over the next several years, while barely scraping together a living from a series of odd jobs, he published his first stories in the Philadelphia *Saturday Courier* and the Baltimore *Saturday Visiter.* Poe's story "Ms. Found in a Bottle" won a first prize of fifty dollars in a literary contest sponsored by the *Visiter* in October 1833. In March of the following year, John Allan, who had mostly rebuffed Poe's occasional attempts to contact him in the years since he had left West Point, died; he did not provide for Poe in his will. Winning the *Visiter* prize, though, led Poe to a promising association with a Richmond magazine, the *Southern Literary Messenger*, which published his stories and reviews and, in August 1835, took him on as a staff editor.

Meanwhile, with the death of Poe's grandmother in July 1835, the Clemms lost their sole means of support. When Maria Clemm wrote to her nephew that she and Virginia were to be taken into the home of another relative, Poe became distraught. His life with the Clemms had been the closest thing to a loving family life he had known. Promising that he could support them with his position at the *Messenger*, he proposed to marry Virginia and to bring her and her mother to Richmond. Virginia was thirteen at the time. They likely married in secret in Baltimore in September 1835, and in May 1836 took out a second marriage license in Richmond, on which it was claimed that Virginia was "of the full age of twenty-one years." Poe wrote prolifically for the *Messenger* during this time, including hundreds of reviews that frequently offended the literary establishment of the day with their cutting judgments. By the end of 1836, after disputes with *Messenger* owner T. W. White, Poe was again out of work.

Poe relocated to New York City in February 1837, seeking new prospects in the publishing capital of the still-young United States. Since New York was also at the center of a financial depression that afflicted the country beginning a few months later, it was a particularly unpromising time and place to attempt to support a household. Poe, his wife, and mother-in-law lived on bread and molasses for weeks at a time. Little is known about what he did in New York over the following year. He published two stories and wrote his longest work, the short novel *The Narrative of Arthur Gordon Pym*. Around the time *Pym* was published, in July 1838, Poe moved his family again, this time to Philadelphia, where they lived for the next five years.

In the spring of 1839, Poe entered into a partnership with actor and playwright William Burton to serve as coeditor of a new periodical, *Burton's Gentleman's Magazine*. Poe wrote most of the reviews that appeared in the magazine over the next year and published some of his best-known stories: "Ligeia," "The Fall of the House of Usher," and "William Wilson." These stories appeared along with twenty-two others in Poe's first collection of short fiction, the two-volume *Tales of the Grotesque and Arabesque*, which was published in 1840. He also attempted to start his own magazine, even soliciting subscriptions, but was unable to raise enough money. In late 1840 *Burton's* was sold and became *Graham's Magazine*, and Poe stayed on as editor.

Poe's editorial positions were inevitably short-lived. He struggled with alcoholism and gained a reputation for unreliability, although he contributed prodigiously to the periodicals for which he wrote. In *Graham's* he published "A Descent into the Maelström" and "The Murders in the Rue Morgue," among other stories and many reviews. He had his greatest success when he published "The Raven" in the New York *Evening Mirror* in January 1845, which made him one of the most famous poets of his time. Yet he was preoccupied with his inability to care for Virginia, who was suffering from tuberculosis. The New York newspaper editors, who sometimes waged contentious wars of words with Poe, published appeals for donations on his family's behalf. After Virginia's death

in January 1847, Poe's health collapsed. He was unable
to appear in court for the libel suit he brought against the
owners of the New York *Mirror*, who had published al-
legations of fraud and embezzlement against him;
though he won the suit, he received about two hundred
dollars in damages, considerably less than the five thousand dollars he claimed.

Poe had recovered somewhat by the end of 1847,
when he published the poem "Ulalume" in the *American
Review*. In February 1848, a few days after the first anniversary of Virginia's death, he gave a public lecture on
"The Universe," which became the basis for his philosophical treatise *Eureka*, published in July. A pseudosci-
entific speculative essay about the "Heart Divine" that
remakes the universe with each throb, *Eureka* was generally derided by critics (whom Poe thought misunderstood it) and failed to make much of an impact. Poe
wooed a series of women during this time, sometimes
dedicating verse to them, but the courtships tended to
end badly. He attempted suicide when his affair with
Sarah Helen Whitman failed; she broke off their engagement in January 1849 when he started drinking
again.

Poe made another attempt to revive his literary career, publishing new stories and giving lectures. His
health was deteriorating, however, and friends reported
that he was suffering from occasional bouts of hallucina-
tions. He returned to Richmond for the first time in
more than ten years, seeking money for another magazine project, the *Stylus*. While there, he renewed his acquaintance with Elmira Royster Shelton, his childhood
sweetheart whose family had kept them apart years be-

fore. She was now a widow, and she had never completely gotten over her youthful affection for Poe. When he left Richmond for business on September 27, 1849, Poe believed that he and Elmira had become engaged.

But Poe never returned to Richmond. A week later, on October 3, he turned up in Baltimore, under circumstances that will likely always be a mystery. He was apparently drunk and delirious, and wearing ill-fitting, shabby clothes that did not seem to be his. He lingered in a hospital for four days before succumbing to a fever, possibly encephalitis. He was never coherent enough to explain what had happened during the week he had vanished. He was buried in Baltimore, attended by a small group of mourners.

Historical and Literary Context of Poe's Writings

The Young Republic

Poe lived from 1809 until 1849, a turbulent early period in American history after the nation gained its independence and before regional and political tensions exploded into civil war. He was a proponent of "art for art's sake," and so he rarely engaged, at least directly, with the controversial issues of the day in his poems, stories, or criticism. But no American of the time could be unaffected by the rapid changes in the country, namely the westward expansion and the explosion of population of the cities of the Northeast. Poe was one of the many who came to these metropolitan centers—New York, Philadelphia, Boston, Baltimore—seeking fortune. He made a name for himself in his brief literary career, but as an adult he was plagued by the poverty that was common in the United States of the early nineteenth century. His circumstances are an example of how precarious life in the city could be at the time: Poverty contributed to his ill health and death at forty and to the early deaths of his mother, brother, and wife.

Some critics have argued that Poe's morbid fantasies, though frequently set in faraway places and a mythical timeless past, are psychological projections of the anxieties of the young United States: the pains of starvation and illness; the violence of urban crime and the threat of war; the grief of orphanhood and the loss of loved ones. If Walt Whitman was the nineteenth century's optimistic voice of the American dream, Poe was his nightmare counterpart. (Incidentally, Whitman was the only poet to attend the service when a memorial to Poe was dedicated in Baltimore in 1875.) At the same time, in his puzzle stories such as "The Murders in the Rue Morgue" and "The Gold-Bug" and in his literary criticism, he asserted the power of the rational mind to impose some sort of order on the chaos of life.

Romanticism

As a poet, Poe's role models were the English poets of the late eighteenth and early nineteenth century known as the Romantics. He was especially influenced by Samuel Taylor Coleridge, whose best-known poem, "The Rime of the Ancient Mariner," is a desolate maritime fantasy that Poe no doubt had in mind when he created the ghost ship of "Ms. Found in a Bottle." Coleridge was also known for his writings about poetry, which Poe drew from for his own theories of the poetic imagination in lectures and essays. In "Letter to Mr.— ——," written to the publisher Elam Bliss and published as the preface to Poe's 1831 collection *Poems*, he wrote: "In reading his poetry I tremble, like one who stands upon a volcano. . . ." Poe shared with Coleridge the ideas that poetry comes to the poet in dreams and visions, that poets should strive to attain beauty rather than truth, and that the most poetically beautiful subjects are sad ones.

Poe was born in the same year as Alfred Lord Tennyson, an English Romantic poet he admired. Tennyson lived until nearly the end of the nineteenth century, long enough to become *the* English poet of the Victorian era; Poe, on the other hand, died the year before the first great flowering of American Romanticism, known as the American Renaissance, began. And he was not acknowledged as much of an influence by great contributors to the American Renaissance such as Herman Melville, Nathaniel Hawthorne, Ralph Waldo Emerson (who once referred to Poe as "the jingle man"), and Whitman. Europeans were much more enthusiastic about Poe. Tennyson returned the compliments of his American admirer, calling him "the most original genius that America has produced." Charles Baudelaire, who translated Poe into French in Paris, was his great champion; in his magazine, Fyodor Dostoyevsky published Russian translations of the "strange, though enormously talented" Poe. Overseas he was widely appreciated for his fevered, dreamlike tales and poems—a morbid dark side to the Romantic celebration of the individual imagination.

Early American Literary Journalism

Poe was a widely recognized participant in the media wars of his day, the free-for-all competition among hundreds of American newspapers and magazines in the 1830s and 1840s. There were dozens of newspapers in New York City alone in the 1830s, all clamoring for the attention of a growing urban reading public. Especially given the lax copyright laws of the day, publishing books was not a viable way for writers of the time to make a living. Many of them supported themselves, and found a regular outlet for their writing, by editing newspapers or journals. Walt Whitman was an editor of several New York newspapers of the time, as were Margaret Fuller, John Greenleaf Whittier, and William Cullen Bryant. Among his fellow literary journalists, Poe earned a reputation as a biting critic. He was known, and in some circles held in contempt, for his attacks on fellow writers such as Theodore S. Fay (who Poe said wrote like a schoolboy) and Henry Wadsworth Longfellow. Poe took it upon himself to offer a comprehensive appraisal of the literary landscape of the time called "The Literati of New York City," which appeared in six parts in *Godey's Lady's Book* in May through October 1846. Not surprisingly, he was also on the receiving end of satire from rivals. James Russell Lowell, for example, in his "The Fable for the Critics," wrote: "Here comes Poe with his Raven, like Barnaby Rudge— / Three-fifths of him genius, and two-fifths sheer fudge; / Who talks like a book of iambs and pentameters, / In a way to make all men of common sense d—n metres. . . ."

Poe's pioneering gothic and detective stories were

written for magazine audiences. His greatest popular successes in his lifetime, "The Gold-Bug" and "The Raven," were introduced to the world in this format. And the essays he wrote for magazines—such as "The Poetic Principle" and "The Philosophy of Composition" (published in *Graham's Magazine* in April 1846), in which he gave a detailed description of the process he followed in writing "The Raven"—are essentially the earliest examples of literary criticism in the United States. Poe also wrote for less reputable periodicals than *Graham's*, though; his hoax account of a hot-air balloon crossing the Atlantic Ocean earned him more notoriety when it appeared in the *New York Sun*—a newspaper known for its sensationalist and frankly untrue stories—in April 1844.

CHRONOLOGY OF EDGAR ALLAN POE'S LIFE AND WORK

1809: Born January 19, Boston, Massachusetts.

1810: Poe's father, David, abandons the family and likely dies soon thereafter (death date uncertain).

1811: Poe's mother, Elizabeth, dies, December 8, leaving Edgar; his brother, Henry; and his sister, Rosalie, without support. Edgar is taken into the home of Richmond tobacco merchant John Allan and his wife, Frances.

1815–1820: Lives in England with the Allans, attending boarding schools while John Allan tries unsuccessfully to expand his business.

1825: Courts Sarah Elmira Royster, to whom he may have become engaged.

1826: Registers at the University of Virginia on February 14.

1827: After Allan refuses to allow Poe to continue his studies at the University of Virginia, he leaves home for Boston on April 3. Publishes first collection of poems, *Tamerlane and Other Poems*. Enlists in the U.S. Army under the name Edgar A. Perry.

1828: Rises to rank of sergeant major in the army before seeking a discharge in order to apply to attend West Point.

1829: Second collection of poems, *Al Aaraaf, Tamerlane, and Minor Poems*, is published in Baltimore.

1830: Enters West Point.

1831: Is court-martialed and leaves West Point. Moves to Baltimore and into the home of the Clemms, his grandmother, aunt, and cousins. His brother, Henry, also a Baltimore resident, dies, August 1. Poe's third collection of verse, *Poems by Edgar A. Poe. Second Edition*, is published in New York.

1833: Story "Ms. Found in a Bottle" wins Baltimore *Saturday Visiter* literary contest.

1834: Foster father, John Allan, dies on March 27, leaving Poe nothing in his will.

1835: Moves to Richmond to become an editor of the *Southern Literary Messenger,* in which he publishes stories and reviews that gain him a reputation as a caustic critic.

1836: On May 16, marries cousin Virginia Clemm, at the time thirteen years old.

1837: Resigns as editor of the *Messenger* and moves with his wife and aunt to New York City but is unable to find employment there.

1838: Moves with his family to Philadelphia; his novel *The Narrative of Arthur Gordon Pym* is published in July.

1839: Becomes an editor of *Burton's Gentleman's Maga-*

zine, writing reviews and publishing stories, including "The Fall of the House of Usher."

1840: Attempts unsuccessfully to found his own magazine, the *Penn*, and becomes editor of *Graham's Magazine*, as *Burton's* is renamed after changing owners. *Tales of the Grotesque and Arabesque* published in Philadelphia.

1841: Publishes "A Descent into the Maelström," "The Murders in the Rue Morgue," and other stories in *Graham's*.

1843: "The Gold Bug" wins literary contest sponsored by the Philadelphia *Dollar Newspaper*. *Prose Romances* published in Philadelphia.

1844: Returning to New York, Poe goes to work for the New York *Evening Mirror*.

1845: "The Raven" is published in the New York *Evening Mirror*, becoming an immediate popular success. Poe becomes editor of the *Broadway Journal* and then in October buys the newspaper himself with borrowed money.

1847: Virginia Poe dies of tuberculosis on January 30. Poe published "Ulalume" in the *American Review* at the end of the year.

1848: Continues lecturing and publishes a philosophical treatise, *Eureka*, in July.

1849: Becomes engaged to the now widowed Elmira Royster Shelton, a childhood sweetheart.

1849: Found in a delirious stupor in Baltimore on October 3 and dies on October 7. "The Bells" and "Annabel Lee" are published posthumously.

HISTORICAL CONTEXT OF
THE WRITINGS OF EDGAR ALLAN POE

1809: Abraham Lincoln is born.

1812–1815: War of 1812 with Great Britain results in the burning of Washington, D.C., in August 1814.

1819: University of Virginia founded.

1823: President James Monroe declares that nations in the Americas would be free from European colonization, later called the Monroe Doctrine.

1825: Erie Canal opens.

1831: Nat Turner leads slave rebellion in Virginia.

1832: Samuel Morse invents the telegraph.

1835: Alexis de Tocqueville publishes *Democracy in America*, his observations from his extensive travels in the United States.

1836: Battle of the Alamo.

1837: Victoria becomes queen of England. Financial panic in the United States causes widespread unemployment and bank closings.

1838–1839: Trail of Tears, the forced migration of the

Cherokee from Georgia to Oklahoma, resulting in the deaths of more than four thousand Indians.

1839: Louis Daguerre invents early form of photography.

1845: Texas and Florida become U.S. states. Potato famine in Ireland begins.

1846: War with Mexico (1846–1848); Smithsonian Institution is founded.

1847: Mormons establish Salt Lake City.

1848: Karl Marx and Friedrich Engels publish *The Communist Manifesto*; Women's Rights Convention in Seneca Falls, New York.

1849: California Gold Rush.

TALES

THE TELL-TALE HEART[1]

TRUE!—NERVOUS—very, very dreadfully nervous I had been—and am; but why *will* you say that I am mad? The disease had sharpened my senses—not destroyed—not dulled them. Above all was the sense of hearing acute. I heard all things in the heaven and in the earth. I heard many things in hell. How, then, am I mad? Hearken! and observe how healthily—how calmly I can tell you the whole story.

It is impossible to say how first the idea entered my brain; but once conceived, it haunted me day and night. Object there was none. Passion there was none. I loved the old man. He had never wronged me. He had never given me insult. For his gold I had no desire. I think it was his eye! yes, it was this! One of his eyes resembled that of a vulture—a pale blue eye, with a film over it. Whenever it fell upon me, my blood ran cold; and so by degrees—very gradually—I made up my mind to take the life of the old man, and thus rid myself of the eye for ever.

Now this is the point. You fancy me mad. Madmen know nothing. But you should have seen *me*. You should have seen how wisely I proceeded—with what caution— with what foresight—with what dissimulation I went to work! I was never kinder to the old man than during the whole week before I killed him. And every night, about midnight, I turned the latch of his door and opened it— oh, so gently! And then, when I had made an opening sufficient for my head, I put in a dark lantern, all closed, closed, so that no light shone out, and then I thrust in my head. Oh, you would have laughed to see how cunningly I thrust it in! I moved it slowly—very, very slowly, so that I might not disturb the old man's sleep. It took me an hour to place my whole head within the opening so far that I could see him as he lay upon his bed. Ha!—would a madman have been so wise as this? And then when my head was well in the room, I undid the lantern cautiously—oh, so cautiously—cautiously (for the hinges creaked)—I undid it just so much that a single thin ray fell upon the vulture eye. And this I did for seven long nights—every night just at midnight—but I found the eye always closed; and so it was impossible to do the work; for it was not the old man who vexed me, but his Evil Eye. And every morning, when the day broke, I went boldly into the chamber, and spoke courageously to him, calling him by name in a hearty tone, and inquiring how he had passed the night. So you see he would have been a very profound old man, indeed, to suspect that every night, just at twelve, I looked in upon him while he slept.

Upon the eighth night I was more than usually cautious in opening the door. A watch's minute hand moves more quickly than did mine. Never before that night had I *felt* the extent of my own powers—of my sagacity. I could scarcely contain my feelings of triumph. To think that there I was, opening the door, little by little, and he not even to dream of my secret deeds or thoughts. I fairly chuckled at the idea; and perhaps he heard me; for he moved on the bed suddenly, as if startled. Now you may think that I drew back—but no. His room was as black as pitch with the thick darkness (for the shutters were close fastened, through fear of robbers), and so I knew that he could not see the opening of the door, and I kept pushing it on steadily, steadily.

I had my head in, and was about to open the lantern, when my thumb slipped upon the tin fastening, and the old man sprang up in the bed, crying out—"Who's there?"

I kept quite still and said nothing. For a whole hour I did not move a muscle, and in the meantime I did not hear him lie down. He was still sitting up in the bed listening;—just as I have done, night after night, hearkening to the death watches[2] in the wall.

Presently I heard a slight groan, and I knew it was the groan of mortal terror. It was not a groan of pain or of grief—oh, no!—it was the low stifled sound that arises from the bottom of the soul when overcharged with awe. I knew the sound well. Many a night, just at midnight, when all the world slept, it has welled up from my own bosom, deepening, with its dreadful echo, the terrors that distracted me. I say I knew it well. I knew what the old man felt, and pitied him, although I chuckled at heart. I knew that he had been lying awake ever since the first slight noise, when he had turned in the bed. His fears had been ever since growing upon him. He had been trying to fancy them causeless, but could not. He had been saying to himself—"It is nothing but the wind in the chimney—it is only a mouse crossing the floor," or "it is merely a cricket which has made a single chirp." Yes, he has been trying to comfort himself with these suppositions; but he had found all in vain. *All in vain;* because Death, in approaching him, had stalked with his black shadow before him, and enveloped the victim. And it was the mournful influence of the unperceived shadow that caused him to feel—although he neither saw nor heard—to *feel* the presence of my head within the room.

When I had waited a long time, very patiently, without hearing him lie down, I resolved to open a little—a very, very little crevice in the lantern. So I opened it—you cannot imagine how stealthily, stealthily—until, at length, a single dim ray, like the thread of a spider, shot from out the crevice and full upon the vulture eye.

It was open—wide, wide open—and I grew furious as I gazed upon it. I saw it with perfect distinctness—all a dull blue, with a hideous veil over it that chilled the very marrow in my bones; but I could see nothing else of the old man's face or person: for I had directed the ray as if by instinct, precisely upon the damned spot.

And now have I not told you that what you mistake for madness is but over-acuteness of the senses?—now, I say, there came to my ears a low, dull, quick sound, such as a watch makes when enveloped in cotton. I knew *that* sound well too. It was the beating of the old man's heart. It increased my fury, as the beating of a drum stimulates the soldier into courage.

But even yet I refrained and kept still. I scarcely

breathed. I held the lantern motionless. I tried how steadily I could maintain the ray upon the eye. Meantime the hellish tattoo of the heart increased. It grew quicker and quicker, and louder and louder every instant. The old man's terror *must* have been extreme! It grew louder, I say, louder every moment!—do you mark me well? I have told you that I am nervous: so I am. And now at the dead hour of the night, amid the dreadful silence of that old house, so strange a noise as this excited me to uncontrollable terror. Yet, for some minutes longer I refrained and stood still. But the beating grew louder, louder! I thought the heart must burst. And now a new anxiety seized me—the sound would be heard by a neighbor! The old man's hour had come! With a loud yell, I threw open the lantern and leaped into the room. He shrieked once—once only. In an instant I dragged him to the floor, and pulled the heavy bed over him. I then smiled gaily, to find the deed so far done. But, for many minutes, the heart beat on with a muffled sound. This, however, did not vex me; it would not be heard through the wall. At length it ceased. The old man was dead. I removed the bed and examined the corpse. Yes, he was stone, stone dead. I placed my hand upon the heart and held it there many minutes. There was no pulsation. He was stone dead. His eye would trouble me no more.

If still you think me mad, you will think so no longer when I describe the wise precautions I took for the concealment of the body. The night waned, and I worked hastily, but in silence. First of all I dismembered the corpse. I cut off the head and the arms and the legs.

I then took up three planks from the flooring of the

chamber, and deposited all between the scantlings.³ I then replaced the boards so cleverly, so cunningly, that no human eye—not even *his*—could have detected any thing wrong. There was nothing to wash out—no stain of any kind—no blood-spot whatever. I had been too wary for that. A tub had caught all—ha! ha!

When I had made an end of these labors, it was four o'clock—still dark as midnight. As the bell sounded the hour, there came a knocking at the street door. I went down to open it with a light heart,—for what had I *now* to fear? There entered three men, who introduced themselves, with perfect suavity, as officers of the police. A shriek had been heard by a neighbor during the night; suspicion of foul play had been aroused; information had been lodged at the police office, and they (the officers) had been deputed to search the premises.

I smiled,—for *what* had I to fear? I bade the gentlemen welcome. The shriek, I said, was my own in a dream. The old man, I mentioned, was absent in the country. I took my visitors all over the house. I bade them search—search *well*. I led them, at length, to *his* chamber. I showed them his treasures, secure, undisturbed. In the enthusiasm of my confidence, I brought chairs into the room, and desired them *here* to rest from their fatigues, while I myself, in the wild audacity of my perfect triumph, placed my own seat upon the very spot beneath which reposed the corpse of the victim.

The officers were satisfied. My *manner* had convinced them. I was singularly at ease. They sat, and while I answered cheerily, they chatted familiar things. But, ere long, I felt myself getting pale and wished them gone. My head ached, and I fancied a ringing in my ears: but still they sat and still chatted. The ringing became more distinct:—it continued and became more distinct: I talked more freely to get rid of the feeling: but it continued and gained definitiveness—until, at length, I found that the noise was *not* within my ears.

No doubt I now grew *very* pale;—but I talked more fluently, and with a heightened voice. Yet the sound increased—and what could I do? It was *a low, dull, quick sound—much such a sound as a watch makes when enveloped in cotton.* I gasped for breath—and yet the officers heard it not. I talked more quickly—more vehemently; but the noise steadily increased. I arose and argued about trifles, in a high key and with violent gesticulations, but the noise steadily increased. Why *would* they not be gone? I paced the floor to and fro with heavy strides, as if excited to fury by the observation of the men—but the noise steadily increased. Oh God! what *could* I do? I foamed—I raved—I swore! I swung the chair upon which I had been sitting, and grated it upon the boards, but the noise arose over all and continually increased. It grew louder—louder—*louder!* And still the men chatted pleasantly, and smiled. Was it possible they heard not? Almighty God!—no, no! They heard!—they suspected!—they *knew!*—they were making a mockery of my horror!—this I thought, and this I think. But any thing was better than this agony! Any thing was more tolerable than this derision! I could bear those hypocritical smiles no longer! I felt that I must scream or die!—and now—again!—hark! louder! louder! louder! *louder!*—

"Villains!" I shrieked, "dissemble no more! I admit the deed!—tear up the planks!—here, here!—it is the beating of his hideous heart!"

THE CASK OF AMONTILLADO[1]

THE THOUSAND INJURIES of Fortunato I had borne as I best could; but when he ventured upon insult, I vowed revenge. You, who so well know the nature of my soul, will not suppose, however, that I gave utterance to a threat. *At length* I would be avenged; this was a point definitively settled—but the very definitiveness with which it was resolved, precluded the idea of risk. I must not only punish, but punish with impunity. A wrong is unredressed when retribution overtakes its redresser. It is equally unredressed when the avenger fails to make himself felt as such to him who has done the wrong.

It must be understood, that neither by word nor deed had I given Fortunato cause to doubt my good-will. I continued, as was my wont, to smile in his face, and he did not perceive that my smile *now* was at the thought of his immolation.

He had a weak point—this Fortunato—although in other regards he was a man to be respected and even feared. He prided himself on his connoisseurship in wine. Few Italians have the true virtuoso spirit. For the most part their enthusiasm is adopted to suit the time and opportunity—to practise imposture upon the British and Austrian *millionaires*. In painting and gemmary Fortunato, like his countrymen, was a quack—but in the matter of old wines he was sincere. In this respect I did not differ from him materially: I was skilful in the Italian vintages myself, and bought largely whenever I could.

It was about dusk, one evening during the supreme madness of the carnival season, that I encountered my friend. He accosted me with excessive warmth, for he had been drinking much. The man wore motley. He had on a tight-fitting parti-striped dress, and his head was surmounted by the conical cap and bells. I was so pleased to see him, that I thought I should never have done wringing his hand.

I said to him: "My dear Fortunato, you are luckily met. How remarkably well you are looking to-day! But I have received a pipe of what passes for Amontillado,[2] and I have my doubts."

"How?" said he. "Amontillado? A pipe? Impossible! And in the middle of the carnival!"

"I have my doubts," I replied; "and I was silly enough to pay the full Amontillado price without consulting you in the matter. You were not to be found, and I was fearful of losing a bargain."

"Amontillado!"

"I have my doubts."

"Amontillado!"

"And I must satisfy them."

"Amontillado!"

"As you are engaged, I am on my way to Luchesi. If any one has a critical turn, it is he. He will tell me——"

"Luchesi cannot tell Amontillado from Sherry."

"And yet some fools will have it that his taste is a match for your own."

"Come, let us go."

"Whither?"

"To your vaults."

"My friend, no; I will not impose upon your good nature. I perceive you have an engagement. Luchesi——"

"I have no engagement;—come."

"My friend, no. It is not the engagement, but the severe cold with which I perceive you are afflicted. The vaults are insufferably damp. They are encrusted with nitre."[3]

"Let us go, nevertheless. The cold is merely nothing. Amontillado! You have been imposed upon. And as for Luchesi, he cannot distinguish Sherry from Amontillado."

Thus speaking, Fortunato possessed himself of my arm. Putting on a mask of black silk, and drawing a *roquelaire*[4] closely about my person, I suffered him to hurry me to my palazzo.

There were no attendants at home; they had absconded to make merry in honor of the time. I had told them that I should not return until the morning, and had given them explicit orders not to stir from the house. These orders were sufficient, I well knew, to insure their immediate disappearance, one and all, as soon as my back was turned.

I took from their sconces two flambeaux, and giving one to Fortunato, bowed him through several suites of rooms to the archway that led into the vaults. I passed down a long and winding staircase, requesting him to be cautious as he followed. We came at length to the foot of the descent, and stood together on the damp ground of the catacombs of the Montresors.

The gait of my friend was unsteady, and the bells upon his cap jingled as he strode.

"The pipe?" said he.

"It is farther on," said I; "but observe the white web-work which gleams from these cavern walls."

He turned toward me, and looked into my eyes with two filmy orbs that distilled the rheum of intoxication.

"Nitre?" he asked, at length.

"Nitre," I replied. "How long have you had that cough?"

"Ugh! ugh! ugh!—ugh! ugh! ugh!—ugh! ugh! ugh!— ugh! ugh! ugh!—ugh! ugh! ugh!"

My poor friend found it impossible to reply for many minutes.

"It is nothing," he said, at last.

"Come," I said with decision, "we will go back; your health is precious. You are rich, respected, admired, be-loved; you are happy, as once I was. You are a man to be missed. For me it is no matter. We will go back; you will be ill, and I cannot be responsible. Besides, there is Luchesi——"

"Enough," he said; "the cough is a mere nothing; it will not kill me. I shall not die of a cough."

"True—true," I replied; "and, indeed, I had no inten-tion of alarming you unnecessarily; but you should use all proper caution. A draught of this Medoc[5] will defend us from the damps."

Here I knocked off the neck of a bottle which I drew from a long row of its fellows that lay upon the mould.

"Drink," I said, presenting him the wine.

He raised it to his lips with a leer. He paused and nodded to me familiarly, while his bells jingled.

"I drink," he said, "to the buried that repose around us."

"And I to your long life."

He again took my arm, and we proceeded.

"These vaults," he said, "are extensive."

"The Montresors," I replied, "were a great and numerous family."

"I forget your arms."

"A huge human foot d'or, in a field azure; the foot crushes a serpent rampant whose fangs are imbedded in the heel."

"And the motto?"

"Nemo me impune lacessit."[6]

"Good!" he said.

The wine sparkled in his eyes and the bells jingled. My own fancy grew warm with the Medoc. We had passed through walls of piled bones, with casks and puncheons[7] intermingling, into the inmost recesses of the catacombs. I paused again, and this time I made bold to seize Fortunato by an arm above the elbow.

"The nitre!" I said; "see, it increases. It hangs like moss upon the vaults. We are below the river's bed. The drops of moisture trickle among the bones. Come, we will go back ere it is too late. Your cough——"

"It is nothing," he said; "let us go on. But first, another draught of the Medoc."

I broke and reached him a flagon of De Grâve.[8] He emptied it at a breath. His eyes flashed with a fierce light. He laughed and threw the bottle upward with a gesticulation I did not understand.

I looked at him in surprise. He repeated the movement—a grotesque one.

"You do not comprehend?" he said.

"Not I," I replied.

"Then you are not of the brotherhood."

"How?"

"You are not of the masons."

"Yes, yes," I said; "yes, yes."

"You? Impossible! A mason?"

"A mason," I replied.

"A sign," he said.

"It is this," I answered, producing a trowel from beneath the folds of my *roquelaire*.

"You jest," he exclaimed, recoiling a few paces. "But let us proceed to the Amontillado."

"Be it so," I said, replacing the tool beneath the cloak, and again offering him my arm. He leaned upon it heavily. We continued our route in search of the Amontillado. We passed through a range of low arches, descended, passed on, and descending again, arrived at a deep crypt, in which the foulness of the air caused our flambeaux rather to glow than flame.

At the most remote end of the crypt there appeared another less spacious. Its walls had been lined with human remains, piled to the vault overhead, in the fashion of the great catacombs of Paris. Three sides of this interior crypt were still ornamented in this manner. From the fourth the bones had been thrown down, and lay promiscuously upon the earth, forming at one point a mound of some size. Within the wall thus exposed by the displacing of the bones, we perceived a still interior recess, in depth about four feet, in width three, in height six or seven. It seemed to have been constructed for no especial use within itself, but formed merely the interval between two of the colossal supports of the roof of the catacombs, and was backed by one of their circumscribing walls of solid granite.

It was in vain that Fortunato, uplifting his dull torch, endeavored to pry into the depth of the recess. Its termination the feeble light did not enable us to see.

"Proceed," I said; "herein is the Amontillado. As for Luchesi——"

"He is an ignoramus," interrupted my friend, as he stepped unsteadily forward, while I followed immediately at his heels. In an instant he had reached the extremity of the niche, and finding his progress arrested by the rock, stood stupidly bewildered. A moment more and I had fettered him to the granite. In its surface were two iron staples, distant from each other about two feet, horizontally. From one of these depended a short chain, from the other a padlock. Throwing the links about his waist, it was but the work of a few seconds to secure it. He was too much astounded to resist. Withdrawing the key I stepped back from the recess.

"Pass your hand," I said, "over the wall; you cannot help feeling the nitre. Indeed it is *very* damp. Once more let me *implore* you to return. No? Then I must positively leave you. But I must first render you all the little attentions in my power."

"The Amontillado!" ejaculated my friend, not yet recovered from his astonishment.

"True," I replied; "the Amontillado."

As I said these words I busied myself among the pile of bones of which I have before spoken. Throwing them aside, I soon uncovered a quantity of building stone and mortar. With these materials and with the aid of my trowel, I began vigorously to wall up the entrance of the niche.

I had scarcely laid the first tier of the masonry when I discovered that the intoxication of Fortunato had in a great measure worn off. The earliest indication I had of this was a low moaning cry from the depth of the recess. It was *not* the cry of a drunken man. There was then a long and obstinate silence. I laid the second tier, and the third, and the fourth; and then I heard the furious vibrations of the chain. The noise lasted for several minutes, during which, that I might hearken to it with the more satisfaction, I ceased my labors and sat down upon the bones. When at last the clanking subsided, I resumed the trowel, and finished without interruption the fifth, the sixth, and the seventh tier. The wall was now nearly upon a level with my breast. I again paused, and holding the flambeaux over the mason-work, threw a few feeble rays upon the figure within.

A succession of loud and shrill screams, bursting suddenly from the throat of the chained form, seemed to thrust me violently back. For a brief moment I hesitated—I trembled. Unsheathing my rapier, I began to grope with it about the recess; but the thought of an instant reassured me. I placed my hand upon the solid fabric of the catacombs, and felt satisfied. I reapproached the wall. I replied to the yells of him who clamored. I reechoed—I aided—I surpassed them in volume and in strength. I did this, and the clamorer grew still.

It was now midnight, and my task was drawing to a

close. I had completed the eighth, the ninth, and the tenth tier. I had finished a portion of the last and the eleventh; there remained but a single stone to be fitted and plastered in. I struggled with its weight; I placed it partially in its destined position. But now there came from out the niche a low laugh that erected the hairs upon my head. It was succeeded by a sad voice, which I had difficulty in recognizing as that of the noble Fortunato. The voice said—

"Ha! ha! ha!—he! he!—a very good joke indeed—an excellent jest. We will have many a rich laugh about it at the palazzo—he! he! he!—over our wine—he! he! he!"

"The Amontillado!" I said.

"He! he! he!—he! he! he!—yes, the Amontillado. But is it not getting late? Will not they be awaiting us at the palazzo, the Lady Fortunato and the rest? Let us be gone."

"Yes," I said, "let us be gone."

"For the love of God, Montresor!"

"Yes," I said, "for the love of God!"

But to these words I hearkened in vain for a reply. I grew impatient. I called aloud:

"Fortunato!"

No answer. I called again:

"Fortunato!"

No answer still. I thrust a torch through the remaining aperture and let it fall within. There came forth in return only a jingling of the bells. My heart grew sick—on account of the dampness of the catacombs. I hastened to make an end of my labor. I forced the last stone into its position; I plastered it up. Against the new masonry I re-erected the old rampart of bones. For half of a century no mortal has disturbed them. *In pace requiescat!*[9]

THE BLACK CAT[1]

FOR THE MOST wild yet most homely narrative which I am about to pen, I neither expect nor solicit belief. Mad indeed would I be to expect it, in a case where my very senses reject their own evidence. Yet, mad am I not—and very surely do I not dream. But to-morrow I die, and to-day I would unburden my soul. My immediate purpose is to place before the world, plainly, succinctly, and without comment, a series of mere household events. In their consequences, these events have terrified—have tortured—have destroyed me. Yet I will not attempt to expound them. To me, they have presented little but horror—to many they will seem less terrible than *baroques*.[2] Hereafter, perhaps, some intellect may be found which will reduce my phantasm to the commonplace—some intellect more calm, more logical, and far less excitable than my own, which will perceive, in the circumstances I detail with awe, nothing more than an ordinary succession of very natural causes and effects.

From my infancy I was noted for the docility and humanity of my disposition. My tenderness of heart was even so conspicuous as to make me the jest of my companions. I was especially fond of animals, and was indulged by my parents with a great variety of pets. With these I spent most of my time, and never was so happy as when feeding and caressing them. This peculiarity of character grew with my growth, and, in my manhood, I derived from it one of my principal sources of pleasure. To those who have cherished an affection for a faithful and sagacious dog, I need hardly be at the trouble of explaining the nature or the intensity of the gratification thus derivable. There is something in the unselfish and self-sacrificing love of a brute, which goes directly to the heart of him who has had frequent occasion to test the paltry friendship and gossamer fidelity of mere *Man*.

I married early, and was happy to find in my wife a disposition not uncongenial with my own. Observing my partiality for domestic pets, she lost no opportunity of procuring those of the most agreeable kind. We had birds, gold-fish, a fine dog, rabbits, a small monkey, and a *cat*.

This latter was a remarkably large and beautiful animal, entirely black, and sagacious to an astonishing degree. In speaking of his intelligence, my wife, who at heart was not a little tinctured with superstition, made frequent allusion to the ancient popular notion, which regarded all black cats as witches in disguise. Not that she was ever *serious* upon this point—and I mention the matter at all for no better reason than that it happens, just now, to be remembered.

Pluto[3]—this was the cat's name—was my favorite pet and playmate. I alone fed him, and he attended me wherever I went about the house. It was even with difficulty that I could prevent him from following me through the streets.

Our friendship lasted, in this manner, for several years, during which my general temperament and character—through the instrumentality of the Fiend Intemperance[4]—had (I blush to confess it) experienced a radical alteration for the worse. I grew, day by day, more moody, more irritable, more regardless of the feelings of others. I suffered myself to use intemperate language to my wife. At length, I even offered her personal violence. My pets, of course, were made to feel the change in my disposition. I not only neglected, but ill-used them. For Pluto, however, I still retained sufficient regard to restrain me from maltreating him, as I made no scruple of maltreating the rabbits, the monkey, or even the dog, when, by accident, or through affection, they came in my way. But my disease grew upon me—for what disease is like Alcohol!—and at length even Pluto, who was now becoming old, and consequently somewhat peevish—even Pluto began to experience the effects of my ill temper.

One night, returning home, much intoxicated, from one of my haunts about town, I fancied that the cat avoided my presence. I seized him; when, in his fright at my violence, he inflicted a slight wound upon my hand with his teeth. The fury of a demon instantly possessed me. I knew myself no longer. My original soul seemed, at once, to take its flight from my body; and a more than fiendish malevolence, gin-nurtured, thrilled every fibre of my frame. I took from my waistcoat-pocket a penknife, opened it, grasped the poor beast by the throat, and deliberately cut one of its eyes from the socket! I blush, I burn, I shudder, while I pen the damnable atrocity.

When reason returned with the morning—when I had slept off the fumes of the night's debauch—I experienced a sentiment half of horror, half of remorse, for the crime of which I had been guilty; but it was, at best, a feeble and equivocal feeling, and the soul remained untouched. I again plunged into excess, and soon drowned in wine all memory of the deed.

In the meantime the cat slowly recovered. The socket of the lost eye presented, it is true, a frightful appearance, but he no longer appeared to suffer any pain. He went about the house as usual, but, as might be expected, fled in extreme terror at my approach. I had so much of my old heart left, as to be at first grieved by this evident dislike on the part of a creature which had once so loved me. But this feeling soon gave place to irritation. And then came, as if to my final and irrevocable overthrow, the spirit of PERVERSENESS. Of this spirit philosophy takes no account. Yet I am not more sure that my soul lives, than I am that perverseness is one of the primitive impulses of the human heart—one of the indivisible primary faculties, or sentiments, which give direction to the character of Man. Who has not, a hundred times, found himself committing a vile or a stupid action, for no other reason than because he knows he should *not?* Have we not a perpetual inclination, in the teeth of our best judgment, to violate that which is *Law,* merely because we understand it to be such? This spirit of perverseness, I say, came to my final overthrow. It was this unfathomable longing of the soul *to vex itself*—to offer violence to its own nature—to do wrong for the wrong's sake only—that urged me to continue and finally to consummate the injury I had inflicted upon the unoffending brute. One morning, in cold blood, I slipped a noose about its neck and hung it to the limb of a tree;—hung it with the tears streaming from my eyes, and with the bitterest remorse at my heart;—hung it *because* I knew that it had loved me, and *because* I felt it had given me no reason of offence;—hung it *because* I knew that in so doing I was committing a sin—a deadly sin that would so jeopardize my immortal soul as to place it—if such a thing were possible—even beyond the reach of the infinite mercy of the Most Merciful and Most Terrible God.

On the night of the day on which this most cruel deed was done, I was aroused from sleep by the cry of fire. The curtains of my bed were in flames. The whole house was blazing. It was with great difficulty that my wife, a servant, and myself, made our escape from the conflagration. The destruction was complete. My entire worldly wealth was swallowed up, and I resigned myself thenceforward to despair.

I am above the weakness of seeking to establish a sequence of cause and effect, between the disaster and the atrocity. But I am detailing a chain of facts—and wish not to leave even a possible link imperfect. On the day succeeding the fire, I visited the ruins. The walls, with one exception, had fallen in. This exception was found in a compartment wall, not very thick, which stood about the middle of the house, and against which had rested the head of my bed. The plastering had here, in great measure, resisted the action of the fire—a fact which I attributed to its having been recently spread. About this wall a dense crowd were collected, and many persons seemed to be examining a particular portion of it with very minute and eager attention. The words "strange!" "singular!" and other similar expressions excited my curiosity. I approached and saw, as if graven in *bas-relief* upon the white surface, the figure of a gigantic *cat*. The impression was given with an accuracy truly marvellous. There was a rope about the animal's neck.

When I first beheld this apparition—for I could scarcely regard it as less—my wonder and my terror were extreme. But at length reflection came to my aid. The cat, I remembered, had been hung in a garden adjacent to the house. Upon the alarm of fire, the garden had been immediately filled by the crowd—by some one of whom the animal must have been cut from the tree and thrown, through an open window, into my chamber. This had probably been done with the view of arousing me from sleep. The falling of other walls had compressed the victim of my cruelty into the substance of the freshly-spread plaster; the lime of which, with the flames, and the *ammonia* from the carcass, had then accomplished the portraiture as I saw it.

Although I thus readily accounted to my reason, if not altogether to my conscience, for the startling fact just detailed, it did not the less fail to make a deep impression upon my fancy. For months I could not rid myself of the phantasm of the cat; and, during this period, there came back into my spirit a half-sentiment that seemed, but was not, remorse. I went so far as to regret the loss of the animal, and to look about me, among the vile haunts which I now habitually frequented, for another pet of the same species, and of somewhat similar appearance, with which to supply its place.

One night as I sat, half stupefied, in a den of more than infamy, my attention was suddenly drawn to some black object, reposing upon the head of one of the immense hogsheads of gin, or of rum, which constituted the chief furniture of the apartment. I had been looking steadily at the top of this hogshead for some minutes, and what now caused me surprise was the fact that I had not sooner perceived the object thereupon. I approached it, and touched it with my hand. It was a black cat—a very large one—fully as large as Pluto, and closely resembling him in every respect but one. Pluto had not a white hair upon any portion of his body; but this cat had a large, although indefinite splotch of white, covering nearly the whole region of the breast.

Upon my touching him, he immediately arose, purred loudly, rubbed against my hand, and appeared delighted with my notice. This, then, was the very creature of which I was in search. I at once offered to purchase it of the landlord; but this person made no claim to it—knew nothing of it—had never seen it before.

I continued my caresses, and when I prepared to go home, the animal evinced a disposition to accompany me. I permitted it to do so; occasionally stooping and patting it as I proceeded. When it reached the house it domesticated itself at once, and became immediately a great favorite with my wife.

For my own part, I soon found a dislike to it arising within me. This was just the reverse of what I had anticipated; but—I know not how or why it was—its evident fondness for myself rather disgusted and annoyed me. By slow degrees these feelings of disgust and annoyance rose into the bitterness of hatred. I avoided the creature;

a certain sense of shame, and the remembrance of my former deed of cruelty, preventing me from physically abusing it. I did not, for some weeks, strike, or otherwise violently ill use it; but gradually—very gradually—I came to look upon it with unutterable loathing, and to flee silently from its odious presence, as from the breath of a pestilence.

What added, no doubt, to my hatred of the beast, was the discovery, on the morning after I brought it home, that, like Pluto, it also had been deprived of one of its eyes. This circumstance, however, only endeared it to my wife, who, as I have already said, possessed, in a high degree, that humanity of feeling which had once been my distinguishing trait, and the source of many of my simplest and purest pleasures.

With my aversion to this cat, however, its partiality for myself seemed to increase. It followed my footsteps with a pertinacity which it would be difficult to make the reader comprehend. Whenever I sat, it would crouch beneath my chair, or spring upon my knees, covering me with its loathsome caresses. If I arose to walk it would get between my feet and thus nearly throw me down, or, fastening its long and sharp claws in my dress, clamber, in this manner, to my breast. At such times, although I longed to destroy it with a blow, I was yet withheld from so doing, partly by a memory of my former crime, but chiefly—let me confess it at once—by absolute *dread* of the beast.

This dread was not exactly a dread of physical evil—and yet I should be at a loss how otherwise to define it. I am almost ashamed to own—yes, even in this felon's cell, I am almost ashamed to own—that the terror and horror

with which the animal inspired me, had been heightened
by one of the merest chimeras it would be possible to
conceive. My wife had called my attention, more than
once, to the character of the mark of white hair, of which
I have spoken, and which constituted the sole visible difference between the strange beast and the one I had destroyed. The reader will remember that this mark,
although large, had been originally very indefinite; but,
by slow degrees—degrees nearly imperceptible, and
which for a long time my reason struggled to reject as
fanciful—it had, at length, assumed a rigorous distinctness of outline. It was now the representation of an object that I shudder to name—and for this, above all, I
loathed, and dreaded, and would have rid myself of the
monster *had I dared*—it was now, I say, the image of a
hideous—of a ghastly thing—of the GALLOWS!—oh,
mournful and terrible engine of Horror and of Crime—
of Agony and of Death!

And now was I indeed wretched beyond the
wretchedness of mere Humanity. And *a brute beast*—
whose fellow I had contemptuously destroyed—*a brute
beast* to work out for *me*—for me, a man fashioned in the
image of the High God—so much of insufferable woe!
Alas! neither by day nor by night knew I the blessing of
rest any more! During the former the creature left me
no moment alone, and in the latter I started hourly from
dreams of unutterable fear to find the hot breath of *the
thing* upon my face, and its vast weight—an incarnate
nightmare that I had no power to shake off—incumbent
eternally upon my *heart!*

Beneath the pressure of torments such as these the
feeble remnant of the good within me succumbed. Evil

thoughts became my sole intimates—the darkest and most evil of thoughts. The moodiness of my usual temper increased to hatred of all things and of all mankind; while from the sudden, frequent, and ungovernable outbursts of a fury to which I now blindly abandoned myself, my uncomplaining wife, alas, was the most usual and the most patient of sufferers.

One day she accompanied me, upon some household errand, into the cellar of the old building which our poverty compelled us to inhabit. The cat followed me down the steep stairs, and, nearly throwing me headlong, exasperated me to madness. Uplifting an axe, and forgetting in my wrath the childish dread which had hitherto stayed my hand, I aimed a blow at the animal, which, of course, would have proved instantly fatal had it descended as I wished. But this blow was arrested by the hand of my wife. Goaded by the interference into a rage more than demoniacal, I withdrew my arm from her grasp and buried the axe in her brain. She fell dead upon the spot without a groan.

This hideous murder accomplished, I set myself forthwith, and with entire deliberation, to the task of concealing the body. I knew that I could not remove it from the house, either by day or by night, without the risk of being observed by the neighbors. Many projects entered my mind. At one period I thought of cutting the corpse into minute fragments, and destroying them by fire. At another, I resolved to dig a grave for it in the floor of the cellar. Again, I deliberated about casting it in the well in the yard—about packing it in a box, as if merchandise, with the usual arrangements, and so getting a porter to take it from the house. Finally I hit upon what

I considered a far better expedient than either of these. I determined to wall it up in the cellar, as the monks of the Middle Ages are recorded to have walled up their victims.

For a purpose such as this the cellar was well adapted. Its walls were loosely constructed, and had lately been plastered throughout with a rough plaster, which the dampness of the atmosphere had prevented from hardening. Moreover, in one of the walls was a projection, caused by a false chimney, or fireplace, that had been filled up and made to resemble the rest of the cellar. I made no doubt that I could readily displace the bricks at this point, insert the corpse, and wall the whole up as before, so that no eye could detect any thing suspicious.

And in this calculation I was not deceived. By means of a crowbar I easily dislodged the bricks, and, having carefully deposited the body against the inner wall, I propped it in that position, while with little trouble I relaid the whole structure as it originally stood. Having procured mortar, sand, and hair, with every possible precaution, I prepared a plaster which could not be distinguished from the old, and with this I very carefully went over the new brick-work. When I had finished, I felt satisfied that all was right. The wall did not present the slightest appearance of having been disturbed. The rubbish on the floor was picked up with the minutest care. I looked around triumphantly, and said to myself: "Here at least, then, my labor has not been in vain."

My next step was to look for the beast which had been the cause of so much wretchedness; for I had, at length, firmly resolved to put it to death. Had I been able to meet with it at the moment, there could have been no doubt of its fate; but it appeared that the crafty animal had been alarmed at the violence of my previous anger, and forbore to present itself in my present mood. It is impossible to describe or to imagine the deep, the blissful sense of relief which the absence of the detested creature occasioned in my bosom. It did not make its appearance during the night; and thus for one night, at least, since its introduction into the house, I soundly and tranquilly slept; aye, *slept* even with the burden of murder upon my soul.

The second and the third day passed, and still my tormentor came not. Once again I breathed as a freeman. The monster, in terror, had fled the premises for ever! I should behold it no more! My happiness was supreme! The guilt of my dark deed disturbed me but little. Some few inquiries had been made, but these had been readily answered. Even a search had been instituted—but of course nothing was to be discovered. I looked upon my future felicity as secured.

Upon the fourth day of the assassination, a party of the police came, very unexpectedly, into the house, and proceeded again to make rigorous investigation of the premises. Secure, however, in the inscrutability of my place of concealment, I felt no embarrassment whatever. The officers bade me accompany them in their search. They left no nook or corner unexplored. At length, for the third or fourth time, they descended into the cellar. I quivered not in a muscle. My heart beat calmly as that of one who slumbers in innocence. I walked the cellar from end to end. I folded my arms upon my bosom, and roamed easily to and fro. The police were thoroughly satisfied and prepared to depart. The glee at my heart was too strong to be restrained. I burned to say if but one word, by way of triumph, and to render doubly sure their assurance of my guiltlessness.

"Gentlemen," I said at last, as the party ascended the steps, "I delight to have allayed your suspicions. I wish you all health and a little more courtesy. By the bye, gentlemen, this—this is a very well-constructed house," (in the rabid desire to say something easily, I scarcely knew what I uttered at all),—"I may say an *excellently* well-constructed house. These walls—are you going, gentlemen?—these walls are solidly put together"; and here, through the mere frenzy of bravado, I rapped heavily with a cane which I held in my hand, upon that very portion of the brick-work behind which stood the corpse of the wife of my bosom.

But may God shield and deliver me from the fangs of the Arch-Fiend! No sooner had the reverberation of my blows sunk into silence, than I was answered by a voice from within the tomb!—by a cry, at first muffled and broken, like the sobbing of a child, and then quickly swelling into one long, loud, and continuous scream, utterly anomalous and inhuman—a howl—a wailing shriek, half of horror and half of triumph, such as might have arisen only out of hell, conjointly from the throats of the damned in their agony and of the demons that exult in the damnation.

Of my own thoughts it is folly to speak. Swooning, I staggered to the opposite wall. For one instant the party on the stairs remained motionless, through extremity of terror and awe. In the next a dozen stout arms were toiling at the wall. It fell bodily. The corpse, already greatly decayed and clotted with gore, stood erect before the eyes of the spectators. Upon its head, with red extended mouth and solitary eye of fire, sat the hideous beast whose craft had seduced me into murder, and whose informing voice had consigned me to the hangman. I had walled the monster up within the tomb.

LIGEIA[1]

And the will therein lieth, which dieth not. Who knoweth the mysteries of the will, with its vigor? For God is but a great will pervading all things by nature of its intentness. Man doth not yield himself to the angels, nor unto death utterly, save only through the weakness of his feeble will.

—*Joseph Glanvill*[2]

I CANNOT, FOR MY SOUL, remember how, when, or even precisely where, I first became acquainted with the lady Ligeia. Long years have since elapsed, and my memory is feeble through much suffering. Or, perhaps, I cannot *now* bring these points to mind, because, in truth, the character of my beloved, her rare learning, her singular yet placid cast of beauty, and the thrilling and enthralling eloquence of her low musical language, made their way into my heart by paces so steadily and stealthily progressive, that they have been unnoticed and unknown.

Yet I believe that I met her first and most frequently in some large, old, decaying city near the Rhine. Of her family—I have surely heard her speak. That it is of a remotely ancient date cannot be doubted. Ligeia! Ligeia! Buried in studies of a nature more than all else adapted to deaden impressions of the outward world, it is by that sweet word alone—by Ligeia—that I bring before mine eyes in fancy the image of her who is no more. And now, while I write, a recollection flashes upon me that I have *never known* the paternal name of her who was my friend and my betrothed, and who became the partner of my studies, and finally the wife of my bosom. Was it a playful charge on the part of my Ligeia? or was it a test of my strength of affection, that I should institute no inquiries upon this point? or was it rather a caprice of my own—a wildly romantic offering on the shrine of the most passionate devotion? I but indistinctly recall the fact itself—what wonder that I have utterly forgotten the circumstances which originated or attended it? And, indeed, if ever that spirit which is entitled *Romance*—if ever she, the wan and the misty-winged *Ashtophet*[3] of idolatrous Egypt, presided, as they tell, over marriages ill-omened, then most surely she presided over mine.

There is one dear topic, however, on which my memory fails me not. It is the *person* of Ligeia. In stature she was tall, somewhat slender, and, in her latter days, even emaciated. I would in vain attempt to portray the majesty, the quiet ease of her demeanor, or the incomprehensible lightness and elasticity of her footfall. She came and departed as a shadow. I was never made aware of her entrance into my closed study, save by the dear music of her low sweet voice, as she placed her marble

hand upon my shoulder. In beauty of face no maiden
ever equalled her. It was the radiance of an opium-
dream—an airy and spirit-lifting vision more wildly divine than the phantasies which hovered about the
slumbering souls of the daughters of Delos.[4] Yet her features were not of that regular mould which we have been
falsely taught to worship in the classical labors of the
heathen. "There is no exquisite beauty," says Bacon,
Lord Verulam, speaking truly of all the forms and *genera*
of beauty, "without some *strangeness* in the proportion."[5]
Yet, although I saw that the features of Ligeia were not
of a classic regularity—although I perceived that her
loveliness was indeed "exquisite," and felt that there was
much of "strangeness" pervading it, yet I have tried in
vain to detect the irregularity and to trace home my own
perception of "the strange." I examined the contour of
the lofty and pale forehead—it was faultless—how cold
indeed that word when applied to a majesty so divine!—
the skin rivalling the purest ivory, the commanding extent and repose, the gentle prominence of the regions
above the temples; and then the raven-black, the glossy,
the luxuriant, and naturally-curling tresses, setting forth
the full force of the Homeric epithet, "hyacinthine!" I
looked at the delicate outlines of the nose—and nowhere
but in the graceful medallions of the Hebrews had I beheld a similar perfection. There were the same luxurious
smoothness of surface, the same scarcely perceptible
tendency to the aquiline, the same harmoniously curved
nostrils speaking the free spirit. I regarded the sweet
mouth. Here was indeed the triumph of all things heavenly—the magnificent turn of the short upper lip—the
soft, voluptuous slumber of the under—the dimples

which sported, and the color which spoke—the teeth glancing back, with a brilliancy almost startling, every ray of the holy light which fell upon them in her serene and placid yet most exultingly radiant of all smiles. I scrutinized the formation of the chin—and, here too, I found the gentleness of breadth, the softness and the majesty, the fullness and the spirituality, of the Greek—the contour which the god Apollo revealed but in a dream, to Cleomenes,[6] the son of the Athenian. And then I peered into the large eyes of Ligeia.

For eyes we have no models in the remotely antique. It might have been, too, that in these eyes of my beloved lay the secret to which Lord Verulam alludes. They were, I must believe, far larger than the ordinary eyes of our own race. They were even fuller than the fullest of the gazelle eyes of the tribe of the valley of Nourjahad.[7] Yet it was only at intervals—in moments of intense excitement—that this peculiarity became more than slightly noticeable in Ligeia. And at such moments was her beauty—in my heated fancy thus it appeared perhaps— the beauty of beings either above or apart from the earth—the beauty of the fabulous Houri[8] of the Turk. The hue of the orbs was the most brilliant of black, and, far over them, hung jetty lashes of great length. The brows, slightly irregular in outline, had the same tint. The "strangeness," however, which I found in the eyes was of a nature distinct from the formation, or the color, or the brilliancy of the features, and must, after all, be referred to as the *expression*. Ah, word of no meaning! behind whose vast latitude of mere sound we intrench our ignorance of so much of the spiritual. The expression of the eyes of Ligeia! How for long hours have I pondered upon it! How have I, through the whole of a midsummer night, struggled to fathom it! What was it—that something more profound than the well of Democritus[9]—which lay far within the pupils of my beloved? What *was* it? I was possessed with a passion to discover. Those eyes! those large, those shining, those divine orbs! they became to me twin stars of Leda,[10] and I to them devoutest of astrologers.

There is no point, among the many incomprehensible anomalies of the science of mind, more thrillingly exciting than the fact—never, I believe, noticed in the schools—that in our endeavors to recall to memory something long forgotten, we often find ourselves *upon the very verge* of remembrance, without being able, in the end, to remember. And thus how frequently, in my intense scrutiny of Ligeia's eyes, have I felt approaching the full knowledge of their expression—felt it approaching—yet not quite be mine—and so at length entirely depart! And (strange, oh, strangest mystery of all!) I found, in the commonest objects of the universe, a circle of analogies to that expression. I mean to say that, subsequently to the period when Ligeia's beauty passed into my spirit, there dwelling as in a shrine, I derived, from many existences in the material world, a sentiment such as I felt always around, within me, by her large and luminous orbs. Yet not the more could I define that sentiment, or analyze, or even steadily view it. I recognized it, let me repeat, sometimes in the survey of a rapidly growing vine—in the contemplation of a moth, a butterfly, a chrysalis, a stream of running water. I have felt it in the ocean—in the falling of a meteor. I have felt it in the glances of unusually aged people. And there are one or two stars in heaven (one especially, a star of the sixth magnitude, double and changeable, to be found near the large star in Lyra[11]) in a telescopic scrutiny of which I have been made aware of the feeling. I have been filled with it by certain sounds from stringed instruments, and not unfrequently by passages from books. Among innumerable other instances, I well remember something in a volume of Joseph Glanvill, which (perhaps merely from its quaintness—who shall say?) never failed to inspire me with the sentiment: "And the will therein lieth, which dieth not. Who knoweth the mysteries of the will, with its vigor? For God is but a great will pervading all things by nature of its intentness. Man doth not yield him to the angels, nor unto death, utterly, save only through the weakness of his feeble will."

Length of years and subsequent reflection have enabled me to trace, indeed, some remote connection between this passage in the English moralist and a portion of the character of Ligeia. An *intensity* in thought, action, or speech was possibly, in her, a result, or at least an index, of that gigantic volition which, during our long intercourse, failed to give other and more immediate evidence of its existence. Of all the women whom I have ever known, she, the outwardly calm, the ever-placid Ligeia, was the most violently a prey to the tumultuous vultures of stern passion. And of such passion I could form no estimate, save by the miraculous expansion of those eyes which at once so delighted and appalled me,—by the almost magical melody, modulation, distinctness, and placidity of her very low voice,—and by the fierce energy (rendered doubly effective by contrast with her manner of utterance) of the wild words which she habitually uttered.

I have spoken of the learning of Ligeia: it was immense—such as I have never known in woman. In the classical tongues was she deeply proficient, and as far as my own acquaintance extended in regard to the modern dialects of Europe, I have never known her at fault. Indeed upon any theme of the most admired because simply the most abstruse of the boasted erudition of the Academy, have I *ever* found Ligeia at fault? How singularly—how thrillingly, this one point in the nature of my wife has forced itself, at this late period only, upon my attention! I said her knowledge was such as I have never known in woman—but where breathes the man who has traversed, and successfully, *all* the wide areas of moral, physical, and mathematical science? I saw not then what I now clearly perceive, that the acquisitions of Ligeia were gigantic, were astounding; yet I was sufficiently aware of her infinite supremacy to resign myself, with a child-like confidence, to her guidance through the chaotic world of metaphysical investigation at which I was most busily occupied during the earlier years of our marriage. With how vast a triumph—with how vivid a delight—with how much of all that is ethereal in hope did I *feel*, as she bent over me in studies but little sought—but less known,—that delicious vista by slow degrees expanding before me, down whose long, gorgeous, and all untrodden path, I might at length pass onward to the goal of a wisdom too divinely precious not to be forbidden!

How poignant, then, must have been the grief with which, after some years, I beheld my well-grounded expectations take wings to themselves and fly away! Without Ligeia I was but as a child groping benighted. Her presence, her readings alone, rendered vividly luminous the many mysteries of the transcendentalism in which we were immersed. Wanting the radiant lustre of her eyes, letters, lambent and golden, grew duller than Saturnian[12] lead. And now those eyes shone less and less frequently upon the pages over which I pored. Ligeia grew ill. Her wild eyes blazed with a too—too glorious effulgence; the pale fingers became of the transparent waxen hue of the grave; and the blue veins upon the lofty forehead swelled and sank impetuously with the tides of the most gentle emotion. I saw that she must die—and I struggled desperately in spirit with the grim Azrael.[13] And the struggles of the passionate wife were, to my astonishment, even more energetic than my own. There had been much in her stern nature to impress me with the belief that, to her, death would have come without its terrors; but not so. Words are impotent to convey any just idea of the fierceness of resistance with which she wrestled with the Shadow. I groaned in anguish at the pitiable spectacle. I would have soothed—I would have reasoned; but in the intensity of her wild desire for life—for life—*but* for life—solace and reason were alike the uttermost of folly. Yet not until the last instance, amid the most convulsive writhings of her fierce spirit, was shaken the external placidity of her demeanor. Her voice grew more gentle—grew more low— yet I would not wish to dwell upon the wild meaning of the quietly uttered words. My brain reeled as I hearkened, entranced, to a melody more than mortal—to assumptions and aspirations which mortality had never before known.

That she loved me I should not have doubted; and I might have been easily aware that, in a bosom such as hers, love would have reigned no ordinary passion. But

in death only was I fully impressed with the strength of
her affection. For long hours, detaining my hand, would
she pour out before me the overflowing of a heart whose
more than passionate devotion amounted to idolatry.
How had I deserved to be so blessed by such confes-
sions?—how had I deserved to be so cursed with the removal of my beloved in the hour of my making them?
But upon this subject I cannot bear to dilate. Let me say
only, that in Ligeia's more than womanly abandonment
to a love, alas! all unmerited, all unworthily bestowed, I
at length recognized the principle of her longing, with so
wildly earnest a desire, for the life which was now fleeing
so rapidly away. It is this wild longing—it is this eager ve-
hemence of desire for life—*but* for life—that I have no
power to portray—no utterance capable of expressing.

At high noon of the night in which she departed,
beckoning me, peremptorily, to her side, she bade me
repeat certain verses composed by herself not many days
before. I obeyed her. They were these:—

Lo! 'tis a gala night
　　Within the lonesome latter years!
An angel throng, bewinged, bedight
　　In veils, and drowned in tears,
Sit in a theatre, to see
　　A play of hopes and fears,
While the orchestra breathes fitfully
　　The music of the spheres.

Mimes, in the form of God on high,
　　Mutter and mumble low,
And hither and thither fly;
　　Mere puppets they, who come and go

At bidding of vast formless things
    That shift the scenery to and fro,
Flapping from out their condor wings
    Invisible Woe!

That motley drama!—oh, be sure
    It shall not be forgot!
With its Phantom chased for evermore,
    By a crowd that seize it not,
Through a circle that ever returneth in
    To the self-same spot;
And much of Madness, and more of Sin
    And Horror, the soul of the plot!

But see, amid the mimic rout
    A crawling shape intrude!
A blood-red thing that writhes from out
    The scenic solitude!
It writhes!—it writhes!—with mortal pangs
    The mimes become its food,
And the seraphs sob at vermin fangs
    In human gore imbued.

Out—out are the lights—out all!
    And over each quivering form,
The curtain, a funeral pall,
    Comes down with the rush of a storm—
And the angels, all pallid and wan,
    Uprising, unveiling, affirm
That the play is the tragedy, "Man,"
    And its hero, the Conqueror Worm.

"O God!" half shrieked Ligeia, leaping to her feet and extending her arms aloft with a spasmodic movement, as

I made an end of these lines—"O God! O Divine Father!—shall these things be undeviatingly so?—shall this conqueror be not once conquered? Are we not part and parcel in Thee? Who—who knoweth the mysteries of the will with its vigor? Man doth not yield him to the angels, *nor unto death utterly,* save only through the weakness of his feeble will."

And now, as if exhausted with emotion, she suffered her white arms to fall, and returned solemnly to her bed of death. And as she breathed her last sighs, there came mingled with them a low murmur from her lips. I bent to them my ear, and distinguished, again, the concluding words of the passage in Glanvill: *"Man doth not yield him to the angels, nor unto death utterly, save only through the weakness of his feeble will."*

She died: and I, crushed into the very dust with sorrow, could no longer endure the lonely desolation of my dwelling in the dim and decaying city by the Rhine. I had no lack of what the world calls wealth. Ligeia had brought me far more, very far more, than ordinarily falls to the lot of mortals. After a few months, therefore, of weary and aimless wandering, I purchased and put in some repair, an abbey, which I shall not name, in one of the wildest and least frequented portions of fair England. The gloomy and dreary grandeur of the building, the almost savage aspect of the domain, the many melancholy and time-honored memories connected with both, had much in unison with the feelings of utter abandonment which had driven me into that remote and unsocial region of the country. Yet although the external abbey, with its verdant decay hanging about it, suffered but little alteration, I gave way, with a child-like perversity, and perchance with a faint hope of alleviating my sorrows, to a display of more than regal magnificence within. For such follies, even in childhood, I had imbibed a taste, and now they came back to me as if in the dotage of grief. Alas, I feel how much even of incipient madness might have been discovered in the gorgeous and fantastic draperies, in the solemn carvings of Egypt, in the wild cornices and furniture, in the Bedlam patterns of the carpets of tufted gold! I had become a bounden slave in the trammels of opium, and my labors and my orders had taken a coloring from my dreams. But these absurdities I must not pause to detail. Let me speak only of that one chamber, ever accursed, whither, in a moment of mental alienation, I led from the altar as my bride—as the successor of the unforgotten Ligeia—the fair-haired and blue-eyed Lady Rowena Trevanion, of Tremaine.

There is no individual portion of the architecture and decoration of that bridal chamber which is not now visibly before me. Where were the souls of the haughty family of the bride, when, through thirst of gold, they permitted to pass the threshold of an apartment *so* bedecked, a maiden and a daughter so beloved? I have said, that I minutely remember the details of the chamber—yet I am sadly forgetful on topics of deep moment; and here there was no system, no keeping, in the fantastic display, to take hold upon the memory. The room lay in a high turret of the castellated abbey, was pentagonal in shape, and of capacious size. Occupying the whole southern face of the pentagon was the sole window—an immense sheet of unbroken glass from Venice—a single pane, and tinted of a leaden hue, so that the rays of either the sun or moon passing through it, fell with a ghastly lustre on the objects within. Over the upper portion of this huge window, extended the trellis-work of an aged vine, which clambered up the massy walls of the turret. The ceiling, of gloomy-looking oak, was excessively lofty, vaulted, and elaborately fretted with the wildest and most grotesque specimens of a semi-Gothic, semi-Druidical device. From out the most central recess of this melancholy vaulting, depended, by a single chain of gold with long links, a huge censer of the same metal, Saracenic in pattern, and with many perforations so contrived that there writhed in and out of them, as if endued with a serpent vitality, a continual succession of parti colored fires.

Some few ottomans and golden candelabra, of Eastern figure, were in various stations about; and there was the couch, too—the bridal couch—of an Indian model, and low, and sculptured of solid ebony, with a pall-like canopy above. In each of the angles of the chamber stood on end a gigantic sarcophagus of black granite, from the tombs of the kings over against Luxor, with their aged lids full of immemorial sculpture. But in the draping of the apartment lay, alas! the chief phantasy of all. The lofty walls, gigantic in height—even unproportionably so—were hung from summit to foot, in vast folds, with a heavy and massive-looking tapestry—tapestry of a material which was found alike as a carpet on the floor, as a covering for the ottomans and the ebony bed, as a canopy for the bed and as the gorgeous volutes of the curtains which partially shaded the window. The material was the richest cloth of gold. It was spotted all over, at irregular intervals, with arabesque figures, about a foot in diameter, and wrought upon the cloth in patterns of the most jetty black. But these figures partook of the true character of the arabesque only when regarded from a single point of view. By a contrivance now common, and indeed traceable to a very remote period of antiquity, they were made changeable in aspect. To one entering the room, they bore the appearance of simple monstrosities; but upon a farther advance, this appearance gradually departed; and, step by step, as the visitor moved his station in the chamber, he saw himself surrounded by an endless succession of the ghastly forms which belong to the superstition of the Norman, or arise in the guilty slumbers of the monk. The phantasmagoric effect was vastly heightened by the artificial introduction of a strong continual current of wind behind the draperies—giving a hideous and uneasy animation to the whole.

In halls such as these—in a bridal chamber such as this—I passed, with the Lady of Tremaine, the unhallowed hours of the first month of our marriage—passed them with but little disquietude. That my wife dreaded the fierce moodiness of my temper—that she shunned me, and loved me but little—I could not help perceiving; but it gave me rather pleasure than otherwise. I loathed her with a hatred belonging more to demon than to man. My memory flew back (oh, with what intensity of regret!) to Ligeia, the beloved, the august, the beautiful, the entombed. I revelled in recollections of her purity, of her wisdom, of her lofty—her ethereal nature, of her passionate, her idolatrous love. Now, then, did my spirit fully and freely burn with more than all the fires of her own. In the excitement of my opium-dreams (for I was habitually fettered in the shackles of the drug), I would call aloud upon her name, during the silence of the night, or among the sheltered recesses of the glens by day, as if, through the wild eagerness, the solemn passion, the consuming ardor of my longing for the departed, I could restore her to the pathways she had abandoned—ah, *could* it be for ever?—upon the earth.

About the commencement of the second month of the marriage, the Lady Rowena was attacked with sudden illness, from which her recovery was slow. The fever which consumed her rendered her nights uneasy; and in her perturbed state of half-slumber, she spoke of sounds, and of motions, in and about the chamber of the turret, which I concluded had no origin save in the distemper of her fancy, or perhaps in the phantasmagoric influences of the chamber itself. She became at length convalescent—finally, well. Yet but a brief period elapsed, ere a second more violent disorder again threw her upon a bed of suffering; and from this attack her frame, at all times feeble, never altogether recovered. Her illnesses were, after this epoch, of alarming character, and of more alarming recurrence, defying alike the knowledge and the great exertions of her physicians. With the increase of the chronic disease, which had thus, apparently, taken too sure hold upon her constitution to be eradicated by human means, I could not fail to observe a similar increase in the nervous irritation of her temperament, and in her excitability by trivial causes of fear. She spoke again, and now more frequently and pertinaciously, of the sounds—of the slight sounds—and of the unusual motions among the tapestries, to which she had formerly alluded.

One night, near the closing in of September, she pressed this distressing subject with more than usual emphasis upon my attention. She had just awakened from an unquiet slumber, and I had been watching, with feelings half of anxiety, half of vague terror, the workings of her emaciated countenance. I sat by the side of her ebony bed, upon one of the ottomans of India. She partly arose, and spoke, in an earnest low whisper, of sounds which she *then* heard, but which I could not hear—of motions which she *then* saw, but which I could not perceive. The wind was rushing hurriedly behind the tapestries, and I wished to show her (what, let me confess it, I could not *all* believe) that those almost inarticulate breathings, and those very gentle variations of the figures upon the wall, were but the natural effects of that customary rushing of the wind. But a deadly pallor, overspreading her face, had proved to me that my exertions to reassure her would be fruitless. She appeared to be fainting, and no attendants were within call. I remembered where was deposited a decanter of light wine which had been ordered by her physicians, and hastened across the chamber to procure it. But, as I stepped beneath the light of the censer, two circumstances of a startling nature attracted my attention. I had felt that some palpable although invisible object had passed lightly by my person; and I saw that there lay upon the golden carpet, in the very middle of the rich lustre thrown from the censer, a shadow—a faint, indefinite shadow of angelic aspect—such as might be fancied for the shadow of a shade. But I was wild with the excitement of an immoderate dose of opium, and heeded these things but little, nor spoke of them to Rowena. Having found the wine, I recrossed the chamber, and poured out a gobletful, which I held to the lips of the fainting lady. She had now partially recovered, however, and took the vessel herself, while I sank upon an ottoman near me, with my eyes fastened upon her person. It was then that I became distinctly aware of a gentle footfall upon the carpet, and near the couch; and in a second thereafter, as Rowena was in the act of raising the wine to her lips, I saw, or may have dreamed that I saw, fall within the goblet, as if from some invisible spring in the atmosphere of the room three or four large drops of a brilliant and ruby colored fluid. If this I saw not so Rowena. She swallowed the wine unhesitatingly, and I forbore to speak to her of a circumstance which must, after all, I considered, have been but the suggestion of a vivid imagination, rendered morbidly active by the terror of the lady, by the opium, and by the hour.

Yet I cannot conceal it from my own perception that, immediately subsequent to the fall of the ruby-drops, a rapid change for the worse took place in the disorder of my wife; so that, on the third subsequent night, the hands of her menials prepared her for the tomb, and on the fourth, I sat alone, with her shrouded body, in that fantastic chamber which had received her as my bride. Wild visions, opium-engendered, flitted, shadow-like, before me. I gazed with unquiet eye upon the sarcophagi in the angles of the room, upon the varying figures of the drapery, and upon the writhing of the parti-colored fires in the censer overhead. My eyes then fell, as I called to mind the circumstances of a former night, to the spot beneath the glare of the censer where I had seen the faint traces of the shadow. It was there, however, no longer;

and breathing with greater freedom, I turned my glances to the pallid and rigid figure upon the bed. Then rushed upon me a thousand memories of Ligeia—and then came back upon my heart, with the turbulent violence of a flood, the whole of that unutterable woe with which I had regarded *her* thus enshrouded. The night waned; and still, with a bosom full of bitter thoughts of the one only and supremely beloved, I remained gazing upon the body of Rowena.

It might have been midnight, or perhaps earlier, or later, for I had taken no note of time, when a sob, low, gentle, but very distinct, startled me from my revery. I *felt* that it came from the bed of ebony—the bed of death. I listened in an agony of superstitious terror—but there was no repetition of the sound. I strained my vision to detect any motion in the corpse—but there was not the slightest perceptible. Yet I could not have been deceived. I *had* heard the noise, however faint, and my soul was awakened within me. I resolutely and perseveringly kept my attention riveted upon the body. Many minutes elapsed before any circumstance occurred tending to throw light upon the mystery. At length it became evident that a slight, a very feeble, and barely noticeable tinge of color had flushed up within the cheeks, and along the sunken small veins of the eyelids. Through a species of unutterable horror and awe, for which the language of mortality has no sufficiently energetic expression, I felt my heart cease to beat, my limbs grow rigid where I sat. Yet a sense of duty finally operated to restore my self-possession. I could no longer doubt that we had been precipitate in our preparations—that Rowena still lived. It was necessary that some immediate exertion be made; yet the turret was altogether apart from the portion of the abbey tenanted by the servants—there were none within call—I had no means of summoning them to my aid without leaving the room for many minutes—and this I could not venture to do. I therefore struggled alone in my endeavors to call back the spirit still hovering. In a short period it was certain, however, that a relapse had taken place; the color disappeared from both eyelid and cheek, leaving a wanness even more than that of marble; the lips became doubly shrivelled and pinched up in the ghastly expression of death; a repulsive clamminess and coldness overspread rapidly the surface of the body; and all the usual rigorous stiffness immediately supervened. I fell back with a shudder upon the couch from which I had been so startlingly aroused, and again gave myself up to passionate waking visions of Ligeia.

An hour thus elapsed, when (could it be possible?) I was a second time aware of some vague sound issuing from the region of the bed. I listened—in extremity of horror. The sound came again—it was a sigh. Rushing to the corpse, I saw—distinctly saw—a tremor upon the lips. In a minute afterward they relaxed, disclosing a bright line of the pearly teeth. Amazement now struggled in my bosom with the profound awe which had hitherto reigned there alone. I felt that my vision grew dim, that my reason wandered; and it was only by a violent effort that I at length succeeded in nerving myself to the task which duty thus once more had pointed out. There was now a partial glow upon the forehead and upon the cheek and throat; a perceptible warmth pervaded the whole frame; there was even a slight pulsation at the heart. The lady *lived;* and with redoubled ardor I betook myself to the task of restoration. I chafed and bathed the temples and the hands, and used every exertion which experience, and no little medical reading, could suggest. But in vain. Suddenly, the color fled, the pulsation ceased, the lips resumed the expression of the dead, and, in an instant afterward, the whole body took upon itself the icy chilliness, the livid hue, the intense rigidity, the sunken outline, and all the loathsome peculiarities of that which has been, for many days, a tenant of the tomb.

And again I sunk into visions of Ligeia—and again (what marvel that I shudder while I write?), *again* there reached my ears a low sob from the region of the ebony bed. But why shall I minutely detail the unspeakable horrors of that night? Why shall I pause to relate how, time after time, until near the period of the gray dawn, this hideous drama of revivification was repeated; how each terrific relapse was only into a sterner end apparently more irredeemable death; how each agony wore the aspect of a struggle with some invisible foe; and how each struggle was succeeded by I know not what of wild change in the personal appearance of the corpse? Let me hurry to a conclusion.

The greater part of the fearful night had worn away, and she who had been dead once again stirred—and now more vigorously than hitherto, although arousing from a dissolution more appalling in its utter hopelessness than any. I had long ceased to struggle or to move, and remained sitting rigidly upon the ottoman, a helpless prey to a whirl of violent emotions, of which extreme awe was perhaps the least terrible, the least consuming. The corpse, I repeat, stirred, and now more vigorously than before. The hues of life flushed up with unwonted energy into the countenance—the limbs relaxed—and, save that the eyelids were yet pressed heavily together, and that the bandages and draperies of the grave still imparted their charnel character to the figure, I might have dreamed that Rowena had indeed shaken off, utterly, the fetters of Death. But if this idea was not, even then, altogether adopted, I could at least doubt no longer, when, arising from the bed, tottering, with feeble steps, with closed eyes, and with the manner of one bewildered in a dream, the thing that was enshrouded advanced boldly and palpably into the middle of the apartment.

I trembled not—I stirred not—for a crowd of unutterable fancies connected with the air, the stature, the demeanor, of the figure, rushing hurriedly through my brain, had paralyzed—had chilled me into stone. I stirred not—but gazed upon the apparition. There was a mad disorder in my thoughts—a tumult unappeasable. Could it, indeed, be the *living* Rowena who confronted me? Could it, indeed, be Rowena *at all*—the fair-haired, the blue-eyed Lady Rowena Trevanion of Tremaine? Why, *why* should I doubt it? The bandage lay heavily about the mouth—but then might it not be the mouth of the breathing Lady of Tremaine? And the cheeks—there were the roses as in her noon of life—yes, these might indeed be the fair cheeks of the living Lady of Tremaine. And the chin, with its dimples, as in health, might it not be hers?—but *had she then grown taller since her malady?* What inexpressible madness seized me with that thought? One bound, and I had reached her feet! Shrinking from my touch, she let fall from her head, unloosened, the ghastly cerements which had confined it, and there streamed forth into the rushing atmosphere of the chamber huge masses of long and dishevelled hair; *it was blacker than the raven wings of midnight!* And now slowly opened *the eyes* of the figure which stood before me. "Here then, at least," I shrieked aloud, "can I never—can I never be mistaken—these are the full, and the black, and the wild eyes—of my lost love—of the Lady—of the LADY LIGEIA."

THE MASQUE OF THE RED DEATH[1]

THE "RED DEATH" had long devastated the country. No pestilence had ever been so fatal, or so hideous. Blood was its Avatar[2] and its seal—the redness and the horror of blood. There were sharp pains, and sudden dizziness, and then profuse bleeding at the pores, with dissolution. The scarlet stains upon the body and especially upon the face of the victim, were the pest ban[3] which shut him out from the aid and from the sympathy of his fellow-men. And the whole seizure, progress, and termination of the disease, were the incidents of half an hour.

But the Prince Prospero was happy and dauntless and sagacious. When his dominions were half depopulated, he summoned to his presence a thousand hale and light-hearted friends from among the knights and dames of his court, and with these retired to the deep seclusion of one of his castellated abbeys. This was an extensive and magnificent structure, the creation of the prince's own eccentric yet august taste. A strong and lofty wall girdled it in. This wall had gates of iron. The courtiers, having entered, brought furnaces and massy hammers and welded the bolts. They resolved to leave means neither of ingress nor egress to the sudden impulses of despair or of frenzy from within. The abbey was amply provisioned. With such precautions the courtiers might bid defiance to contagion. The external world could take care of itself. In the meantime it was folly to grieve, or to think. The prince had provided all the appliances of pleasure. There were buffoons, there were improvisatori,[4] there were ballet-dancers, there were musicians, there was Beauty, there was wine. All these and security were within. Without was the "Red Death."

It was toward the close of the fifth or sixth month of his seclusion, and while the pestilence raged most furiously abroad, that the Prince Prospero entertained his thousand friends at a masked ball of the most unusual magnificence.

It was a voluptuous scene, that masquerade. But first let me tell of the rooms in which it was held. There were seven—an imperial suite. In many palaces, however, such suites form a long and straight vista, while the folding doors slide back nearly to the walls on either hand, so that the view of the whole extent is scarcely impeded. Here the case was very different; as might have been expected from the duke's love of the *bizarre*. The apartments were so irregularly disposed that the vision embraced but little more than one at a time. There was a sharp turn at every twenty or thirty yards, and at each turn a novel effect. To the right and left, in the middle of each wall, a tall and narrow Gothic window looked out upon a closed corridor which pursued the windings of the suite. These windows were of stained glass whose color varied in accordance with the prevailing hue of the decorations of the chamber into which it opened. That at the eastern extremity was hung, for example, in blue—and vividly blue were its windows. The second chamber was purple in its ornaments and tapestries, and here the panes were purple. The third was green throughout, and so were the casements. The fourth was furnished and lighted with orange—the fifth with white—the sixth with violet. The seventh apartment was closely shrouded in black velvet tapestries that hung all over the ceiling and down the walls, falling in heavy folds upon a carpet of the same material and hue. But in this chamber only, the color of the windows failed to correspond with the decorations. The panes here were scarlet—a deep blood color. Now in no one of the seven apartments was there any lamp or candelabrum, amid the profusion of golden ornaments that lay scattered to and fro or depended from the roof. There was no light of any kind emanating from lamp or candle within the suite of chambers. But in the corridors that followed the suite, there stood, opposite to each window, a heavy tripod, bearing a brazier of fire, that projected its rays through the tinted glass and so glaringly illumined the room. And thus were produced a multitude of gaudy and fantastic appearances. But in the western or black chamber the effect of the fire-light that streamed upon the dark hangings through the blood-tinted panes was ghastly in the extreme, and produced so wild a look upon the countenances of those who entered, that there were few of the company bold enough to set foot within its precincts at all.

It was in this apartment, also, that there stood against the western wall, a gigantic clock of ebony. Its pendulum swung to and fro with a dull, heavy, monotonous clang; and when the minute-hand made the circuit of the face, and the hour was to be stricken, there came from the brazen lungs of the clock a sound which was clear and loud and deep and exceedingly musical, but of so peculiar a note and emphasis that, at each lapse of an hour, the musicians of the orchestra were constrained to pause, momentarily, in their performance, to hearken to the sound; and thus the waltzers perforce ceased their evolutions; and there was a brief disconcert of the whole gay company; and, while the chimes of the clock yet rang, it was observed that the giddiest grew pale, and the more aged and sedate passed their hands over their brows as if in confused revery or meditation. But when the echoes had fully ceased, a light laughter at once pervaded the assembly; the musicians looked at each other and smiled as if at their own nervousness and folly, and made whispering vows, each to the other, that the next chiming of the clock should produce in them no similar emotion; and then, after the lapse of sixty minutes (which embrace three thousand and six hundred seconds of the Time that flies), there came yet another chiming of the clock, and then were the same disconcert and tremulousness and meditation as before.

But, in spite of these things, it was a gay and magnificent revel. The tastes of the duke were peculiar. He had a fine eye for colors and effects. He disregarded the *decora*[5] of mere fashion. His plans were bold and fiery, and his conceptions glowed with barbaric lustre. There are some who would have thought him mad. His followers felt that he was not. It was necessary to hear and see and touch him to be *sure* that he was not.

He had directed, in great part, the movable embellishments of the seven chambers, upon occasion of this great *fête;* and it was his own guiding taste which had given character to the masqueraders. Be sure they were grotesque. There were much glare and glitter and piquancy and phantasm—much of what has been since seen in "Hernani."[6] There were arabesque figures with unsuited limbs and appointments. There were delirious fancies such as the madman fashions. There were much of the beautiful, much of the wanton, much of the *bizarre*, something of the terrible, and not a little of that which might have excited disgust. To and fro in the seven chambers there stalked, in fact, a multitude of dreams. And these—the dreams—writhed in and about, taking hue from the rooms, and causing the wild music of the orchestra to seem as the echo of their steps. And, anon, there strikes the ebony clock which stands in the hall of the velvet. And then, for a moment, all is still, and all is silent save the voice of the clock. The dreams are stiff-frozen as they stand. But the echoes of the chime die away—they have endured but an instant—and a light, half-subdued laughter floats after them as they depart. And now again the music swells, and the dreams live, and writhe to and fro more merrily than ever, taking hue from the many-tinted windows through which stream the rays from the tripods. But to the chamber which lies most westwardly of the seven there are now none of the maskers who venture; for the night is waning away; and there flows a ruddier light through the blood-colored panes; and the blackness of the sable drapery appals; and to him whose foot falls upon the sable carpet, there comes from the near clock of ebony a muffled peal more solemnly emphatic than any which reaches *their* ears who indulge in the more remote gaieties of the other apartments.

But these other apartments were densely crowded, and in them beat feverishly the heart of life. And the revel went whirlingly on, until at length there commenced the sounding of midnight upon the clock. And then the music ceased, as I have told; and the evolutions of the waltzers were quieted; and there was an uneasy cessation of all things as before. But now there were twelve strokes to be sounded by the bell of the clock; and thus it happened, perhaps, that more of thought crept, with more of time, into the meditations of the thoughtful among those who revelled. And thus too, it happened, perhaps, that before the last echoes of the last chime had utterly sunk into silence, there were many individuals in the crowd who had found leisure to become aware of the presence of a masked figure which had arrested the attention of no single individual before. And the rumor of this new presence having spread itself whisperingly around, there arose at length from the whole company a buzz, or murmur, expressive of disapprobation and surprise—then, finally, of terror, of horror, and of disgust.

In an assembly of phantasms such as I have painted, it may well be supposed that no ordinary appearance could have excited such sensation. In truth the masquerade license of the night was nearly unlimited; but the figure in question had out-Heroded Herod,[7] and gone beyond the bounds of even the prince's indefinite decorum. There are chords in the hearts of the most reckless which cannot be touched without emotion. Even with the utterly lost, to whom life and death are equally jests, there are matters of which no jest can be made. The whole company, indeed, seemed now deeply to feel that in the costume and bearing of the stranger neither wit nor propriety existed. The figure was tall and gaunt, and shrouded from head to foot in the habiliments[8] of the grave. The mask which concealed the visage was made so nearly to resemble the countenance of a stiffened corpse that the closest scrutiny must have had difficulty in detecting the cheat. And yet all this might have been endured, if not approved, by the mad revellers around. But the mummer[9] had gone so far as to assume the type of the Red Death. His vesture was dabbled in *blood*—and his broad brow, with all the features of the face, was besprinkled with the scarlet horror.

When the eyes of Prince Prospero fell upon this spectral image (which, with a slow and solemn movement, as if more fully to sustain its *rôle*, stalked to and fro among the waltzers) he was seen to be convulsed, in the first moment with a strong shudder either of terror or distaste; but, in the next, his brow reddened with rage.

"Who dares"—he demanded hoarsely of the courtiers who stood near him—"who dares insult us with this blasphemous mockery? Seize him and unmask him—that we may know whom we have to hang, at sunrise, from the battlements!"

It was in the eastern or blue chamber in which stood the Prince Prospero as he uttered these words. They rang throughout the seven rooms loudly and clearly, for the prince was a bold and robust man, and the music had become hushed at the waving of his hand.

It was in the blue room where stood the prince, with a group of pale courtiers by his side. At first, as he spoke, there was a slight rushing movement of this group in the direction of the intruder, who, at the moment was also near at hand, and now, with deliberate and stately step, made closer approach to the speaker. But from a certain nameless awe with which the mad assumptions of the mummer had inspired the whole party, there were found none who put forth hand to seize him; so that, unimpeded, he passed within a yard of the prince's person; and, while the vast assembly, as if with one impulse, shrank from the centres of the rooms to the walls, he made his way uninterruptedly, but with the same solemn and measured step which had distinguished him from the first, through the blue chamber to the purple— through the purple to the green—through the green to the orange—through this again to the white—and even thence to the violet, ere a decided movement had been made to arrest him. It was then, however, that the Prince Prospero, maddening with rage and the shame of his own momentary cowardice, rushed hurriedly through the six chambers, while none followed him on account of a deadly terror that had seized upon all. He bore aloft a drawn dagger, and had approached, in rapid impetuosity, to within three or four feet of the retreating figure, when the latter, having attained the extremity of the velvet apartment, turned suddenly and confronted his pursuer. There was a sharp cry—and the dagger dropped gleaming upon the sable carpet, upon which, instantly afterward, fell prostrate in death the Prince Prospero. Then, summoning the wild courage of despair, a throng of the revellers at once threw themselves into the black apartment, and, seizing the mummer, whose tall figure stood erect and motionless within the shadow of the ebony clock, gasped in unutterable horror at finding the grave cerements and corpse-like mask, which they handled with so violent a rudeness, untenanted by any tangible form.

And now was acknowledged the presence of the Red Death. He had come like a thief in the night.[10] And one by one dropped the revellers in the blood-bedewed halls of their revel, and died each in the despairing posture of his fall. And the life of the ebony clock went out with that of the last of the gay. And the flames of the tripods expired. And Darkness and Decay and the Red Death held illimitable dominion over all.

THE FALL OF THE HOUSE OF USHER[1]

Son cœur est un luth suspendu;
Sitôt qu'on le touche il résonne.
—*De Béranger*[2]

DURING THE WHOLE of a dull, dark, and soundless day in the autumn of the year, when the clouds hung oppressively low in the heavens, I had been passing alone, on horseback, through a singularly dreary tract of country, and at length found myself, as the shades of the evening drew on, within view of the melancholy House of Usher. I know not how it was—but, with the first glimpse of the building, a sense of insufferable gloom pervaded my spirit. I say insufferable; for the feeling was unrelieved by any of that half-pleasurable, because poetic, sentiment with which the mind usually receives even the sternest natural images of the desolate or terrible. I looked upon the scene before me—upon the mere house, and the simple landscape features of the domain—upon the bleak walls—upon the vacant eye-like windows—upon a few rank sedges—and upon a few white trunks of decayed trees—with an utter depression of soul which I can compare to no earthly sensation more properly than to the after-dream of the reveller upon opium—the bitter lapse into everyday life—the hideous dropping off of the veil. There was an iciness, a sinking, a sickening of the heart—an unredeemed dreariness of thought which no goading of the imagination could torture into aught of the sublime. What was it—I paused to think—what was it that so unnerved me in the contemplation of the House of Usher? It was a mystery all insoluble; nor could I grapple with the shadowy fancies that crowded upon me as I pondered. I was forced to fall back upon the unsatisfactory conclusion, that while, beyond doubt, there *are* combinations of very simple natural objects which have the power of thus affecting us, still the analysis of this power lies among considerations beyond our depth. It was possible, I reflected, that a mere different arrangement of the particulars of the scene, of the details of the picture, would be sufficient to modify, or perhaps to annihilate its capacity for sorrowful impression; and, acting upon this idea, I reined my horse to the precipitous brink of a black and lurid tarn that lay in unruffled lustre by the dwelling, and gazed down—but with a shudder even more thrilling than before—upon the remodelled and inverted images of the gray sedge, and the ghastly tree-stems, and the vacant and eye-like windows.

Nevertheless, in this mansion of gloom I now proposed to myself a sojourn of some weeks. Its proprietor, Roderick Usher, had been one of my boon companions in boyhood; but many years had elapsed since our last meeting. A letter, however, had lately reached me in a distant part of the country—a letter from him—which, in its wildly importunate nature, had admitted of no other than a personal reply. The MS. gave evidence of nervous agitation. The writer spoke of acute bodily illness—of a mental disorder which oppressed him—and of an earnest desire to see me, as his best and indeed his only personal friend, with a view of attempting, by the cheerfulness of my society, some alleviation of his malady. It was the manner in which all this, and much more, was said—it was the apparent *heart* that went with his request—which allowed me no room for hesitation; and I accordingly obeyed forthwith what I still considered a very singular summons.

Although, as boys, we had been even intimate associates, yet I really knew little of my friend. His reserve had been always excessive and habitual. I was aware, however, that his very ancient family had been noted, time out of mind, for a peculiar sensibility of temperament, displaying itself, through long ages, in many works of exalted art, and manifested, of late, in repeated deeds of munificent yet unobtrusive charity, as well as in a passionate devotion to the intricacies, perhaps even more than to the orthodox and easily recognizable beauties, of musical science. I had learned, too, the very remarkable fact, that the stem of the Usher race, all time-honored as it was, had put forth, at no period, any enduring branch; in other words, that the entire family lay in the direct line of descent,[3] and had always, with very trifling and very temporary variation, so lain. It was this deficiency, I considered, while running over in thought the perfect keeping of the character of the premises with the accredited character of the people, and while speculating upon the possible influence which the one, in the long lapse of centuries, might have exercised upon the other—it was this deficiency, perhaps, of collateral issue, and the consequent undeviating transmission, from sire to son, of the patrimony with the name, which had, at length, so identified the two as to merge the original title of the estate in the quaint and equivocal appellation of the "House of Usher"—an appellation which seemed to include, in the minds of the peasantry who used it, both the family and the family mansion.

I have said that the sole effect of my somewhat childish experiment—that of looking down within the tarn—had been to deepen the first singular impression. There can be no doubt that the consciousness of the rapid increase of my superstition—for why should I not so term it?—served mainly to accelerate the increase itself. Such, I have long known, is the paradoxical law of all sentiments having terror as a basis. And it might have been for this reason only, that, when I again uplifted my eyes to the house itself, from its image in the pool, there grew in my mind a strange fancy—a fancy so ridiculous, indeed, that I but mention it to show the vivid force of the sensations which oppressed me. I had so worked upon my imagination as really to believe that about the whole mansion and domain there hung an atmosphere peculiar to themselves and their immediate vicinity—an atmosphere which had no affinity with the air of heaven, but which had reeked up from the decayed trees, and the gray wall, and the silent tarn—a pestilent and mystic vapor, dull, sluggish, faintly discernible, and leaden-hued.

Shaking off from my spirit what *must* have been a dream, I scanned more narrowly the real aspect of the building. Its principal feature seemed to be that of an excessive antiquity. The discoloration of ages had been great. Minute fungi overspread the whole exterior, hanging in a fine tangled web-work from the eaves. Yet all this was apart from any extraordinary dilapidation. No portion of the masonry had fallen; and there appeared to be a wild inconsistency between its still perfect adaptation of parts, and the crumbling condition of the individual stones. In this there was much that reminded me of the specious totality of old wood-work which has rotted for long years in some neglected vault, with no disturbance from the breath of the external air. Beyond this indication of extensive decay, however, the fabric gave little token of instability. Perhaps the eye of a scrutinizing observer might have discovered a barely perceptible fissure, which, extending from the roof of the building in front, made its way down the wall in a zigzag direction, until it became lost in the sullen waters of the tarn.

Noticing these things, I rode over a short causeway to the house. A servant in waiting took my horse, and I entered the Gothic archway of the hall. A valet, of stealthy step, thence conducted me, in silence, through many dark and intricate passages in my progress to the *studio* of his master. Much that I encountered on the way contributed, I know not how, to heighten the vague sentiments of which I have already spoken. While the objects around me—while the carvings of the ceilings, the sombre tapestries of the walls, the ebon blackness of the floors, and the phantasmagoric armorial trophies which rattled as I strode, were but matters to which, or to such

as which, I had been accustomed from my infancy—
while I hesitated not to acknowledge how familiar was all
this—I still wondered to find how familiar were the fancies which ordinary images were stirring up. On one of
the staircases, I met the physician of the family. His
countenance, I thought, wore a mingled expression of
low cunning and perplexity. He accosted me with trepidation and passed on. The valet now threw open a door
and ushered me into the presence of his master.

The room in which I found myself was very large and
lofty. The windows were long, narrow, and pointed, and
at so vast a distance from the black oaken floor as to be
altogether inaccessible from within. Feeble gleams of
encrimsoned light made their way through the trellissed
panes, and served to render sufficiently distinct the more
prominent objects around; the eye, however, struggled in
vain to reach the remoter angles of the chamber, or the
recesses of the vaulted and fretted ceiling. Dark
draperies hung upon the walls. The general furniture
was profuse, comfortless, antique, and tattered. Many
books and musical instruments lay scattered about, but
failed to give any vitality to the scene. I felt that I
breathed an atmosphere of sorrow. An air of stern, deep,
and irredeemable gloom hung over and pervaded all.

Upon my entrance, Usher arose from a sofa on which
he had been lying at full length, and greeted me with a
vivacious warmth which had much in it, I at first thought,
of an overdone cordiality—of the constrained effort of
the *ennuyé*[4] man of the world. A glance, however, at his
countenance convinced me of his perfect sincerity. We
sat down; and for some moments, while he spoke not, I
gazed upon him with a feeling half of pity, half of awe.

Surely, man had never before so terribly altered, in so brief a period, as had Roderick Usher! It was with difficulty that I could bring myself to admit the identity of the wan being before me with the companion of my early boyhood. Yet the character of his face had been at all times remarkable. A cadaverousness of complexion; an eye large, liquid, and luminous beyond comparison; lips somewhat thin and very pallid, but of a surpassingly beautiful curve; a nose of a delicate Hebrew model, but with a breadth of nostril unusual in similar formations; a finely moulded chin, speaking, in its want of prominence, of a want of moral energy; hair of a more than web-like softness and tenuity;—these features, with an inordinate expansion above the regions of the temple, made up altogether a countenance not easily to be forgotten. And now in the mere exaggeration of the prevailing character of these features, and of the expression they were wont to convey, lay so much of change that I doubted to whom I spoke. The now ghastly pallor of the skin, and the now miraculous lustre of the eye, above all things startled and even awed me. The silken hair, too, had been suffered to grow all unheeded, and as, in its wild gossamer texture, it floated rather than fell about the face, I could not, even with effort, connect its Arabesque expression with any idea of simple humanity.

In the manner of my friend I was at once struck with an incoherence—an inconsistency; and I soon found this to arise from a series of feeble and futile struggles to overcome an habitual trepidancy—an excessive nervous agitation. For something of this nature I had indeed been prepared, no less by his letter, than by reminiscences of certain boyish traits, and by conclusions deduced from his peculiar physical confirmation and temperament. His action was alternately vivacious and sullen. His voice varied rapidly from a tremulous indecision (when the animal spirits seemed utterly in abeyance) to that species of energetic concision—that abrupt, weighty, unhurried, and hollow-sounding enunciation—that leaden, self-balanced, and perfectly modulated guttural utterance, which may be observed in the lost drunkard, or the irreclaimable eater of opium, during the periods of his most intense excitement.

It was thus that he spoke of the object of my visit, of his earnest desire to see me, and of the solace he expected me to afford him. He entered, at some length, into what he conceived to be the nature of his malady. It was, he said, a constitutional and a family evil, and one for which he despaired to find a remedy—a mere nervous affection, he immediately added, which would undoubtedly soon pass off. It displayed itself in a host of unnatural sensations. Some of these, as he detailed them, interested and bewildered me; although, perhaps, the terms and the general manner of their narration had their weight. He suffered much from a morbid acuteness of the senses; the most insipid food was alone endurable; he could wear only garments of certain texture; the odors of all flowers were oppressive; his eyes were tortured by even a faint light; and there were but peculiar sounds, and these from stringed instruments, which did not inspire him with horror.

To an anomalous species of terror I found him a bounden slave. "I shall perish," said he, "I *must* perish in this deplorable folly. Thus, thus, and not otherwise, shall I be lost. I dread the events of the future, not in themselves, but in their results. I shudder at the thought of any, even the most trivial, incident, which may operate upon this intolerable agitation of soul. I have, indeed, no abhorrence of danger, except in its absolute effect—in terror. In this unnerved, in this pitiable, condition I feel that the period will sooner or later arrive when I must abandon life and reason together, in some struggle with the grim phantasm, FEAR."

I learned, moreover, at intervals, and through broken and equivocal hints, another singular feature of his mental condition. He was enchained by certain superstitious impressions in regard to the dwelling which he tenanted, and whence, for many years, he had never ventured forth—in regard to an influence whose supposititious force was conveyed in terms too shadowy here to be restated—an influence which some peculiarities in the mere form and substance of his family mansion had, by dint of long sufferance, he said, obtained over his spirit—an effect which the *physique* of the gray walls and turrets, and of the dim tarn into which they all looked down, had, at length, brought about upon the *morale* of his existence.

He admitted, however, although with hesitation, that much of the peculiar gloom which thus afflicted him could be traced to a more natural and far more palpable origin—to the severe and long-continued illness—indeed to the evidently approaching dissolution—of a tenderly beloved sister, his sole companion for long years, his last and only relative on earth. "Her decease," he said, with a bitterness which I can never forget, "would leave him (him, the hopeless and the frail) the last of the ancient race of the Ushers." While he spoke, the lady

Madeline (for so was she called) passed through a remote portion of the apartment, and, without having noticed my presence, disappeared. I regarded her with an utter astonishment not unmingled with dread; and yet I found it impossible to account for such feelings. A sensation of stupor oppressed me as my eyes followed her retreating steps. When a door, at length, closed upon her, my glance sought instinctively and eagerly the countenance of the brother; but he had buried his face in his hands, and I could only perceive that a far more than ordinary wanness had overspread the emaciated fingers through which trickled many passionate tears.

The disease of the lady Madeline had long baffled the skill of her physicians. A settled apathy, a gradual wasting away of the person, and frequent although transient affections of a partially cataleptical character[5] were the unusual diagnosis. Hitherto she had steadily borne up against the pressure of her malady, and had not betaken herself finally to bed; but on the closing in of the evening of my arrival at the house, she succumbed (as her brother told me at night with inexpressible agitation) to the prostrating power of the destroyer; and I learned that the glimpse I had obtained of her person would thus probably be the last I should obtain—that the lady, at least while living, would be seen by me no more.

For several days ensuing, her name was unmentioned by either Usher or myself; and during this period I was busied in earnest endeavors to alleviate the melancholy of my friend. We painted and read together, or I listened, as if in a dream, to the wild improvisations of his speaking guitar. And thus, as a closer and still closer intimacy admitted me more unreservedly into the recesses of his spirit, the more bitterly did I perceive the futility of all attempts at cheering a mind from which darkness, as if an inherent positive quality, poured forth upon all objects of the moral and physical universe in one unceasing radiation of gloom.

I shall ever bear about me a memory of the many solemn hours I thus spent alone with the master of the House of Usher. Yet I should fail in any attempt to convey an idea of the exact character of the studies, or of the occupations, in which he involved me, or led me the way. An excited and highly distempered ideality[6] threw a sulphureous lustre over all. His long improvised dirges will ring forever in my ears. Among other things, I hold painfully in mind a certain singular perversion and amplification of the wild air of the last waltz of Von Weber.[7] From the paintings over which his elaborate fancy brooded, and which grew, touch by touch, into vaguenesses at which I shuddered the more thrillingly, because I shuddered knowing not why—from these paintings (vivid as their images now are before me) I would in vain endeavor to educe more than a small portion which should lie within the compass of merely written words. By the utter simplicity, by the nakedness of his designs, he arrested and overawed attention. If ever mortal painted an idea, that mortal was Roderick Usher. For me at least, in the circumstances then surrounding me, there arose out of the pure abstractions which the hypochondriac contrived to throw upon his canvas, an intensity of intolerable awe, no shadow of which felt I ever yet in the contemplation of the certainly glowing yet too concrete reveries of Fuseli.[8]

One of the phantasmagoric conceptions of my friend,

partaking not so rigidly of the spirit of abstraction, may be shadowed forth, although feebly, in words. A small picture presented the interior of an immensely long and rectangular vault or tunnel, with low walls, smooth, white, and without interruption or device. Certain accessory points of the design served well to convey the idea that this excavation lay at an exceeding depth below the surface of the earth. No outlet was observed in any portion of its vast extent, and no torch or other artificial source of light was discernible; yet a flood of intense rays rolled throughout, and bathed the whole in a ghastly and inappropriate splendor.

I have just spoken of that morbid condition of the auditory nerve which rendered all music intolerable to the sufferer, with the exception of certain effects of stringed instruments. It was, perhaps, the narrow limits to which he thus confined himself upon the guitar which gave birth, in great measure, to the fantastic character of his performances. But the fervid *facility* of his *impromptus* could not be so accounted for. They must have been, and were, in the notes, as well as in the words of his wild fantasies (for he not unfrequently accompanied himself with rhymed verbal improvisations), the result of that intense mental collectedness and concentration to which I have previously alluded as observable only in particular moments of the highest artificial excitement. The words of one of these rhapsodies I have easily remembered. I was, perhaps, the more forcibly impressed with it as he gave it, because, in the under or mystic current of its meaning, I fancied that I perceived, and for the first time, a full consciousness on the part of Usher of the tottering of his lofty reason upon her throne. The verses, which were entitled "The Haunted Palace," ran very nearly, if not accurately, thus:—

I.

In the greenest of our valleys,
  By good angels tenanted,
Once a fair and stately palace—
  Radiant palace—reared its head.
In the monarch Thought's dominion—
  It stood there!
Never seraph spread a pinion[9]
  Over fabric half so fair.

II.

Banners yellow, glorious, golden,
  On its roof did float and flow
(This—all this—was in the olden
  Time long ago);
And every gentle air that dallied,
  In that sweet day,
Along the ramparts plumed and pallid,
  A winged odor went away.

III.

Wanderers in that happy valley
  Through two luminous windows saw
Spirits moving musically
  To a lute's well-timed law;
Round about a throne, where sitting
  (Porphyrogene!)[10]
In state his glory well befitting,
  The ruler of the realm was seen.

IV.

And all with pearl and ruby glowing
    Was the fair palace door,
Through which came flowing, flowing, flowing
    And sparkling evermore,
A troop of Echoes whose sweet duty
    Was but to sing,
In voices of surpassing beauty,
    The wit and wisdom of their king.

V.

But evil things, in robes of sorrow,
    Assailed the monarch's high estate;
(Ah, let us mourn, for never morrow
    Shall dawn upon him, desolate!)
And, round about his home, the glory
    That blushed and bloomed
Is but a dim-remembered story
    Of the old time entombed.

VI.

And travellers now within that valley,
    Through the red-litten windows see
Vast forms that move fantastically
    To a discordant melody;
While, like a rapid ghastly river,
    Through the pale door;
A hideous throng rush out forever,
    And laugh—but smile no more.

I well remember that suggestions arising from this ballad led us into a train of thought wherein there became manifest an opinion of Usher's which I mention not so much on account of its novelty (for other men° have thought thus), as on account of the pertinacity with which he maintained it. This opinion, in its general form, was that of the sentience of all vegetable things. But, in his disordered fancy, the idea had assumed a more daring character, and trespassed, under certain conditions, upon the kingdom of inorganization. I lack words to express the full extent, or the earnest *abandon* of his persuasion. The belief, however, was connected (as I have previously hinted) with the gray stones of the home of his forefathers. The conditions of the sentence had been here, he imagined, fulfilled in the method of collocation of these stones—in the order of their arrangement, as well as in that of the many *fungi* which overspread them, and of the decayed trees which stood around—above all, in the long undisturbed endurance of this arrangement, and in its reduplication in the still waters of the tarn. Its evidence—the evidence of the sentience—was to be seen, he said (and I here started as he spoke), in the gradual yet certain condensation of an atmosphere of their own about the waters and the walls. The result was discoverable, he added, in that silent yet importunate and terrible influence which for centuries had moulded the destinies of his family, and which made *him* what I now saw him—what he was. Such opinions need no comment, and I will make none.

Our books—the books which, for years, had formed no small portion of the mental existence of the invalid—

° Watson, Dr. Percival, Spallanzani, and especially the Bishop of Llandaff.—See "Chemical Essays," vol v.[11]

were, as might be supposed, in strict keeping with this character of phantasm. We pored together over such works as the "Ververt et Chartreuse" of Gresset; the "Belphegor" of Machiavelli; the "Heaven and Hell" of Swedenborg; the "Subterranean Voyage of Nicholas Klimm" of Holberg; the "Chiromancy" of Robert Flud, of Jean D'Indaginé, and of Dela Chambre; the "Journey into the Blue Distance" of Tieck; and the "City of the Sun" of Campanella.[12] One favorite volume was a small octavo edition of the "Directorium Inquisitorium," by the Dominican Eymeric de Gironne; and there were passages in Pomponius Mela, about the old African Satyrs and Œgipans,[13] over which Usher would sit dreaming for hours. His chief delight, however, was found in the perusal of an exceedingly rare and curious book in quarto Gothic—the manual of a forgotten church—the *Vigiliæ Mortuorum Secundum Chorum Ecclesiæ Maguntinæ.*[14]

I could not help thinking of the wild ritual of this work, and of its probable influence upon the hypochondriac, when, one evening, having informed me abruptly that the lady Madeline was no more, he stated his intention of preserving her corpse for a fortnight (previously to its final interment), in one of the numerous vaults within the main walls of the building. The worldly reason, however, assigned for this singular proceeding, was one which I did not feel at liberty to dispute. The brother had been led to his resolution (so he told me) by consideration of the unusual character of the malady of the deceased, of certain obtrusive and eager inquiries on the part of her medical men, and of the remote and exposed situation of the burial-ground of the family. I will not deny that when I called to mind the sinister countenance of the person whom I met upon the staircase, on the day of my arrival at the house, I had no desire to oppose what I regarded as at best but a harmless, and by no means an unnatural, precaution.

At the request of Usher, I personally aided him in the arrangements for the temporary entombment. The body having been encoffined, we two alone bore it to its rest. The vault in which we placed it (and which had been so long unopened that our torches, half smothered in its oppressive atmosphere, gave us little opportunity for investigation) was small, damp, and entirely without means of admission for light; lying, at great depth, immediately beneath that portion of the building in which was my own sleeping apartment. It had been used, apparently, in remote feudal times, for the worst purposes of a donjon-keep,[15] and, in later days, as a place of deposit for powder, or some other highly combustible substance, as a portion of its floor, and the whole interior of a long archway through which we reached it, were carefully sheathed with copper. The door, of massive iron, had been, also, similarly protected. Its immense weight caused an unusually sharp, grating sound, as it moved upon its hinges.

Having deposited our mournful burden upon tressels within this region of horror, we partially turned aside the yet unscrewed lid of the coffin, and looked upon the face of the tenant. A striking similitude between the brother and sister now first arrested my attention; and Usher, divining, perhaps, my thoughts, murmured out some few words from which I learned that the deceased and himself had been twins, and that sympathies of a scarcely intelligible nature had always existed between them. Our glances, however, rested not long upon the dead—for we could not regard her unawed. The disease which had thus entombed the lady in the maturity of youth, had left, as usual in all maladies of a strictly cataleptical character, the mockery of a faint blush upon the bosom and the face, and that suspiciously lingering smile upon the lip which is so terrible in death. We replaced and screwed down the lid, and, having secured the door of iron, made our way, with toil, into the scarcely less gloomy apartments of the upper portion of the house.

And now, some days of bitter grief having elapsed, an observable change came over the features of the mental disorder of my friend. His ordinary manner had vanished. His ordinary occupations were neglected or forgotten. He roamed from chamber to chamber with hurried, unequal, and objectless step. The pallor of his countenance had assumed, if possible, a more ghastly hue—but the luminousness of his eye had utterly gone out. The once occasional huskiness of his tone was heard no more; and a tremendous quaver, as if of extreme terror, habitually characterized his utterance. There were times, indeed, when I thought his unceasingly agitated mind was laboring with some oppressive secret, to divulge which he struggled for the necessary courage. At times, again, I was obliged to resolve all into the mere inexplicable vagaries of madness, for I beheld him gazing upon vacancy for long hours, in an attitude of the profoundest attention, as if listening to some imaginary sound. It was no wonder that his condition terrified—that it infected me. I felt creeping upon me, by slow yet certain degrees, the wild influences of his own fantastic yet impressive superstitions.

It was, especially, upon retiring to bed late in the night of the seventh or eighth day after the placing of the lady Madeline within the donjon, that I experienced the full power of such feelings. Sleep came not near my couch— while the hours waned and waned away. I struggled to reason off the nervousness which had dominion over me. I endeavored to believe that much, if not all of what I felt, was due to the bewildering influence of the gloomy furniture of the room—of the dark and tattered draperies, which, tortured into motion by the breath of a rising tempest, swayed fitfully to and fro upon the walls, and rustled uneasily about the decorations of the bed. But my efforts were fruitless. An irrepressible tremor gradually pervaded my frame; and, at length, there sat upon my very heart an incubus of utterly causeless alarm. Shaking this off with a gasp and a struggle, I uplifted myself upon the pillows, and, peering earnestly within the intense darkness of the chamber, hearkened—I know not why, except that an instinctive spirit prompted me—to certain low and indefinite sounds which came, through the pauses of the storm, at long intervals, I knew not whence. Overpowered by an intense sentiment of horror, unaccountable yet unendurable, I threw on my clothes with haste (for I felt that I should sleep no more during the night), and endeavored to arouse myself from the pitiable condition into which I had fallen, by pacing rapidly to and fro through the apartment.

I had taken but few turns in this manner, when a light step on an adjoining staircase arrested my attention. I presently recognized it as that of Usher. In an instant afterward he rapped, with a gentle touch, at my door, and entered, bearing a lamp. His countenance was, as usual, cadaverously wan—but, moreover, there was a species of mad hilarity in his eyes—an evidently restrained *hysteria* in his whole demeanor. His air appalled me—but any thing was preferable to the solitude which I had so long endured, and I even welcomed his presence as a relief.

"And you have not seen it?" he said abruptly, after having stared about him for some moments in silence—"you have not then seen it?—but, stay! you shall." Thus speaking, and having carefully shaded his lamp, he hurried to one of the casements, and threw it freely open to the storm.

The impetuous fury of the entering gust nearly lifted us from our feet. It was, indeed, a tempestuous yet sternly beautiful night, and one wildly singular in its terror and its beauty. A whirlwind had apparently collected its force in our vicinity; for there were frequent and violent alterations in the direction of the wind; and the exceeding density of the clouds (which hung so low as to press upon the turrets of the house) did not prevent our perceiving the life-like velocity with which they flew careering from all points against each other, without passing away into the distance. I say that even their exceeding density did not prevent our perceiving this—yet we had no glimpse of the moon or stars, nor was there any flashing forth of the lightning. But the under surfaces of the huge masses of agitated vapor, as well as all terrestrial objects immediately around us, were glowing in the unnatural light of a faintly luminous and distinctly visible gaseous exhalation which hung about and enshrouded the mansion.

"You must not—you shall not behold this!" said I, shuddering, to Usher, as I led him, with a gentle violence, from the window to a seat. "These appearances, which bewilder you, are merely electrical phenomena not uncommon—or it may be that they have their ghastly origin in the rank miasma of the tarn. Let us close this casement;—the air is chilling and dangerous to your frame. Here is one of your favorite romances. I will read, and you shall listen:—and so we will pass away this terrible night together."

The antique volume which I had taken up was the "Mad Trist" of Sir Launcelot Canning;[16] but I had called it a favorite of Usher's more in sad jest than in earnest; for, in truth, there is little in its uncouth and unimaginative prolixity which could have had interest for the lofty and spiritual ideality of my friend. It was, however, the only book immediately at hand; and I indulged a vague hope that the excitement which now agitated the hypochondriac, might find relief (for the history of mental disorder is full of similar anomalies) even in the extremeness of the folly which I should read. Could I have judged, indeed, by the wild overstrained air of vivacity with which he hearkened, or apparently hearkened, to the words of the tale, I might well have congratulated myself upon the success of my design.

I had arrived at that well-known portion of the story where Ethelred, the hero of the Trist, having sought in vain for peaceable admission into the dwelling of the hermit, proceeds to make good an entrance by force. Here, it will be remembered, the words of the narrative run thus:

"And Ethelred, who was by nature of a doughty[17] heart, and who was now mighty withal, on account of the powerfulness of the wine which he had drunken, waited no longer to hold parley with the hermit, who, in sooth, was of an obstinate and maliceful turn, but, feeling the rain upon his shoulders, and fearing the rising of the tempest, uplifted his mace outright, and, with blows, made quickly room in the plankings of the door for his gauntleted hand; and now pulling therewith sturdily, he so cracked, and ripped, and tore all asunder, that the noise of the dry and hollow-sounding wood alarumed[18] and reverberated throughout the forest."

At the termination of this sentence I started and, for a moment, paused; for it appeared to me (although I at once concluded that my excited fancy had deceived me)—it appeared to me that, from some very remote portion of the mansion, there came, indistinctly to my ears, what might have been, in its exact similarity of character, the echo (but a stifled and dull one certainly) of the very cracking and ripping sound which Sir Launcelot had so particularly described. It was, beyond doubt, the coincidence alone which had arrested my attention; for, amid the rattling of the sashes of the casements, and the ordinary commingled noises of the still increasing storm, the sound, in itself, had nothing, surely, which should have interested or disturbed me. I continued the story:

"But the good champion Ethelred, now entering within the door, was sore enraged and amazed to perceive no signal of the maliceful hermit; but, in the stead thereof, a dragon of a scaly and prodigious demeanor, and of a fiery tongue, which sate in guard before a palace of gold, with a floor of silver; and upon the wall there hung a shield of shining brass with this legend enwritten—

Who entereth herein, a conqueror hath bin;
Who slayeth the dragon, the shield he shall win.

And Ethelred uplifted his mace, and struck upon the head of the dragon, which fell before him, and gave up his pesty breath, with a shriek so horrid and harsh, and withal so piercing, that Ethelred had fain to close his ears with his hands against the dreadful noise of it, the like whereof was never before heard."

Here again I paused abruptly, and now with a feeling of wild amazement—for there could be no doubt whatever that, in this instance, I did actually hear (although from what direction it proceeded I found it impossible to say) a low and apparently distant, but harsh, protracted, and most unusual screaming or grating sound—the exact counterpart of what my fancy had already conjured up for the dragon's unnatural shriek as described by the romancer.

Oppressed, as I certainly was, upon the occurrence of this second and most extraordinary coincidence, by a thousand conflicting sensations, in which wonder and extreme terror were predominant, I still retained sufficient presence of mind to avoid exciting, by any observation, the sensitive nervousness of my companion. I was by no means certain that he had noticed the sounds in question; although, assuredly, a strange alteration had, during the last few minutes, taken place in his demeanor. From a position fronting my own, he had gradually brought round his chair, so as to sit with his face to the door of the chamber; and thus I could but partially perceive his features, although I saw that his lips trembled as if he were murmuring inaudibly. His head had dropped upon his breast—yet I knew that he was not asleep, from the wide and rigid opening of the eye as I caught a glance of it in profile. The motion of his body, too, was at variance with this idea—for he rocked from side to side with a gentle yet constant and uniform sway. Having rapidly taken notice of all this, I resumed the narrative of Sir Launcelot, which thus proceeded:

"And now, the champion, having escaped from the terrible fury of the dragon, bethinking himself of the brazen shield, and of the breaking up of the enchantment which was upon it, removed the carcass from out of the way before him, and approached valorously over the silver pavement of the castle to where the shield was upon the wall; which in sooth tarried not for his full coming, but fell down at his feet upon the silver floor, with a mighty great and terrible ringing sound."

No sooner had these syllables passed my lips, than—as if a shield of brass had indeed, at the moment, fallen heavily upon a floor of silver—I became aware of a distinct, hollow, metallic, and clangorous, yet apparently muffled, reverberation. Completely unnerved, I leaped to my feet; but the measured rocking movement of Usher was undisturbed. I rushed to the chair in which he sat. His eyes were bent fixedly before him, and throughout his whole countenance there reigned a stony rigidity. But, as I placed my hand upon his shoulder, there came a strong shudder over his whole person; a sickly smile quivered about his lips; and I saw that he spoke in a low, hurried, and gibbering murmur, as if unconscious of my presence. Bending closely over him, I at length drank in the hideous import of his words.

"Now hear it?—yes, I hear it, and *have* heard it. Long—long—long—many minutes, many hours, many days, have I heard it—yet I dared not—oh, pity me, miserable wretch that I am!—I dared not—I *dared* not speak! *We have put her living in the tomb!* Said I not that my senses were acute? I *now* tell you that I heard her first feeble movements in the hollow coffin. I heard them—many, many days ago—yet I dared not—*I dared not speak!* And now—to-night—Ethelred—ha! ha!—the breaking of the hermit's door, and the death-cry of the dragon, and the clangor of the shield—say, rather, the rending of her coffin, and the grating of the iron hinges of her prison, and her struggles within the coppered archway of the vault! Oh! whither shall I fly? Will she not be here anon? Is she not hurrying to upbraid me for my haste? Have I not heard her footstep on the stair? Do I not distinguish that heavy and horrible beating of her heart? Madman!"—here he sprang furiously to his feet, and shrieked out his syllables, as if in the effort he were giving up his soul—*"Madman! I tell you that she now stands without the door!"*

As if in the superhuman energy of his utterance there had been found the potency of a spell, the huge antique panels to which the speaker pointed threw slowly back, upon the instant, their ponderous and ebony jaws. It was the work of the rushing gust—but then without those doors there *did* stand the lofty and enshrouded figure of the lady Madeline of Usher. There was blood upon her white robes, and the evidence of some bitter struggle upon every portion of her emaciated frame. For a moment she remained trembling and reeling to and fro upon the threshold—then, with a low moaning cry, fell heavily inward upon the person of her brother, and in her violent and now final death-agonies, bore him to the floor a corpse, and a victim to the terrors he had anticipated.

From that chamber, and from that mansion, I fled aghast. The storm was still abroad in all its wrath as I found myself crossing the old causeway. Suddenly there shot along the path a wild light, and I turned to see whence a gleam so unusual could have issued; for the vast house and its shadows were alone behind me. The radiance was that of the sun, setting, and blood-red moon, which now shone vividly through that once barely discernible fissure, of which I have before spoken as extending from the roof of the building, in a zigzag direction, to the base. While I gazed, this fissure rapidly widened—there came a fierce breath of the whirlwind— the entire orb of the satellite burst at once upon my sight—my brain reeled as I saw the mighty walls rushing asunder—there was a long tumultuous shouting sound like the voice of a thousand waters—and the deep and dank tarn at my feet closed sullenly and silently over the fragments of the *"House of Usher."*

THE MURDERS IN THE RUE MORGUE[1]

> What song the Syrens sang, or what name Achilles assumed when he hid himself among women, although puzzling questions, are not beyond *all* conjecture.
> —*Sir Thomas Browne*[2]

THE MENTAL FEATURES discoursed of as the analytical, are, in themselves, but little susceptible of analysis. We appreciate them only in their effects. We know of them, among other things, that they are always to their possessor, when inordinately possessed, a source of the liveliest enjoyment. As the strong man exults in his physical ability, delighting in such exercises as call his muscles into action, so glories the analyst in that moral activity which *disentangles*. He derives pleasure from even the most trivial occupations bringing his talent into play. He is fond of enigmas, of conundrums, hieroglyphics; exhibiting in his solutions of each a degree of *acumen* which appears to the ordinary apprehension præternatural. His results, brought about by the very soul and essence of method, have, in truth, the whole air of intuition.

The faculty of re-solution is possibly much invigorated by mathematical study, and especially by that highest branch of it which, unjustly, and merely on account of its retrograde operations, has been called, as if *par excellence*, analysis. Yet to calculate is not in itself to analyze. A chess-player, for example, does the one, without effort at the other. It follows that the game of chess, in its effects upon mental character, is greatly misunderstood. I am not now writing a treatise, but simply prefacing a somewhat peculiar narrative by observations very much at random; I will, therefore, take occasion to assert that the higher powers of the reflective intellect are more decidedly and more usefully tasked by the unostentatious game of draughts[3] than by all the elaborate frivolity of chess. In this latter, where the pieces have different and *bizarre* motions, with various and variable values, what is only complex, is mistaken (a not unusual error) for what is profound. The *attention* is here called powerfully into play. If it flag for an instant, an oversight is committed, resulting in injury or defeat. The possible moves being not only manifold, but involute,[4] the chances of such oversights are multiplied; and in nine cases out of ten, it is the more concentrative rather than the more acute player who conquers. In draughts, on the contrary, where the moves are *unique* and have but little variation, the probabilities of inadvertence are diminished, and the mere attention being left comparatively unemployed, what advantages are obtained by either party are obtained by superior *acumen*. To be less abstract, let us

suppose a game of draughts where the pieces are reduced to four kings, and where, of course, no oversight is
to be expected. It is obvious that here the victory can be
decided (the players being at all equal) only by some
recherché[5] movement, the result of some strong exertion of the intellect. Deprived of ordinary resources, the
analyst throws himself into the spirit of his opponent,
identifies himself therewith, and not unfrequently sees
thus, at a glance, the sole methods (sometimes indeed
absurdly simple ones) by which he may seduce into error
or hurry into miscalculation.

Whist[6] has long been known for its influence upon what
is termed the calculating power; and men of the highest
order of intellect have been known to take an apparently
unaccountable delight in it, while eschewing chess as frivolous. Beyond doubt there is nothing of a similar nature so
greatly tasking the faculty of analysis. The best chess-
player in Christendom *may* be little more than the best
player of chess; but proficiency in whist implies capacity
for success in all these more important undertakings
where mind struggles with mind. When I say proficiency,
I mean that perfection in the game which includes a comprehension of *all* the sources whence legitimate advantage
may be derived. These are not only manifold, but multi-
form, and lie frequently among recesses of thought altogether inaccessible to the ordinary understanding. To
observe attentively is to remember distinctly; and, so far,
the concentrative chess-player will do very well at whist;
while the rules of Hoyle[7] (themselves based upon the
mere mechanism of the game) are sufficiently and generally comprehensible. Thus to have a retentive memory,
and proceed by "the book" are points commonly regarded

as the sum total of good playing. But it is in matters beyond the limits of mere rule that the skill of the analyst is evinced. He makes, in silence, a host of observations and inferences. So, perhaps, do his companions; and the difference in the extent of the information obtained, lies not so much in the validity of the inference as in the quality of the observation. The necessary knowledge is that of *what* to observe. Our player confines himself not at all; nor, because the game is the object, does he reject deductions from things external to the game. He examines the countenance of his partner, comparing it carefully with that of each of his opponents. He considers the mode of assorting the cards in each hand; often counting trump by trump, and honor by honor, through the glances bestowed by their holders upon each. He notes every variation of face as the play progresses, gathering a fund of thought from the differences in the expression of certainty, of surprise, of triumph, or chagrin. From the manner of gathering up a trick he judges whether the person taking it, can make another in the suit. He recognizes what is played through feint, by the manner with which it is thrown upon the table. A casual or inadvertent word; the accidental dropping or turning of a card, with the accompanying anxiety or carelessness in regard to its concealment; the counting of the tricks, with the order of their arrangement; embarrassment, hesitation, eagerness, or trepidation—all afford, to his apparently intuitive perception, indications of the true state of affairs. The first two or three rounds having been played, he is in full possession of the contents of each hand, and thenceforward puts down his cards with as absolute a precision of purpose as if the rest of the party had turned outward the faces of their own.

The analytical power should not be confounded with simple ingenuity; for while the analyst is necessarily ingenious, the ingenious man is often remarkably incapable of analysis. The constructive or combining power, by which ingenuity is usually manifested, and to which the phrenologists[8] (I believe erroneously) have assigned a separate organ, supposing it a primitive faculty, has been so frequently seen in those whose intellect bordered otherwise upon idiocy, as to have attracted general observation among writers on morals. Between ingenuity and the analytic ability there exists a difference far greater, indeed, than that between the fancy and the imagination, but of a character very strictly analogous. It will be found, in fact, that the ingenious are always fanciful, and the *truly* imaginative never otherwise than analytic.

The narrative which follows will appear to the reader somewhat in the light of a commentary upon the propositions just advanced.

Residing in Paris during the spring and part of the summer of 18—, I there became acquainted with a Monsieur C. Auguste Dupin. This young gentleman was of an excellent, indeed of an illustrious family, but, by a variety of untoward events, had been reduced to such poverty that the energy of his character succumbed beneath it, and he ceased to bestir himself in the world, or to care for the retrieval of his fortunes. By courtesy of his creditors, there still remained in his possession a small remnant of his patrimony; and, upon the income arising from this, he managed, by means of a rigorous economy, to procure the necessities of life, without troubling himself about its superfluities. Books, indeed, were his sole luxuries, and in Paris these are easily obtained.

Our first meeting was at an obscure library in the Rue Montmartre, where the accident of our both being in search of the same very rare and very remarkable volume, brought us into closer communion. We saw each other again and again. I was deeply interested in the little family history which he detailed to me with all that candor which a Frenchman indulges whenever mere self is the theme. I was astonished, too, at the vast extent of his reading; and, above all, I felt my soul enkindled within me by the wild fervor, and the vivid freshness of his imagination. Seeking in Paris the objects I then sought, I felt that the society of such a man would be to me a treasure beyond price; and this feeling I frankly confided to him. It was at length arranged that we should live together during my stay in the city; and as my worldly circumstances were somewhat less embarrassed than his own, I was permitted to be at the expense of renting, and furnishing in a style which suited the rather fantastic gloom of our common temper, a time-eaten and grotesque mansion, long deserted through superstitions into which we did not inquire, and tottering to its fall in a retired and desolate portion of the Faubourg St. Germain.

Had the routine of our life at this place been known to the world, we should have been regarded as madmen—although, perhaps, as madmen of a harmless nature. Our seclusion was perfect. We admitted no visitors. Indeed the locality of our retirement had been carefully kept a secret from my own former associates; and it had been many years since Dupin had ceased to know or be known in Paris. We existed within ourselves alone.

It was a freak of fancy in my friend (for what else shall I call it?) to be enamored of the night for her own sake;

and into this *bizarrerie*, as into all his others, I quietly fell; giving myself up to his wild whims with a perfect *abandon*. The sable divinity would not herself dwell with us always; but we could counterfeit her presence. At the first dawn of the morning we closed all the massy shutters of our old building; lighted a couple of tapers which, strongly perfumed, threw out only the ghastliest and feeblest of rays. By the aid of these we then busied our souls in dreams—reading, writing, or conversing, until warned by the clock of the advent of true Darkness. Then we sallied forth into the streets, arm in arm, continuing the topics of the day, or roaming far and wide until a late hour, seeking, amid the wild lights and shadows of the populous city, that infinity of mental excitement which quiet observation can afford.

At such times I could not help remarking and admiring (although from his rich ideality I had been prepared to expect it) a peculiar analytic ability in Dupin. He seemed, too, to take an eager delight in its exercise—if not exactly in its display—and did not hesitate to confess the pleasure thus derived. He boasted to me, with a low chuckling laugh, that most men, in respect to himself, wore windows in their bosoms, and was wont to follow up such assertions by direct and very startling proofs of his intimate knowledge of my own. His manner at these moments was frigid and abstract; his eyes were vacant in expression; while his voice, usually a rich tenor, rose into a treble which would have sounded petulant but for the deliberateness and entire distinctness of the enunciation. Observing him in these moods, I often dwelt meditatively upon the old philosophy of the Bi-Part Soul, and amused myself with the fancy of a double Dupin—the creative and the resolvent.

Let it not be supposed, from what I have just said, that I am detailing any mystery, or penning any romance. What I have described in the Frenchman was merely the result of an excited, or perhaps of a diseased, intelligence. But of the character of his remarks at the periods in question an example will best convey the idea.

We were strolling one night down a long dirty street, in the vicinity of the Palais Royal. Being both, apparently, occupied with thought, neither of us had spoken a syllable for fifteen minutes at least. All at once Dupin broke forth with these words:

"He is a very little fellow, that's true, and would do better for the *Théâtre des Variétés*."⁹

"There can be no doubt of that," I replied, unwittingly, and not at first observing (so much had I been absorbed in reflection) the extraordinary manner in which the speaker had chimed in with my meditations. In an instant afterward I recollected myself, and my astonishment was profound.

"Dupin," said I, gravely, "this is beyond my comprehension. I do not hesitate to say that I am amazed, and can scarcely credit my senses. How was it possible you should know I was thinking of——?" Here I paused, to ascertain beyond a doubt whether he really knew of whom I thought.

"——of Chantilly," said he, "why do you pause? You were remarking to yourself that his diminutive figure unfitted him for tragedy."

This was precisely what had formed the subject of my reflections. Chantilly was a *quondam*¹⁰ cobbler of the Rue St. Denis, who, becoming stage-mad, had attempted the *rôle* of Xerxes, in Crébillon's tragedy[11] so called, and been notoriously Pasquinaded[12] for his pains.

"Tell me, for Heaven's sake," I exclaimed, "the method—if method there is—by which you have been enabled to fathom my soul in this matter." In fact, I was even more startled than I would have been willing to express.

"It was the fruiterer," replied my friend, "who brought you to the conclusion that the mender of soles was not of sufficient height for Xerxes *et id genus omne*."[13]

"The fruiterer!—you astonish me—I know no fruiterer whomsoever."

"The man who ran up against you as we entered the street—it may have been fifteen minutes ago."

I now remembered that, in fact, a fruiterer, carrying upon his head a large basket of apples, had nearly thrown me down, by accident, as we passed from the Rue C—— into the thoroughfare where we stood; but what this had to do with Chantilly I could not possibly understand.

There was not a particle of *charlatânerie*[14] about Dupin. "I will explain," he said, "and that you may comprehend all clearly, we will first retrace the course of your meditations, from the moment in which I spoke to you until that of the *rencontre*[15] with the fruiterer in question. The larger links of the chain run thus—Chantilly, Orion, Dr. Nichols,[16] Epicurus, Stereotomy,[17] the street stones, the fruiterer."

There are few persons who have not, at some period of their lives, amused themselves in retracing the steps by which particular conclusions of their own minds have been attained. The occupation is often full of interest;

and he who attempts it for the first time is astonished by the apparently illimitable distance and incoherence between the starting-point and the goal. What, then, must have been my amazement, when I heard the Frenchman speak what he had just spoken, and when I could not help acknowledging that he had spoken the truth. He continued:

"We had been talking of horses, if I remember aright, just before leaving the Rue C——. This was the last subject we discussed. As we crossed into this street, a fruiterer, with a large basket upon his head, brushing quickly past us, thrust you upon a pile of paving-stones collected at a spot where the causeway is undergoing repair. You stepped upon one of the loose fragments, slipped, slightly strained your ankle, appeared vexed or sulky, muttered a few words, turned to look at the pile, and then proceeded in silence. I was not particularly attentive to what you did; but observation has become with me, of late, a species of necessity.

"You kept your eyes upon the ground—glancing, with a petulant expression, at the holes and ruts in the pavement (so that I saw you were still thinking of the stones), until we reached the little alley called Lamartine, which has been paved, by way of experiment, with the overlapping and riveted blocks. Here your countenance brightened up, and, perceiving your lips move, I could not doubt that you murmured the word 'stereotomy,' a term very affectedly applied to this species of pavement. I knew that you could not say to yourself 'stereotomy' without being brought to think of atomies, and thus of the theories of Epicurus;[18] and since, when we discussed this subject not very long ago, I mentioned to you how singularly, yet with how little notice, the vague guesses of that noble Greek had met with confirmation in the late nebular cosmogony, I felt that you could not avoid casting your eyes upward to the great *nebula* in Orion, and I certainly expected that you would do so. You did look up; and I was now assured that I had correctly followed your steps. But in that bitter *tirade* upon Chantilly, which appeared in yesterday's *'Musée,'* the satirist, making some disgraceful allusions to the cobbler's change of name upon assuming the buskin, quoted a Latin line about which we have often conversed. I mean the line

Perdidit antiquum litera prima sonum.[19]

I had told you that this was in reference to Orion, formerly written Urion; and, from certain pungencies connected with this explanation, I was aware that you could not have forgotten it. It was clear, therefore, that you would not fail to combine the two ideas of Orion and Chantilly. That you did combine them I saw by the character of the smile which passed over your lips. You thought of the poor cobbler's immolation. So far, you had been stooping in your gait; but now I saw you draw yourself up to your full height. I was then sure that you reflected upon the diminutive figure of Chantilly. At this point I interrupted your meditations to remark that as, in fact, he *was* a very little fellow—that Chantilly—he would do better at the *Théâtre des Variétés.*"

Not long after this, we were looking over an evening edition of the *Gazette des Tribunaux,* when the following paragraphs arrested our attention.

"EXTRAORDINARY MURDERS.—This morning, about

three o'clock, the inhabitants of the Quartier St. Roch were roused from sleep by a succession of terrific shrieks, issuing, apparently, from the fourth story of a house in the Rue Morgue, known to be in the sole occupancy of one Madame L'Espanaye, and her daughter, Mademoiselle Camille L'Espanaye. After some delay, occasioned by a fruitless attempt to procure admission in the usual manner, the gateway was broken in with a crowbar, and eight or ten of the neighbors entered, accompanied by two *gendarmes*. By this time the cries had ceased; but, as the party rushed up the first flight of stairs, two or more rough voices, in angry contention, were distinguished, and seemed to proceed from the upper part of the house. As the second landing was reached, these sounds, also, had ceased, and every thing remained perfectly quiet. The party spread themselves, and hurried from room to room. Upon arriving at a large back chamber in the fourth story (the door of which, being found locked, with the key inside, was forced open), a spectacle presented itself which struck every one present not less with horror than with astonishment.

"The apartment was in the wildest disorder—the furniture broken and thrown about in all directions. There was only one bedstead; and from this the bed had been removed, and thrown into the middle of the floor. On a chair lay a razor, besmeared with blood. On the hearth were two or three long and thick tresses of gray human hair, also dabbled with blood, and seeming to have been pulled out by the roots. Upon the floor were found four Napoleons,[20] an ear-ring of topaz, three large silver spoons, three smaller of *métal d'Alger*,[21] and two bags, containing nearly four thousand francs in gold. The drawers of a *bureau,* which stood in one corner, were open, and had been, apparently, rifled, although many articles still remained in them. A small iron safe was discovered under the *bed* (not under the bedstead). It was open, with the key still in the door. It had no contents beyond a few old letters, and other papers of little consequence.

"Of Madame L'Espanaye no traces were here seen; but an unusual quantity of soot being observed in the fire-place, a search was made in the chimney, and (horrible to relate!) the corpse of the daughter, head downward, was dragged therefrom; it having been thus forced up the narrow aperture for a considerable distance. The body was quite warm. Upon examining it, many excoriations were perceived, no doubt occasioned by the violence with which it had been thrust up and disengaged. Upon the face were many severe scratches, and, upon the throat, dark bruises, and deep indentations of finger nails, as if the deceased had been throttled to death.

"After a thorough investigation of every portion of the house without farther discovery, the party made its way into a small paved yard in the rear of the building, where lay the corpse of the old lady, with her throat so entirely cut that, upon an attempt to raise her, the head fell off. The body, as well as the head, was fearfully mutilated— the former so much so as scarcely to retain any semblance of humanity.

"To this horrible mystery there is not as yet, we believe, the slightest clue."

The next day's paper had these additional particulars:

"*The Tragedy in the Rue Morgue.*—Many individuals have been examined in relation to this most extraordinary and frightful affair," [the word *'affaire'* has not yet, in France, that levity of import which it conveys with us] "but nothing whatever has transpired to throw light upon it. We give below all the material testimony elicited.

"*Pauline Dubourg*, laundress, deposes that she has known both the deceased for three years, having washed for them during that period. The old lady and her daughter seemed on good terms—very affectionate toward each other. They were excellent pay. Could not speak in regard to their mode or means of living. Believe that Madame L. told fortunes for a living. Was reputed to have money put by. Never met any person in the house when she called for the clothes or took them home. Was sure that they had no servant in employ. There appeared to be no furniture in any part of the building except in the fourth story.

"*Pierre Moreau*, tobacconist, deposes that he has been in the habit of selling small quantities of tobacco and snuff to Madame L'Espanaye for nearly four years. Was born in the neighborhood, and has always resided there. The deceased and her daughter had occupied the house in which the corpses were found, for more than six years. It was formerly occupied by a jeweller, who under-let the upper rooms to various persons. The house was the property of Madame L. She became dissatisfied with the abuse of the premises by her tenant, and moved into them herself, refusing to let any portion. The old lady was childish. Witness had seen the daughter some five or six times during the six years. The two lived an exceedingly retired life—were reputed to have money. Had heard it said among the neighbors that Madame L. told fortunes—did not believe it. Had never seen any person enter the door except the old lady and her daughter, a porter once or twice, and a physician some eight or ten times.

"Many other persons, neighbors, gave evidence to the same effect. No one was spoken of as frequenting the house. It was not known whether there were any living connections of Madame L. and her daughter. The shutters of the front windows were seldom opened. Those in the rear were always closed, with the exception of the large back room, fourth story. The house was a good house—not very old.

"*Isidore Musèt, gendarme,* deposes that he was called to the house about three o'clock in the morning, and found some twenty or thirty persons at the gateway, endeavoring to gain admittance. Forced it open, at length, with a bayonet—not with a crowbar. Had but little difficulty in getting it open, on account of its being a double or folding gate, and bolted neither at bottom nor top. The shrieks were continued until the gate was forced— and then suddenly ceased. They seemed to be screams of some person (or persons) in great agony—were loud and drawn out, not short and quick. Witness led the way up stairs. Upon reaching the first landing, heard two voices in loud and angry contention—the one a gruff voice, the other much shriller—a very strange voice. Could distinguish some words of the former, which was that of a Frenchman. Was positive that it was not a woman's voice. Could distinguish the words '*sacré*' and '*diable.*' The shrill voice was that of a foreigner. Could not be sure whether it was the voice of a man or of a woman. Could not make out what was said, but believed the language to be Spanish. The state of the room and of the bodies was described by this witness as we described them yesterday.

"*Henri Duval,* a neighbor, and by trade a silver-smith, deposes that he was one of the party who first entered the house. Corroborates the testimony of Musèt in general. As soon as they forced an entrance, they reclosed the door, to keep out the crowd, which collected very fast, notwithstanding the lateness of the hour. The shrill voice, this witness thinks, was that of an Italian. Was certain it was not French. Could not be sure that it was a man's voice. It might have been a woman's. Was not acquainted with the Italian language. Could not distinguish the words, but was convinced by the intonation that the speaker was an Italian. Knew Madame L. and her daughter. Had conversed with both frequently. Was sure that the shrill voice was not that of either of the deceased.

"——*Odenheimer, restaurateur.*—This witness volunteered his testimony. Not speaking French, was examined through an interpreter. Is a native of Amsterdam. Was passing the house at the time of the shrieks. They lasted for several minutes—probably ten. They were long and loud—very awful and distressing. Was one of those who entered the building. Corroborated the previous evidence in every respect but one. Was sure that the shrill voice was that of a man—of a Frenchman. Could not distinguish the words uttered. They were loud and quick—unequal—spoken apparently in fear as well as in anger. The voice was harsh—not so much shrill as harsh. Could not call it a shrill voice. The gruff voice said repeatedly, '*sacré,*' '*diable,*' and once '*mon Dieu.*'

"*Jules Mignaud,* banker, of the firm of Mignaud et

Fils, Rue Deloraine. Is the elder Mignaud. Madame L'Espanaye had some property. Had opened an account with his banking house in the spring of the year —— (eight years previously). Made frequent deposits in small sums. Had checked for nothing until the third day before her death, when she took out in person the sum of 4000 francs. This sum was paid in gold, and a clerk sent home with the money.

"*Adolphe Le Bon,* clerk to Mignaud et Fils, deposes that on the day in question, about noon, he accompanied Madame L'Espanaye to her residence with the 4000 francs, put up in two bags. Upon the door being opened, Mademoiselle L. appeared and took from his hands one of the bags, while the old lady relieved him of the other. He then bowed and departed. Did not see any person in the street at the time. It is a by-street—very lonely.

"*William Bird,* tailor, deposes that he was one of the party who entered the house. Is an Englishman. Has lived in Paris two years. Was one of the first to ascend the stairs. Heard the voices in contention. The gruff voice was that of a Frenchman. Could make out several words, but cannot now remember all. Heard distinctly '*sacré*' and '*mon Dieu.*' There was a sound at the moment as if of several persons struggling—a scraping and scuffling sound. The shrill voice was very loud—louder than the gruff one. Is sure that it was not the voice of an Englishman. Appeared to be that of a German. Might have been a woman's voice. Does not understand German.

"Four of the above-named witnesses, being recalled, deposed that the door of the chamber in which was found the body of Mademoiselle L. was locked on the inside when the party reached it. Every thing was perfectly silent—no groans or noises of any kind. Upon forcing the door no person was seen. The windows, both of the back and front room, were down and firmly fastened from within. A door between the two rooms was closed but not locked. The door leading from the front room into the passage was locked, with the key on the inside. A small room in the front of the house, on the fourth story, at the head of the passage, was open, the door being ajar. This room was crowded with old beds, boxes, and so forth. These were carefully removed and searched. There was not an inch of any portion of the house which was not carefully searched. Sweeps were sent up and down the chimneys. The house was a four-story one, with garrets (*mansardes*). A trap-door on the roof was nailed down very securely—did not appear to have been opened for years. The time elapsing between the hearing of the voices in contention and the breaking open of the room door was variously stated by the witnesses. Some made it as short as three minutes—some as long as five. The door was opened with difficulty.

"*Alfonzo Garcio*, undertaker, deposes that he resides in the Rue Morgue. Is a native of Spain. Was one of the party who entered the house. Did not proceed up stairs. Is nervous, and was apprehensive of the consequences of agitation. Heard the voices in contention. The gruff voice was that of a Frenchman. Could not distinguish what was said. The shrill voice was that of an Englishman—is sure of this. Does not understand the English language, but judges by the intonation.

"*Alberto Montani*, confectioner, deposes that he was among the first to ascend the stairs. Heard the voices in question. The gruff voice was that of a Frenchman. Distinguished several words. The speaker appeared to be expostulating. Could not make out the words of the shrill voice. Spoke quick and unevenly. Thinks it the voice of a Russian. Corroborates the general testimony. Is an Italian. Never conversed with a native of Russia.

"Several witnesses, recalled, here testified that the chimneys of all the rooms on the fourth story were too narrow to admit the passage of a human being. By 'sweeps' were meant cylindrical sweeping-brushes, such as are employed by those who clean chimneys. These brushes were passed up and down every flue in the house. There is no back passage by which any one could have descended while the party proceeded up stairs. The body of Mademoiselle L'Espanaye was so firmly wedged in the chimney that it could not be got down until four or five of the party united their strength.

"*Paul Dumas,* physician, deposes that he was called to view the bodies about daybreak. They were both then lying on the sacking of the bedstead in the chamber where Mademoiselle L. was found. The corpse of the young lady was much bruised and excoriated. The fact that it had been thrust up the chimney would sufficiently account for these appearances. The throat was greatly chafed. There were several deep scratches just below the chin, together with a series of livid spots which were evidently the impression of fingers. The face was fearfully discolored, and the eyeballs protruded. The tongue had been partially bitten through. A large bruise was discovered upon the pit of the stomach, produced, apparently, by the pressure of a knee. In the opinion of M. Dumas, Mademoiselle L'Espanaye had been throttled to death by some person or persons unknown. The corpse of the mother was horribly mutilated. All the bones of the right leg and arm were more or less shattered. The left *tibia* much splintered, as well as all the ribs of the left side. Whole body dreadfully bruised and discolored. It was not possible to say how the injuries had been inflicted. A heavy club of wood, or a broad bar of iron—a chair—any large, heavy, and obtuse weapon would have produced such results, if wielded by the hands of a very powerful man. No woman could have inflicted the blows with any weapon. The head of the deceased, when seen by witness, was entirely separated from the body, and was also greatly shattered. The throat had evidently been cut with some very sharp instrument—probably with a razor.

"*Alexandre Etienne,* surgeon, was called with M. Dumas to view the bodies. Corroborated the testimony, and the opinions of M. Dumas.

"Nothing further of importance was elicited, although several other persons were examined. A murder so mysterious, and so perplexing in all its particulars, was never before committed in Paris—if indeed a murder has been committed at all. The police are entirely at fault—an unusual occurrence in affairs of this nature. There is not, however, the shadow of a clew apparent."

The evening edition of the paper stated that the greatest excitement still continued in the Quartier St. Roch—that the premises in question had been carefully re-searched, and fresh examinations of witnesses instituted, but all to no purpose. A postscript, however, mentioned that Adolphe Le Bon had been arrested and imprisoned—although nothing appeared to criminate him beyond the facts already detailed.

Dupin seemed singularly interested in the progress of this affair—at least so I judged from his manner, for he made no comments. It was only after the announcement that Le Bon had been imprisoned, that he asked me my opinion respecting the murders.

I could merely agree with all Paris in considering them an insoluble mystery. I saw no means by which it would be possible to trace the murderer.

"We must not judge of the means," said Dupin, "by this shell of an examination. The Parisian police, so much extolled for *acumen*, are cunning, but no more. There is no method in their proceedings, beyond the method of the moment. They make a vast parade of measures; but, not unfrequently, these are so ill-adapted to the objects proposed, as to put us in mind of Monsieur Jourdain's calling for his *robe-de-chambre—pour mieux entendre la musique.*[22] The results attained by them are not unfrequently surprising, but, for the most part, are brought about by simple diligence and activity. When these qualities are unavailing, their schemes fail. Vidocq,[23] for example, was a good guesser, and a persevering man. But, without educated thought, he erred continually by the very intensity of his investigations. He impaired his vision by holding the object too close. He might see, perhaps, one or two points with unusual clearness, but in so doing he, necessarily, lost sight of the matter as a whole. Thus there is such a thing as being too profound. Truth is not always in a well.[24] In fact, as regards the more important knowledge, I do believe that she is invariably superficial. The depth lies in the valleys where we seek her, and not upon the mountain-tops where she is found. The modes and sources of this kind of error are well typified

in the contemplation of the heavenly bodies. To look at a
star by glances—to view it in a side-long way, by turning
toward it the exterior portions of the *retina* (more susceptible of feeble impressions of light than the interior),
is to behold the star distinctly—is to have the best appreciation of its lustre—a lustre which grows dim just in
proportion as we turn our vision *fully* upon it. A greater
number of rays actually fall upon the eye in the latter
case, but in the former, there is the more refined capacity for comprehension. By undue profundity we perplex
and enfeeble thought; and it is possible to make even
Venus herself vanish from the firmament by a scrutiny
too sustained, too concentrated, or too direct.

"As for these murders, let us enter into some examinations for ourselves, before we make up an opinion respecting them. An inquiry will afford us amusement," [I
thought this an odd term, so applied, but said nothing]
"and besides, Le Bon once rendered me a service for
which I am not ungrateful. We will go and see the premises with our own eyes. I know G——, the Prefect of Police, and shall have no difficulty in obtaining the
necessary permission."

The permission was obtained, and we proceeded at
once to the Rue Morgue. This is one of those miserable
thoroughfares which intervene between the Rue Riche-
lieu and the Rue St. Roch. It was late in the afternoon
when we reached it, as this quarter is at a great distance
from that in which we resided. The house was readily
found; for there were still many persons gazing up at the
closed shutters, with an objectless curiosity, from the opposite side of the way. It was an ordinary Parisian house,
with a gateway, on one side of which was a glazed watch-

box, with a sliding panel in the window, indicating a *loge de concierge.*[25] Before going in we walked up the street, turned down an alley, and then, again turning, passed in the rear of the building—Dupin, meanwhile, examining the whole neighborhood, as well as the house, with a minuteness of attention for which I could see no possible object.

Retracing our steps we came again to the front of the dwelling, rang, and, having shown our credentials, were admitted by the agents in charge. We went up stairs— into the chamber where the body of Mademoiselle L'Espanaye had been found, and where both the deceased still lay. The disorders of the room had, as usual, been suffered to exist. I saw nothing beyond what had been stated in the *Gazette des Tribunaux.* Dupin scrutinized every thing—not excepting the bodies of the victims. We then went into the other rooms, and into the yard; a *gendarme* accompanying us throughout. The examination occupied us until dark, when we took our departure. On our way home my companion stepped in for a moment at the office of one of the daily papers.

I have said that the whims of my friend were manifold, and that *Je les ménageais:*[26]—for this phrase there is no English equivalent. It was his humor, now, to decline all conversation on the subject of the murder, until about noon the next day. He then asked me, suddenly, if I had observed any thing *peculiar* at the scene of the atrocity.

There was something in his manner of emphasizing the word *"peculiar,"* which caused me to shudder, without knowing why.

"No, nothing *peculiar,*" I said; "nothing more, at least, than we both saw stated in the paper."

"The *Gazette*," he replied, "has not entered, I fear, into the unusual horror of the thing. But dismiss the idle opinions of this print. It appears to me that this mystery is considered insoluble, for the very reason which should cause it to be regarded as easy of solution—I mean for the *outré*[27] character of its features. The police are confounded by the seeming absence of motive—not for the murder itself—but for the atrocity of the murder. They are puzzled, too, by the seeming impossibility of reconciling the voices heard in contention, with the facts that no one was discovered upstairs but the assassinated Mademoiselle L'Espanaye, and that there were no means of egress without the notice of the party ascending. The wild disorder of the room; the corpse thrust, with the head downward, up the chimney; the frightful mutilation of the body of the old lady; these considerations, with those just mentioned, and others which I need not mention, have sufficed to paralyze the powers, by putting completely at fault the boasted *acumen*, of the government agents. They have fallen into the gross but common error of confounding the unusual with the abstruse. But it is by these deviations from the plane of the ordinary, that reason feels its way, if at all, in its search for the true. In investigations such as we are now pursuing, it should not be so much asked 'what has occurred,' as 'what has occurred that has never occurred before.' In fact, the facility with which I shall arrive, or have arrived, at the solution of this mystery, is in the direct ratio of its apparent insolubility in the eyes of the police."

I stared at the speaker in mute astonishment.

"I am now awaiting," continued he, looking toward the door of our apartment—"I am now awaiting a person who, although perhaps not the perpetrator of these butcheries, must have been in some measure implicated in their perpetration. Of the worst portion of the crimes committed, it is probable that he is innocent. I hope that I am right in this supposition; for upon it I build my expectation of reading the entire riddle. I look for the man here—in this room—every moment. It is true that he may not arrive; but the probability is that he will. Should he come, it will be necessary to detain him. Here are pistols; and we both know how to use them when occasion demands their use."

I took the pistols, scarcely knowing what I did, or believing what I heard, while Dupin went on, very much as if in a soliloquy. I have already spoken of his abstract manner at such times. His discourse was addressed to myself; but his voice, although by no means loud, had that intonation which is commonly employed in speaking to some one at a great distance. His eyes, vacant in expression, regarded only the wall.

"That the voices heard in contention," he said, "by the party upon the stairs, were not the voices of the women themselves, was fully proved by the evidence. This relieves us of all doubt upon the question whether the old lady could have first destroyed the daughter, and afterward have committed suicide. I speak of this point chiefly for the sake of method; for the strength of Madame L'Espanaye would have been utterly unequal to the task of thrusting her daughter's corpse up the chimney as it was found; and the nature of the wounds upon her own person entirely precludes the idea of self-destruction. Murder, then, has been committed by some third party; and the voices of this third party were those heard in contention. Let me now advert—not to the whole testimony respecting these voices—but to what was *peculiar* in that testimony. Did you observe any thing peculiar about it?"

I remarked that, while all the witnesses agreed in supposing the gruff voice to be that of a Frenchman, there was much disagreement in regard to the shrill or as one individual termed it, the harsh voice.

"That was the evidence itself," said Dupin, "but it was not the peculiarity of the evidence. You have observed nothing distinctive. Yet there *was* something to be observed. The witnesses, as you remark, agreed about the gruff voice; they were here unanimous. But in regard to the shrill voice, the peculiarity is—not that they disagreed—but that, while an Italian, an Englishman, a Spaniard, a Hollander, and a Frenchman attempted to describe it, each one spoke of it as that *of a foreigner.* Each is sure that it was not the voice of one of his own countrymen. Each likens it—not to the voice of an individual of any nation with whose language he is conversant—but the converse. The Frenchman supposes it the voice of a Spaniard, and 'might have distinguished some words *had he been acquainted with the Spanish.*' The Dutchman maintains it to have been that of a Frenchman; but we find it stated that '*not understanding French this witness was examined through an interpreter.*' The Englishman thinks it the voice of a German, and '*does not understand German.*' The Spaniard 'is sure' that it was that of an Englishman, but 'judges by the intonation' altogether, '*as he has no knowledge of the English.*' The Italian believes it the voice of a Russian, but '*has never conversed with a native of Russia.*' A second

Frenchman differs, moreover, with the first, and is positive that the voice was that of an Italian; but *not being cognizant of that tongue,* is like the Spaniard, 'convinced by the intonation.' Now, how strangely unusual must that voice have really been, about which such testimony as this *could* have been elicited!—in whose *tones,* even denizens of the five great divisions of Europe could recognize nothing familiar! You will say that it might have been the voice of an Asiatic—of an African. Neither Asiatics nor Africans abound in Paris; but, without denying the inference, I will now merely call your attention to three points. The voice is termed by one witness 'harsh rather than shrill.' It is represented by two others to have been 'quick and *unequal.*' No words—no sounds resembling words—were by any witness mentioned as distinguishable.

"I know not," continued Dupin, "what impression I may have made, so far, upon your own understanding; but I do not hesitate to say that legitimate deductions even from this portion of the testimony—the portion respecting the gruff and shrill voices—are in themselves sufficient to engender a suspicion which should give direction to all farther progress in the investigation of the mystery. I said 'legitimate deductions'; but my meaning is not thus fully expressed. I designed to imply that the deductions are the *sole* proper ones, and that the suspicion arises *inevitably* from them as a single result. What the suspicion is, however, I will not say just yet. I merely wish you to bear in mind that, with myself, it was sufficiently forcible to give a definite form—a certain tendency—to my inquiries in the chamber.

"Let us now transport ourselves, in fancy, to this

chamber. What shall we first seek here? The means of egress employed by the murderers. It is not too much to say that neither of us believes in præternatural events. Madame and Mademoiselle L'Espanaye were not destroyed by spirits. The doers of the deed were material and escaped materially. Then how? Fortunately there is but one mode of reasoning upon the point, and that mode *must* lead us to a definite decision. Let us examine, each by each, the possible means of egress. It is clear that the assassins were in the room where Mademoiselle L'Espanaye was found, or at least in the room adjoining, when the party ascended the stairs. It is, then, only from these two apartments that we have to seek issues. The police have laid bare the floors, the ceiling, and the masonry of the walls, in every direction. No *secret* issues could have escaped their vigilance. But, not trusting to *their* eyes, I examined with my own. There were, then, *no* secret issues. Both doors leading from the rooms into the passage were securely locked, with the keys inside. Let us turn to the chimneys. These, although of ordinary width for some eight or ten feet above the hearths, will not admit, throughout their extent, the body of a large cat. The impossibility of egress, by means already stated, being thus absolute, we are reduced to the windows. Through those of the front room no one could have escaped without notice from the crowd in the street. The murderers *must* have passed, then, through those of the back room. Now, brought to this conclusion in so unequivocal a manner as we are, it is not our part, as reasoners, to reject it on account of apparent impossibilities. It is only left for us to prove that these apparent 'impossibilities' are, in reality, not such.

"There are two windows in the chamber. One of them is unobstructed by furniture, and is wholly visible. The lower portion of the other is hidden from view by the head of the unwieldy bedstead which is thrust close up against it. The former was found securely fastened from within. It resisted the utmost force of those who endeavored to raise it. A large gimlet-hole had been pierced in its frame to the left, and a very stout nail was found fitted therein, nearly to the head. Upon examining the other window, a similar nail was seen similarly fitted in it; and a vigorous attempt to raise this sash failed also. The police were now entirely satisfied that egress had not been in these directions. And, *therefore*, it was thought a matter of supererogation to withdraw the nails and open the windows.

"My own examination was somewhat more particular, and was so for the reason I have just given—because here it was, I knew, that all apparent impossibilities *must* be proved to be not such in reality.

"I proceeded to think thus—*a posteriori*.[28] The murderers *did* escape from one of these windows. This being so, they could not have re-fastened the sashes from the inside, as they were found fastened;—the consideration which put a stop, through its obviousness, to the scrutiny of the police in this quarter. Yet the sashes *were* fastened. They *must*, then, have the power of fastening themselves. There was no escape from this conclusion. I stepped to the unobstructed casement, withdrew the nail with some difficulty, and attempted to raise the sash. It resisted all my efforts, as I had anticipated. A concealed spring must, I now knew, exist; and this corroboration of my idea convinced me that my premises, at least, were correct, however mysterious still appeared the circumstances attending the nails. A careful search soon brought to light the hidden spring. I pressed it, and, satisfied with the discovery, forbore to upraise the sash.

"I now replaced the nail and regarded it attentively. A person passing out through this window might have reclosed it, and the spring would have caught—but the nail could not have been replaced. The conclusion was plain, and again narrowed in the field of my investigations. The assassins *must* have escaped through the other window. Supposing, then, the springs upon each sash to be the same, as was probable, there *must* be found a difference between the nails, or at least between the modes of their fixture. Getting upon the sacking of the bedstead, I looked over the head-board minutely at the second casement. Passing my hand down behind the board, I readily discovered and pressed the spring, which was, as I had supposed, identical in character with its neighbor. I now looked at the nail. It was as stout as the other, and apparently fitted in the same manner—driven in nearly up to the head.

"You will say that I was puzzled; but, if you think so, you must have misunderstood the nature of the inductions. To use a sporting phrase, I had not been once 'at fault.' The scent had never for an instant been lost. There was no flaw in any link of the chain. I had traced the secret to its ultimate result,—and that result was *the nail*. It had, I say, in every respect, the appearance of its fellow in the other window; but this fact was an absolute nullity (conclusive as it might seem to be) when compared with the consideration that here, at this point, terminated the clew. 'There *must* be something wrong,' I said, 'about the nail.' I touched it; and the head, with about a quarter of an inch of the shank, came off in my fingers. The rest of the shank was in the gimlet-hole, where it had been broken off. The fracture was an old one (for its edges were incrusted with rust), and had apparently been accomplished by the blow of a hammer, which had partially imbedded, in the top of the bottom sash, the head portion of the nail. I now carefully replaced this head portion in the indentation whence I had taken it, and the resemblance to a perfect nail was complete—the fissure was invisible. Pressing the spring, I gently raised the sash for a few inches; the head went up with it, remaining firm in its bed. I closed the window, and the semblance of the whole nail was again perfect.

"This riddle, so far, was now unriddled. The assassin had escaped through the window which looked upon the bed. Dropping of its own accord upon his exit (or perhaps purposely closed), it had become fastened by the spring; and it was the retention of this spring which had been mistaken by the police for that of the nail,—farther inquiry being thus considered unnecessary.

"The next question is that of the mode of descent. Upon this point I had been satisfied in my walk with you around the building. About five feet and a half from the casement in question there runs a lightning-rod. From this rod it would have been impossible for any one to reach the window itself, to say nothing of entering it. I observed, however, that the shutters of the fourth story were of the peculiar kind called by Parisian carpenters *ferrades*—a kind rarely employed at the present day, but frequently seen upon very old mansions at Lyons and Bordeaux. They are in the form of an ordinary door (a single, not a folding door), except that the lower half is latticed or worked in open trellis—thus affording an excellent hold for the hands. In the present instance these shutters are fully three feet and a half broad. When we saw them from the rear of the house, they were both about half open—that is to say they stood off at right angles from the wall. It is probable that the police, as well as myself, examined the back of the tenement; but, if so, in looking at these *ferrades* in the line of their breadth (as they must have done), they did not perceive this great breadth itself, or, at all events, failed to take it into due consideration. In fact, having once satisfied themselves that no egress could have been made in this quarter, they would naturally bestow here a very cursory examination. It was clear to me, however, that the shutter belonging to the window at the head of the bed, would, if swung fully back to the wall, reach to within two feet of the lightning-rod. It was also evident that, by exertion of a very unusual degree of activity and courage, an entrance into the window, from the rod, might have been thus effected. By reaching to the distance of two feet and a half (we now suppose the shutter open to its whole extent) a robber might have taken a firm grasp upon the trellis-work. Letting go, then, his hold upon the rod, placing his feet securely against the wall, and springing boldly from it, he might have swung the shutter so as to close it, and, if we imagine the window open at the time, might even have swung himself into the room.

"I wish you to bear especially in mind that I have spoken of a *very* unusual degree of activity as requisite to success in so hazardous and so difficult a feat. It is my design to show you first, that the thing might possibly have been accomplished:—but, secondly and *chiefly*, I wish to impress upon your understanding the *very extraordinary*—the almost præternatural character of that agility which could have accomplished it.

"You will say, no doubt, using the language of the law, that 'to make out my case, I should rather undervalue than insist upon a full estimation of the activity required in this matter.' This may be the practice in law, but it is not the usage of reason. My ultimate object is only the truth. My immediate purpose is to lead you to place in juxtaposition, that *very unusual* activity of which I have just spoken, with that *very peculiar* shrill (or harsh) and *unequal* voice, about whose nationality no two persons could be found to agree, and in whose utterance no syllabification could be detected."

At these words a vague and half-formed conception of the meaning of Dupin flitted over my mind. I seemed to be upon the verge of comprehension, without power to comprehend—as men, at times, find themselves upon the brink of remembrance, without being able, in the end, to remember. My friend went on with his discourse.

"You will see," he said, "that I have shifted the question from the mode of egress to that of ingress. It was my design to convey the idea that both were effected in the same manner, at the same point. Let us now revert to the interior of the room. Let us survey the appearances here. The drawers of the bureau, it is said, had been rifled, although many articles of apparel still remained within them. The conclusion here is absurd. It is a mere guess—a very silly one—and no more. How are we to know that the articles found in the drawers were not all these drawers had originally contained? Madame L'Espanaye and her daughter lived an exceedingly retired life—saw no company—seldom went out—had little use for numerous changes of habiliment. Those found were at least of as good quality as any likely to be possessed by these ladies. If a thief had taken any, why did he not take the best—why did he not take all? In a word, why did he abandon four thousand francs in gold to encumber himself with a bundle of linen? The gold *was* abandoned. Nearly the whole sum mentioned by Monsieur Mignaud, the banker, was discovered, in bags, upon the floor. I wish you therefore, to discard from your thoughts the blundering idea of *motive*, engendered in the brains of the police by that portion of the evidence which speaks of money delivered at the door of the house. Coincidences ten times as remarkable as this (the delivery of the money, and murder committed within three days upon the party receiving it), happen to all of us every hour of our lives, without attracting even momentary notice. Coincidences, in general, are great stumbling-blocks in the way of that class of thinkers who have been educated to know nothing of the theory of probabilities—that theory to which the most glorious objects of human research are indebted for the most glorious of illustration. In the present instance, had the gold been gone, the fact of its delivery three days before would have formed something more than a coincidence. It would have been corroborative of this idea of motive. But, under the real circumstances of the case, if we are to suppose gold the motive of this outrage, we must also imagine the perpetrator so vacillating an idiot as to have abandoned his gold and his motive together.

"Keeping now steadily in mind the points to which I

have drawn your attention—that peculiar voice, that unusual agility, and that startling absence of motive in a murder so singularly atrocious as this—let us glance at the butchery itself. Here is a woman strangled to death by manual strength, and thrust up a chimney head downward. Ordinary assassins employ no such mode of murder as this. Least of all, do they thus dispose of the murdered. In the manner of thrusting the corpse up the chimney, you will admit that there was something *excessively outré*—something altogether irreconcilable with our common notions of human action, even when we suppose the actors the most depraved of men. Think, too, how great must have been that strength which could have thrust the body *up* such an aperture so forcibly that the united vigor of several persons was found barely sufficient to drag it *down!*

"Turn, now, to other indications of the employment of a vigor most marvellous. On the hearth were thick tresses—very thick tresses—of gray human hair. These had been torn out by the roots. You are aware of the great force necessary in tearing thus from the head even twenty or thirty hairs together. You saw the locks in question as well as myself. Their roots (a hideous sight!) were clotted with fragments of the flesh of the scalp—sure token of the prodigious power which had been exerted in uprooting perhaps half a million of hairs at a time. The throat of the old lady was not merely cut, but the head absolutely severed from the body: the instrument was a mere razor. I wish you also to look at the *brutal* ferocity of these deeds. Of the bruises upon the body of Madame L'Espa   e I do not speak. Monsieur Dumas, and his worthy coadjutor Monsieur Etienne, have pronounced that they were inflicted by some obtuse instrument; and so far these gentlemen are very correct. The obtuse instrument was clearly the stone pavement in the yard, upon which the victim had fallen from the window which looked in upon the bed. This idea, however simple it may now seem, escaped the police for the same reason that the breadth of the shutters escaped them—because, by the affair of the nails, their perceptions had been hermetically sealed against the possibility of the windows having ever been opened at all.

"If now, in addition to all these things, you have properly reflected upon the odd disorder of the chamber, we have gone so far as to combine the ideas of an agility astounding, a strength superhuman, a ferocity brutal, a butchery without motive, a *grotesquerie* in horror absolutely alien from humanity, and a voice foreign in tone to the ears of men of many nations, and devoid of all distinct or intelligible syllabification. What result, then, has ensued? What impression have I made upon your fancy?"

I felt a creeping of the flesh as Dupin asked me the question. "A madman," I said, "has done this deed—some raving maniac, escaped from a neighboring *Maison de Santé*."[29]

"In some respects," he replied, "your idea is not irrelevant. But the voices of madmen, even in their wildest paroxysms, are never found to tally with that peculiar voice heard upon the stairs. Madmen are of some nation, and their language, however incoherent in its words, has always the coherence of syllabification. Besides, the hair of a madman is not such as I now hold in my hand. I disentangled this little tuft from the rigidly clutched fingers of Madame L'Espanaye. Tell me what you can make of it."

"Dupin!" I said, completely unnerved; "this hair is most unusual—this is no *human* hair."

"I have not asserted that it is," said he; "but, before we decide this point, I wish you to glance at the little sketch I have here traced upon this paper. It is a *facsimile* drawing of what has been described in one portion of the testimony as 'dark bruises and deep indentations of finger nails' upon the throat of Mademoiselle L'Espanaye, and in another (by Messrs. Dumas and Etienne) as a 'series of livid spots, evidently the impression of fingers.'

"You will perceive," continued my friend, spreading out the paper upon the table before us, "that this drawing gives the idea of a firm and fixed hold. There is no *slipping* apparent. Each finger has retained—possibly until the death of the victim—the fearful grasp by which it originally imbedded itself. Attempt, now, to place all your fingers, at the same time, in the respective impressions as you see them."

I made the attempt in vain.

"We are possibly not giving this matter a fair trial," he said. "The paper is spread out upon a plane surface; but the human throat is cylindrical. Here is a billet of wood, the circumference of which is about that of the throat. Wrap the drawing around it, and try the experiment again."

I did so; but the difficulty was even more obvious than before. "This," I said, "is the mark of no human hand."

"Read now," replied Dupin, "this passage from Cuvier."[30]

It was a minute anatomical and generally descriptive account of the large fulvous Ourang-Outang of the East

Indian Islands. The gigantic stature, the prodigious strength and activity, the wild ferocity, and the imitative propensities of these mammalia are sufficiently well known to all. I understood the full horrors of the murder at once.

"The description of the digits," said I, as I made an end of the reading, "is in exact accordance with this drawing. I see that no animal but an Ourang-Outang, of the species here mentioned, could have impressed the indentations as you have traced them. This tuft of tawny hair, too, is identical in character with that of the beast of Cuvier. But I cannot possibly comprehend the particulars of this frightful mystery. Besides, there were *two* voices heard in contention, and one of them was unquestionably the voice of a Frenchman."

"True; and you will remember an expression attributed at most unanimously, by the evidence, to this voice,—the expression, *'mon Dieu!'* This, under the circumstances, has been justly characterized by one of the witnesses (Montani, the confectioner) as an expression of remonstrance or expostulation. Upon these two words, therefore, I have mainly built my hopes of a full solution of the riddle. A Frenchman was cognizant of the murder. It is possible—indeed it is far more than probable—that he was innocent of all participation in the bloody transactions which took place. The Ourang-Outang may have escaped from him. He may have traced it to the chamber; but, under the agitating circumstances which ensued, he could never have recaptured it. It is still at large. I will not pursue these guesses—for I have no right to call them more—since the shades of reflection upon which they are based are scarcely of sufficient depth to be appreciable by my own intellect, and since I could not pretend to make them intelligible to the understanding of another. We will call them guesses, then, and speak of them as such. If the Frenchman in question is indeed, as I suppose, innocent of this atrocity, this advertisement, which I left last night, upon our return home, at the office of *Le Monde* (a paper devoted to the shipping interest, and much sought by sailors), will bring him to our residence."

He handed me a paper, and I read thus:

"CAUGHT—*In the Bois de Boulogne, early in the morning of the —— inst.* (the morning of the murder), *a very large, tawny Ourang-Outang of the Bornese species. The owner (who is ascertained to be a sailor, belonging to a Maltese vessel) may have the animal again, upon identifying it satisfactorily, and paying a few charges arising from its capture and keeping. Call at No. —— Rue ——, Faubourg St. Germain—au troisième.*"[31]

"How was it possible," I asked, "that you should know the man to be a sailor, and belonging to a Maltese vessel?"

"I do *not* know it," said Dupin. "I am not *sure* of it. Here, however, is a small piece of ribbon, which from its form, and from its greasy appearance, has evidently been used in tying the hair in one of those long *queues* of which sailors are so fond. Moreover, this knot is one which few besides sailors can tie, and is peculiar to the Maltese. I picked the ribbon up at the foot of the lightning-rod. It could not have belonged to either of the deceased. Now if, after all, I am wrong in my induction from this ribbon, that the Frenchman was a sailor belonging to a Maltese vessel, still I can have done no harm in saying what I did in the advertisement. If I am in error, he will merely suppose that I have been misled by some circumstance into which he will not take the trouble to inquire. But if I am right, a great point is gained. Cognizant although innocent of the murder, the Frenchman will naturally hesitate about replying to the advertisement—about demanding the Ourang-Outang. He will reason thus:—'I am innocent; I am poor; my Ourang-Outang is of great value—to one in my circumstance a fortune of itself—why should I lose it through idle apprehensions of danger? Here it is, within my grasp. It was found in the Bois de Boulogne—at a vast distance from the scene of that butchery. How can it ever be suspected that a brute beast should have done the deed? The police are at fault—they have failed to procure the slightest clew. Should they even trace the animal, it would be impossible to prove me cognizant of the murder, or to implicate me in guilt on account of that cognizance. Above all, *I am known*. The advertiser designates me as the possessor of the beast. I am not sure to what limit his knowledge may extend. Should I avoid claiming a property of so great value, which it is known that I possess, I will render the animal at least, liable to suspicion. It is not my policy to attract attention either to myself or to the beast. I will answer the advertisement, get the Ourang-Outang, and keep it close until this matter has blown over.'"

At this moment we heard a step upon the stairs.

"Be ready," said Dupin, "with your pistols, but neither use them nor show them until at a signal from myself."

The front door of the house had been left open, and the visitor had entered, without ringing, and advanced several steps upon the staircase. Now, however, he seemed to hesitate. Presently we heard him descending. Dupin was moving quickly to the door, when we again heard him coming up. He did not turn back a second time, but stepped up with decision, and rapped at the door of our chamber.

"Come in," said Dupin, in a cheerful and hearty tone.

A man entered. He was a sailor, evidently,—a tall, stout, and muscular-looking person, with a certain dare-devil expression of countenance, not altogether unprepossessing. His face, greatly sunburnt, was more than half hidden by whisker and *mustachio*. He had with him a huge oaken cudgel, but appeared to be otherwise unarmed. He bowed awkwardly, and bade us "good evening," in French accents, which, although somewhat Neufchâtelish,[32] were still sufficiently indicative of a Parisian origin.

"Sit down, my friend," said Dupin. "I suppose you have called about the Ourang-Outang. Upon my word, I almost envy you the possession of him; a remarkably fine, and no doubt a very valuable animal. How old do you suppose him to be?"

The sailor drew a long breath, with the air of a man relieved of some intolerable burden, and then replied, in an assured tone:

"I have no way of telling—but he can't be more than four or five years old. Have you got him here?"

"Oh, no; we had no conveniences for keeping him here. He is at a livery stable in the Rue Dubourg, just by. You can get him in the morning. Of course you are prepared to identify the property?"

"To be sure I am, sir."

"I shall be sorry to part with him," said Dupin.

"I don't mean that you should be at all this trouble for nothing, sir," said the man. "Couldn't expect it. Am very willing to pay a reward for the finding of the animal—that is to say, any thing in reason."

"Well," replied my friend, "that is all very fair, to be sure. Let me think!—what should I have? Oh! I will tell you. My reward shall be this. You shall give me all the information in your power about these murders in the Rue Morgue."

Dupin said the last words in a very low tone, and very quietly. Just as quietly, too, he walked toward the door, locked it, and put the key in his pocket. He then drew a pistol from his bosom and placed it, without the least flurry, upon the table.

The sailor's face flushed up as if he were struggling with suffocation. He started to his feet and grasped his cudgel; but the next moment he fell back into his seat, trembling violently, and with the countenance of death itself. He spoke not a word. I pitied him from the bottom of my heart.

"My friend," said Dupin, in a kind tone, "you are alarming yourself unnecessarily—you are indeed. We mean you no harm whatever. I pledge you the honor of a gentleman, and of a Frenchman, that we intend you no injury. I perfectly well know that you are innocent of the atrocities in the Rue Morgue. It will not do, however, to deny that you are in some measure implicated in them. From what I have already said, you must know that I have had means of information about this matter—means of which you could never have dreamed. Now the thing stands thus. You have done nothing which you could have avoided—nothing, certainly, which renders you culpable. You were not even guilty of robbery, when you might nave robbed with impunity. You have nothing to conceal. You have no reason for concealment. On the other hand, you are bound by every principle of honor to confess all you know. An innocent man is now imprisoned, charged with that crime of which you can point out the perpetrator."

The sailor had recovered his presence of mind, in a great measure, while Dupin uttered these words; but his original boldness of bearing was all gone.

"So help me God!" said he, after a brief pause, "I *will* tell you all I know about this affair;—but I do not expect you to believe one half I say—I would be a fool indeed if I did. Still, I *am* innocent, and I will make a clean breast if I die for it."

What he stated was, in substance, this. He had lately made a voyage to the Indian Archipelago. A party, of which he formed one, landed at Borneo, and passed into the interior on an excursion of pleasure. Himself and a companion had captured the Ourang-Outang. This companion dying, the animal fell into his own exclusive possession. After great trouble, occasioned by the intractable ferocity of his captive during the home voyage, he at length succeeded in lodging it safely at his own residence in Paris, where, not to attract toward himself the unpleasant curiosity of his neighbors, he kept it carefully secluded, until such time as it should recover from a wound in the foot, received from a splinter on board ship. His ultimate design was to sell it.

Returning home from some sailors' frolic on the

night, or rather in the morning, of the murder, he found the beast occupying his own bedroom, into which it had broken from a closet adjoining, where it had been, as was thought, securely confined. Razor in hand, and fully lathered, it was sitting before a looking-glass, attempting the operation of shaving, in which it had no doubt previously watched its master through the keyhole of the closet. Terrified at the sight of so dangerous a weapon in the possession of an animal so ferocious, and so well able to use it, the man, for some moments, was at a loss what to do. He had been accustomed, however, to quiet the creature, even in its fiercest moods, by the use of a whip, and to this he now resorted. Upon sight of it, the Ourang-Outang sprang at once through the door of the chamber, down the stairs, and thence through a window, unfortunately open, into the street.

The Frenchman followed in despair; the ape, razor still in hand, occasionally stopping to look back and gesticulate at his pursuer, until the latter had nearly come up with it. It then again made off. In this manner the chase continued for a long time. The streets were profoundly quiet, as it was nearly three o'clock in the morning. In passing down an alley in the rear of the Rue Morgue, the fugitive's attention was arrested by a light gleaming from the open window of Madame L'Espanaye's chamber, in the fourth story of her house. Rushing to the building, it perceived the lightning-rod, clambered up with inconceivable agility, grasped the shutter, which was thrown fully back against the wall, and, by its means, swung itself directly upon the headboard of the bed. The whole feat did not occupy a minute. The shutter was kicked open again by the Ourang-Outang as it entered the room.

The sailor, in the meantime, was both rejoiced and perplexed. He had strong hopes of now recapturing the brute, as it could scarcely escape from the trap into which it had ventured, except by the rod, where it might be intercepted as it came down. On the other hand, there was much cause for anxiety as to what it might do in the house. This latter reflection urged the man still to follow the fugitive. A lightning-rod is ascended without difficulty, especially by a sailor; but, when he had arrived as high as the window, which lay far to his left, his career was stopped; the most that he could accomplish was to reach over so as to obtain a glimpse of the interior of the room. At this glimpse he nearly fell from his hold through excess of horror. Now it was that those hideous shrieks arose upon the night, which had startled from slumber the inmates of the Rue Morgue. Madame L'Espanaye and her daughter, habited in their night clothes, had apparently been occupied in arranging some papers in the iron chest already mentioned, which had been wheeled into the middle of the room. It was open, and its contents lay beside it on the floor. The victims must have been sitting with their backs toward the window; and, from the time elapsing between the ingress of the beast and the screams, it seems probable that it was not immediately perceived. The flapping-to of the shutter would naturally have been attributed to the wind.

As the sailor looked in, the gigantic animal had seized Madame L'Espanaye by the hair (which was loose, as she had been combing it), and was flourishing the razor about her face, in imitation of the motions of a barber.

The daughter lay prostrate and motionless; she had swooned. The screams and struggles of the old lady (during which the hair was torn from her head) had the effect of changing the probably pacific purposes of the Ourang-Outang into those of wrath. With one determined sweep of its muscular arm it nearly severed her head from her body. The sight of blood inflamed its anger into phrensy. Gnashing its teeth, and flashing fire from its eyes, it flew upon the body of the girl, and imbedded its fearful talons in her throat, retaining its grasp until she expired. Its wandering and wild glances fell at this moment upon the head of the bed, over which the face of its master, rigid with horror, was just discernible. The fury of the beast, who no doubt bore still in mind the dreaded whip, was instantly converted into fear. Conscious of having deserved punishment, it seemed desirous of concealing its bloody deeds, and skipped about the chamber in an agony of nervous agitation; throwing down and breaking the furniture as it moved, and dragging the bed from the bedstead. In conclusion, it seized first the corpse of the daughter, and thrust it up the chimney, as it was found; then that of the old lady, which it immediately hurled through the window headlong.

As the ape approached the casement with its mutilated burden, the sailor shrank aghast to the rod, and, rather gliding than clambering down it, hurried at once home—dreading the consequences of the butchery, and gladly abandoning, in his terror, all solicitude about the fate of the Ourang-Outang. The words heard by the party upon the staircase were the Frenchman's exclamations of horror and affright, commingled with the fiendish jabberings of the brute.

I have scarcely any thing to add. The Ourang-Outang must have escaped from the chamber, by the rod, just before the breaking of the door. It must have closed the window as it passed through it. It was subsequently caught by the owner himself, who obtained for it a very large sum at the *Jardin des Plantes.*[33] Le Bon was instantly released, upon our narration of the circumstances (with some comments from Dupin) at the *bureau* of the Prefect of Police. This functionary, however well disposed to my friend, could not altogether conceal his chagrin at the turn which affairs had taken, and was fain to indulge in a sarcasm or two about the propriety of every person minding his own business.

"Let him talk," said Dupin, who had not thought it necessary to reply. "Let him discourse; it will ease his conscience. I am satisfied with having defeated him in his own castle. Nevertheless, that he failed in the solution of this mystery, is by no means that matter for wonder which he supposes it; for, in truth, our friend the Prefect is somewhat too cunning to be profound. In his wisdom is no *stamen.* It is all head and no body, like the pictures of the Goddess Laverna[34]—or, at best, all head and shoulders, like a codfish. But he is a good creature after all. I like him especially for one master stroke of cant, by which he has attained his reputation for ingenuity. I mean the way he has *'de nier ce qui est, et d'expliquer ce qui n'est pas.'* "[*][35]

---

[*] Rousseau—*Nouvelle Héloise.*

THE PURLOINED LETTER[1]

Nil sapientiæ odiosius acumine nimio.

—Seneca[2]

A T PARIS, just after dark one gusty evening in the autumn of 18—, I was enjoying the twofold luxury of meditation and a meerschaum,[3] in company with my friend, C. Auguste Dupin, in his little back library, or book-closet, *au troisième*,[4] No. 33 *Rue Dunôt, Faubourg St. Germain.* For one hour at least we had maintained a profound silence; while each, to any casual observer, might have seemed intently and exclusively occupied with the curling eddies of smoke that oppressed the atmosphere of the chamber. For myself, however, I was mentally discussing certain topics which had formed matter for conversation between us at an earlier period of the evening; I mean the affair of the Rue Morgue, and the mystery attending the murder of Marie Rogêt. I looked upon it, therefore, as something of a coincidence, when the door of our apartment was thrown open and admitted our old acquaintance, Monsieur G——, the Prefect of the Parisian police.

We gave him a hearty welcome; for there was nearly half as much of the entertaining as of the contemptible about the man, and we had not seen him for several years. We had been sitting in the dark, and Dupin now arose for the purpose of lighting a lamp, but sat down again, without doing so, upon G.'s saying that he had called to consult us, or rather to ask the opinion of my friend, about some official business which had occasioned a great deal of trouble.

"If it is any point requiring reflection," observed Dupin, as he forbore to enkindle the wick, "we shall examine it to better purpose in the dark."

"That is another of your odd notions," said the Prefect, who had the fashion of calling everything "odd" that was beyond his comprehension, and thus lived amid an absolute legion of "oddities."

"Very true," said Dupin, as he supplied his visitor with a pipe, and rolled toward him a comfortable chair.

"And what is the difficulty now?" I asked. "Nothing more in the assassination way I hope?"

"Oh, no; nothing of that nature. The fact is, the business is *very* simple indeed, and I make no doubt that we can manage it sufficiently well ourselves; but then I thought Dupin would like to hear the details of it, because it is so excessively *odd*."

"Simple and odd," said Dupin.

"Why, yes; and not exactly that either. The fact is, we have all been a good deal puzzled because the affair *is* so simple, and yet baffles us altogether."

"Perhaps it is the very simplicity of the thing which puts you at fault," said my friend.

"What nonsense you *do* talk!" replied the Prefect, laughing heartily.

"Perhaps the mystery is a little *too* plain," said Dupin.

"Oh, good heavens! who ever heard of such an idea?"

"A little *too* self-evident."

"Ha! ha! ha!— ha! ha! ha!—ho! ho! ho!" roared our visitor, profoundly amused, "oh, Dupin, you will be the death of me yet!"

"And what, after all, *is* the matter on hand?" I asked.

"Why, I will tell you," replied the Prefect, as he gave a long, steady, and contemplative puff, and settled himself in his chair. "I will tell you in a few words; but, before I begin, let me caution you that this is an affair demanding the greatest secrecy, and that I should most probably lose the position I now hold, were it known that I confided it to any one."

"Proceed," said I.

"Or not," said Dupin.

"Well, then; I have received personal information, from a very high quarter, that a certain document of the last importance has been purloined from the royal apartments. The individual who purloined it is known; this beyond a doubt; he was seen to take it. It is known, also, that it still remains in his possession."

"How is this known?" asked Dupin.

"It is clearly inferred," replied the Prefect, "from the nature of the document, and from the non-appearance of certain results which would at once arise from its passing *out* of the robber's possession—that is to say, from his employing it as he must design in the end to employ it."

"Be a little more explicit," I said.

"Well, I may venture so far as to say that the paper gives its holder a certain power in a certain quarter where such power is immensely valuable." The Prefect was fond of the cant of diplomacy.

"Still I do not quite understand," said Dupin.

"No? Well; the disclosure of the document to a third person, who shall be nameless, would bring in question the honor of a personage of most exalted station; and this fact gives the holder of the document an ascendancy over the illustrious personage whose honor and peace are so jeopardized."

"But this ascendancy," I interposed, "would depend upon the robber's knowledge of the loser's knowledge of the robber. Who would dare—"

"The thief," said G., "is the Minister D——, who dares all things, those unbecoming as well as those becoming a man. The method of the theft was not less ingenious than bold. The document in question—a letter, to be frank—had been received by the personage robbed while alone in the royal *boudoir.* During its perusal she was suddenly interrupted by the entrance of the other exalted personage from whom especially it was her wish to conceal it. After a hurried and vain endeavor to thrust it in a drawer, she was forced to place it, open it was, upon a table. The address, however, was uppermost, and, the contents thus unexposed, the letter escaped notice. At this juncture enters the Minister D——. His lynx eye immediately perceives the paper, recognizes the handwriting of the address, observes the confusion of the personage addressed, and fathoms her secret. After some business transactions, hurried through in his ordinary manner, he produces a letter somewhat similar to the one in question, opens it, pretends to read it, and then places it in close juxtaposition to the other. Again he converses, for some fifteen minutes, upon the public affairs. At length, in taking leave, he takes also from the table the letter to which he had no claim. Its rightful owner saw, but, of course, dared not call attention to the act, in the presence of the third personage who stood at her elbow. The minister decamped; leaving his own letter—one of no importance—upon the table."

"Here, then," said Dupin to me, "you have precisely what you demand to make the ascendancy complete—the robber's knowledge of the loser's knowledge of the robber."

"Yes," replied the Prefect; "and the power thus attained has, for some months past, been wielded, for political purposes, to a very dangerous extent. The personage robbed is more thoroughly convinced, every day, of the necessity of reclaiming her letter. But this, of course, cannot be done openly. In fine, driven to despair, she has committed the matter to me."

"Than whom," said Dupin, amid a perfect whirlwind of smoke, "no more sagacious agent could, I suppose, be desired, or even imagined."

"You flatter me," replied the Prefect; "but it is possible that some such opinion may have been entertained."

"It is clear," said I, "as you observe, that the letter is still in the possession of the minister; since it is this possession, and not any employment of the letter, which bestows the power. With the employment the power departs."

"True," said G.; "and upon this conviction I proceeded. My first care was to make thorough search of the minister's hotel; and here my chief embarrassment lay in the necessity of searching without his knowledge. Beyond all things, I have been warned of the danger which would result from giving him reason to suspect our design."

"But," said I, "you are quite *au fait*⁵ in these investigations. The Parisian police have done this thing often before."

"Oh, yes; and for this reason I did not despair. The habits of the minister gave me, too, a great advantage. He is frequently absent from home an night. His servants are by no means numerous. They sleep at a distance from their master's apartment, and, being chiefly Neapolitans, are readily made drunk. I have keys, as you know, with which I can open any chamber or cabinet in Paris. For three months a night has not passed, during the greater part of which I have not been engaged, personally, in ransacking the D—— Hotel. My honor is interested, and, to mention a great secret, the reward is enormous. So I did not abandon the search until I had become fully satisfied that the thief is a more astute man than myself. I fancy that I have investigated every nook and corner of the premises in which it is possible that the paper can be concealed."

"But is it not possible," I suggested, "that although the letter may be in possession of the minister, as it unquestionably is, he may have concealed it elsewhere than upon his own premises?"

"This is barely possible," said Dupin. "The present peculiar condition of affairs at court, and especially of those intrigues in which D—— is known to be involved,

would render the instant availability of the document—
its susceptibility of being produced at a moment's notice—a point of nearly equal importance with its
possession."

"Its susceptibility of being produced?" said I.

"That is to say, of being *destroyed*," said Dupin.

"True," I observed; "the paper is clearly then upon the
premises. As for its being upon the person of the minister, we may consider that as out of the question."

"Entirely," said the Prefect. "He has been twice way-
laid, as if by footpads, and his person rigidly searched
under my own inspection."

"You might have spared yourself this trouble," said
Dupin. "D——, I presume, is not altogether a fool, and,
if not, must have anticipated these waylayings, as a matter of course."

"Not *altogether* a fool," said G., "but then he is a poet,
which I take to be only one remove from a fool."

"True," said Dupin, after a long and thoughtful whiff
from his meerschaum, "although I have been guilty of
certain doggerel myself."

"Suppose you detail," said I, "the particulars of your
search."

"Why, the fact is, we took our time, and we searched
everywhere. I have had long experience in these affairs. I
took the entire building, room by room; devoting the
nights of a whole week to each. We examined, first, the
furniture of each apartment. We opened every possible
drawer; and I presume you know that, to a properly
trained police-agent, such a thing as a *'secret'* drawer is
impossible. Any man is a dolt who permits a *'secret'*
drawer to escape him in a search of this kind. The thing

is *so* plain. There is a certain amount of bulk—of space—to be accounted for in every cabinet. Then we have accurate rules. The fiftieth part of a line could not escape us. After the cabinets we took the chairs. The cushions we probed with the fine long needles you have seen me employ. From the tables we removed the tops."

"Why so?"

"Sometimes the top of a table, or other similarly arranged piece of furniture, is removed by the person wishing to conceal an article; then the leg is excavated, the article deposited within the cavity, and the top replaced. The bottoms and tops of bedposts are employed in the same way."

"But could not the cavity be detected by sounding?" I asked.

"By no means, if, when the article is deposited, a sufficient wadding of cotton be placed around it. Besides, in our case, we were obliged to proceed without noise."

"But you could not have removed—you could not have taken to pieces *all* articles of furniture in which it would have been possible to make a deposit in the manner you mention. A letter may be compressed into a thin spiral roll, not differing much in shape or bulk from a large knitting-needle, and in this form it might be inserted into the rung of a chair, for example. You did not take to pieces all the chairs?"

"Certainly not; but we did better—we examined the rungs of every chair in the hotel, and, indeed, the jointings of every description of furniture, by the aid of a most powerful microscope. Had there been any traces of recent disturbance we should not have failed to detect it instantly. A single grain of gimlet-dust, for example, would have been as obvious as an apple. Any disorder in the gluing—any unusual gaping in the joints—would have sufficed to insure detection."

"I presume you looked to the mirrors, between the boards and the plates, and you probed the beds and the bedclothes, as well as the curtains and carpets."

"That of course; and when we had absolutely completed every particle of the furniture in this way, then we examined the house itself. We divided its entire surface into compartments, which we numbered, so that none might be missed; then we scrutinized each individual square inch throughout the premises, including the two houses immediately adjoining, with the microscope, as before."

"The two houses adjoining!" I exclaimed; "you must have had a great deal of trouble."

"We had; but the reward offered is prodigious."

"You include the *grounds* about the houses?"

"All the grounds are paved with brick. They gave us comparatively little trouble. We examined the moss between the bricks, and found it undisturbed."

"You looked among D——'s papers, of course, and into the books of the library?"

"Certainly; we opened every package and parcel; we not only opened every book, but we turned over every leaf in each volume, not contenting ourselves with a mere shake, according to the fashion of some of our police officers. We also measured the thickness of every book-*cover*, with the most accurate admeasurement and applied to each the most jealous scrutiny of the microscope. Had any of the bindings been recently meddled with, it would have been utterly impossible that the fact should have escaped observation. Some five or six volumes, just from the hands of the binder, we carefully probed, longitudinally, with the needles."

"You explored the floors beneath the carpets?"

"Beyond doubt. We removed every carpet, and examined the boards with the microscope."

"And the paper on the walls?"

"Yes."

"You looked into the cellars?"

"We did."

"Then," I said, "you have been making a miscalculation and the letter is *not* upon the premises, as you suppose."

"I fear you are right there," said the Prefect. "And now, Dupin, what would you advise me to do?"

"To make a thorough research of the premises."

"That is absolutely needless," replied G——. "I am not more sure that I breathe than I am that the letter is not at the hotel."

"I have no better advice to give you," said Dupin. "You have, of course, an accurate description of the letter?"

"Oh, yes!"—And here the Prefect, producing a memorandum-book, proceeded to read aloud a minute account of the internal, and especially of the external, appearance of the missing document. Soon after finishing the perusal of this description, he took his departure, more entirely depressed in spirits than I had ever known the good gentleman before.

In about a month afterward he paid us another visit, and found us occupied very nearly as before. He took a pipe and a chair and entered into some ordinary conversation. At length I said:

"Well, but G., what of the purloined letter? I presume you have at last made up your mind that there is no such thing as overreaching the Minister?"

"Confound him, say I—yes; I made the re-examination, however, as Dupin suggested—but it was all labor lost, as I knew it would be."

"How much was the reward offered, did you say?" asked Dupin.

"Why, a very great deal—a *very* liberal reward—I don't like to say how much, precisely; but one thing I *will* say, that I wouldn't mind giving my individual check for fifty thousand francs to any one who could obtain me that letter. The fact is, it is becoming of more and more importance every day; and the reward has been lately doubled. If it were trebled, however, I could do no more than I have done."

"Why, yes," said Dupin, drawlingly, between the whiffs of his meerschaum, "I really—think, G., you have not exerted yourself—to the utmost in this matter. You might—do a little more, I think, eh?"

"How?—in what way?"

"Why—puff, puff—you might—puff, puff—employ counsel in the matter, eh?— puff, puff, puff. Do you remember the story they tell of Abernethy?"[6]

"No; hang Abernethy!"

"To be sure! hang him and welcome. But, once upon a time, a certain rich miser conceived the design of spunging upon this Abernethy for a medical opinion. Getting up, for this purpose, an ordinary conversation in a private company, he insinuated his case to the physician, as that of an imaginary individual."

" 'We will suppose,' said the miser, that his symptoms

are such and such; now, doctor, what would *you* have directed him to take?'

" 'Take!' said Abernethy, 'Why, take *advice,* to be sure.' "

"But," said the Prefect, a little discomposed, "*I* am *perfectly* willing to take advice, and to pay for it. I would *really* give fifty thousand francs to any one who would aid me in the matter."

"In that case," replied Dupin, opening a drawer, and producing a check-book, "you may as well fill me up a check for the amount mentioned. When you have signed it, I will hand you the letter."

I was astounded. The Prefect appeared absolutely thunder-stricken. For some minutes he remained speechless and motionless, looking incredulously at my friend with open mouth, and eyes that seemed starting from their sockets; then apparently recovering himself in some measure, he seized a pen, and after several pauses and vacant stares, finally filled up and signed a check for fifty thousand francs, and handed it across the table to Dupin. The latter examined it carefully and deposited it in his pocket-book; then, unlocking an *escritoire,*[7] took thence a letter and gave it to the Prefect. This functionary grasped it in a perfect agony of joy, opened it with a trembling hand, cast a rapid glance at its contents, and then, scrambling and struggling to the door, rushed at length unceremoniously from the room and from the house, without having uttered a syllable since Dupin had requested him to fill up the check.

When he had gone, my friend entered into some explanations.

"The Parisian police," he said, "are exceedingly able in

their way. They are persevering, ingenious, cunning, and
thoroughly versed in the knowledge which their duties
seem chiefly to demand. Thus, when G—— detailed to us
his mode of searching the premises at the Hotel D——, I
felt entire confidence in his having made a satisfactory
investigation—so far as his labors extended."

"So far as his labors extended?" said I.

"Yes," said Dupin. "The measures adopted were not
only the best of their kind, but carried out to absolute
perfection. Had the letter been deposited within the
range of their search, these fellows would, beyond a
question, have found it."

I merely laughed—but he seemed quite serious in all
that he said.

"The measures, then," he continued, "were good in
their kind, and well executed; their defect lay in their
being inapplicable to the case and to the man. A certain
set of highly ingenious resources are, with the Prefect, a
sort of Procrustean bed,[8] to which he forcibly adapts his
designs. But he perpetually errs by being too deep or too
shallow for the matter in hand; and many a school-boy is
a better reasoner than he. I knew one about eight years
of age, whose success at guessing in the game of 'even
and odd' attracted universal admiration. This game is
simple, and is played with marbles. One player holds in
his hand a number of these toys, and demands of another whether that number is even or odd. If the guess is
right, the guesser wins one; if wrong, he loses one. The
boy to whom I allude won all the marbles of the school.
Of course he had some principle of guessing; and this lay
in mere observation and admeasurement of the astute-
ness of his opponents. For example, an arrant simpleton

is his opponent, and, holding up his closed hand, asks, 'Are they even or odd?' Our school-boy replies, 'Odd,' and loses; but upon the second trial he wins, for he then says to himself: 'The simpleton had them even upon the first trial, and his amount of cunning is just sufficient to make him have them odd upon the second; I will therefore guess odd';—he guesses odd, and wins. Now, with a simpleton a degree above the first, he would have reasoned that: 'This fellow finds that in the first instance I guessed odd, and, in the second, he will propose to himself, upon the first impulse, a simple variation from even to odd, as did the first simpleton; but then a second thought will suggest that this is too simple a variation, and finally he will decide upon putting it even as before. I will therefore guess even';—he guesses even, and wins. Now this mode of reasoning in the school-boy, whom his fellows termed 'lucky,'—what, in its last analysis, is it?"

"It is merely," I said, "an identification of the reasoner's intellect with that of his opponent."

"It is," said Dupin; "and, upon inquiring of the boy by what means he effected the *thorough* identification in which his success consisted, I received answer as follows: 'When I wish to find out how wise, or how stupid, or how good, or how wicked is any one, or what are his thoughts at the moment, I fashion the expression of my face, as accurately as possible, in accordance with the expression of his, and then wait to see what thoughts or sentiments arise in my mind or heart, as if to match or correspond with the expression.' This response of the school-boy lies at the bottom of all the spurious profundity which has been attributed to Rochefoucault, to La Bougive, to Machiavelli, and to Campanella."[9]

"And the identification," I said, "of the reasoner's intellect with that of his opponent, depends, if I understand you aright, upon the accuracy with which the opponent's intellect is admeasured."

"For its practical value it depends upon this," replied Dupin; "and the Prefect and his cohort fail so frequently, first, by default of this identification, and, secondly, by ill-admeasurement, or rather through non-admeasurement, of the intellect with which they are engaged. They consider only their own ideas of ingenuity; and, in searching for any thing hidden, advert only to the modes in which *they* would have hidden it. They are right in this much— that their own ingenuity is a faithful representative of that of *the mass;* but when the cunning of the individual felon is diverse in character from their own, the felon foils them, of course. This always happens when it is above their own, and very usually when it is below. They have no variation of principle in their investigations; at best, when urged by some unusual emergency—by some extraordinary reward—they extend or exaggerate their old modes of *practice,* without touching their principles. What, for example, in this case of D——, has been done to vary the principle of action? What is all this boring, and probing, and sounding, and scrutinizing with the microscope, and dividing the surface of the building into registered square inches—what is it all but an exaggeration *of the application* of the one principle or set of principles of search, which are based upon the one set of notions regarding human ingenuity, to which the Prefect, in the long routine of his duty, has been accustomed? Do you not see he has taken it for granted that *all* men proceed to conceal a letter, not exactly in a gimlet-hole bored in a chair-leg, but, at least, in *some* out-of-the-way hole or corner suggested by the same tenor of thought which would urge a man to secrete a letter in a gimlet-hole bored in a chair-leg? And do you not see also, that such *recherchés*[10] nooks for concealment are adapted only for ordinary occasions, and would be adopted only by ordinary intellects; for, in all cases of concealment, a disposal of the article concealed—a disposal of it in this *recherché* manner,—is, in the very first instance, presumable and presumed; and thus its discovery depends, not at all upon the acumen, but altogether upon the mere care, patience, and determination of the seekers; and where the case is of importance—or, what amounts to the same thing in the political eyes, when the reward is of magnitude,—the qualities in question have *never* been known to fail. You will now understand what I meant in suggesting that, had the purloined letter been hidden anywhere within the limits of the Prefect's examination—in other words, had the principle of its concealment been comprehended within the principles of the Prefect—its discovery would have been a matter altogether beyond question. This functionary, however, has been thoroughly mystified; and the remote source of his defeat lies in the supposition that the Minister is a fool, because he has acquired renown as a poet. All fools are poets; this the Prefect *feels;* and he is merely guilty of a *non distributio medii*[11] in thence inferring that all poets are fools."

"But is this really the poet?" I asked. "There are two brothers, I know; and both have attained reputation in letters. The Minister I believe has written learnedly on the Differential Calculus. He is a mathematician, and no poet."

"You are mistaken; I know him well; he is both. As poet *and* mathematician, he would reason well; as mere mathematician, he could not have reasoned at all, and thus would have been at the mercy of the Prefect."

"You surprise me," I said, "by these opinions, which have been contradicted by the voice of the world. You do not mean to set at naught the well-digested idea of centuries. The mathematical reason has long been regarded as *the* reason *par excellence*."

" '*Il y a à parier,*' " replied Dupin, quoting from Chamfort, " '*que toute idée publique, toute convention reçue, est une sottise, car elle a convenue au plus grand nombre.*'[12] The mathematicians, I grant you, have done their best to promulgate the popular error to which you allude, and which is none the less an error for its promulgation as truth. With an art worthy a better cause, for example, they have insinuated the term 'analysis' into application to algebra. The French are the originators of this particular deception; but if a term is of any importance—if words derive any value from applicability—then 'analysis' conveys 'algebra' about as much as, in Latin, '*ambitus*' implies 'ambition,' '*religio*' 'religion,' or '*homines honesti*' a set of '*honorable* men.' "[13]

"You have a quarrel on hand, I see," said I, "with some of the algebraists of Paris; but proceed."

"I dispute the availability, and thus the value, of that reason which is cultivated in any especial form other than the abstractly logical. I dispute, in particular, the reason educed by mathematical study. The mathematics are the science of form and quantity; mathematical reasoning is merely logic applied to observation upon form and quantity. The great error lies in supposing that even the truths of what is called *pure* algebra are abstract or general truths. And this error is so egregious that I am confounded at the universality with which it has been received. Mathematical axioms are *not* axioms of general truth. What is true of *relation*—of form and quantity—is often grossly false in regard to morals, for example. In this latter science it is very usually untrue that the aggregated parts are equal to the whole. In chemistry also the axiom fails. In the consideration of motive it fails; for two motives, each of a given value, have not, necessarily, a value when united, equal to the sum of their values apart. There are numerous other mathematical truths which are only truths within the limits of *relation*. But the mathematician argues from his *finite truths*, through habit, as if they were of an absolutely general applicability—as the world indeed imagines them to be. Bryant,[14] in his very learned 'Mythology,' mentions an analogous source of error, when he says that 'although the pagan fables are not believed, yet we forget ourselves continually, and make inferences from them as existing realities.' With the algebraists, however, who are pagans themselves, the 'pagan fables' *are* believed, and the inferences are made, not so much through lapse of memory as through an unaccountable addling of the brains. In short, I never yet encountered the mere mathematician who would be trusted out of equal roots, or one who did not clandestinely hold it as a point of his faith that $x^2 + px$ was absolutely and unconditionally equal to q. Say to one of these gentlemen, by way of experiment, if you please, that you believe occasions may occur where $x^2 + px$ is *not* altogether equal to q, and, having made him understand what you mean, get out of his reach as speedily as convenient, for, beyond doubt, he will endeavor to knock you down.

"I mean to say," continued Dupin, while I merely laughed at his last observations, "that if the Minister had been no more than a mathematician, the Prefect would have been under no necessity of giving me this check. I knew him, however, as both mathematician and poet, and my measures were adapted to his capacity, with reference to the circumstances by which he was surrounded. I knew him as a courtier, too, and as a bold *intrigant*.[15] Such a man, I considered, could not fail to be aware of the ordinary policial modes of action. He could not have failed to anticipate—and events have proved that he did not fail to anticipate—the waylayings to which he was subjected. He must have foreseen, I reflected, the secret investigations of his premises. His frequent absences from home at night, which were hailed by the Prefect as certain aids to his success, I regarded only as *ruses,* to afford opportunity for thorough search to the police, and thus the sooner to impress them with the conviction to which G——, in fact, did finally arrive—the conviction that the letter was not upon the premises. I felt, also, that the whole train of thought, which I was at some pains in detailing to you just now, concerning the invariable principle of policial action in searches for articles concealed—I felt that this whole train of thought would necessarily pass through the mind of the minister. It would imperatively lead him to despise all the ordinary *nooks* of concealment. *He* could not, I reflected, be so weak as not to see that the most intricate and remote recess of his hotel would be as open as his commonest closets to the eyes, to the probes, to the gimlets, and to the microscopes of the Prefect. I saw, in fine, that he would be driven, as a matter of course, to *simplicity,* if not deliberately induced to it as a matter of choice. You will remember, perhaps, how desperately the Prefect laughed when I suggested, upon our first interview, that it was just possible this mystery troubled him so much on account of its being so *very* self-evident."

"Yes," said I. "I remember his merriment well. I really thought he would have fallen into convulsions."

"The material world," continued Dupin, "abounds with very strict analogies to the immaterial; and thus some color of truth has been given to the rhetorical dogma, that metaphor, or simile, may be made to strengthen an argument as well as to embelish a description. The principle of the *vis inertiœ,*[16] for example, seems to be identical in physics and metaphysics. It is not more true in the former, that a large body is with more difficulty set in motion than a smaller one, and that its subsequent *momentum* is commensurate with this difficulty, than it is, in the latter, that intellects of the vaster capacity, while more forcible, more constant, and more eventful in their movements than those of inferior grade, are yet the less readily moved, and more embarrassed, and full of hesitation in the first few steps of their progress. Again: have you ever noticed which of the street signs, over the shop doors, are the most attractive of attention?"

"I have never given the matter a thought," I said.

"There is a game of puzzles," he resumed, "which is played upon a map. One party playing requires another to find a given word—the name of town, river, state, or empire—any word, in short, upon the motley and perplexed surface of the chart. A novice in the game generally seeks to embarrass his opponents by giving them the most minutely lettered names; but the adept selects such words as stretch, in large characters, from one end of the chart to the other. These, like the over-largely lettered signs and placards of the street, escape observation by dint of being excessively obvious; and here the physical oversight is precisely analogous with the moral inapprehension by which the intellect suffers to pass unnoticed those considerations which are too obtrusively and too palpably self-evident. But this is a point, it appears, somewhat above or beneath the understanding of the Prefect. He never once thought it probable, or possible, that the minister had deposited the letter immediately beneath the nose of the whole world, by way of best preventing any portion of that world from perceiving it.

"But the more I reflected upon the daring, dashing, and discriminating ingenuity of D——; upon the fact that the document must always have been *at hand,* if he intended to use it to good purpose; and upon the decisive evidence, obtained by the Prefect, that it was not hidden within the limits of that dignitary's ordinary search—the more satisfied I became that, to conceal this letter, the minister had resorted to the comprehensive and sagacious expedient of not attempting to conceal it at all.

"Full of these ideas, I prepared myself with a pair of green spectacles, and called one fine morning, quite by accident, at the Ministerial hotel. I found D—— at home, yawning, lounging, and dawdling, as usual, and pretending to be in the last extremity of *ennui*. He is, perhaps, the most really energetic human being now alive—but that is only when nobody sees him.

"To be even with him, I complained of my weak eyes, and lamented the necessity of the spectacles, under cover of which I cautiously and thoroughly surveyed the whole apartment, while seemingly intent only upon the conversation of my host.

"I paid especial attention to a large writing-table near which he sat, and upon which lay confusedly, some miscellaneous letters and other papers, with one or two musical instruments and a few books. Here, however, after a long and very deliberate scrutiny, I saw nothing to excite particular suspicion.

"At length my eyes, in going the circuit of the room, fell upon a trumpery filigree card-rack of pasteboard, that hung dangling by a dirty blue ribbon, from a little brass knob just beneath the middle of the mantelpiece. In this rack, which had three or four compartments, were five or six visiting cards and a solitary letter. This last was much soiled and crumpled. It was torn nearly in two, across the middle—as if a design, in the first instance, to tear it entirely up as worthless, had been altered, or stayed, in the second. It had a large black seal bearing the D—— cipher *very* conspicuously, and was addressed, in a diminutive female hand, to D——, the minister, himself. It was thrust carelessly, and even, as it seemed contemptuously, into one of the uppermost divisions of the rack.

"No sooner had I glanced at this letter than I concluded it to be that of which I was in search. To be sure, it was, to all appearance, radically different than the one of which the Prefect had read us so minute a description. Here the seal was large and black, with the D—— cipher; there it was small and red, with the ducal arms of the S—— family. Here, the address, to the minister, was diminutive and feminine; there the superscription, to a certain royal personage, was markedly bold and decided; the size alone formed a point of correspondence. But, then, the *radicalness* of these differences, which was excessive; the dirt; the soiled and torn condition of the paper, so inconsistent with the true *methodical* habits of D——, and so suggestive of a design to delude the beholder into an idea of the worthlessness of the document;—these things, together with the hyperobtrusive situation of this document, full in the view of every visitor, and thus exactly in accordance with the conclusions to which I had previously arrived; these things, I say, were strongly corroborative of suspicion, in one who came with the intention to suspect.

"I protracted my visit as long as possible, and, while I maintained a most animated discussion with the minister, upon a topic which I knew well had never failed to interest and excite him, I kept my attention really riveted upon the letter. In this examination, I committed to memory its external appearance and arrangement in the rack; and also fell, at length, upon a discovery which set at rest whatever trivial doubt I might have entertained. In scrutinizing the edges of the paper, I observed them to be more *chafed* than seemed necessary. They presented the *broken* appearance which is manifested when a stiff paper, having been once folded and pressed with a folder, is refolded in a reversed direction, in the same creases or edges which had formed the original fold. This discovery was sufficient. It was clear to me that the letter had been turned, as a glove, inside out, re-directed and re-sealed. I bade the minister good-morning, and took my departure at once, leaving a gold snuff-box upon the table.

"The next morning I called for the snuff-box, when we resumed, quite eagerly, the conversation of the preceding day. While thus engaged, however, a loud report, as if of a pistol, was heard immediately beneath the windows of the hotel, and was succeeded by a series of fearful screams, and the shoutings of a terrified mob. D—— rushed to a casement, threw it open, and looked out. In the meantime I stepped to the card-rack, took the letter, put it in my pocket, and replaced it by a *fac-simile*, (so far as regards externals) which I had carefully prepared at my lodgings—imitating the D—— cipher, very readily, by means of a seal formed of bread.

The disturbance in the street had been occasioned by the frantic behavior of a man with a musket. He had fired it among a crowd of women and children. It proved, however, to have been without ball, and the fellow was suffered to go his way as a lunatic or a drunkard. When he had gone, D—— came from the window, whither I had followed him immediately upon securing the object in view. Soon afterward I bade him farewell. The pretended lunatic was a man in my own pay."

"But what purpose had you," I asked, "in replacing the letter by a *fac-simile?* Would it not have been better, at the first visit, to have seized it openly, and departed?"

"D——," replied Dupin, "is a desperate man, and a man of nerve. His hotel, too, is not without attendants devoted to his interests. Had I made the wild attempt you suggest, I might never have left the Ministerial presence alive. The good people of Paris might have heard of me no more. But I had an object apart from these considerations. You know my political prepossessions. In this matter, I act as a partisan of the lady concerned. For eighteen months the Minister has had her in his power. She has now him in hers—since, being unaware that the letter is not in his possession, he will proceed with his exactions as if it was. Thus will he inevitably commit himself, at once, to his political destruction. His downfall, too, will not be more precipitate than awkward. It is all very well to talk about the *facilis descensus Averni;*[17] but in all kinds of climbing, as Catalani[18] said of singing, it is far more easy to get up than to come down. In the present instance I have no sympathy—at least no pity—for him who descends. He is that *monstrum horrendum,*[19] an unprincipled man of genius. I confess, however, that I should like very well to know the precise character of his thoughts, when, being defied by her whom the Prefect terms 'a certain personage,' he is reduced to opening the letter which I left to him in the card-rack."

"How? Did you put any thing particular in it?"

"Why—it did not seem altogether right to leave the interior blank—that would have been insulting. D—— at Vienna once, did me an evil turn, which I told him, quite good-humoredly, that I should remember. So, as I knew he would feel some curiosity in regard to the identity of the person who had outwitted him, I thought it a pity not to give him a clew. He is well acquainted with my MS., and I just copied into the middle of the blank sheet the words—

" '——   ——Un dessein si funeste,
S'il n'est digne d'Atrée, est digne de Thyeste.'[20]

They are to be found in Crébillon's 'Atrée.' "

THE GOLD-BUG[1]

What ho! what ho! this fellow is dancing mad!
He hath been bitten by the Tarantula.
　　　　　　　　　　　—*All in the Wrong*[2]

M ANY YEARS AGO, I contracted an intimacy with a
Mr. William Legrand. He was of an ancient
Huguenot[3] family, and had once been wealthy; but a se-
ries of misfortunes had reduced him to want. To avoid
the mortification consequent upon his disasters, he left
New Orleans, the city of his forefathers, and took up his
residence at Sullivan's Island, near Charleston, South
Carolina.

This island is a very singular one. It consists of little
else than the sea sand, and is about three miles long. Its
breadth at no point exceeds a quarter of a mile. It is separated from the mainland by a scarcely perceptible
creek, oozing its way through a wilderness of reeds and
slime, a favorite resort of the marsh-hen. The vegetation,

as might be supposed, is scant, or at least dwarfish. No trees of any magnitude are to be seen. Near the western extremity, where Fort Moultrie[4] stands, and where are some miserable frame buildings, tenanted, during summer, by the fugitives from Charleston dust and fever, may be found, indeed, the bristly palmetto; but the whole island, with the exception of this western point, and a line of hard, white beach on the sea-coast, is covered with a dense undergrowth of the sweet myrtle so much prized by the horticulturists of England. The shrub here often attains the height of fifteen or twenty feet, and forms an almost impenetrable coppice, burthening the air with its fragrance.

In the inmost recesses of this coppice, not far from the eastern or more remote end of the island, Legrand had built himself a small hut, which he occupied when I first, by mere accident, made his acquaintance. This soon ripened into friendship—for there was much in the recluse to excite interest and esteem. I found him well educated, with unusual powers of mind, but infected with misanthropy, and subject to perverse moods of alternate enthusiasm and melancholy. He had with him many books, but rarely employed them. His chief amusements were gunning and fishing, or sauntering along the beach and through the myrtles, in quest of shells or entomological specimens—his collection of the latter might have been envied by a Swammerdamm.[5] In these excursions he was usually accompanied by an old Negro, called Jupiter, who had been manumitted before the reverses of the family, but who could be induced, neither by threats nor by promises, to abandon what he considered his right of attendance upon the footsteps of his young

"Massa Will." It is not improbable that the relatives of Legrand, conceiving him to be somewhat unsettled in intellect, had contrived to instil this obstinacy into Jupiter, with a view to the supervision and guardianship of the wanderer.

The winters in the latitude of Sullivan's Island are seldom very severe, and in the fall of the year it is a rare event indeed when a fire is considered necessary. About the middle of October, 18—, there occurred, however, a day of remarkable chilliness. Just before sunset I scrambled my way through the evergreens to the hut of my friend, whom I had not visited for several weeks—my residence being, at that time, in Charleston, a distance of nine miles from the island, while the facilities of passage and re-passage were very far behind those of the present day. Upon reaching the hut I rapped, as was my custom, and getting no reply, sought for the key where I knew it was secreted, unlocked the door, and went in. A fine fire was blazing upon the hearth. It was a novelty, and by no means an ungrateful one. I threw off an overcoat, took an arm-chair by the crackling logs, and awaited patiently the arrival of my hosts.

Soon after dark they arrived, and gave me a most cordial welcome. Jupiter, grinning from ear to ear, bustled about to prepare some marsh-hens for supper. Legrand was in one of his fits—how else shall I term them?—of enthusiasm. He had found an unknown bivalve, forming a new genus, and, more than this, he had hunted down and secured, with Jupiter's assistance, a *scarabœus* which he believed to be totally new, but in respect to which he wished to have my opinion on the morrow.

"And why not to-night?" I asked, rubbing my hands

over the blaze, and wishing the whole tribe of *scarabœi* at the devil.

"Ah, if I had only known you were here!" said Legrand, "but it's so long since I saw you; and how could I foresee that you would pay me a visit this very night of all others? As I was coming home I met Lieutenant G——, from the fort, and very foolishly, I lent him the bug; so it will be impossible for you to see it until the morning. Stay here to-night, and I will send Jup down for it at sunrise. It is the loveliest thing in creation!"

"What?—sunrise?"

"Nonsense! no!—the bug. It is of a brilliant gold color—about the size of a large hickory-nut—with two jet black spots near one extremity of the back, and another, somewhat longer, at the other. The *antennœ* are—"

"Dey aint *no* tin in him, Massa Will, I keep a tellin' on you," here interrupted Jupiter; "de bug is a goole-bug, solid, ebery bit of him, inside and all, sep him wing—neber feel half so hebby a bug in my life."

"Well, suppose it is, Jup," replied Legrand, somewhat more earnestly, it seemed to me, than the case demanded; "is that any reason for your letting the birds burn? The color"—here he turned to me—"is really almost enough to warrant Jupiter's idea. You never saw a more brilliant metallic lustre than the scales emit—but of this you cannot judge till to-morrow. In the meantime I can give you some idea of the shape." Saying this, he seated himself at a small table, on which were a pen and ink, but no paper. He looked for some in a drawer, but found none.

"Never mind," he said at length, "this will answer"; and he drew from his waistcoat pocket a scrap of what I took to be very dirty foolscap,[6] and made upon it a rough drawing with the pen. While he did this, I retained my seat by the fire, for I was still chilly. When the design was complete, he handed it to me without rising. As I received it, a loud growl was heard, succeeded by a scratching at the door. Jupiter opened it, and a large Newfoundland, belonging to Legrand, rushed in, leaped upon my shoulders, and loaded me with caresses; for I had shown him much attention during previous visits. When his gambols were over, I looked at the paper, and, to speak the truth, found myself not a little puzzled at what my friend had depicted.

"Well!" I said, after contemplating it for some minutes, "this *is* a strange *scarabœus*, I must confess; new to me; never saw any thing like it before—unless it was a skull, or a death's-head, which it more nearly resembles than any thing else that has come under *my* observation."

"A death's-head!" echoed Legrand. "Oh—yes—well, it has something of that appearance upon paper, no doubt. The two upper black spots look like eyes, eh? and the longer one at the bottom like a mouth—and then the shape of the whole is oval."

"Perhaps so," said I; "but, Legrand, I fear you are no artist. I must wait until I see the beetle itself, if I am to form any idea of its personal appearance."

"Well, I don't know," said he, a little nettled, "I draw tolerably—*should* do it at least—have had good masters, and flatter myself that I am not quite a blockhead."

"But, my dear fellow, you are joking then," said I, "this is a very passable *skull*—indeed, I may say that it is a very *excellent* skull, according to the vulgar notions about such specimens of physiology—and your *scarabœus* must be the queerest *scarabœus* in the world if it resembles it. Why, we may get up a very thrilling bit of superstition upon this hint. I presume you will call the bug *scarabœus caput hominis*,[7] or something of that kind—there are many similar titles in the Natural Histories. But where are the *antennœ* you spoke of?"

"The *antennœ!*" said Legrand, who seemed to be getting unaccountably warm upon the subject; "I am sure you must see the *antennœ*. I made them as distinct as they are in the original insect, and I presume that is sufficient."

"Well, well," I said, "perhaps you have—still I don't see them"; and I handed him the paper without additional remark, not wishing to ruffle his temper; but I was much surprised at the turn affairs had taken; his ill humor puzzled me—and, as for the drawing of the beetle, there were positively *no antennœ* visible, and the whole *did* bear a very close resemblance to the ordinary cuts of a death's-head.

He received the paper very peevishly, and was about to crumple it, apparently to throw it in the fire, when a casual glance at the design seemed suddenly to rivet his attention. In an instant his face grew violently red—in another as excessively pale. For some minutes he continued to scrutinize the drawing minutely where he sat. At length he arose, took a candle from the table, and proceeded to seat himself upon a sea-chest in the farthest corner of the room. Here again he made an anxious examination of the paper; turning it in all directions. He said nothing, however, and his conduct greatly astonished me; yet I thought it prudent not to exacerbate the growing moodiness of his temper by any comment. Presently he took from his coat-pocket a wallet, placed the paper carefully in it, and deposited both in a writing-desk, which he locked. He now grew more composed in his demeanor; but his original air of enthusiasm had quite disappeared. Yet he seemed not so much sulky as abstracted. As the evening wore away he became more and more absorbed in revery, from which no sallies of mine could arouse him. It had been my intention to pass the night at the hut, as I had frequently done before, but, seeing my host in this mood, I deemed it proper to take leave. He did not press me to remain, but, as I departed, he shook my hand with even more than his usual cordiality.

It was about a month after this (and during the interval I had seen nothing of Legrand) when I received a visit, at Charleston, from his man, Jupiter. I had never seen the good old Negro look so dispirited, and I feared that some serious disaster had befallen my friend.

"Well, Jup," said I, "what is the matter now?—how is your master?"

"Why, to speak de troof, massa, him not so berry well as mought be."

"Not well! I am truly sorry to hear it. What does he complain of?"

"Dar! dat's it!—him nebcr 'plain of notin'—but him berry sick for all dat."

"*Very* sick, Jupiter!—why didn't you say so at once? Is he confined to bed?"

"No, dat he aint!—he aint 'fin'd nowhar—dat's just whar de shoe pinch—my mind is got to be berry hebby 'bout poor Massa Will."

"Jupiter, I should like to understand what it is you are talking about. You say your master is sick. Hasn't he told you what ails him?"

"Why, massa, 'taint worf while for to git mad about de matter—Massa Will say noffin at all aint de matter wid him—but den what make him go about looking dis here way, wid he head down and he soldiers up, and as white as a gose? And den he keep a syphon all de time—"

"Keeps a what, Jupiter?"

"Keeps a syphon wid de figgurs on de slate—de queerest figgurs I ebber did see. Ise gittin' to be skeered, I tell you. Hab for to keep mighty tight eye 'pon him 'noovers.[8] Todder day he gib me slip 'fore de sun up and was gone de whole ob de blessed day. I had a big stick ready cut for to gib him deuced good beating when he did come—but Ise sich a fool dat I hadn't de heart arter all—he looked so berry poorly."

"Eh?—what?—ah yes!—upon the whole I think you had better not be too severe with the poor fellow—don't flog him, Jupiter—he can't very well stand it—but can you form no idea of what has occasioned this illness, or rather this change of conduct? Has any thing unpleasant happened since I saw you?"

"No, massa, dey aint bin noffin onpleasant *since* den—'twas 'fore den I'm feared—'twas de berry day you was dare."

"How? what do you mean?"

"Why, massa, I mean de bug—dare now."

"The what?"

"De bug—I'm berry sartain dat Massa Will bin bit somewhere 'bout de head by dat goole-bug."

"And what cause have you, Jupiter, for such a supposition?"

"Claws enuff, massa, and mouff too. I nebber did see sich a deuced bug—he kick and he bite ebery ting what cum near him. Massa Will cotch him fuss, but had for to let him go 'gin mighty quick, I tell you—den was de time he must ha' got de bite. I didn't like de look ob de bug mouff, myself, nohow, so I wouldn't take hold ob him wid my finger, but I cotch him wid a piece ob paper dat I found. I rap him up in de paper and stuff a piece of it in he mouff—dat was de way."

"And you think, then, that your master was really bitten by the beetle, and that the bite made him sick?"

"I don't think noffin' about it—I nose it. What make him dream 'bout de goole so much, if 'taint cause he bit by de goole-bug? Ise heerd 'bout dem goole-bugs 'fore dis."

"But how do you know he dreams about gold?"

"How I know? why, 'cause he talk about it in he sleep—dat's how I nose."

"Well, Jup, perhaps you are right; but to what fortunate circumstance am I to attribute the honor of a visit from you to-day?"

"What de matter, massa?"

"Did you bring any message from Mr. Legrand?"

"No, massa, I bring dis her pissel";[9] and here Jupiter handed me a note which ran thus:

My Dear——

"Why have I not seen you for so long a time? I hope you have not been so foolish as to take offence at any little *brusquerie*[10] of mine; but no, that is improbable.

"Since I saw you I have had great cause for anxiety. I have something to tell you, yet scarcely know how to tell it, or whether I should tell it at all.

"I have not been quite well for some days past, and poor old Jup annoys me, almost beyond endurance, by his well-meant attentions. Would you believe it?—he had prepared a huge stick, the other day, with which to chastise me for giving him the slip, and spending the day, *solus*,[11] among the hills on the main land. I verily believe that my ill looks alone saved me a flogging.

"I have made no addition to my cabinet since we met.

"If you can, in any way, make it convenient, come over with Jupiter. *Do* come. I wish to see you *to-night*, upon business of importance. I assure you that it is of the *highest* importance.

"Ever yours,
"William Legrand"

There was something in the tone of this note which gave me great uneasiness. Its whole style differed materially from that of Legrand. What could he be dreaming of? What new crotchet possessed his excitable brain? What "business of the highest importance" could *he* possibly have to transact? Jupiter's account of him boded no good. I dreaded lest the continued pressure of misfortune had, at length, fairly unsettled the reason of my friend. Without a moment's hesitation, therefore, I prepared to accompany the Negro.

Upon reaching the wharf, I noticed a scythe and three spades, all apparently new, lying in the bottom of the boat in which we were to embark.

"What is the meaning of all this, Jup?" I inquired.

"Him syfe, massa, and spade."

"Very true; but what are they doing here?"

"Him de syfe and de spade what Massa Will sis 'pon my buying for him in de town, and de debbil's own lot of money I had to gib for 'em."

"But what, in the name of all that is mysterious, is your 'Massa Will' going to do with scythes and spades?"

"Dat's more dan *I* know, and debbil take me if I don't b'lieve 'tis more dan he know too. But it's all cum ob do bug."

Finding that no satisfaction was to be obtained of Jupiter, whose whole intellect seemed to be absorbed by "de bug," I now stepped into the boat, and made sail. With a fair and strong breeze we soon ran into the little cove to the northward of Fort Moultrie, and a walk of some two miles brought us to the hut. It was about three in the afternoon when we arrived. Legrand had been waiting us in eager expectation. He grasped my hand with a nervous *empressement*[12] which alarmed me and strengthened the suspicions already entertained. His countenance was pale even to ghastliness, and his deep-set eyes glared with unnatural lustre. After some inquiries respecting his health, I asked him, not knowing what better to say, if he had yet obtained the *scarabœus* from Lieutenant G——.

"Oh, yes," he replied, coloring violently, "I got it from him the next morning. Nothing should tempt me to part with that *scarabœus*. Do you know that Jupiter is quite right about it?"

"In what way?" I asked, with a sad foreboding at heart.

"In supposing it to be a bug of *real gold*." He said this

with an air of profound seriousness, and I felt inexpressibly shocked,

"This bug is to make my fortune," he continued, with a triumphant smile; "to reinstate me in my family possessions. Is it any wonder, then, that I prize it? Since Fortune has thought fit to bestow it upon me, I have only to use it properly, and I shall arrive at the gold of which it is the index. Jupiter, bring me that *scarabœus!*"

"What! de bug, massa? I'd rudder not go fer trubble dat bug; you mus' git him for your own self." Hereupon Legrand arose, with a grave and stately air, and brought me the beetle from a glass case in which it was enclosed. It was a beautiful *scarabœus*, and, at that time, unknown to naturalists—of course a great prize in a scientific point of view. There were two round black spots near one extremity of the back, and a long one near the other. The scales were exceedingly hard and glossy, with all the appearance of burnished gold. The weight of the insect was very remarkable, and taking all things into consideration, I could hardly blame Jupiter for his opinion respecting it; but what to make of Legrand's concordance with that opinion, I could not, for the life of me, tell.

"I sent for you," said he, in a grandiloquent tone, when I had completed my examination of the beetle, "I sent for you that I might have your counsel and assistance in furthering the views of Fate and of the bug—"

"My dear Legrand," I cried, interrupting him, "you are certainly unwell, and had better use some little precautions. You shall go to bed, and I will remain with you a few days, until you get over this. You are feverish and—"

"Feel my pulse," said he.

I felt it, and, to say the truth, found not the slightest indication of fever.

"But you may be ill and yet have no fever. Allow me this once to prescribe for you. In the first place go to bed. In the next—"

"You are mistaken," he interposed, "I am as well as I can expect to be under the excitement which I suffer. If you really wish me well, you will relieve this excitement."

"And how is this to be done?"

"Very easily. Jupiter and myself are going upon an expedition into the hills, upon the main land, and, in this expedition, we shall need the aid of some person in whom we can confide. You are the only one we can trust. Whether we succeed or fail, the excitement which you now perceive in me will be equally allayed."

"I am anxious to oblige you in any way," I replied; "but do you mean to say that this infernal beetle has any connection with your expedition into the hills?"

"It has."

"Then, Legrand, I can become a party to no such absurd proceeding."

"I am sorry—very sorry—for we shall have to try it by ourselves."

"Try it by yourselves! The man is surely mad!—but stay!—how long do you propose to be absent?"

"Probably all night. We shall start immediately, and be back, at all events, by sunrise."

"And will you promise me, upon your honor, that when this freak of yours is over, and the bug business (good God!) settled to your satisfaction, you will then return home and follow my advice implicitly, as that of your physician."

"Yes; I promise; and now let us be off, for we have no time to lose."

With a heavy heart I accompanied my friend. We started about four o'clock—Legrand, Jupiter, the dog, and myself, Jupiter had with him the scythe and spades—the whole of which he insisted upon carrying—more through fear, it seemed to me, of trusting either of the implements within reach of his master, than from any excess of industry or complaisance. His demeanor was dogged in the extreme, and "dat deuced bug" were the sole words which escaped his lips during the journey. For my own part, I had charge of a couple of dark lanterns, while Legrand contented himself with the *scarabœus*, which he carried attached to the end of a bit of whip-cord; twirling it to and fro, with the air of a conjuror, as he went. When I observed this last, plain evidence of my friend's aberation of mind, I could scarcely refrain from tears. I thought it best, however, to humor his fancy, at least for the present, or until I could adopt some more energetic measures with a chance of success. In the meantime, I endeavored, but all in vain, to sound him in regard to the object of the expedition. Having succeeded in inducing me to accompany him, he seemed unwilling to hold conversation upon any topic of minor importance, and to all my questions vouchsafed no other reply than "we shall see!"

We crossed the creek at the head of the island by means of a skiff, and, ascending the high grounds on the shore of the main land, proceeded in a northwesterly direction, through a tract of country excessively wild and desolate, where no trace of a human footstep was to be seen. Legrand led the way with decision; pausing only for an instant, here and there, to consult what appeared to be certain landmarks of his own contrivance upon a former occasion.

In this manner we journed for about two hours, and the sun was just setting when we entered a region infinitely more dreary than any yet seen. It was a species of table-land, near the summit of an almost inaccessible hill, densely wooded from base to pinnacle, and interspersed with huge crags that appeared to lie loosely upon the soil, and in many cases were prevented from precipitating themselves into the valleys below, merely by the support of the trees against which they reclined. Deep ravines, in various directions, gave an air of still sterner solemnity to the scene.

The natural platform to which we had clambered was thickly overgrown with brambles, through which we soon discovered that it would have been impossible to force our way but for the scythe; and Jupiter, by direction of his master, proceeded to clear for us a path to the foot of an enormously tall tulip-tree, which stood, with some eight or ten oaks, upon the level, and far surpassed them all, and all other trees which I had then ever seen, in the beauty of its foliage and form, in the wide spread of its branches, and in the general majesty of its appearance. When we reached this tree, Legrand turned to Jupiter, and asked him if he thought he could climb it. The old man seemed a little staggered by the question, and for some moments made no reply. At length he approached the huge trunk, walked slowly around it, and examined it with minute attention. When he had completed his scrutiny, he merely said:

"Yes, massa, Jup climb any tree he ebber see in he life."

"Then up with you as soon as possible, for it will soon be too dark to see what we are about."

"How far mus' go up, massa?" inquired Jupiter.

"Get up the main trunk first, and then I will tell you which way to go—and here—stop! take this beetle with you."

"De bug, Massa Will!—de goole-bug!" cried the Negro, drawing back in dismay—"what for mus' tote de bug way up de tree?—d—n if I do!"

"If you are afraid, Jup, a great big Negro like you, to take hold of a harmless little dead beetle, why you can carry it up by this string—but, if you do not take it up with you in some way, I shall be under the necessity of breaking your head with this shovel."

"What de matter now, massa?" said Jup, evidently shamed into compliance; "always want for to raise fuss wid old nigger. Was only funnin anyhow. *Me* feered de bug! what I keer for de bug?" Here he took cautiously hold of the extreme end of the string, and, maintaining the insect as far from his person as circumstances would permit, prepared to ascend the tree.

In youth, the tulip-tree, or *Liriodendron Tulipiferum*, the most magnificent of American foresters, has a trunk peculiarly smooth, and often rises to a great height without lateral branches; but, in its riper age, the bark becomes gnarled and uneven, while many short limbs make their appearance on the stem. Thus the difficulty of ascension, in the present case, lay more in semblance than in reality. Embracing the huge cylinder, as closely as possible, with his arms and knees, seizing with his hands some projections, and resting his naked toes upon others, Jupiter, after one or two narrow escapes from falling, at length wriggled himself into the first great fork, and seemed to consider the whole business as virtually accomplished. The *risk* of the achievement was, in fact, now over, although the climber was some sixty or seventy feet from the ground.

"Which way mus' go now, Massa Will?" he asked.

"Keep up the largest branch—the one on this side," said Legrand. The Negro obeyed him promptly, and apparently with but little trouble; ascending higher and higher, until no glimpse of his squat figure could be obtained through the dense foliage which enveloped it. Presently his voice was heard in a sort of halloo.

"How much fudder is got for go?"

"How high up are you?" asked Legrand.

"Ebber so fur," replied the Negro; "can see de sky fru de top ob de tree."

"Never mind the sky, but attend to what I say. Look down the trunk and count the limbs below you on this side. How many limbs have you passed?"

"One, two, tree, four, fibe—I done pass fibe big limb, massa, 'pon dis side."

"Then go one limb higher."

In a few minutes the voice was heard again, announcing that the seventh limb was attained.

"Now, Jup," cried Legrand, evidently much excited, "I want you to work your way out upon that limb as far as you can. If you see any thing strange let me know."

By this time what little doubt I might have entertained of my poor friend's insanity was put finally at rest. I had no alternative but to conclude him stricken with lunacy, and I became seriously anxious about getting him home. While I was pondering upon what was best to be done, Jupiter's voice was again heard.

"Mos' feerd for to venture 'pon dis limb berry far—'tis dead limb putty much all de way."

"Did you say it was a *dead* limb, Jupiter?" cried Legrand in a quavering voice.

"Yes, massa, him dead as de door-nail—done up for sartain—done departed dis here life."

"What in the name of heaven shall I do?" asked Legrand, seemingly in the greatest distress.

"Do!" said I, glad of an opportunity to interpose a word, "why come home and go to bed. Come now!— that's a fine fellow. It's getting late, and, besides, you remember your promise."

"Jupiter," cried he, without heeding me in the least, "do you hear me?"

"Yes, Massa Will, hear you ebber so plain."

"Try the wood well, then, with your knife, and see if you think it *very* rotten."

"Him rotten, massa, sure nuff," replied the Negro in a few moments, "but not so berry rotten as mought be. Mought venture out leetle way 'pon de limb by myself, dat's true."

"By yourself!—what do you mean?"

"Why, I mean de bug. 'Tis *berry* hebby bug. Spose I drop him down fuss, and den de limb won't break wid just de weight ob one nigger."

"You infernal scoundrel!" cried Legrand, apparently much relieved, "what do you mean by telling me such nonsense as that? As sure as you drop that beetle I'll break your neck. Look here, Jupiter, do you hear me?"

"Yes, massa, needn't hollo at poor nigger dat style."

"Well! now listen!—if you will venture out on the limb as far as you think safe, and not let go the beetle, I'll make you a present of a silver dollar as soon as you get down."

"I'm gwine, Massa Will—deed I is," replied the Negro very promptly—"mos' out to the eend now."

"*Out to the end!*" here fairly screamed Legrand; "do you say you are out to the end of that limb?"

"Soon be on de eend, massa—o-o-o-o-oh! Lor-gol-a-marcy! what *is* dis here pon de tree?"

"Well!" cried Legrand, highly delighted, "what is it?"

"Why taint noffin but a skull—somebody bin left him head up de tree, and de crows done gobble ebery bit ob de meat off."

"A skull, you say!—very well,—how is it fastened to the limb?—what holds it on?"

"Sure nuff, massa; mus' look. Why dis berry curous sarcumstance, 'pon my word—dare's a great big nail in de skull, what fastens ob it on to de tree."

"Well now, Jupiter, do exactly as I tell you—do you hear?"

"Yes, massa."

"Pay attention, then—find the left eye of the skull."

"Hum! hoo! dat's good! why dey aint no eye lef' at all."

"Curse your stupidity! do you know your right hand from your left?"

"Yes, I knows dat—know all bout dat—'tis my lef' hand what I chops de wood wid."

"To be sure! you are left-handed; and your left eye is on the same side as your left hand. Now, I suppose, you can find the left eye of the skull, or the place where the left eye has been. Have you found it?"

Here was a long pause. At length the Negro asked:

"Is de lef' eye ob de skull 'pon de same side as de lef'

hand ob de skull too?—cause de skull aint got not a bit ob a hand at all—nebber mind! I got de lef' eye now— here de lef' eye! what mus' do wid it?"

"Let the beetle drop through it, as far as the string will reach—but be careful and not let go your hold of the string."

"All dat done, Massa Will; mighty easy ting for to put the bug fru de hole—look out for him dare below!"

During this colloquy no portion of Jupiter's person could be seen; but the beetle, which he had suffered to descend, was now visible at the end of the string, and glistened, like a globe of burnished gold, in the last rays of the setting sun, some of which still faintly illumined the eminence upon which we stood. The *scarabœus* hung quite clear of any branches, and, if allowed to fall, would have fallen at our feet. Legrand immediately took the scythe, and cleared with it a circular space, three or four yards in diameter, just beneath the insect, and, having accomplished this, ordered Jupiter to let go the string and come down from the tree.

Driving a peg, with great nicety, into the ground, at the precise spot where the beetle fell, my friend now produced from his pocket a tape measure. Fastening one end of this at that point of the trunk of the tree which was nearest the peg, he unrolled it till it reached the peg and thence further unrolled it, in the direction already established by the two points of the tree and the peg, for the distance of fifty feet—Jupiter clearing away the brambles with the scythe. At the spot thus attained a second peg was driven, and about this, as a centre, a rude circle, about four feet in diameter, described. Taking now a spade himself, and giving one to Jupiter and one to me, Legrand begged us to set about digging as quickly as possible.

To speak the truth, I had no especial relish for such amusement at any time, and, at that particular moment, would most willingly have declined it; for the night was coming on, and I felt much fatigued with the exercise already taken; but I saw no mode of escape, and was fearful of disturbing my poor friend's equanimity by a refusal. Could I have depended, indeed upon Jupiter's aid, I would have had no hesitation in attempting to get the lunatic home by force; but I was too well assured of the old Negro's disposition, to hope that he would assist me, under any circumstances, in a personal contest with his master. I made no doubt that the latter had been infected with some of the innumerable Southern superstitions about money buried, and that his phantasy had received confirmation by the finding of the *scarabœus*, or, perhaps, by Jupiter's obstinacy in maintaining it to be "a bug of real gold." A mind disposed to lunacy would readily be led away by such suggestions—especially if chiming in with favorite preconceived ideas—and then I called to mind the poor fellow's speech about the beetle's being "the index of his fortune." Upon the whole, I was sadly vexed and puzzled, but, at length, I concluded to make a virtue of necessity—to dig with a good will, and thus the sooner to convince the visionary, by ocular demonstration, of the fallacy of the opinions he entertained.

The lanterns having been lit, we all fell to work with a zeal worthy a more rational cause; and, as the glare fell upon our persons and implements, I could not help thinking how picturesque a group we composed, and how strange and suspicious our labors must have appeared to any interloper who, by chance, might have stumbled upon our whereabouts.

We dug very steadily for two hours. Little was said; and our chief embarrassment lay in the yelpings of the dog, who took exceeding interest in our proceedings. He, at length, became so obstreperous that we grew fearful of his giving the alarm to some stragglers in the vicinity,—or, rather, this was the apprehension of Legrand;—for myself, I should have rejoiced at any interruption which might have enabled me to get the wanderer home. The noise was, at length, very effectually silenced by Jupiter, who, getting out of the hole with a dogged air of deliberation, tied the brute's mouth up with one of his suspenders, and then returned, with a grave chuckle, to his task.

When the time mentioned had expired, we had reached a depth of five feet, and yet no signs of any treasure became manifest. A general pause ensued, and I began to hope that the farce was at an end. Legrand, however, although evidently much disconcerted, wiped his brow thoughtfully and recommenced. We had excavated the entire circle of four feet diameter, and now we slightly enlarged the limit, and went to the farther depth of two feet. Still nothing appeared. The gold-seeker, whom I sincerely pitied, at length clambered from the pit, with the bitterest disappointment imprinted upon every feature, and proceeded, slowly and reluctantly, to put on his coat, which he had thrown off at the beginning of his labor. In the meantime I made no remark. Jupiter, at a signal from his master, began to gather up his tools. This done, and the dog having been unmuzzled, we turned in profound silence toward home.

We had taken, perhaps, a dozen steps in this direction, when, with a loud oath, Legrand strode up to Jupiter, and seized him by the collar. The astonished Negro opened his eyes and mouth to the fullest extent, let fall the spades, and fell upon his knees.

"You scoundrel!" said Legrand, hissing out the syllables from between his clenched teeth—"you infernal black villain!—speak, I tell you!—answer me this instant, without prevarication!—which—which is your left eye?"

"Oh, my golly, Massa Will! aint dis here my lef' eye for sartain?" roared the terrified Jupiter, placing his hand upon his *right* organ of vision, and holding it there with a desperate pertinacity, as if in immediate dread of his master's attempt at a gouge.

"I thought so!—I knew it! hurrah!" vociferated Legrand, letting the Negro go and executing a series of curvets and caracols,[13] much to the astonishment of his valet, who, arising from his knees, looked, mutely, from his master to myself, and then from myself to his master.

"Come! we must go back," said the latter, "the game's not up yet"; and he again led the way to the tulip-tree.

"Jupiter," said he, when we reached its foot, "come here! was the skull nailed to the limb with the face outward, or with the face to the limb?"

"De face was out, massa, so dat de crows could get at de eyes good, widout any trouble."

"Well, then, was it this eye or that through which you dropped the beetle?"—here Legrand touched each of Jupiter's eyes.

" 'Twas dis eye,—massa—de lef' eye—jis as you tell me," and here it was his right eye that the Negro indicated.

"That will do—we must try it again."

Here my friend, about whose madness I now saw, or fancied that I saw, certain indications of method, removed the peg which marked the spot where the beetle fell, to a spot about three inches to the westward of its former position. Taking, now, the tape measure from the nearest point of the trunk to the peg, as before, and continuing the extension in a straight line to the distance of fifty feet, a spot was indicated, removed, by several yards, from the point at which we had been digging.

Around the new position a circle, somewhat larger than in the former instance, was now described, and we again set to work with the spade. I was dreadfully weary, but, scarcely understanding what had occasioned the change in my thoughts, I felt no longer any great aversion from the labor imposed. I had become most unaccountably interested—nay, even excited. Perhaps there was something, amid all the extravagant demeanor of Legrand—some air of forethought, or of deliberation, which impressed me. I dug eagerly, and now and then caught myself actually looking, with something that very much resembled expectation, for the fancied treasure, the vision of which had demented my unfortunate companion. At a period when such vagaries of thought most fully possessed me, and when we had been at work perhaps an hour and a half, we were again interrupted by the violent howlings of the dog. His uneasiness, in the first instance, had been, evidently, but the result of playfulness or caprice, but he now assumed a bitter and serious tone. Upon Jupiter's again attempting to muzzle him, he made furious resistance, and, leaping into the hole, tore up the mould frantically with his claws. In a few seconds he had uncovered a mass of human bones, forming two complete skeletons, intermingled with several buttons of metal, and what appeared to be the dust of decayed woollen. One or two strokes of a spade up-turned the blade of a large Spanish knife, and, as we dug farther, three or four loose pieces of gold and silver coin came to light.

At sight of these the joy of Jupiter could scarcely be restrained, but the countenance of his master wore an air of extreme disappointment. He urged us, however, to continue our exertions, and the words were hardly uttered when I stumbled and fell forward, having caught the toe of my boot in a large ring of iron that lay half buried in the loose earth.

We now worked in earnest, and never did I pass ten minutes of more intense excitement. During this interval we had fairly unearthed an oblong chest of wood, which, from its perfect preservation and wonderful hardness, had plainly been subjected to some mineralizing process—perhaps that of the bi-chloride of mercury.[14] This box was three feet and a half long, three feet broad, and two and a half feet deep. It was firmly secured by bands of wrought iron, riveted, and forming a kind of open trellis-work over the whole. On each side of the chest, near the top, were three rings of iron— six in all— by means of which a firm hold could be obtained by six persons. Our utmost united endeavors served only to disturb the coffer very slightly in its bed. We at once saw the impossibility of removing so great a weight. Luckily, the sole fastenings of the lid consisted of two sliding bolts. These we drew back—trembling and panting with anxiety. In an instant, a treasure of incalculable value lay gleaming before us. As the rays of the lanterns fell within the pit, there flashed upward a glow and a glare, from a confused heap of gold and of jewels, that absolutely dazzled our eyes.

I shall not pretend to describe the feelings with which I gazed. Amazement was, of course, predominant. Legrand appeared exhausted with excitement, and spoke very few words. Jupiter's countenance wore, for some minutes, as deadly a pallor as it is possible, in the nature of things, for any Negro's visage to assume. He seemed stupefied—thunderstricken. Presently he fell upon his knees in the pit, and burying his naked arms up to the elbows in gold, let them there remain, as if enjoying the luxury of a bath. At length, with a deep sigh, he exclaimed, as if in a soliloquy:

"And dis all cum ob de goole-bug! de putty goole-bug! the poor little goole-bug, what I boosed in dat sabage kind ob style! Aint you shamed ob yourself, nigger?—answer me dat!"

It became necessary, at last, that I should arouse both master and valet to the expediency of removing the treasure. It was growing late, and it behooved us to make exertion, that we might get every thing housed before daylight. It was difficult to say what should be done, and much time was spent in deliberation—so confused were the ideas of all. We, finally, lightened the box by removing two thirds of its contents, when we were enabled, with some trouble, to raise it from the hole. The articles taken out were deposited among the brambles, and the dog left to guard them, with strict orders from Jupiter neither, upon any pretence, to stir from the spot, nor to open his mouth until our return. We then hurriedly made for home with the chest; reaching the hut in safety, but after excessive toil, at one o'clock in the morning. Worn out as we were, it was not in human nature to do more immediately. We rested until two, and had supper; starting for the hills immediately afterward, armed with three stout sacks, which, by good luck, were upon the premises. A little before four we arrived at the pit, divided the remainder of the booty, as equally as might be, among us, and, leaving the holes unfilled, again set out for the hut, at which, for the second time, we deposited our golden burthens, just as the first faint streaks of the dawn gleamed from over the tree-tops in the east.

We were now thoroughly broken down; but the intense excitement of the time denied us repose. After an unquiet slumber of some three or four hours' duration, we arose, as if by preconcert, to make examination of our treasure.

The chest had been full to the brim, and we spent the whole day, and the greater part of the next night, in a scrutiny of its contents. There had been nothing like order or arrangement. Every thing had been heaped in promiscuously. Having assorted all with care, we found ourselves possessed of even vaster wealth than we had at first supposed. In coin there was rather more than four hundred and fifty thousand dollars—estimating the value of the pieces, as accurately as we could, by the tables of the period. There was not a particle of silver. All was gold of antique date and of great variety—French, Spanish, and German money, with a few English guineas, and some counters, of which we had never seen specimens before. There were several very large and heavy coins, so worn that we could make nothing of their inscriptions.

There was no American money. The value of the jewels we found more difficulty in estimating. There were diamonds—some of them exceedingly large and fine—a hundred and ten in all, and not one of them small; eighteen rubies of remarkable brilliancy;—three hundred and ten emeralds, all very beautiful; and twenty-one sapphires, with an opal. These stones had all been broken from their settings and thrown loose in the chest. The settings themselves, which we picked out from among the other gold, appeared to have been beaten up with hammers, as if to prevent identification. Besides all this, there was a vast quantity of solid gold ornaments: nearly two hundred massive finger- and ear-rings; rich chains— thirty of these, if I remember; eighty-three very large and heavy crucifixes; five gold censers of great value; a prodigious golden punch-bowl, ornamented with richly chased vine-leaves and Bacchanalian figures; with two sword-handles exquisitely embossed, and many other smaller articles which I cannot recollect. The weight of these valuables exceeded three hundred and fifty pounds avoirdupois; and in this estimate I have not included one hundred and ninety-seven superb gold watches; three of the number being worth each five hundred dollars, if one. Many of them were very old, and as timekeepers valueless; the works having suffered, more or less, from corrosion—but all were richly jewelled and in cases of great worth. We estimated the entire contents of the chest, that night, at a million and a half of dollars; and upon the subsequent disposal of the trinkets and jewels (a few being retained for our own use), it was found that we had greatly undervalued the treasure.

When, at length, we had concluded our examination,

and the intense excitement of the time had, in some
measure, subsided, Legrand, who saw that I was dying
with impatience for a solution of this most extraordinary
riddle, entered into a full detail of all the circumstances
connected with it.

"You remember," said he, "the night when I handed
you the rough sketch I had made of the *scarabœus*. You
recollect also, that I became quite vexed at you for insisting that my drawing resembled a death's-head. When
you first made this assertion I thought you were jesting;
but afterward I called to mind the peculiar spots on the
back of the insect, and admitted to myself that your remark had some little foundation in fact. Still, the sneer at
my graphic powers irritated me—for I am considered a
good artist—and, therefore, when you handed me the
scrap of parchment, I was about to crumple it up and
throw it angrily into the fire."

"The scrap of paper, you mean," said I.

"No; it had much of the appearance of paper, and at
first I supposed it to be such, but when I came to draw
upon it, I discovered it at once to be a piece of very thin
parchment. It was quite dirty, you remember. Well, as I
was in the very act of crumpling it up, my glance fell
upon the sketch at which you had been looking, and you
may imagine my astonishment when I perceived, in fact,
the figure of a death's-head just where, it seemed to me,
I had made the drawing of the beetle. For a moment I
was too much amazed to think with accuracy. I knew that
my design was very different in detail from this—although there was a certain similarity in general outline.
Presently I took a candle, and seating myself at the other
end of the room, proceeded to scrutinize the parchment

more closely. Upon turning it over, I saw my own sketch
upon the reverse, just as I had made it. My first idea,
now, was mere surprise at the really remarkable similarity of outline—at the singular coincidence involved in
the fact that, unknown to me, there should have been a
skull upon the other side of the parchment, immediately
beneath my figure of the *scarabœus,* and that this skull,
not only in outline, but in size, should so closely resemble my drawing. I say the singularity of this coincidence
absolutely stupefied me for a time. This is the usual effect of such coincidences. The mind struggles to establish a connection—a sequence of cause and effect—and,
being unable to do so, suffers a species of temporary
paralysis. But, when I recovered from this stupor, there
dawned upon me gradually a conviction which startled
me even far more than the coincidence. I began distinctly, positively, to remember that there had been *no*
drawing upon the parchment when I made my sketch of
the *scarabœus.* I became perfectly certain of this; for I
recollected turning up first one side and then the other,
in search of the cleanest spot. Had the skull been then
there, of course I could not have failed to notice it. Here
was indeed a mystery which I felt it impossible to explain; but, even at that early moment, there seemed to
glimmer, faintly, within the most remote and secret
chambers of my intellect, a glow-worm-like conception
of that truth which last night's adventure brought to so
magnificent a demonstration. I arose at once, and putting the parchment securely away, dismissed all further
reflection until I should be alone.

"When you had gone, and when Jupiter was fast
asleep, I betook myself to a more methodical investiga-

tion of the affair. In the first place I considered the manner in which the parchment had come into my possession. The spot where we discovered the *scarabœus* was on the coast of the main-land, about a mile eastward of the island, and but a short distance above high-water mark. Upon my taking hold of it, it gave me a sharp bite, which caused me to let it drop. Jupiter, with his accustomed caution, before seizing the insect, which had flown toward him, looked about him for a leaf, or something of that nature, by which to take hold of it. It was at this moment that his eyes, and mine also, fell upon the scrap of parchment, which I then supposed to be paper. It was lying half buried in the sand, a corner sticking up. Near the spot where we found it, I observed the remnants of the hull of what appeared to have been a ship's long-boat. The wreck seemed to have been there for a very great while; for the resemblance to boat timbers could scarcely be traced.

"Well, Jupiter picked up the parchment, wrapped the beetle in it, and gave it to me. Soon afterward we turned to go home, and on the way met Lieutenant G——. I showed him the insect, and he begged me to let him take it to the fort. Upon my consenting, he thrust it forthwith into his waistcoat pocket, without the parchment in which it had been wrapped, and which I had continued to hold in my hand during his inspection. Perhaps he dreaded my changing my mind, and thought it best to make sure of the prize at once—you know how enthusiastic he is on all subjects connected with Natural History. At the same time, without being conscious of it, I must have deposited the parchment in my own pocket.

"You remember that when I went to the table, for the

purpose of making a sketch of the beetle, I found no paper where it was usually kept. I looked in the drawer, and found none there. I searched my pockets, hoping to find an old letter, when my hand fell upon the parchment. I thus detail the precise mode in which it came into my possession; for the circumstances impressed me with peculiar force.

"No doubt you will think me fanciful—but I had already established a kind of *connection*. I had put together two links of a great chain. There was a boat lying upon the sea-coast, and not far from the boat was a parchment—*not a paper*—with a skull depicted upon it. You will, of course, ask 'where is the connection?' I reply that the skull, or death's-head is the well-known emblem of the pirate. The flag of the death's-head is hoisted in all engagements.

"I have said that the scrap was parchment, and not paper. Parchment is durable—almost imperishable. Matters of little moment are rarely consigned to parchment; since, for the mere ordinary purposes of drawing or writing, it is not nearly so well adapted as paper. This reflection suggested some meaning—some relevancy—in the death's-head. I did not fail to observe, also, the *form* of the parchment. Although one of its corners had been, by some accident, destroyed, it could be seen that the original form was oblong. It was just such a slip, indeed, as might have been chosen for a memorandum—for a record of something to be long remembered and carefully preserved."

"But," I interposed, "you say that the skull was *not* upon the parchment when you made the drawing of the beetle. How then do you trace any connection between the boat and the skull—since this latter, according to your own admission, must have been designed (God only knows how or by whom) at some period subsequent to your sketching the *scarabœus*?"

"Ah, hereupon turns the whole mystery; although the secret, at this point, I had comparatively little difficulty in solving. My steps were sure, and could afford a single result. I reasoned, for example, thus: When I drew the *scarabœus*, there was no skull apparent upon the parchment. When I had completed the drawing I gave it to you, and observed you narrowly until you returned it. *You*, therefore, did not design the skull, and no one else was present to do it. Then it was not done by human agency. And nevertheless it was done.

"At this stage of my reflections I endeavored to remember, and *did* remember, with entire distinctness, every incident which occurred about the period in question. The weather was chilly (oh, rare and happy accident!), and a fire was blazing upon the hearth. I was heated with exercise and sat near the table. You, however, had drawn a chair close to the chimney. Just as I placed the parchment in your hand, and as you were in the act of inspecting it, Wolf, the Newfoundland, entered, and leaped upon your shoulders. With your left hand you caressed him and kept him off, while your right, holding the parchment, was permitted to fall listlessly between your knees, and in close proximity to the fire. At one moment I thought the blaze had caught it, and was about to caution you, but, before I could speak, you had withdrawn it, and were engaged in its examination. When I considered all these particulars, I doubted not for a moment that *heat* had been the agent in bringing to light, upon the parchment, the skull which I saw designed upon it. You are well aware that chemical preparations exist, and have existed time out of mind, by means of which it is possible to write upon either paper or vellum, so that the characters shall become visible only when subjected to the action of fire. Zaffre, digested in *aqua regia*,[15] and diluted with four times its weight of water, is sometimes employed; a green tint results. The regulus[16] of cobalt, dissolved in spirit of nitre, gives a red. These colors disappear at longer or shorter intervals after the material written upon cools, but again become apparent upon the re-application of heat.

"I now scrutinized the death's-head with care. Its outer edges—the edges of the drawing nearest the edge of the vellum —were far more *distinct* than the others. It was clear that the action of the caloric[17] had been imperfect or unequal. I immediately kindled a fire, and subjected every portion of the parchment to a glowing heat. At first, the only effect was the strengthening of the faint lines in the skull; but, upon persevering in the experiment, there became visible, at the corner of the slip, diagonally opposite to the spot in which the death's-head was delineated, the figure of what I at first supposed to be a goat. A closer scrutiny, however, satisfied me that it was intended for a kid."

"Ha! ha!" said I, "to be sure I have no right to laugh at you—a million and a half of money is too serious a matter for mirth—but you are not about to establish a third link in your chain—you will not find any especial connection between your pirates and a goat—pirates, you know, have nothing to do with goats; they appertain to the farming interest."

"But I have just said that the figure was *not* that of a goat."

"Well, a kid then—pretty much the same thing."

"Pretty much, but not altogether," said Legrand. "You may have heard of one *Captain* Kidd. I at once looked upon the figure of the animal as a kind of punning or hierogryphical signature. I say signature; because its position upon the vellum suggested this idea. The death's-head at the corner diagonally opposite, had, in the same manner, the air of a stamp, or seal. But I was sorely put out by the absence of all else—of the body to my imagined instrument—of the text for my context."

"I presume you expected to find a letter between the stamp and the signature."

"Something of that kind. The fact is, I felt irresistibly impressed with a presentiment of some vast good fortune impending. I can scarcely say why. Perhaps, after all, it was rather a desire than an actual belief;—but do you know that Jupiter's silly words, about the bug being of solid gold, had a remarkable effect upon my fancy? And then the series of accidents and coincidences—these were so *very* extraordinary. Do you observe how mere an accident it was that these events should have occurred upon the *sole* day of all the year in which it has been, or may be sufficiently cool for fire, and that without the fire, or without the intervention of the dog at the precise moment in which he appeared, I should never have become aware of the death's-head, and so never the possessor of the treasure?"

"But proceed—I am all impatience."

"Well; you have heard, of course, the many stories current—the thousand vague rumors afloat about money buried, somewhere upon the Atlantic coast, by Kidd and his associates. These rumors must have had some foundation in fact. And that the rumors have existed so long and so continuous, could have resulted, it appeared to me, only from the circumstance of the buried treasure still *remaining* entombed. Had Kidd concealed his plunder for a time, and afterward reclaimed it, the rumors would scarcely have reached us in their present unvarying form. You will observe that the stories told are all about money-seekers, not about money-finders. Had the pirate recovered his money, there the affair would have dropped. It seemed to me that some accident—say the loss of a memorandum indicating its locality—had deprived him of the means of recovering it, and that this accident had become known to his followers, who otherwise might never have heard that treasure had been concealed at all, and who, busying themselves in vain, because unguided, attempts to regain it, had given first birth, and then universal currency, to the reports which are now so common. Have you ever heard of any important treasure being unearthed along the coast?"

"Never."

"But that Kidd's accumulations were immense, is well known. I took it for granted, therefore, that the earth still held them; and you will scarcely be surprised when I tell you that I felt a hope, nearly amounting to certainty, that the parchment so strangely found involved a lost record of the place of deposit."

"But how did you proceed?"

"I held the vellum again to the fire, after increasing the heat, but nothing appeared. I now thought it possible that the coating of dirt might have something to do with

the failure: so I carefully rinsed the parchment by pour-
ing warm water over it, and, having done this, I placed it
in a tin pan, with the skull downward, and put the pan
upon a furnace of lighted charcoal. In a few minutes, the
pan having become thoroughly heated, I removed the
slip, and, to my inexpressible joy, found it spotted, in several places, with what appeared to be figures arranged in
lines. Again I placed it in the pan, and suffered it to remain another minute. Upon taking it off, the whole was
just as you see it now."

Here Legrand, having re-heated the parchment, sub-
mitted it to my inspection. The following characters were
rudely traced, in a red tint, between the death's-head and
the goat:

53‡‡†305))6*;4826)4‡.)4‡);806*;48†8¶60))85;1‡(;:‡*8†8
3(88)5*†;46(;88*96*?;8)*‡(;485);5*†2:*‡(;4956*2(5*—
4)8¶8*;4069285);)6†8)4‡‡;1(‡9;48081;8:8‡1;48†85;4)48
5†528806*81(‡9;48;88;4(‡?34;48)4‡;161;:188;‡?;

"But," said I, returning him the slip, I am as much in
the dark as ever. Were all the jewels of Golconda[18] awaiting me upon my solution of this enigma, I am quite sure
that I should be unable to earn them."

"And yet," said Legrand, "the solution is by no means
so difficult as you might be led to imagine from the first
hasty inspection of the characters. These characters, as
any one might readily guess, form a cipher—that is to
say, they convey a meaning; but then from what is known
of Kidd, I could not suppose him capable of constructing
any of the more abstruse cryptographs. I made up my
mind, at once, that this was of a simple species—such,

however, as would appear, to the crude intellect of the sailor, absolutely insoluble without the key."

"And you really solved it?"

"Readily; I have solved others of an abstruseness ten thousand times greater. Circumstances, and a certain bias of mind, have led me to take interest in such riddles, and it may well be doubted whether human ingenuity can construct an enigma of the kind which human ingenuity may not, by proper application, resolve. In fact, having once established connected and legible characters, I scarcely gave a thought to the mere difficulty of developing their import.

"In the present case—indeed in all cases of secret writing—the first question regards the *language* of the cipher; for the principles of solution, so far, especially, as the more simple ciphers are concerned, depend upon, and are varied by, the genius of the particular idiom. In general, there is no alternative but experiment (directed by probabilities) of every tongue known to him who attempts the solution, until the true one be attained. But, with the cipher now before us all difficulty was removed by the signature. The pun upon the word 'Kidd' is appreciable in no other language than the English. But for this consideration I should have begun my attempts with the Spanish and French, as the tongues in which a secret of this kind would most naturally have been written by a pirate of the Spanish main. As it was, I assumed the cryptograph to be English.

"You observe there are no divisions between the words. Had there been divisions the task would have been comparatively easy. In such cases I should have commenced with a collation and analysis of the shorter

words, and, had a word of a single letter occurred, as is
most likely (*a* or *I*, for example), I should have considered the solution as assured. But, there being no division, my first step was to ascertain the predominant
letters, as well as the least frequent. Counting all, I constructed a table thus:

Of the character 8 there are 33.

;	"	20.
4	"	19.
‡)	"	16.
°	"	13.
5	"	12.
6	"	11.
† 1	"	8.
0	"	6.
9 2	"	5.
: 3	"	4.
?	"	3.
¶	"	2.
—.	"	1.

"Now, in English, the letter which most frequently occurs is *e*. Afterward, the succession runs thus: *a o i d h n
r s t u y c f g l m w b k p q x z*. E predominates so remarkably, that an individual sentence of any length is
rarely seen in which it is not the prevailing character.

"Here, then, we have, in the very beginning, the
groundwork for something more than a mere guess.
The general use which may be made of the table is obvious—but, in this particular cipher, we shall only very
partially require its aid. As our predominant character

is 8, we will commence by assumming it as the *e* of the natural alphabet. To verify the supposition, let us observe if the 8 be seen often in couples—for *e* is doubled with great frequency in English—in such words, for example, as 'meet,' 'fleet,' 'speed,' 'seen,' 'been,' 'agree,' etc. In the present instance we see it doubled no less than five times, although the cryptograph is brief.

"Let us assume 8, then, as *e*. Now, of all *words* in the language, 'the' is most usual; let us see, therefore, whether there are not repetitions of any three characters, in the same order of collocation, the last of them being 8. If we discover repetitions of such letters, so arranged, they will most probably represent the word 'the.' Upon inspection, we find no less than seven such arrangements, the characters being ;48. We may, therefore, assume that ; represents *t,* 4 represents *h,* and 8 represents *e*—the last being now well confirmed. Thus a great step has been taken.

"But, having established a single word, we are enabled to establish a vastly important point; that is to say, several commencements and terminations of other words. Let us refer, for example, to the last instance but one, in which the combination ;48 occurs—not far from the end of the cipher. We know that the ; immediately ensuing is the commencement of a word, and, of the six characters succeeding this 'the', we are cognizant of no less than five. Let us set these characters down, thus, by the letters we know them to represent, leaving a space for the unknown—

t eeth.

"Here we are enabled, at once, to discard the '*th*,' as forming no portion of the word commencing with the first *t*; since, by experiment of the entire alphabet for a letter adapted to the vacancy, we perceive that no word can be formed of which this *th* can be a part. We are thus narrowed into

t ee,

and, going through the alphabet, if necessary, as before, we arrive at the word 'tree,' as the sole possible reading. We thus gain another letter, *r*, represented by (, with the words 'the tree' in juxtaposition.

"Looking beyond these words, for a short distance, we again see the combination ;48, and employ it by way of *termination* to what immediately precedes. We have thus this arrangement:

the tree ;4(‡?34 the,

or, substituting the natural letters, where known, it reads thus:

the tree thr‡?3h the.

"Now, if, in place of the unknown characters, we leave blank spaces, or substitute dots, we read thus:

the tree thr...h the,

when the word '*through*' makes itself evident at once. But this discovery gives us three new letters, *o*, *u*, and *g*, represented by ‡, ?, and 3.

"Looking now, narrowly, through the cipher for combinations of known characters, we find, not very far from the beginning, this arrangement,

83(88, or †egree,

which, plainly, is the conclusion of the word 'degree,' and gives us another letter, *d*, represented by †.

"Four letters beyond the word 'degree,' we perceive the combination

;46(;88.

"Translating the known characters, and representing the unknown by dots, as before, we read thus:

th.rtee,

an arrangement immediately suggestive of the word thirteen, and again furnishing us with two new characters, *i* and *n*, represented by 6 and °.

"Referring, now, to the beginning of the cryptograph, we find the combination,

53‡‡†

"Translating as before, we obtain

.good,

which assures us that the first letter is *A*, and that the first two words are 'A good.'

"It is now time that we arrange our key, as far as discovered, in a tabular form, to avoid confusion. It will stand thus:

5	represents	a
†	"	d
8	"	e
3	"	g
4	"	h
6	"	i
°	"	n
‡	"	o
(	"	r
;	"	t
?	"	u

"We have, therefore, no less than eleven of the most important letters represented, and it will be unnecessary to proceed with the details of the solution. I have said enough to convince you that ciphers of this nature are readily soluble, and to give you some insight into the *rationale* of their development. But be assured that the specimen before us appertains to the very simplest species of cryptograph. It now only remains to give you the full translation of the characters upon the parchment, as unriddled. Here it is:

" 'A good glass in the bishop's hostel in the devil's seat forty-one degrees and thirteen minutes northeast and by north main branch seventh limb east side shoot from the left eye of the death's-head a bee-line from the tree through the shot fifty feet out.' "

"But," said I, "the enigma seems still in as bad a condition as ever. How is it possible to extort a meaning from all this jargon about 'devil's seats,' 'death's-heads,' and 'bishop's hostels'?"

"I confess," replied Legrand, "that the matter still wears a serious aspect, when regarded with a casual glance. My first endeavor was to divide the sentence into the natural division intended by the cryptographist."

"You mean, to punctuate it?"

"Something of that kind."

"But how was it possible to effect this?"

"I reflected that it had been a *point* with the writer to run his words together without division, so as to increase the difficulty of solution. Now, a not over-acute man, in pursuing such an object, would be nearly certain to overdo the matter. When, in the course of his composition, he arrived at a break in his subject which would naturally require a pause, or a point, he would be exceedingly apt to run his characters, at this place, more than usually close together. If you will observe the MS., in the present instance, you will easily detect five such cases of unusual crowding. Acting upon this hint, I made the division thus:

" '*A good glass in the bishop's hostel in the devil's seat—forty-one degrees and thirteen minutes—northeast and by north—main branch seventh limb east side—shoot from the left eye of the death's-head—a beeline from the tree through the shot fifty feet out.*' "

"Even this division," said I, "leaves me still in the dark."

"It left me also in the dark," replied Legrand, "for a few days; during which I made diligent inquiry, in the neighborhood of Sullivan's Island, for any building which went by the name of the 'Bishop's Hotel'; for, of course, I dropped the obsolete word 'hostel.' Gaining no information on the subject, I was on the point of extending my sphere of search, and proceeding in a more systematic manner, when, one morning, it entered into my head, quite suddenly, that this 'Bishop's Hostel' might have some reference to an old family, of the name of Bessop, which, time out of mind, had held possession of an ancient manor-house, about four miles to the northward of the island. I accordingly went over to the plantation, and re-instituted my inquiries among the older Negroes of the place. At length one of the most aged of the women said that she had heard of such a place as *Bessop's Castle*, and thought that she could guide me to it, but that it was not a castle, nor a tavern, but a high rock.

"I offered to pay her well for her trouble, and, after some demur, she consented to accompany me to the spot. We found it without much difficulty, when, dismissing her, I proceeded to examine the place. The 'castle' consisted of an irregular assemblage of cliffs and rocks—one of the latter being quite remarkable for its height as well as for its insulated and artificial appearance. I clambered to its apex, and then felt much at a loss as to what should be next done.

"While I was busied in reflection, my eyes fell upon a narrow ledge in the eastern face of the rock, perhaps a yard below the summit upon which I stood. This ledge projected about eighteen inches, and was not more than a foot wide, while a niche in the cliff just above it gave it a rude resemblance to one of the hollow-backed chairs used by our ancestors. I made no doubt that here was the 'devil's-seat' alluded to in the MS., and now I seemed to grasp the full secret of the riddle.

"The 'good glass,' I knew, could have reference to nothing but a telescope; for the word 'glass' is rarely employed in any other sense by seamen. Now here, I at once saw, was a telescope to be used, and a definite point of view, *admitting no variation,* from which to use it. Nor did I hesitate to believe that the phrases, 'forty-one degrees and thirteen minutes,' and 'northeast and by north,' were intended as directions for the levelling of the glass. Greatly excited by these discoveries, I hurried home, procured a telescope, and returned to the rock.

"I let myself down to the ledge, and found that it was impossible to retain a seat upon it except in one particular position. This fact confirmed my preconceived idea. I proceeded to use the glass. Of course, the 'forty-one degrees and thirteen minutes' could allude to nothing but elevation above the visible horizon, since the horizontal direction was clearly indicated by the words, 'northeast and by north.' This latter direction I at once established by means of a pocket-compass; then, pointing the glass as nearly at an angle of forty-one degrees of elevation as I could do it by guess, I moved it cautiously up or down, until my attention was arrested by a circular rift or opening in the foliage of a large tree that overtopped its fellows in the distance. In the centre of this rift I perceived a white spot, but could not, at first, distinguish what it was. Adjusting the focus of the telescope, I again looked, and now made it out to be a human skull.

"Upon this discovery I was so sanguine as to consider

the enigma solved; for the phrase 'main branch, seventh limb, east side,' could refer only to the position of the skull upon the tree, while 'shoot from the left eye of the death's-head' admitted, also, of but one interpretation, in regard to a search for buried treasure. I perceived that the design was to drop a bullet from the left eye of the skull, and that a bee-line, or, in other words, a straight line, drawn from the nearest point of the trunk through 'the shot' (or the spot where the bullet fell), and thence extended to a distance of fifty feet, would indicate a definite point—and beneath this point I thought it at least *possible* that a deposit of value lay concealed."

"All this," I said, "is exceedingly clear, and, although ingenious, still simple and explicit. When you left the 'Bishop's Hotel,' what then?"

"Why, having carefully taken the bearings of the tree, I turned homeward. The instant that I left the 'devil's seat,' however, the circular rift vanished; nor could I get a glimpse of it afterward, turn as I would. What seems to me the chief ingenuity in this whole business is the fact (for repeated experiment has convinced me it *is* a fact) that the circular opening in question is visible from no other attainable point of view than that afforded by the narrow ledge upon the face of the rock.

"In the expedition to the 'Bishop's Hotel' I had been attended by Jupiter, who had, no doubt, observed, for some weeks past, the abstraction of my demeanor, and took especial care not to leave me alone. But, on the next day, getting up very early, I contrived to give him the slip, and went into the hills in search of the tree. After much toil I found it. When I came home at night my valet proposed to give me a flogging. With the rest of the adventure I believe you are as well acquainted as myself."

"I suppose,' said I, "you missed the spot, in the first attempt at digging, through Jupiter's stupidity in letting the bug fall through the right instead of through the left eye of the skull."

"Precisely. This mistake made a difference of about two inches and a half in the 'shot'—that is to say, in the position of the peg nearest the tree; and had the treasure been *beneath* the 'shot,' the error would have been of little moment; but the 'shot,' together with the nearest point of the tree, were merely two points for the establishment of a line of direction; of course the error, however trivial in the beginning, increased as we proceeded with the line, and by the time we had gone fifty feet threw us quite off the scent. But for my deep-seated impressions that treasure was here somewhere actually buried, we might have had all our labor in vain."

"But your grandiloquence, and your conduct in swinging the beetle—how excessively odd! I was sure you were mad. And why did you insist upon letting fall the bug, instead of a bullet, from the skull?"

"Why, to be frank, I felt somewhat annoyed by your evident suspicions touching my sanity, and so resolved to punish you quietly, in my own way, by a little bit of sober mystification. For this reason I swung the beetle, and for this reason I let it fall from the tree. An observation of yours about its great weight suggested the latter idea."

"Yes, I perceive; and now there is only one point which puzzles me. What are we to make of the skeletons found in the hole?"

"That is a question I am no more able to answer than

yourself. There seems, however, only one plausible way of accounting for them—and yet it is dreadful to believe in such atrocity as my suggestion would imply. It is clear that Kidd—if Kidd indeed secreted this treasure, which I doubt not—it is clear that he must have had assistance in the labor. But this labor concluded, he may have thought it expedient to remove all participants in his secret. Perhaps a couple of blows with a mattock were sufficient, while his coadjutors were busy in the pit; perhaps it required a dozen—who shall tell?"

Ms. Found in a Bottle[1]

Qui n'a plus qu'un moment à vivre
N'a plus rien à dissimuler.

Quinault—Atys[2]

O F MY COUNTRY and of my family I have little to say. Ill usage and length of years have driven me from the one, and estranged me from the other. Hereditary wealth afforded me an education of no common order, and a contemplative turn of mind enabled me to methodise the stories which early study diligently garnered up. Beyond all things, the works of the German moralists[3] gave me great delight; not from my ill-advised admiration of their eloquent madness, but from the ease with which my habits of rigid thoughts enabled me to detect their falsities. I have often been reproached with the aridity of my genius; a deficiency of imagination has been imputed to me as a crime; and the Pyrrhonism[4] of my opinions has at all times rendered me notorious. Indeed,

a strong relish for physical philosophy has, I fear, tinctured my mind with a very common error of this age—I
mean the habit of referring occurrences, even the least
susceptible of such reference, to the principles of that
science. Upon the whole, no person could be less liable
than myself to be led away from the severe precincts of
truth by the *ignes fatui*[5] of superstition. I have thought
proper to premise thus much, lest the incredible tale I
have to tell should be considered rather the raving of a
crude imagination, than the positive experience of a
mind to which the reveries of fancy have been a dead letter and a nullity.

After many years spent in foreign travel, I sailed in the
year 18—, from the port of Batavia, in the rich and populous island of Java, on a voyage to the Archipelago Islands. I went as passenger—having no other inducement
than a kind of nervous restlessness which haunted me as
a fiend.

Our vessel was a beautiful ship of about four hundred
tons, copper-fastened, and built at Bombay of Malabar
teak. She was freighted with cotton-wool and oil, from
the Lachadive Islands.[6] We had also on board coir, jaggeree, ghee,[7] cocoanuts, and a few cases of opium. The
stowage was clumsily done, and the vessel consequently
crank.[8]

We got under way with a mere breath of wind, and for
many days stood along the eastern coast of Java, without
any other incident to beguile the monotony of our course
than the occasional meeting with some of the small
grabs[9] of the Archipelago to which we were bound.

One evening, leaning over the taffrail, I observed a
very singular isolated cloud, to the N.W. It was remark-

able, as well from its color as from its being the first we
had seen since our departure from Batavia. I watched it
attentively until sunset, when it spread all at once to the
eastward and westward, girting in the horizon with a narrow strip of vapor, and looking like a long line of low
beach. My notice was soon afterward attracted by the
dusky-red appearance of the moon, and the peculiar
character of the sea. The latter was undergoing a rapid
change, and the water seemed more than usually transparent. Although I could distinctly see the bottom, yet,
heaving the lead, I found the ship in fifteen fathoms. The
air now became intolerably hot, and was loaded with spiral exhalations similar to those arising from heated iron.
As night came on, every breath of wind died away, and a
more entire calm it is impossible to conceive. The flame
of a candle burned upon the poop without the least perceptible motion, and a long hair, held between the finger
and thumb, hung without the possibility of detecting a
vibration. However, as the captain said he could perceive
no indication of danger, and as we were drifting in bodily
to shore, he ordered the sails to be furled, and the anchor let go. No watch was set, and the crew, consisting
principally of Malays,[10] stretched themselves deliberately
upon deck. I went below—not without a full presentiment of evil. Indeed, every appearance warranted me in
apprehending a simoon.[11] I told the captain of my fears;
but he paid no attention to what I said, and left me without deigning to give a reply. My uneasiness, however,
prevented me from sleeping, and about midnight I went
upon deck. As I placed my foot upon the upper step of
the companion-ladder, I was startled by a loud, humming
noise, like that occasioned by the rapid revolution of a

mill-wheel, and before I could ascertain its meaning, I found the ship quivering to its centre. In the next instant a wilderness of foam hurled us upon our beam-ends, and, rushing over us fore and aft, swept the entire decks from stem to stern.

The extreme fury of the blast proved, in a great measure, the salvation of the ship. Although completely water-logged, yet, as her masts had gone by the board, she rose, after a minute, heavily from the sea, and, staggering awhile beneath the immense pressure of the tempest, finally righted.

By what miracle I escaped destruction, it is impossible to say. Stunned by the shock of the water, I found myself, upon recovery, jammed in between the stern-post and rudder. With great difficulty I regained my feet, and looking dizzily around, was at first struck with the idea of our being among breakers; so terrific, beyond the wildest imagination, was the whirlpool of mountainous and foaming ocean within which we were engulfed. After a while I heard the voice of an old Swede, who had shipped with us at the moment of leaving port. I hallooed to him with all my strength, and presently he came reeling aft. We soon discovered that we were the sole survivors of the accident. All on deck, with the exception of ourselves, had been swept overboard; the captain and mates must have perished while they slept, for the cabins were deluged with water. Without assistance we could expect to do little for the security of the ship, and our exertions were at first paralyzed by the momentary expectation of going down. Our cable had, of course, parted like pack-thread, at the first breath of the hurricane, or we should have been instantaneously overwhelmed. We scudded with frightful velocity before the sea, and the water made clear breaches over us. The framework of our stern was shattered excessively, and, in almost every respect, we had received considerable injury; but to our extreme joy we found the pumps unchoked, and that we had made no great shifting of our ballast. The main fury of the blast had already blown over, and we apprehended little danger from the violence of the wind; but we looked forward to its total cessation with dismay; well believing, that in our shattered condition, we should inevitably perish in the tremendous swell which would ensue. But this very just apprehension seemed by no means likely to be soon verified. For five entire days and nights—during which our only subsistence was a small quantity of jaggeree, procured with great difficulty from the forecastle—the hulk flew at a rate defying computation, before rapidly succeeding flaws of wind, which, without equalling the first violence of the simoon, were still more terrific than any tempest I had before encountered. Our course for the first four days was, with trifling variations, S.E. and by S.; and we must have run down the coast of New Holland.[12] On the fifth day the cold became extreme, although the wind had hauled round a point more to the northward. The sun arose with a sickly yellow lustre, and clambered a very few degrees above the horizon—emitting no decisive light. There were no clouds apparent, yet the wind was upon the increase, and blew with a fitful and unsteady fury. About noon, as nearly as we could guess, our attention was again arrested by the appearance of the sun. It gave out no light, properly so called, but a dull and sullen glow without reflection, as if all its rays were polarized. Just before sinking within the turgid sea, its central fires suddenly went out, as if hurriedly extinguished by some unaccountable power. It was a dim, silver-like rim, alone, as it rushed down the unfathomable ocean.

We waited in vain for the arrival of the sixth day—that day to me has not yet arrived—to the Swede never did arrive. Thenceforward we were enshrouded in pitchy darkness, so that we could not have seen an object at twenty paces from the ship. Eternal night continued to envelop us, all unrelieved by the prosphoric sea-brilliancy to which we had been accustomed in the tropics. We observed, too, that, although the tempest continued to rage with unabated violence, there was no longer to be discovered the usual appearance of surf, or foam, which had hitherto attended us. All around were horror, and thick gloom, and a black sweltering desert of ebony. Superstitious terror crept by degrees into the spirit of the old Swede, and my own soul was wrapt in silent wonder. We neglected all care of the ship, as worse than useless, and securing ourselves as well as possible, to the stump of the mizen-mast, looked out bitterly into the world of ocean. We had no means of calculating time, nor could we form any guess of our situation. We were, however, well aware of having made farther to the southward than any previous navigators, and felt great amazement at not meeting with the usual impediments of ice. In the meantime every moment threatened to be our last—every mountainous billow hurried to overwhelm us. The swell surpassed anything I had imagined possible, and that we were not instantly buried is a miracle. My companion spoke of the lightness of our cargo, and reminded me of the excellent qualities of our ship;

but I could not help feeling the utter hopelessness of hope itself, and prepared myself gloomily for that death which I thought nothing could defer beyond an hour, as, with every knot of way the ship made, the swelling of the black stupendous seas became more dismally appalling. At times we gasped for breath at an elevation beyond the albatross—at times became dizzy with the velocity of our descent into some watery hell, where the air grew stagnant, and no sound disturbed the slumbers of the kraken.[13]

We were at the bottom of one of these abysses, when a quick scream from my companion broke fearfully upon the night. "See! see!" cried he, shrieking in my ears, "Almighty God! see! see!" As he spoke I became aware of a dull sullen glare of red light which streamed down the sides of the vast chasm where we lay, and threw a fitful brilliancy upon our deck. Casting my eyes upwards, I beheld a spectacle which froze the current of my blood. At a terrific height directly above us, and upon the very verge of the precipitous descent, hovered a gigantic ship of perhaps four thousand tons. Although upreared upon the summit of a wave more than a hundred times her own altitude, her apparent size still exceeded that of any ship of the line or East Indiaman[14] in existence. Her huge hull was of a deep dingy black, unrelieved by any of the customary carvings of a ship. A single row of brass cannon protruded from her open ports, and dashed from the polished surfaces the fires of innumerable battle-lanterns which swung to and fro about her rigging. But what mainly inspired us with horror and astonishment, was that she bore up under a press of sail[15] in the very teeth of that supernatural sea, and of that ungovernable hurricane. When we first discovered her, her bows were alone to be seen, as she rose slowly from the dim and horrible gulf beyond her. For a moment of intense terror she paused upon the giddy pinnacle as if in contemplation of her own sublimity, then trembled, and tottered, and—came down.

At this instant, I know not what sudden self-possession came over my spirit. Staggering as far aft as I could, I awaited fearlessly the ruin that was to overwhelm. Our own vessel was at length ceasing from her struggles, and sinking with her head to the sea. The shock of the descending mass struck her, consequently in that portion of her frame which was nearly under water, and the inevitable result was to hurl me, with irresistible violence, upon the rigging of the stranger.

As I fell, the ship hove in stays,[16] and went about; and to the confusion ensuing I attributed my escape from the notice of the crew. With little difficulty I made my way, unperceived, to the main hatchway, which was partially open, and soon found an opportunity of secreting myself in the hold. Why I did so I can hardly tell. An indefinite sense of awe, which at first sight of the navigators of the ship had taken hold of my mind, was perhaps the principle of my concealment. I was unwilling to trust myself with a race of people who had offered, to the cursory glance I had taken, so many points of vague novelty, doubt, and apprehension. I therefore thought proper to contrive a hiding-place in the hold. This I did by removing a small portion of the shifting-boards,[17] in such a manner as to afford me a convenient retreat between the huge timbers of the ship.

I had scarcely completed my work, when a footstep in

the hold forced me to make use of it. A man passed by my place of concealment with a feeble and unsteady gait. I could not see his face, but had an opportunity of observing his general appearance. There was about it an evidence of great age and infirmity. His knees tottered beneath a load of years, and his entire frame quivered under the burthen. He muttered to himself, in a low broken tone, some words of a language which I could not understand, and groped in a corner among a pile of singular-looking instruments, and decayed charts of navigation. His manner was a wild mixture of the peevishness of second childhood, and the solemn dignity of a God. He at length went on deck, and I saw him no more.

     *   *   *   *   *

A feeling, for which I have no name, has taken possession of my soul—a sensation which will admit of no analysis, to which the lessons of bygone time are inadequate, and for which I fear futurity itself will offer me no key. To a mind constituted like my own, the latter consideration is an evil. I shall never—I know that I shall never—be satisfied with regard to the nature of my conceptions. Yet it is not wonderful that these conceptions are indefinite, since they have their origin in sources so utterly novel. A new sense—a new entity is added to my soul.

     *   *   *   *   *

It is long since I first trod the deck of this terrible ship, and the rays of my destiny are, I think, gathering to a focus. Incomprehensible men! Wrapped up in meditations of a kind which I cannot divine, they pass me by unnoticed. Concealment is utter folly on my part, for the people *will not* see. It is but just now that I passed di-

rectly before the eyes of the mate; it was no long while
ago that I ventured into the captain's own private cabin,
and took thence the materials with which I write, and
have written. I shall from time to time continue this journal. It is true that I may not find an opportunity of trans-
mitting it to the world, but I will not fail to make the
endeavor. At the last moment I will enclose the MS. in a
bottle, and cast it within the sea.

    *   *   *   *   *

An incident has occurred which has given me new room for
meditation. Are such things the operation of ungoverned
chance? I had ventured upon deck and thrown myself
down, without attracting any notice, among a pile of ratlin-
stuff[18] and old sails, in the bottom of the yawl.[19] While mus-
ing upon the singularity of my fate, I unwittingly daubed
with a tar-brush the edges of a neatly-folded studding-sail[20]
which lay near me on a barrel. The studding-sail is now bent
upon the ship, and the thoughtless touches of the brush are
spread out into the word Discovery.

I have made my observations lately upon the structure
of the vessel. Although well armed, she is not, I think, a
ship of war. Her rigging, build, and general equipment,
all negative a supposition of this kind. What she *is not*, I
can easily perceive; what she *is*, I fear it is impossible to
say. I know not how it is, but in scrutinizing her strange
model and singular cast of spars, her huge size and overgrown suits of canvas, her severely simple bow and anti-
quated stern, there will occasionally flash across my
mind a sensation of familiar things, and there is always
mixed up with such indistinct shadows of recollection, an
unaccountable memory of old foreign chronicles and
ages long ago.   *   *   *

I have been looking at the timbers of the ship. She is built of a material to which I am a stranger. There is a peculiar character about the wood which strikes me as rendering it unfit for the purpose to which it has been applied. I mean its extreme *porousness,* considered independently of the worm-eaten condition which is a consequence of navigation in these seas, and apart from the rottenness attendant upon age. It will appear perhaps an observation somewhat over-curious, but this would have every characteristic of Spanish oak, if Spanish oak were distended by any unnatural means.

In reading the above sentence, a curious apothegm of an old weather-beaten Dutch navigator comes full upon my recollection. "It is as sure," he was wont to say, when any doubt was entertained of his veracity, "as sure as there is a sea where the ship itself will grow in bulk like the living body of the seaman."   °   °   °

About an hour ago, I made bold to trust myself among a group of the crew. They paid me no manner of attention, and, although I stood in the very midst of them all, seemed utterly unconscious of my presence. Like the one I had at first seen in the hold, they all bore about them the marks of a hoary old age. Their knees trembled with infirmity; their shoulders were bent double with decrepitude; their shrivelled skins rattled in the wind; their voices were low, tremulous, and broken; their eyes glistened with the rheum of years; and their gray hairs streamed terribly in the tempest. Around them, on every part of the deck, lay scattered mathematical instruments of the most quaint and obsolete construction.   °   °   °

I mentioned, some time ago, the bending of a studding-sail. From that period, the ship, being thrown dead off the wind, has continued her terrific course due south, with every rag of canvas packed upon her, from her truck to her lower studding-sail booms, and rolling every moment her top-gallant yard-arms[21] into the most appalling hell of water which it can enter into the mind of man to imagine. I have just left the deck, where I find it impossible to maintain a footing, although the crew seem to experience little inconvenience. It appears to me a miracle of miracles that our enormous bulk is not swallowed up at once and forever. We are surely doomed to hover continually upon the brink of eternity, without taking a final plunge into the abyss. From billows a thousand times more stupendous than any I have ever seen, we glide away with the facility of the arrowy sea-gull; and the colossal waters rear their heads above us like demons of the deep, but like demons confined to simple threats, and forbidden to destroy. I am led to attribute these frequent escapes to the only natural cause which can account for such effect. I must suppose the ship to be within the influence of some strong current, or impetuous undertow.   °   °   °

I have seen the captain face to face, and in his own cabin—but, as I expected, he paid me no attention. Although in his appearance there is, to a casual observer, nothing which might bespeak him more or less than man, still, a feeling of irrepressible reverence and awe mingled with the sensation of wonder with which I regarded him. In stature, he is nearly my own height; that is, about five feet eight inches. He is of a well-knit and compact frame of body, neither robust nor remarkable otherwise. But it is the singularity of the expression which reigns upon the face—it is the intense, the wonderful, the thrilling evidence of old age so utter, so extreme, which excites within my spirit a sense—a sentiment ineffable. His forehead, although little wrinkled, seems to bear upon it the stamp of a myriad of years. His gray hairs are records of the past, and his grayer eyes are sibyls[22] of the future. The cabin floor was thickly strewn with strange, iron-clasped folios, and mouldering instruments of science, and obsolete long-forgotten charts. His head was bowed down upon his hands, and he pored, with a fiery, unquiet eye, over a paper which I took to be a commission, and which, at all events, bore the signature of a monarch. He murmured to himself—as did the first whom I saw in the hold—some low peevish syllables of a foreign tongue; and although the speaker was close at my elbow, his voice seemed to reach my ears from the distance of a mile.   °   °   °

The ship and all in it are imbued with the spirit of Eld. The crew glide to and fro like the ghosts of buried centuries; their eyes have an eager and uneasy meaning; and when their fingers fall athwart my path in the wild glare of the battle-lanterns, I feel as I have never felt before, although I have been all my life a dealer in antiquities, and have imbibed the shadows of fallen columns at Balbec, and Tadmor, and Persepolis,[23] until my very soul has become a ruin.   °   °   °

When I look around me, I feel ashamed of my former apprehension. If I trembled at the blast which has hitherto attended us, shall I not stand aghast at a warring of wind and ocean, to convey any idea of which, the words tornado and simoon are trivial and ineffective? All in the immediate vicinity of the ship, is the blackness of eternal night, and a chaos of foamless water; but, about a league on either side of us, may be seen, indistinctly and at intervals, stupendous ramparts of ice, towering away into the desolate sky, and looking like the walls of the universe.   *   *   *

As I imagined, the ship proves to be in a current—if that appellation can properly be given to a tide which, howling and shrieking by the white ice, thunders on to the southward with a velocity like the headlong dashing of a cataract.   *   *   *

To conceive the horror of my sensations is, I presume, utterly impossible; yet a curiosity to penetrate the mysteries of these awful regions, predominates even over my despair, and will reconcile me to the most hideous aspect of death. It is evident that we are hurrying onward to some exciting knowledge—some never-to-be-imparted secret, whose attainment is destruction. Perhaps this current leads us to the southern pole itself. It must be confessed that a supposition apparently so wild has every probability in its favor.   *   *   *

The crew pace the deck with unquiet and tremulous step; but there is upon their countenance an expression more of the eagerness of hope than of the apathy of despair.

In the meantime the wind is still in our poop,[24] and, as we carry a crowd of canvas, the ship is at times lifted bodily from out the sea! Oh, horror upon horror!—the ice opens suddenly to the right, and to the left, and we are whirling dizzily, in immense concentric circles, round and round the borders of a gigantic amphitheatre, the summit of whose walls is lost in the darkness and the distance. But little time will be left me to ponder upon my destiny! The circles rapidly grow small—we are plunging madly within the grasp of the whirlpool—and amid a roaring, and bellowing, and thundering of ocean and tempest, the ship is quivering—oh God! and——going down!

Note.—The "Ms. Found in a Bottle," was originally published in 1831, and it was not until many years afterward that I became acquainted with the maps of Mercator, in which the ocean is represented as rushing, by four mouths into the (northern) Polar Gulf, to be absorbed into the bowels of the earth; the Pole itself being represented by a black rock, towering to a prodigious height.

A Descent into the Maelström[1]

The ways of God in Nature, as in Providence, are not as *our* ways; nor are the models that we frame in any way commensurate to the vastness, profundity, and unsearchableness of His works, *which have a depth in them greater than the well of Democritus.*

—*Joseph Glanvill*[2]

WE HAD NOW reached the summit of the loftiest crag. For some minutes the old man seemed too much exhausted to speak.

"Not long ago," said he at length, "and I could have guided you on this route as well as the youngest of my sons; but, about three years past, there happened to me an event such as never happened before to mortal man—or at least such as no man ever survived to tell of—and the six hours of deadly terror which I then endured have broken me up body and soul. You suppose me a *very* old man—but I am not. It took less than a single day to change these hairs from a jetty black to white, to weaken my limbs, and to unstring my nerves, so that I tremble at the least exertion, and am frightened at a shadow. Do you know I can scarcely look over this little cliff without getting giddy?"

The "little cliff," upon whose edge he had so carelessly thrown himself down to rest that the weightier portion of his body hung over it, while he was only kept from falling by the tenure of his elbow on its extreme and slippery edge—this "little cliff" arose, a sheer unobstructed precipice of black shining rock, some fifteen or sixteen hundred feet from the world of crags beneath us. Nothing would have tempted me to be within half a dozen yards of its brink. In truth so deeply was I excited by the perilous position of my companion, that I fell at full length upon the ground, clung to the shrubs around me, and dared not even glance upward at the sky—while I struggled in vain to divest myself of the idea that the very foundations of the mountain were in danger from the fury of the winds. It was long before I could reason myself into sufficient courage to sit up and look out into the distance.

"You must get over these fancies," said the guide, "for I have brought you here that you might have the best possible view of the scene of that event I mentioned—and to tell you the whole story with the spot just under your eyes.

"We are now," he continued, in that particularizing manner which distinguished him—"we are now close upon the Norwegian coast—in the sixty-eighth degree of latitude—in the great province of Nordland—and in the dreary district of Lofoden.[3] The mountain upon whose top we sit is Helseggen, the Cloudy. Now raise yourself up a little higher—hold on to the grass if you feel giddy—so—and look out, beyond the belt of vapor beneath us, into the sea."

I looked dizzily, and beheld a wide expanse of ocean, whose waters wore so inky a hue as to bring at once to my mind the Nubian geographer's account of the *Mare Tenebrarum*.[4] A panorama more deplorably desolate no human can conceive. To the right and left, as far as the eye could reach, there lay outstretched, like ramparts of the world, lines of horridly black and beetling cliff, whose character of gloom was but the more forcibly illustrated by the surf which reared high up against it its white and ghastly crest, howling and shrieking for ever. Just opposite the promontory upon whose apex we were placed, and at a distance of some five or six miles out at sea, there was visible a small, bleak-looking island; or, more properly, its position was discernible through the wilderness of surge in which it was enveloped. About two miles nearer the land, arose another of smaller size, hideously craggy and barren, and encompassed at various intervals by a cluster of dark rocks.

The appearance of the ocean, in the space between the more distant island and the shore, had something very unusual about it. Although, at the time, so strong a gale was blowing landward that a brig in the remote offing lay to under a double-reefed trysail, and constantly plunged her whole hull out of sight, still there was here nothing like a regular swell, but only a short, quick, angry cross dashing of water in every direction—as well in the teeth of the wind as otherwise. Of foam there was little except in the immediate vicinity of the rocks.

"The island in the distance," resumed the old man, "is called by the Norwegians Vurrgh. The one midway is Moskoe. That a mile to the northward is Ambaaren. Yonder are Islesen, Hotholm, Keildhelm, Suarven, and Buckholm. Further off—between Moskoe and Vurrgh— are Otterholm, Flimen, Sandflesen, and Stockholm. These are the true names of the places—but why it has been thought necessary to name them at all, is more than either you or I can understand. Do you hear any thing? Do you see any change in the water?"

We had now been about ten minutes upon the top of Helseggen, to which we had ascended from the interior of Lofoden, so that we had caught no glimpse of the sea until it had burst upon us from the summit. As the old man spoke, I became aware of a loud and gradually increasing sound, like the moaning of a vast herd of buffaloes upon an American prairie; and at the same moment I perceived that what seamen term the *chopping* character of the ocean beneath us, was rapidly changing into a current which set to the eastward. Even while I gazed, this current acquired a monstrous velocity. Each moment added to its speed—to its headlong impetuosity. In five minutes the whole sea, as far as Vurrgh, was lashed into ungovernable fury; but it was between Moskoe and the coast that the main uproar held its sway. Here the vast bed of the waters, seamed and scarred into a thousand conflicting channels, burst suddenly into phrensied convulsion—heaving, boiling, hissing—gyrating in gigantic sad innumerable vortices, and all whirling and plunging on to the eastward with a rapidity which water never elsewhere assumes, except in precipitous descents.

In a few minutes more, there came over the scene another radical alteration. The general surface grew somewhat more smooth, and the whirlpools, one by one, disappeared, while prodigious streaks of foam became apparent where none had been seen before. These streaks, at length, spreading out to a great distance, and entering into combination, took unto themselves the gyratory motion of the subsided vortices, and seemed to form the germ of another more vast. Suddenly—very suddenly—this assumed a distinct and definite existence, in a circle of more than a mile in diameter. The edge of the whirl was represented by a broad belt of gleaming spray; but no particle of this slipped into the mouth of the terrific funnel, whose interior, as far as the eye could fathom it, was a smooth, shining, and jet-black wall of water, inclined to the horizon at an angle of some forty-five degrees, speeding dizzily round and round with a swaying and sweltering motion, and sending forth to the winds an appalling voice, half shriek, half roar, such as not even the mighty cataract of Niagara ever lifts up in its agony to Heaven.

The mountain trembled to its very base, and the rock rocked. I threw myself upon my face, and clung to the scant herbage in an excess of nervous agitation.

"This," said I at length, to the old man—"this *can* be nothing else than the great whirlpool of the Maelström."

"So it is sometimes termed," said he. "We Norwegians call it the Moskoe-ström, from the island of Moskoe in the midway."

The ordinary account of this vortex had by no means prepared me for what I saw. That of Jonas Ramus,[5] which is perhaps the most circumstantial of any, cannot impart the faintest conception either of the magnificence, or of the horror of the scene—or of the wild bewildering sense of *the novel* which confounds the beholder. I am not sure from what point of view the writer in question surveyed it, nor at what time; but it could neither have been from the summit of Helseggen, nor during a storm. There are some passages of his description, nevertheless, which may be quoted for their details, although their effect is exceedingly feeble in conveying an impression of the spectacle.

"Between Lofoden and Moskoe," he says, "the depth of the water is between thirty-six and forty fathoms; but on the other side, toward Ver (Vurrgh) this depth decreases so as not to afford a convenient passage for a vessel, without the risk of splitting on the rocks, which happens even in the calmest weather. When it is flood, the stream runs up the country between Lofoden and Moskoe with a boisterous rapidity; but the roar of its impetuous ebb to the sea is scarce equalled by the loudest and most dreadful cataracts; the noise being heard several leagues off, and the vortices or pits are of such an extent and depth, that if a ship comes within its attraction, it is inevitably absorbed and carried down to the bottom, and there beat to pieces against the rocks; and when the water relaxes, the fragments thereof are thrown up again. But these intervals of tranquillity are only at the turn of the ebb and flood, and in calm weather, and last but a quarter of an hour, its violence gradually returning. When the stream is most boisterous, and its fury heightened by a storm, it is dangerous to come within a Norway mile[6] of it. Boats, yachts, and ships have been carried away by not guarding against it before they were carried within its reach. It likewise happens frequently, that whales come too near the stream, and are overpowered by its violence; and then it is impossible to describe their howlings and bellowings in their fruitless struggles to disengage themselves. A bear once, attempting to swim from Lofoden to Moskoe, was caught by the stream and borne down, while he roared terribly, so as to be heard on shore. Large stocks of firs and pine trees, after being absorbed by the current, rise again broken and torn to such a degree as if bristles grew upon them. This plainly shows the bottom to consist of craggy rocks, among which they are whirled to and fro. This stream is regulated by the flux and reflux of the sea—it being constantly high and low water every six hours. In the year 1645, early in the morning of Sexagesima Sunday,[7] it raged with such noise and impetuosity that the very stones of the houses on the coast fell to the ground."

In regard to the depth of the water, I could not see how this could have been ascertained at all in the immediate vicinity of the vortex. The "forty fathoms" must have reference only to portions of the channel close upon the shore either of Moskoe or Lofoden. The depth in the centre of the Moskoe-ström must be unmeasurably greater; and no better proof of this fact is necessary than can be obtained from even the sidelong glance into the abyss of the whirl which may be had from the highest crag of Helseggen. Looking down from this pinnacle upon the howling Phlegethon[8] below, I could not help smiling at the simplicity with which the honest Jonas Ramus records, as a matter difficult of belief, the anecdotes of the whales and the bears, for it appeared to me, in fact, a self-evident thing, that the largest ships of the line in existence, coming within the influence of that deadly attraction, could resist it as little as a feather the hurricane, and must disappear bodily and at once.

The attempts to account for the phenomenon—some of which I remember, seemed to me sufficiently plausible in perusal—now wore a very different and unsatisfactory aspect. The idea generally received is that this, as well as three smaller vortices among the Ferroe Islands,[9] "have no other cause than the collision of waves rising and falling, at flux and reflux, against a ridge of rocks and shelves, which confines the water so that it precipitates itself like a cataract; and thus the higher the flood rises, the deeper must the fall be, and the natural result of all is a whirlpool or vortex, the prodigious suction of which is sufficiently known by lesser experiments."—These are the words of the Encyclopædia Britannica. Kircher[10] and others imagine that in the centre of the channel of the maelström is an abyss penetrating the globe, and issuing in some very remote part—the Gulf of Bothnia being somewhat decidedly named in one instance. This opinion, idle in itself, was the one to which, as I gazed, my imagination most readily assented; and, mentioning it to the guide, I was rather surprised to hear him say that, although it was the view almost universally entertained of the subject by the Norwegians, it nevertheless was not his own. As to the former notion he confessed his inability to comprehend it; and here I agreed with him—for, however conclusive on paper, it becomes altogether unintelligible, and even absurd, amid the thunder of the abyss.

"You have had a good look at the whirl now," said the old man, "and if you will creep round this crag, so as to get in its lee, and deaden the roar of the water, I will tell you a story that will convince you I ought to know something of the Moskoe-ström."

I placed myself as desired, and he proceeded.

"Myself and my two brothers once owned a schooner-rigged smack[11] of about seventy tons burthen, with which we were in the habit of fishing among the islands beyond Moskoe, nearly to Vurrgh. In all violent eddies at sea there is good fishing, at proper opportunities, if one has only the courage to attempt it; but among the whole of the Lofoden coastmen, we three were the only ones who made a regular business of going out to the islands, as I tell you. The usual grounds are a great way lower down to the southward. There fish can be got at all hours, without much risk, and therefore these places are preferred. The choice spots over here among the rocks, however, not only yield the finest variety, but in far greater abundance; so that we often got in a single day, what the more timid of the craft could not scrape together in a week. In fact, we made it a matter of desperate speculation—the risk of life standing instead of labor, and courage answering for capital.

"We kept the smack in a cove about five miles higher up the coast than this; and it was our practice, in fine weather, to take advantage of the fifteen minutes' slack to push across the main channel of the Moskoe-ström, far above the pool, and then drop down upon anchorage somewhere near Otterholm, or Sandflesen, where the eddies are not so violent as elsewhere. Here we used to remain until nearly time for slack-water again, when we weighed and made for home. We never set out upon this expedition without a steady side wind for going and coming—one that we felt sure would not fail us before our return—and we seldom made a miscalculation upon this point. Twice, during six years, we were forced to stay all night at anchor on account of a dead calm, which is a rare thing indeed just about here; and once we had to remain on the grounds nearly a week, starving to death, owing to a gale which blew up shortly after our arrival, and made the channel too boisterous to be thought of. Upon this occasion we should have been driven out to sea in spite of every thing (for the whirlpools threw us round and round so violently, that, at length, we fouled our anchor and dragged it), if it had not been that we drifted into one of the innumerable cross currents—here to-day and gone to-morrow—which drove us under the lee of Flimen, where, by good luck, we brought up.

"I could not tell you the twentieth part of the difficulties we encountered 'on the ground'—it is a bad spot to be in, even in good weather—but we make shift always to run the gauntlet of the Moskoe-ström itself without accident; although at times my heart has been in my mouth when we happened to be a minute or so behind or before the slack. The wind sometimes was not as strong as we thought it at starting, and then we made rather less way than we could wish, while the current rendered the smack unmanageable. My eldest brother had a son eighteen years old, and I had two stout boys of my own. These would have been of great assistance at such times, in using the sweeps as well as afterward in fishing—but, somehow, although we ran the risk ourselves, we had not the heart to let the young ones get into the danger—for, after all said and done, it *was* a horrible danger, and that is the truth.

"It is now within a few days of three years since what I

am going to tell you occurred. It was on the tenth of July, 18—, a day which the people of this part of the world will never forget—for it was one in which blew the most terrible hurricane that ever came out of the heavens. And yet all the morning, and indeed until late in the afternoon, there was a gentle and steady breeze from the southwest, while the sun shone brightly, so that the oldest seaman among us could not have foreseen what was to follow.

"The three of us—my two brothers and myself—had crossed over to the islands about two o'clock P.M., and soon nearly loaded the smack with fine fish, which, we all remarked, were more plenty that day than we had ever known them. It was just seven, *by my watch*, when we weighed and started for home, so as to make the worst of the Ström at slack water, which we knew would be at eight.

"We set out with a fresh wind on our starboard quarter, and for some time spanked along at a great rate, never dreaming of danger, for indeed we saw not the slightest reason to apprehend it. All at once we were taken aback by a breeze from over Helseggen. This was most unusual—something that had never happened to us before—and I began to feel a little uneasy, without exactly knowing why. We put the boat on the wind, but could make no headway at all for the eddies, and I was upon the point of proposing to return to the anchorage, when, looking astern, we saw the whole horizon covered with a singular copper-colored cloud that rose with the most amazing velocity.

"In the meantime the breeze that had headed us off fell away and we were dead becalmed, drifting about in every direction. This state of things, however, did not last long enough to give us time to think about it. In less than a minute the storm was upon us—in less than two the sky was entirely overcast—and what with this and the driving spray, it became suddenly so dark that we could not see each other in the smack.

"Such a hurricane as then blew it is folly to attempt describing. The oldest seaman in Norway never experienced any thing like it. We had let our sails go by the run before it cleverly took us; but, at the first puff, both our masts went by the board as if they had been sawed off—the mainmast taking with it my youngest brother, who had lashed himself to it for safety.

"Our boat was the lightest feather of a thing that ever sat upon water. It had a complete flush deck, with only a small hatch near the bow, and this hatch it had always been our custom to batten down when about to cross the Ström, by way of precaution against the chopping seas. But for this circumstance we should have foundered at once—for we lay entirely buried for some moments. How my elder brother escaped destruction I cannot say, for I never had an opportunity of ascertaining. For my part, as soon as I had let the foresail run, I threw myself flat on deck, with my feet against the narrow gunwale of the bow, and with my hands grasping a ring-bolt near the foot of the foremast. It was mere instinct that prompted me to do this—which was undoubtedly the very best thing I could have done—for I was too much flurried to think.

"For some moments we were completely deluged, as I say, and all this time I held my breath, and clung to the bolt. When I could stand it no longer I raised myself upon my knees, still keeping hold with my hands, and thus got my head clear. Presently our little boat gave herself a shake, just as a dog does in coming out of the water, and thus rid herself, in some measure, of the seas. I was now trying to get the better of the stupor that had come over me, and to collect my senses so as to see what was to be done, when I felt somebody grasp my arm. It was my elder brother, and my heart leaped for joy, for I had made sure that he was overboard—but the next moment all this joy was turned into horror—for he put his mouth close to my ear, and screamed out the word *'Moskoe-ström!'*

"No one ever will know what my feelings were at that moment. I shook from head to foot as if I had had the most violent fit of the ague. I knew what he meant by that one word well enough—I knew what he wished to make me understand. With the wind that now drove us on, we were bound for the whirl of the Ström, and nothing could save us!

"You perceive that in crossing the Ström *channel,* we always went a long way up above the whirl, even in the calmest weather, and then had to wait and watch carefully for the slack—but now we were driving right upon the pool itself, and in such a hurricane as this! 'To be sure,' I thought, 'we shall get there just about the slack—there is some little hope in that'—but in the next moment I cursed myself for being so great a fool as to dream of hope at all. I knew very well that we were doomed, had we been ten times a ninety-gun ship.

"By this time the first fury of the tempest had spent itself, or perhaps we did not feel it so much, as we scudded before it, but at all events the seas, which at first had been kept down by the wind, and lay flat and frothing, now got up into absolute mountains. A singular change, too, had come over the heavens. Around in every direction it was still as black as pitch, but nearly overhead there burst out, all at once, a circular rift of clear sky—as clear as I ever saw—and of a deep bright blue—and through it there blazed forth the full moon with a lustre that I never before knew her to wear. She lit up every thing about us with the greatest distinctness—but, oh God, what a scene it was to light up!

"I now made one or two attempts to speak to my brother—but in some manner which I could not understand, the din had so increased that I could not make him hear a single word, although I screamed at the top of my voice in his ear. Presently he shook his head, looking as pale as death, and held up one of his fingers, as if to say '*listen!*'

"At first I could not make out what he meant—but soon a hideous thought flashed upon me. I dragged my watch from its fob. It was not going. I glanced at its face by the moonlight, and then burst into tears as I flung it far away into the ocean. *It had run down at seven o'clock! We were behind the time of the slack, and the whirl of the Ström was in full fury!*

"When a boat is well built, properly trimmed, and not deep laden, the waves in a strong gale, when she is going large, seem always to slip from beneath her—which appears strange to a landsman—and this is what is called *riding*, in sea phrase.

"Well, so far we had ridden the swells very cleverly; but presently a gigantic sea happened to take us right under the counter, and bore us with it as it rose—up—

up—as if into the sky. I would not have believed that any
wave could rise so high. And then down we came with a
sweep, a slide, and a plunge that made me feel sick and
dizzy, as if I was falling from some lofty mountain-top in
a dream. But while we were up I had thrown a quick
glance around—and that one glance was all-sufficient. I
saw our exact position in an instant. The Moskoe-ström
whirlpool was about a quarter of a mile dead ahead—but
no more like the every day Moskoe ström than the whirl,
as you now see it, is like a mill-race. If I had not known
where we were, and what we had to expect, I should not
have recognized the place at all. As it was, I involuntarily
closed my eyes in horror. The lids clenched themselves
together as if in a spasm.

"It could not have been more than two minutes after-
wards until we suddenly felt the waves subside, and were
enveloped in foam. The boat made a sharp half turn to
larboard, and then shot off in its new direction like a
thunderbolt. At the same moment the roaring noise of
the water was completely drowned in a kind of shrill
shriek—such a sound as you might imagine given out by
the water-pipes of many thousand steam-vessels letting
off their steam all together. We were now in the belt of
surf that always surrounds the whirl; and I thought, of
course, that another moment would plunge us into the
abyss, down which we could only see indistinctly on account of the amazing velocity with which we were borne
along. The boat did not seem to sink into the water at all,
but to skim like an air-bubble upon the surface of the
surge. Her starboard side was next the whirl, and on the
larboard arose the world of ocean we had left. It stood
like a huge writhing wall between us and the horizon.

"It may appear strange, but now, when we were in the very jaws of the gulf, I felt more composed than when we were only approaching it. Having made up my mind to hope no more, I got rid of a great deal of that terror which unmanned me at first. I supposed it was despair that strung my nerves.

"It may look like boasting—but what I tell you is truth—I began to reflect how magnificent a thing it was to die in such a manner, and how foolish it was in me to think of so paltry a consideration as my own individual life, in view of so wonderful a manifestation of God's power. I do believe that I blushed with shame when this idea crossed my mind. After a little while I became possessed with the keenest curiosity about the whirl itself. I positively felt a *wish* to explore its depths, even at the sacrifice I was going to make; and my principal grief was that I should never be able to tell my old companions on shore about the mysteries I should see. These, no doubt, were singular fancies to occupy a man's mind in such extremity—and I have often thought since, that the revolutions of the boat around the pool might have rendered me a little light-headed.

"There was another circumstance which tended to restore my self-possession; and this was the cessation of the wind, which could not reach us in our present situation—for, as you saw for yourself, the belt of the surf is considerably lower than the general bed of the ocean, and this latter now towered above us, a high, black, mountainous ridge. If you have never been at sea in a heavy gale, you can form no idea of the confusion of mind occasioned by the wind and spray together. They blind, deafen, and strangle you, and take away all power of action or reflection. But we were now, in a great measure, rid of these annoyances—just as death-condemned felons in prison are allowed petty indulgences, forbidden them while their doom is yet uncertain.

"How often we made the circuit of the belt it is impossible to say. We careered round and round for perhaps an hour, flying rather than floating, getting gradually more and more into the middle of the surge, and then nearer and nearer to its horrible inner edge. All this time I had never let go of the ring-bolt. My brother was at the stern, holding on to a small empty water-cask which had been securely lashed under the coop of the counter, and was the only thing on deck that had not been swept overboard when the gale first took us. As we approached the brink of the pit he let go his hold upon this, and made for the ring, from which, in the agony of his terror, he endeavored to force my hands, as it was not large enough to afford us both a secure grasp. I never felt deeper grief than when I saw him attempt this act—although I knew he was a madman when he did it—a raving maniac through sheer fright. I did not care, however, to contest the point with him. I knew it could make no difference whether either of us held on at all; so I let him have the bolt, and went astern to the cask. This there was no great difficulty in doing; for the smack flew round steadily enough, and upon an even keel—only swaying to and fro with the immense sweeps and swelters of the whirl. Scarcely had I secured myself in my new position, when we gave a wild lurch to starboard, and rushed headlong into the abyss. I muttered a hurried prayer to God, and thought all was over.

"As I felt the sickening sweep of the descent, I had instinctively tightened my hold upon the barrel, and closed my eyes. For some seconds I dared not open them—while I expected instant destruction, and wondered that I was not already in my death-struggles with the water. But moment after moment elapsed. I still lived. The sense of falling had ceased; and the motion of the vessel seemed much as it had been before, while in the belt of foam, with the exception that she now lay more along. I took courage and looked once again upon the scene.

"Never shall I forget the sensation of awe, horror, and admiration with which I gazed about me. The boat appeared to be hanging, as if by magic, midway down, upon the interior surface of a funnel vast in circumference, prodigious in depth, and whose perfectly smooth sides might have been mistaken for ebony, but for the bewildering rapidity with which they spun around, and for the gleaming and ghastly radiance they shot forth, as the rays of the full moon, from that circular rift amid the clouds which I have already described, streamed in a flood of golden glory along the black walls, and far away down into the inmost recesses of the abyss.

"At first I was too much confused to observe any thing accurately. The general burst of terrific grandeur was all that I beheld. When I recovered myself a little, however, my gaze fell instinctively downward. In this direction I was able to obtain an unobstructed view, from the manner in which the smack hung on the inclined surface of the pool. She was quite upon an even keel—that is to say, her deck lay in a plane parallel with that of the water—but this latter sloped at an angle of more than forty-five degrees, so that we seemed to be lying upon our beamends. I could not help observing, nevertheless, that I had scarcely more difficulty in maintaining my hold and footing in this situation, than if we had been upon a dead level; and this, I suppose, was owing to the speed at which we revolved.

"The rays of the moon seemed to search the very bottom of the profound gulf; but still I could make out nothing distinctly on account of a thick mist in which every thing there was enveloped, and over which there hung a magnificent rainbow, like that narrow and tottering bridge which Mussulmen[12] say is the only pathway between Time and Eternity. This mist, or spray, was no doubt occasioned by the clashing of the great walls of the funnel, as they all met together at the bottom—but the yell that went up to the Heavens from out of that mist I dare not attempt to describe.

"Our first slide into the abyss itself, from the belt of foam above, had carried us to a great distance down the slope; but our farther descent was by no means proportionate. Round and round we swept—not with any uniform movement—but in dizzying swings and jerks, that sent us sometimes only a few hundred yards—sometimes nearly the complete circuit of the whirl. Our progress downward, at each revolution, was slow, but very perceptible.

"Looking about me upon the wide waste of liquid ebony on which we were thus borne, I perceived that our boat was not the only object in the embrace of the whirl. Both above and below us were visible fragments of vessels, large masses of building-timber and trunks of trees, with many smaller articles, such as pieces of house furniture, broken boxes, barrels and staves. I have already described the unnatural curiosity which had taken the place of my original terrors. It appeared to grow upon me as I drew nearer and nearer to my dreadful doom. I now began to watch, with a strange interest, the numerous things that floated in our company. I *must* have been delirious, for I even sought *amusement* in speculating upon the relative velocities of their several descents toward the foam below. 'This fir-tree,' I found myself at one time saying, 'will certainly be the next thing that takes the awful plunge and disappears,'—and then I was disappointed to find that the wreck of a Dutch merchant ship overtook it and went down before. At length, after making several guesses of this nature, and being deceived in all—this fact—the fact of my invariable miscalculation, set me upon a train of reflection that made my limbs again tremble, and my heart beat heavily once more.

"It was not a new terror that thus affected me, but the dawn of a more exciting *hope*. This hope arose partly from memory and partly from present observation. I called to mind the great variety of buoyant matter that strewed the coast of Lofoden, having been absorbed and then thrown forth by the Moskoe-ström. By far the greater number of the articles were shattered in the most extraordinary way—so chafed and roughened as to have the appearance of being stuck full of splinters—but then I distinctly recollected that there were *some* of them which were not disfigured at all. Now I could not account for this difference except by supposing that the roughened fragments were the only ones which had been *completely absorbed*—that the others had entered the whirl at so late a period of the tide, or, from some reason, had descended so slowly after entering, that they did not reach the bottom before the turn of the flood came, or of the ebb, as the case might be. I conceived it possible, in either instance, that they might thus be whirled up again to the level of the ocean, without undergoing the fate of those which had been drawn in more early or absorbed more rapidly. I made, also, three important observations. The first was, that as a general rule, the larger the bodies were, the more rapid their descent—the second, that, between two masses of equal extent, the one spherical, and the other *of any other shape,* the superiority in speed of descent was with the sphere—the third, that, between two masses of equal size, the one cylindrical, and the other of any other shape, the cylinder was absorbed the more slowly. Since my escape, I have had several conversations on this subject with an old school-master of the district; and it was from him that I learned the use of the words 'cylinder' and 'sphere.' He explained to me—although I have forgotten the explanation—how what I observed was, in fact, the natural consequence of the forms of the floating fragments—and showed me how it happened that a cylinder, swimming in a vortex, offered more resistance to its suction, and was drawn in with greater difficulty than an equally bulky body, of any form whatever.[*]

"There was one startling circumstance which went a great way in enforcing these observations, and rendering me anxious to turn them to account, and this was that, at every revolution, we passed something like a barrel, or else the yard or the mast of a vessel, while many of these things which had been on our level when I first opened

---

[*] See Archimedes, *"De Incidentibus in Fluido."*—lib. 2.[13]

my eyes upon the wonders of the whirlpool, were now high up above us, and seemed to have moved but little from their original station.

"I no longer hesitated what to do. I resolved to lash myself securely to the water-cask upon which I now held, to cut it loose from the counter, and to throw myself with it into the water. I attracted my brother's attention by signs, pointed to the floating barrels that came near us, and did every thing in my power to make him understand what I was about to do. I thought at length that he comprehended my design—but, whether this was the case or not, he shook his head despairingly, and refused to move from his station by the ring-bolt. It was impossible to reach him; the emergency admitted of no delay; and so, with a bitter struggle, I resigned him to his fate, fastened myself to the cask by means of the lashings which secured it to the counter, and precipitated myself with it into the sea, without another moment's hesitation.

"The result was precisely what I had hoped it might be. As it is myself who now tell you this tale—as you see that I *did* escape—and as you are already in possession of the mode in which this escape was effected, and must therefore anticipate all that I have farther to say—I will bring my story quickly to conclusion. It might have been an hour, or thereabout, after my quitting the smack, when, having descended to a vast distance beneath me, it made three or four wild gyrations in rapid succession, and, bearing my loved brother with it, plunged headlong, at once and forever, into the chaos of foam below. The barrel to which I was attached sunk very little farther than half the distance between the bottom of the gulf and the spot at which I leaped overboard, before a great change took place in the character of the whirlpool. The slope of the sides of the vast funnel became momently less and less steep. The gyrations of the whirl grew, gradually, less and less violent. By degrees, the froth and the rainbow disappeared, and the bottom of the gulf seemed slowly to uprise. The sky was clear, the winds had gone down, and the full moon was setting radiantly in the west, when I found myself on the surface of the ocean, in full view of the shores of Lofoden, and above the spot where the pool of the Moskoe-ström *had been*. It was the hour of the slack—but the sea still heaved in mountainous waves from the effects of the hurricane. I was borne violently into the channel of the Ström, and in a few minutes, was hurried down the coast into the 'grounds' of the fishermen. A boat picked me up—exhausted from fatigue—and (now that the danger was removed) speechless from the memory of its horror. Those who drew me on board were my old mates and daily companions—but they knew me no more than they would have known a traveller from the spirit-land. My hair, which had been raven black the day before, was as white as you see it now. They say too that the whole expression of my countenance had changed. I told them my story— they did not believe it. I now tell it to *you*—and I can scarcely expect you to put more faith in it than did the merry fishermen of Lofoden."

THE PIT AND THE PENDULUM[1]

Impia tortorum longas hic turba furores
Sanguinis innocui, non satiata, aluit.
Sospite nunc patria, fracto nunc funeris antro,
Mors ubi dira fuit vita salusque patent.[2]
[*Quatrain composed for the gates of a market to be erected
upon the site of the Jacobin Club House at Paris.*]

I WAS SICK—SICK unto death with that long agony; and when they at length unbound me, and I was permitted to sit, I felt that my senses were leaving me. The sentence—the dread sentence of death—was the last of distinct accentuation which reached my ears. After that, the sound of the inquisitorial[3] voices seemed merged in one dreamy indeterminate hum. It conveyed to my soul the idea of *revolution*—perhaps from its association in fancy with the burr of a mill-wheel. This only for a brief period, for presently I heard no more. Yet, for a while, I saw—but with how terrible an exaggeration! I saw the lips of the black-robed judges. They appeared to me white—whiter than the sheet upon which I trace these words—and thin even to grotesqueness; thin with the intensity of their expression of firmness—of immovable resolution—of stern contempt of human torture. I saw that the decrees of what to me was Fate were still issuing from those lips. I saw them writhe with a deadly locution. I saw them fashion the syllables of my name; and I shuddered because no sound succeeded. I saw, too, for a few moments of delirious horror, the soft and nearly imperceptible waving of the sable draperies which enwrapped the walls of the apartment. And then my vision fell upon the seven tall candles upon the table. At first they wore the aspect of charity, and seemed white slender angels who would save me; but then, all at once, there came a most deadly nausea over my spirit, and I felt every fibre in my frame thrill as if I had touched the wire of a galvanic battery,[4] while the angel forms became meaningless spectres, with heads of flame, and I saw that from them there would be no help. And then there stole into my fancy, like a rich musical note, the thought of what sweet rest there must be in the grave. The thought came gently and stealthily, and it seemed long before it attained full appreciation; but just as my spirit came at length properly to feel and entertain it, the figures of the judges vanished, as if magically, from before me; the tall candles sank into nothingness; their flames went out utterly; the blackness of darkness supervened; all sensations appeared swallowed up in a mad rushing descent as of the soul into Hades. Then silence, and stillness, and night were the universe.

I had swooned; but still will not say that all of consciousness was lost. What of it there remained I will not attempt to define, or even to describe; yet all was not lost. In the deepest slumber—no! In delirium—no! In a swoon—no! In death—no! even in the grave all *is not* lost. Else there is no immortality for man. Arousing from the most profound of slumbers, we break the gossamer web of *some* dream. Yet in a second afterward (so frail may that web have been) we remember not that we have dreamed. In the return to life from the swoon there are two stages: first, that of the sense of mental or spiritual; secondly, that of the sense of physical, existence. It seems probable that if, upon reaching the second stage, we could recall the impressions of the first, we should find these impressions eloquent in memories of the gulf beyond. And that gulf is—what? How at least shall we distinguish its shadows from those of the tomb? But if the impressions of what I have termed the first stage are not, at will, recalled, yet, after long interval, do they not come unbidden, while we marvel whence they come? He who has never swooned, is not he who finds strange palaces and wildly familiar faces in coals that glow; is not he who beholds floating in mid-air the sad visions that the many may not view; is not he who ponders over the perfume of some novel flower; is not he whose brain grows bewildered with the meaning of some musical cadence which has never before arrested his attention.

Amid frequent and thoughtful endeavors to remember, amid earnest struggles to regather some token of the state of seeming nothingness into which my soul had lapsed, there have been moments when I have dreamed of success; there have been brief, very brief periods when I have conjured up remembrances which the lucid reason of a later epoch assures me could have had reference only to that condition of seeming unconsciousness. These shadows of memory tell, indistinctly, of tall figures that lifted and bore me in silence down—down—still down—till a hideous dizziness oppressed me at the mere idea of the interminableness of the descent. They tell also of a vague horror at my heart, on account of that heart's unnatural stillness. Then comes a sense of sudden motionlessness throughout all things; as if those who bore me (a ghastly train!) had outrun, in their descent, the limits of the limitless, and paused from the wearisomeness of their toil. After this I call to mind flatness and dampness; and then all is *madness*—the madness of a memory which busies itself among forbidden things.

Very suddenly there came back to my soul motion and sound—the tumultuous motion of the heart, and, in my ears, the sound of its beating. Then a pause in which all is blank. Then again sound, and motion, and touch—a tingling sensation pervading my frame. Then the mere consciousness of existence, without thought—a condition which lasted long. Then, very suddenly, *thought,* and shuddering terror, and earnest endeavor to comprehend my true state. Then a strong desire to lapse into insensibility. Then a rushing revival of soul and a successful effort to move. And now a full memory of the trial, of the judges, of the sable draperies, of the sentence, of the sickness, of the swoon. Then entire forgetfulness of all that followed; of all that a later day and much earnestness of endeavor have enabled me vaguely to recall.

So far, I had not opened my eyes. I felt that I lay upon my back, unbound. I reached out my hand and it fell heavily upon something damp and hard. There I suffered it to remain for many minutes, while I strove to imagine where and *what* I could be. I longed, yet dared not, to employ my vision. I dreaded the first glance at objects around me. It was not that I feared to look upon things horrible, but that I grew aghast lest there should be *nothing* to see. At length, with a wild desperation at heart, I quickly unclosed my eyes. My worst thoughts, then, were confirmed. The blackness of eternal night encompassed me. I struggled for breath. The intensity of the darkness seemed to oppress and stifle me. The atmosphere was intolerably close. I still lay quietly, and made effort to exercise my reason. I brought to mind the inquisitorial proceedings, and attempted from that point to deduce my real condition. The sentence had passed; and it appeared to me that a very long interval of time had since elapsed. Yet not for a moment did I suppose myself actually dead. Such a supposition, notwithstanding what we read in fiction, is altogether inconsistent with real existence;—but where and in what state was I? The condemned to death, I knew, perished usually at the *auto-da-fés,*[5] and one of these had been held on the very night of the day of my trial. Had I been remanded to my dungeon, to await the next sacrifice, which would not take place for many months? This I at once saw could not be. Victims had been in immediate demand. Moreover, my dungeon, as well as all the condemned cells at Toledo,[6] had stone floors, and light was not altogether excluded.

A fearful idea now suddenly drove the blood in torrents upon my heart, and for a brief period I once more relapsed into insensibility. Upon recovering, I at once started to my feet, trembling convulsively in every fibre.

I thrust my arms wildly above and around me in all directions. I felt nothing; yet dreaded to move a step, lest I should be impeded by the walls of a *tomb*. Perspiration burst from every pore, and stood in cold big beads upon my forehead. The agony of suspense grew at length intolerable, and I cautiously moved forward, with my arms extended, and my eyes straining from their sockets in the hope of catching some faint ray of light. I proceeded for many paces; but still all was blackness and vacancy. I breathed more freely. It seemed evident that mine was not, at least, the most hideous of fates.[7]

And now, as I still continued to step cautiously onward, there came thronging upon my recollection a thousand vague rumors of the horrors of Toledo. Of the dungeons there had been strange things narrated—fables I had always deemed them,—but yet strange, and too ghastly to repeat, save in a whisper. Was I left to perish of starvation in this subterranean world of darkness; or what fate, perhaps even more fearful, awaited me? That the result would be death, and a death of more than customary bitterness, I knew too well the character of my judges to doubt. The mode and the hour were all that occupied or distracted me.

My outstretched hands at length encountered some solid obstruction. It was a wall, seemingly of stone masonry—very smooth, slimy, and cold. I followed it up; stepping with all the careful distrust with which certain antique narratives had inspired me. This process, however, afforded me no means of ascertaining the dimensions of my dungeon, as I might make its circuit and return to the point whence I set out without being aware of the fact, so perfectly uniform seemed the wall. I therefore sought the knife which had been in my pocket when led into the inquisitorial chamber; but it was gone; my clothes had been exchanged for a wrapper of coarse serge. I had thought of forcing the blade in some minute crevice of the masonry, so as to identify my point of departure. The difficulty, nevertheless, was but trivial; although, in the disorder of my fancy, it seemed at first insuperable. I tore a part of the hem from the robe and placed the fragment at full length, and at right angles to the wall. In groping my way around the prison, I could not fail to encounter this rag upon completing the circuit. So, at least, I thought; but I had not counted upon the extent of the dungeon, or upon my own weakness. The ground was moist and slippery. I staggered onward for some time, when I stumbled and fell. My excessive fatigue induced me to remain prostrate; and sleep soon overtook me as I lay.

Upon awaking, and stretching forth an arm, I found beside me a loaf and a pitcher with water. I was too much exhausted to reflect upon this circumstance, but ate and drank with avidity. Shortly afterward, I resumed my tour around the prison, and with much toil, came at last upon the fragment of the serge. Up to the period when I fell, I had counted fifty-two paces, and, upon resuming my walk, I had counted forty-eight more—when I arrived at the rag. There were in all, then, a hundred paces; and, admitting two paces to the yard, I presumed the dungeon to be fifty yards in circuit. I had met, however, with many angles in the wall, and thus I could form no guess at the shape of the vault, for vault I could not help supposing it to be.

I had little object—certainly no hope—in these researches; but a vague curiosity prompted me to continue them. Quitting the wall, I resolved to cross the area of the enclosure. At first, I proceeded with extreme caution, for the floor, although seemingly of solid material, was treacherous with slime. At length, however, I took courage, and did not hesitate to step firmly—endeavoring to cross in as direct a line as possible. I had advanced some ten or twelve paces in this manner, when the remnant of the torn hem of my robe became entangled between my legs. I stepped on it, and fell violently on my face.

In the confusion attending my fall, I did not immediately apprehend a somewhat startling circumstance, which yet, in a few seconds afterward, and while I still lay prostrate, arrested my attention. It was this: my chin rested upon the floor of the prison, but my lips, and the upper portion of my head, although seemingly at a less elevation than the chin, touched nothing. At the same time, my forehead seemed bathed in a clammy vapor, and the peculiar smell of decayed fungus arose to my nostrils. I put forward my arm, and shuddered to find that I had fallen at the very brink of a circular pit, whose extent, of course, I had no means of ascertaining at the moment. Groping about the masonry just below the margin, I succeeded in dislodging a small fragment, and let it fall into the abyss. For many seconds I hearkened to its reverberations as it dashed against the sides of the chasm in its descent; at length, there was a sullen plunge into water, succeeded by loud echoes. At the same moment, there came a sound resembling the quick opening and as rapid closing of a door overhead, while a faint gleam of light flashed suddenly through the gloom, and as suddenly faded away.

I saw clearly the doom which had been prepared for me, and congratulated myself upon the timely accident by which I had escaped. Another step before my fall, and the world had seen me no more. And the death just avoided was of that very character which I had regarded as fabulous and frivolous in the tales respecting the Inquisition. To the victims of its tyranny, there was the choice of death with its direst physical agonies, or death with its most hideous moral horrors.[8] I had been reserved for the latter. By long suffering my nerves had been unstrung, until I trembled at the sound of my own voice, and had become in every respect a fitting subject for the species of torture which awaited me.

Shaking in every limb, I groped my way back to the wall—resolving there to perish rather than risk the terrors of the wells, of which my imagination now pictured many in various positions about the dungeon. In other conditions of mind, I might have had courage to end my misery at once, by a plunge into one of these abysses; but now I was the veriest of cowards. Neither could I forget what I had read of these pits—that the *sudden* extinction of life formed no part of their most horrible plan.

Agitation of spirit kept me awake for many long hours, but at length I again slumbered. Upon arousing, I found by my side, as before, a loaf and a pitcher of water. A burning thirst consumed me, and I emptied the vessel at a draught. It must have been drugged—for scarcely had I drank, before I became irresistibly drowsy. A deep sleep fell upon me—a sleep like that of death. How long it lasted, of course I know not; but when, once again, I unclosed my eyes, the objects around me were visible. By a wild, sulphurous lustre, the origin of which I could not at first determine, I was enabled to see the extent and aspect of the prison.

In its size I had been greatly mistaken. The whole circuit of its walls did not exceed twenty-five yards. For some minutes this fact occasioned me a world of vain trouble; vain indeed—for what could be of less importance, under the terrible circumstances which environed me, than the mere dimensions of my dungeon? But my soul took a wild interest in trifles, and I busied myself in endeavors to account for the error I had committed in my measurement. The truth at length flashed upon me. In my first attempt at exploration I had counted fifty-two paces, up to the period when I fell: I must then have been within a pace or two of the fragment of serge; in fact, I had nearly performed the circuit of the vault. I then slept—and, upon awaking, I must have returned upon my steps—thus supposing the circuit nearly double what it actually was. My confusion of mind prevented me from observing that I began my tour with the wall to the left, and ended it with the wall to the right.

I had been deceived, too, in respect to the shape of the enclosure. In feeling my way I had found many angles, and thus deduced an idea of great irregularity; so potent is the effect of total darkness upon one arousing from lethargy or sleep! The angles were simply those of a few slight depressions, or niches, at odd intervals. The general shape of the prison was square. What I had taken for masonry seemed now to be iron, or some other metal, in huge plates, whose sutures or joints occasioned the depression. The entire surface of this metallic enclosure was rudely daubed in all the hideous and repulsive devices to which the charnel superstition of the monks has given rise. The figures of fiends in aspects of menace, with skeleton forms, and other more really fearful images, overspread and disfigured the walls. I observed that the outlines of these monstrosities were sufficiently distinct, but that the colors seemed faded and blurred, as if from the effects of a damp atmosphere. I now noticed the floor, too, which was of stone. In the centre yawned the circular pit from whose jaws I had escaped; but it was the only one in the dungeon.

All this I saw indistinctly and by much effort—for my personal condition had been greatly changed during slumber. I now lay upon my back, and at full length, on a species of low framework of wood. To this I was securely bound by a long strap resembling a surcingle.[9] It passed in many convolutions about my limbs and body, leaving at liberty only my head, and my left arm to such extent, that I could, by dint of much exertion, supply myself with food from an earthen dish which lay by my side on the floor. I saw, to my horror, that the pitcher had been removed. I say to my horror—for I was consumed with intolerable thirst. This thirst it appeared to be the design of my persecutors to stimulate—for the food in the dish was meat pungently seasoned.

Looking upward, I surveyed the ceiling of my prison. It was some thirty or forty feet overhead, and constructed much as the side walls. In one of its panels a very singular figure riveted my whole attention. It was the painted figure of Time as he is commonly represented, save that, in lieu of a scythe, he held what, at a casual glance, I supposed to be the pictured image of a huge pendulum, such as we see on antique clocks. There was something, however, in the appearance of this machine which caused me to regard it more attentively. While I gazed directly upward at it (for its position was immediately over my own) I fancied that I saw it in motion. In an instant afterward the fancy was confirmed. Its sweep was brief, and of course slow. I watched it for some minutes somewhat in fear, but more in wonder. Wearied at length with observing its dull movement, I turned my eyes upon the other objects in the cell.

A slight noise attracted my notice, and, looking to the floor, I saw several enormous rats traversing it. They had issued from the well which lay just within view to my right. Even then, while I gazed, they came up in troops, hurriedly, with ravenous eyes, allured by the scent of the meat. From this it required much effort and attention to scare them away.

It might have been half an hour, perhaps even an hour (for I could take but imperfect note of time), before I again cast my eyes upward. What I then saw confounded and amazed me. The sweep of the pendulum had increased in extent by nearly a yard. As a natural consequence its velocity was also much greater. But what mainly disturbed me was the idea that it had perceptibly *descended*. I now observed—with what horror it is needless to say—that its nether extremity was formed of a crescent of glittering steel, about a foot in length from horn to horn; the horns upward, and the under edge evidently as keen as that of a razor. Like a razor also, it seemed massy and heavy, tapering from the edge into a solid and broad structure above. It was appended to a weighty rod of brass, and the whole *hissed* as it swung through the air.

I could no longer doubt the doom prepared for me by

monkish ingenuity in torture. My cognizance of the pit had become known to the inquisitorial agents—*the pit*, whose horrors had been destined for so bold a recusant as myself—*the pit*, typical of hell and regarded by rumor as the Ultima Thule[10] of all their punishments. The plunge into this pit I had avoided by the merest of accidents, and I knew that surprise, or entrapment into torment, formed an important portion of all the grotesquerie of these dungeon deaths. Having failed to fall, it was no part of the demon plan to hurl me into the abyss, and thus (there being no alternative) a different and a milder destruction awaited me. Milder! I half smiled in my agony as I thought of such application of such a term.

What boots it to tell of the long, long hours of horror more than mortal, during which I counted the rushing oscillations of the steel! Inch by inch—line by line—with a descent only appreciable at intervals that seemed ages—down and still down it came! Days passed—it might have been that many days passed—ere it swept so closely over me as to fan me with its acrid breath. The odor of the sharp steel forced itself into my nostrils. I prayed—I wearied heaven with my prayer for its more speedy descent. I grew frantically mad, and struggled to force myself upward against the sweep of the fearful scimitar. And then I fell suddenly calm, and lay smiling at the glittering death, as a child at some rare bauble.

There was another interval of utter insensibility; it was brief; for, upon again lapsing into life, there had been no perceptible descent in the pendulum. But it might have been long—for I knew there were demons who took note of my swoon, and who could have arrested the vi-

bration at pleasure. Upon my recovery, too, I felt very—
oh! inexpressibly—sick and weak, as if through long ina-
nition. Even amid the agonies of that period, the human
nature craved food. With painful effort I outstretched
my left arm as far as my bonds permitted, and took possession of the small remnant which had been spared me
by the rats. As I put a portion of it within my lips, there
rushed to my mind a half-formed thought of joy—of
hope. Yet what business had *I* with hope? It was, as I say,
a half-formed thought—man has many such, which are
never completed. I felt that it was of joy—of hope; but I
felt also that it had perished in its formation. In vain I
struggled to perfect—to regain it. Long suffering had
nearly annihilated all my ordinary powers of mind. I was
an imbecile—an idiot.

The vibration of the pendulum was at right angles to
my length. I saw that the crescent was designed to cross
the region of the heart. It would fray the serge of my
robe—it would return and repeat its operations—
again—and again. Notwithstanding its terrifically wide
sweep (some thirty feet or more), and the hissing vigor of
its descent, sufficient to sunder these very walls of iron,
still the fraying of my robe would be all that, for several
minutes, it would accomplish. And at this thought I
paused. I dared not go further than this reflection. I
dwelt upon it with a pertinacity of attention—as if, in so
dwelling, I could arrest *here* the descent of the steel. I
forced myself to ponder upon the sound of the crescent
as it should pass across the garment—upon the peculiar
thrilling sensation which the friction of cloth produces
on the nerves. I pondered upon all this frivolity until my
teeth were on edge.

Down—steadily down it crept. I took a frenzied pleasure in contrasting its downward with its lateral velocity. To the right—to the left—far and wide—with the shriek of a damned spirit! to my heart, with the stealthy pace of the tiger! I alternately laughed and howled, as the one or the other idea grew predominant.

Down—certainly, relentlessly down! It vibrated within three inches of my bosom! I struggled violently—furiously—to free my left arm. This was free only from the elbow to the hand. I could reach the latter, from the platter beside me, to my mouth, with great effort, but no farther. Could I have broken the fastenings above the elbow, I would have seized and attempted to arrest the pendulum. I might as well have attempted to arrest an avalanche!

Down—still unceasingly—still inevitably down! I gasped and struggled at each vibration. I shrunk convulsively at its every sweep. My eyes followed its outward or upward whirls with the eagerness of the most unmeaning despair; they closed themselves spasmodically at the descent, although death would have been a relief, oh, how unspeakable! Still I quivered in every nerve to think how slight a sinking of the machinery would precipitate that keen, glistening axe upon my bosom. It was *hope* that prompted the nerve to quiver—the frame to shrink. It was *hope*—the hope that triumphs on the rack—that whispers to the death-condemned even in the dungeons of the Inquisition.

I saw that some ten or twelve vibrations would bring the steel in actual contact with my robe—and with this observation there suddenly came over my spirit all the keen, collected calmness of despair. For the first time during many hours—or perhaps days—I *thought*. It now occurred to me, that the bandage, or surcingle, which enveloped me, was *unique*. I was tied by no separate cord. The first stroke of the razor-like crescent athwart any portion of the band would so detach it that it might be unwound from my person by means of my left hand. But how fearful, in that case, the proximity of the steel! The result of the slightest struggle, how deadly! Was it likely, moreover, that the minions of the torturer had not foreseen and provided for this possibility? Was it probable that the bandage crossed my bosom in the track of the pendulum? Dreading to find my faint and, as it seemed, my last hope frustrated, I so far elevated my head as to obtain a distinct view of my breast. The surcingle enveloped my limbs and body close in all directions—*save in the path of the destroying crescent*.

Scarcely had I dropped my head back into its original position, when there flashed upon my mind what I cannot better describe than as the unformed half of that idea of deliverance to which I have previously alluded, and of which a moiety[11] only floated indeterminately through my brain when I raised food to my burning lips. The whole thought was now present—feeble, scarcely sane, scarcely definite—but still entire. I proceeded at once, with the nervous energy of despair, to attempt its execution.

For many hours the immediate vicinity of the low framework upon which I lay had been literally swarming with rats. They were wild, bold, ravenous—their red eyes glaring upon me as if they waited but for motionlessness on my part to make me their prey. "To what food," I thought, "have they been accustomed in the well?"

They had devoured, in spite of all my efforts to prevent them, all but a small remnant of the contents of the dish. I had fallen into an habitual see-saw or wave of the hand about the platter; and, at length, the unconscious uniformity of the movement deprived it of effect. In their voracity, the vermin frequently fastened their sharp fangs in my fingers. With the particles of the oily and spicy viand which now remained, I thoroughly rubbed the bandage wherever I could reach it; then, raising my hand from the floor, I lay breathlessly still.

At first, the ravenous animals were startled and terrified at the change—at the cessation of movement. They shrank alarmedly back; many sought the well. But this was only for a moment. I had not counted in vain upon their voracity. Observing that I remained without motion, one or two of the boldest leaped upon the framework, and smelt at the surcingle. This seemed the signal for a general rush. Forth from the well they hurried in fresh troops. They clung to the wood—they overran it, and leaped in hundreds upon my person. The measured movement of the pendulum disturbed them not at all. Avoiding its strokes, they busied themselves with the anointed bandage. They pressed—they swarmed upon me in ever accumulating heaps. They writhed upon my throat; their cold lips sought my own; I was half stifled by their thronging pressure; disgust, for which the world has no name, swelled my bosom, and chilled, with a heavy clamminess, my heart. Yet one minute, and I felt that the struggle would be over. Plainly I perceived the loosening of the bandage. I knew that in more than one place it must be already severed. With a more than human resolution I lay *still*.

Nor had I erred in my calculations—nor had I endured in vain. I at length felt that I was *free*. The surcingle hung in ribands from my body. But the stroke of the pendulum already pressed upon my bosom. It had divided the serge of the robe. It had cut through the linen beneath. Twice again it swung, and a sharp sense of pain shot through every nerve. But the moment of escape had arrived. At a wave of my hand my deliverers hurried tumultuously away. With a steady movement—cautious, sidelong, shrinking, and slow—I slid from the embrace of the bandage and beyond the reach of the scimitar. For the moment, at least, *I was free*.

Free!—and in the grasp of the Inquisition! I had scarcely stepped from my wooden bed of horror upon the stone floor of the prison, when the motion of the hellish machine ceased, and I beheld it drawn up, by some invisible force, through the ceiling. This was a lesson which I took desperately to heart. My every motion was undoubtedly watched. Free!—I had but escaped death in one form of agony, to be delivered unto worse than death in some other. With that thought I rolled my eyes nervously around on the barriers of iron that hemmed me in. Something unusual—some change which, at first, I could not appreciate distinctly—it was obvious, had taken place in the apartment. For many minutes of a dreamy and trembling abstraction, I busied myself in vain, unconnected conjecture. During this period, I became aware, for the first time, of the origin of the sulphurous light which illumined the cell. It proceeded from a fissure, about half an inch in width, extending entirely around the prison at the base of the walls, which thus appeared, and were completely separated from the floor. I endeavored, but of course in vain, to look through the aperture.

As I arose from the attempt, the mystery of the alteration in the chamber broke at once upon my understanding. I have observed that, although the outlines of the figures upon the walls were sufficiently distinct, yet the colors seemed blurred and indefinite. These colors had now assumed, and were momentarily assuming, a startling and most intense brilliancy, that gave to the spectral and fiendish portraitures an aspect that might have thrilled even firmer nerves than my own. Demon eyes, of a wild and ghastly vivacity, glared upon me in a thousand directions, where none had been visible before and gleamed with the lurid lustre of a fire that I could not force my imagination to regard as unreal.

Unreal!—Even while I breathed there came to my nostrils the breath of the vapor of heated iron! A suffocating odor pervaded the prison! A deeper glow settled each moment in the eyes that glared at my agonies! A richer tint of crimson diffused itself over the pictured horrors of blood. I panted! I gasped for breath! There could be no doubt of the design of my tormentors—oh! most unrelenting! oh! most demoniac of men! I shrank from the glowing metal to the centre of the cell. Amid the thought of the fiery destruction that impended, the idea of the coolness of the well came over my soul like balm. I rushed to its deadly brink. I threw my straining vision below. The glare from the enkindled roof illumined its inmost recesses. Yet, for a wild moment, did my spirit refuse to comprehend the meaning of what I saw. At length it forced—it wrestled its way into my soul—it burned itself in upon my shuddering reason. Oh! for a voice to speak!—oh! horror!—oh! any horror but this! With a shriek, I rushed from the margin, and buried my face in my hands—weeping bitterly.

The heat rapidly increased, and once again I looked up, shuddering as with a fit of ague.[12] There had been a second change in the cell—and now the change was obviously in the *form*. As before, it was in vain that I at first endeavored to appreciate or understand what was taking place. But not long was I left in doubt. The Inquisitorial vengeance had been hurried by my two-fold escape, and there was to be no more dallying with the King of Terrors. The room had been square. I saw that two of its iron angles were now acute—two, consequently, obtuse. The fearful difference quickly increased with a low rumbling or moaning sound. In an instant the apartment had shifted its form into that of a lozenge. But the alteration stopped not here—I neither hoped nor desired it to stop. I could have clasped the red walls to my bosom as a garment of eternal peace. "Death," I said, "any death but that of the pit!" Fool! might I not have known that *into the pit* it was the object of the burning iron to urge me? Could I resist its glow? or if even that, could I withstand its pressure? And now, flatter and flatter grew the lozenge, with a rapidity that left me no time for contemplation. Its centre, and of course its greatest width, came just over the yawning gulf. I shrank back—but the closing walls pressed me resistlessly onward. At length for my seared and writhing body there was no longer an inch of foothold on the firm floor of the prison. I struggled no more, but the agony of my soul found vent in one loud, long, and final scream of despair. I felt that I tottered upon the brink—I averted my eyes—

There was a discordant hum of human voices! There was a loud blast as of many trumpets! There was a harsh grating as of a thousand thunders! The fiery walls rushed back! An outstretched arm caught my own as I fell, fainting, into the abyss. It was that of General Lasalle.[13] The French army had entered Toledo. The Inquisition was in the hands of its enemies.

WILLIAM WILSON[1]

What say of it? what say CONSCIENCE grim,
That spectre in my path?
—CHAMBERLAIN'S *Pharronida*[2]

LET ME CALL myself, for the present, William Wilson. The fair page now lying before me need not be sullied with my real appellation. This has been already too much an object for the scorn—for the horror—for the detestation of my race. To the uttermost regions of the globe have not the indignant winds bruited its unparalleled infamy? Oh, outcast of all outcasts most abandoned!—to the earth art thou not for ever dead? to its honors, to its flowers, to its golden aspirations?—and a cloud, dense, dismal, and limitless, does it not hang eternally between thy hopes and heaven?

I would not, if I could, here or to-day, embody a record of my later years of unspeakable misery, and unpardonable crime. This epoch—these later years—took unto themselves a sudden elevation in turpitude, whose origin alone it is my present purpose to assign. Men usually grow base by degrees. From me, in an instant, all virtue dropped bodily as a mantle. From comparatively trivial wickedness I passed, with the stride of a giant, into more than the enormities of an Elagabalus.[3] What chance—what one event brought this evil thing to pass, bear with me while I relate. Death approaches; and the shadow which foreruns him has thrown a softening influence over my spirit. I long, in passing through the dim valley, for the sympathy—I had nearly said for the pity— of my fellow-men. I would fain have them believe that I have been, in some measure, the slave of circumstances beyond human control. I would wish them to seek out for me, in the details I am about to give, some little oasis of *fatality* amid a wilderness of error. I would have them allow—what they cannot refrain from allowing—that, although temptation may have erewhile existed as great, man was never *thus,* at least, tempted before—certainly, never *thus* fell. And is it therefore that he has never thus suffered? Have I not indeed been living in a dream? And am I not now dying a victim to the horror and the mystery of the wildest of all sublunary visions?

I am the descendant of a race whose imaginative and easily excitable temperament has at all times rendered them remarkable; and, in my earliest infancy, I gave evidence of having fully inherited the family character. As I advanced in years it was more strongly developed; becoming, for many reasons, a cause of serious disquietude to my friends, and of positive injury to myself. I grew self-willed, addicted to the wildest caprices, and a prey to the most ungovernable passions. Weak-minded, and beset with constitutional infirmities akin to my own, my parents could do but little to check the evil propensities which distinguished me. Some feeble and ill-directed efforts resulted in complete failure on their part, and, of course, in total triumph on mine. Thenceforward my voice was a household law; and at an age when few children have abandoned their leading-strings, I was left to the guidance of my own will, and became, in all but name, the master of my own actions.

My earliest recollections of a school-life, are connected with a large, rambling, Elizabethan house, in a misty-looking village of England, where were a vast number of gigantic and gnarled trees, and where all the houses were excessively ancient. In truth, it was a dream-like and spirit-soothing place, that venerable old town. At this moment, in fancy, I feel the refreshing chilliness of its deeply-shadowed avenues, inhale the fragrance of its thousand shrubberies, and thrill anew with undefinable delight, at the deep hollow note of the church-bell, breaking, each hour, with sullen and sudden roar, upon the stillness of the dusky atmosphere in which the fretted Gothic steeple lay imbedded and asleep.

It gives me, perhaps, as much of pleasure as I can now in any manner experience, to dwell upon minute recollections of the school and its concerns. Steeped in misery as I am—misery, alas! only too real—I shall be pardoned for seeking relief, however slight and temporary, in the weakness of a few rambling details. These, moreover, utterly trivial, and even ridiculous in themselves, assume, to my fancy, adventitious importance, as connected with a period and a locality when and where I recognize the first ambiguous monitions of the destiny which afterward so fully overshadowed me. Let me then remember.

The house, I have said, was old and irregular. The grounds were extensive, and a high and solid brick wall, topped with a bed of mortar and broken glass, encompassed the whole. This prison-like rampart formed the limit of our domain; beyond it we saw but thrice a week—once every Saturday afternoon, when, attended by two ushers, we were permitted to take brief walks in a body through some of the neighboring fields—and twice during Sunday, when we were paraded in the same formal manner to the morning and evening service in the one church of the village. Of this church the principal of our school was pastor. With how deep a spirit of wonder and perplexity was I wont to regard him from our remote pew in the gallery, as, with step solemn and slow, he ascended the pulpit! This reverend man, with countenance so demurely benign, with robes so glossy and so clerically flowing, with wig so minutely powdered, so rigid and so vast,—could this be he who, of late, with sour visage, and in snuffy habiliments, administered, ferule in hand, the Draconian Laws of the academy? Oh, gigantic paradox, too utterly monstrous for solution!

At an angle of the ponderous wall frowned a more ponderous gate. It was riveted and studded with iron bolts, and surmounted with jagged iron spikes. What impressions of deep awe did it inspire! It was never opened save for the three periodical egressions and ingressions already mentioned; then, in every creak of its mighty hinges, we found a plenitude of mystery—a world of matter for solemn remark, or for more solemn meditation.

The extensive enclosure was irregular in form, having

many capacious recesses. Of these, three or four of the largest constituted the play-ground. It was level, and covered with fine hard gravel. I well remember it had no trees, nor benches, nor any thing similar within it. Of course it was in the rear of the house. In front lay a small parterre, planted with box and other shrubs, but through this sacred division we passed only upon rare occasions indeed—such as a first advent to school or final departure thence, or perhaps, when a parent or friend having called for us, we joyfully took our way home for the Christmas or Midsummer holidays.

But the house!—how quaint an old building was this!—to me how veritably a palace of enchantment! There was really no end to its windings—to its incomprehensible subdivisions. It was difficult, at any given time, to say with certainty upon which of its two stories one happened to be. From each room to every other there were sure to be found three or four steps either in ascent or descent. Then the lateral branches were innumerable—inconceivable—and so returning in upon themselves, that our most exact ideas in regard to the whole mansion were not very far different from these with which we pondered upon infinity. During the five years of my residence here, I was never able to ascertain with precision, in what remote locality lay the little sleeping apartment assigned to myself and some eighteen or twenty other scholars.

The school-room was the largest in the house—I could not help thinking, in the world. It was very long, narrow, and dismally low, with pointed Gothic windows and a ceiling of oak. In a remote and terror-inspiring angle was a square enclosure of eight or ten feet, comprising the *sanctum,* "during hours," of our principal, the Reverend Dr. Bransby. It was a solid structure, with massy door, sooner than open which in the absence of the "Dominie," we would all have willingly perished by the *peine forte et dure.*[4] In other angles were two other similar boxes, far less reverenced, indeed, but still greatly matters of awe. One of these was the pulpit of the "classical" usher, one of the "English and mathematical." Interspersed about the room, crossing and recrossing in endless irregularity, were innumerable benches and desks, black, ancient, and time-worn, piled desperately with much bethumbed books, and so beseamed with initial letters, names at full length, grotesque figures, and other multiplied efforts of the knife, as to have entirely lost what little of original form might have been their portion in days long departed. A huge bucket with water stood at one extremity of the room, and a clock of stupendous dimensions at the other.

Encompassed by the massy walls of this venerable academy, I passed, yet not in tedium or disgust, the years of the third lustrum[5] of my life. The teeming brain of childhood requires no external world of incident to occupy or amuse it; and the apparently dismal monotony of a school was replete with more intense excitement than my riper youth has derived from luxury, or my full manhood from crime. Yet I must believe that my first mental development had in it much of the uncommon—even much of the *outré.*[6] Upon mankind at large the events of very early existence rarely leave in mature age any definite impression. All is gray shadow—a weak and irregular remembrance—an indistinct regathering of feeble pleasures and phantasmagoric pains. With me this is not

so. In childhood I must have felt with the energy of a
man what I now find stamped upon memory in lines as
vivid, as deep, and as durable as the *exergues* of the
Carthaginian medals.[7]

Yet in fact—in the fact of the world's view—how little
was there to remember! The morning's awakening, the
nightly summons to bed; the connings,[8] the recitations;
the periodical half-holidays, and perambulations; the
play-ground, with its broils, its pastimes, its intrigues;—
these, by a mental sorcery long forgotten, were made to
involve a wilderness of sensation, a world of rich incident, an universe of varied emotion, of excitement the
most passionate and spirit-stirring. *"Oh, le bon temps,
que ce siècle de fer!"*[9]

In truth, the ardor, the enthusiasm, and the imperi-
ousness of my disposition, soon rendered me a marked
character among my schoolmates, and by slow, but natural gradations, gave me an ascendency over all not
greatly older than myself;—over all with a single exception. This exception was found in the person of a scholar,
who, although no relation, bore the same Christian and
surname as myself;—a circumstance, in fact, little remarkable; for, notwithstanding a noble descent, mine
was one of those everyday appellations which seem, by
prescriptive right, to have been, time out of mind, the
common property of the mob. In this narrative I have
therefore designated myself as William Wilson,—a ficti-
tious title not very dissimilar to the real. My namesake
alone, of those who in school phraseology constituted
"our set," presumed to compete with me in the studies of
the class—in the sports and broils of the play-ground—
to refuse implicit belief in my assertions, and submission

to my will—indeed, to interfere with my arbitrary dictation in any respect whatsoever. If there is on earth a supreme and unqualified despotism, it is the despotism of a mastermind in boyhood over the less energetic spirits of its companions.

Wilson's rebellion was to me a source of the greatest embarrassment; the more so as, in spite of the bravado with which in public I made a point of treating him and his pretensions, I secretly felt that I feared him, and could not help thinking the equality which he maintained so easily with myself, a proof of his true superiority; since not to be overcome, cost me a perpetual struggle. Yet this superiority—even this equality—was in truth acknowledged by no one but myself; our associates, by some unaccountable blindness, seemed not even to suspect it. Indeed, his competition, his resistance, and especially his impertinent and dogged interference with my purposes, were not more pointed than private. He appeared to be destitute alike of the ambition which urged, and of the passionate energy of mind which enabled me to excel. In his rivalry he might have been supposed actuated solely by a whimsical desire to thwart, astonish, or mortify myself; although there were times when I could not help observing, with a feeling made up of wonder, abasement, and pique, that he mingled with his injuries, his insults, or his contradictions, a certain most inappropriate, and assuredly most unwelcome *affectionateness* of manner. I could only conceive this singular behavior to arise from a consummate self-conceit assuming the vulgar airs of patronage and protection.

Perhaps it was this latter trait in Wilson's conduct, conjoined with our identity of name, and the mere accident of our having entered the school upon the same day, which set afloat the notion that we were brothers, among the senior classes in the academy. These do not usually inquire with much strictness into the affairs of their juniors. I have before said, or should have said, that Wilson was not, in a most remote degree, connected with my family. But assuredly if we *had* been brothers we must have been twins; for, after leaving Dr. Bransby's, I casually learned that my namesake was born on the nineteenth of January, 1831—and this is a somewhat remarkable coincidence; for the day is precisely that of my own nativity.

It may seem strange that in spite of the continual anxiety occasioned me by the rivalry of Wilson, and his intolerable spirit of contradiction, I could not bring myself to hate him altogether. We had, to be sure, nearly every day a quarrel in which, yielding me publicly the palm of victory, he, in some manner, contrived to make me feel that it was he who had deserved it; yet a sense of pride on my part, and a veritable dignity on his own, kept us always upon what are called "speaking terms," while there were many points of strong congeniality in our tempers, operating to awake in me a sentiment which our position alone, perhaps, prevented from ripening into friendship. It is difficult, indeed, to define, or even to describe, my real feelings toward him. They formed a motley and heterogeneous admixture;—some petulant animosity, which was not yet hatred, some esteem, more respect, much fear, with a world of uneasy curiosity. To the moralist it will be necessary to say, in addition, that Wilson and myself were the most inseparable of companions.

It was no doubt the anomalous state of affairs existing

between us, which turned all my attacks upon him (and there were many, either open or covert) into the channel of banter or practical joke (giving pain while assuming the aspect of mere fun) rather than into a more serious and determined hostility. But my endeavors on this head were by no means uniformly successful, even when my plans were the most wittily concocted; for my namesake had much about him, in character, of that unassuming and quiet austerity which, while enjoying the poignancy of its own jokes, has no heel of Achilles in itself, and absolutely refuses to be laughed at. I could find, indeed, but one vulnerable point, and that, lying in a personal peculiarity, arising, perhaps, from constitutional disease, would have been spared by any antagonist less at his wit's end than myself;—my rival had a weakness in the faucial or guttural organs, which precluded him from raising his voice at any time *above a very low whisper.* Of this defect I did not fail to take what poor advantage lay in my power.

Wilson's retaliations in kind were many; and there was one form of his practical wit that disturbed me beyond measure. How his sagacity first discovered at all that so petty a thing would vex me, is a question I never could solve; but having discovered, he habitually practised the annoyance. I had always felt aversion to my uncourtly patronymic, and its very common, if not plebeian prænomen. The words were venom in my ears; and when, upon the day of my arrival, a second William Wilson came also to the academy, I felt angry with him for bearing the name, and doubly disgusted with the name because a stranger bore it, who would be the cause of its two-fold repetition, who would be constantly in my presence, and whose concerns, in the ordinary routine of the school business, must inevitably, on account of the detestable coincidence, be often confounded with my own.

The feeling of vexation thus engendered grew stronger with every circumstance tending to show resemblance, moral or physical, between my rival and myself. I had not then discovered the remarkable fact that we were of the same age; but I saw that we were of the same height, and I perceived that we were even singularly alike in general contour of person and outline of feature. I was galled, too, by the rumor touching a relationship, which had grown current in the upper forms. In a word, nothing could more seriously disturb me (although I scrupulously concealed such disturbance) than any allusion to a similarity of mind, person, or condition existing between us. But, in truth, I had no reason to believe that (with the exception of the matter of relationship, and in the case of Wilson himself) this similarity had ever been made a subject of comment, or even observed at all by our schoolfellows. That *he* observed it in all its bearings, and as fixedly as I, was apparent; but that he could discover in such circumstances so fruitful a field of annoyance, can only be attributed, as I said before, to his more than ordinary penetration.

His cue, which was to perfect an imitation of myself, lay both in words and in actions; and most admirably did he play his part. My dress it was an easy matter to copy; my gait and general manner were without difficulty, appropriated; in spite of his constitutional defect, even my voice did not escape him. My louder tones were, of course, unattempted, but then the key,—it was identical;

*and his singular whisper, it grew the very echo of my
own.*

How greatly this most exquisite portraiture harassed
me (for it could not justly be termed a caricature), I will
not now venture to describe. I had but one consolation—
in the fact that the imitation, apparently, was noticed by
myself alone, and that I had to endure only the knowing
and strangely sarcastic smiles of my namesake himself.
Satisfied with having produced in my bosom the intended effect, he seemed to chuckle in secret over the
sting he had inflicted, and was characteristically disre-
gardful of the public applause which the success of his
witty endeavors might have so easily elicited. That the
school, indeed, did not feel his design, perceive its ac-
complishment, and participate in his sneer, was, for
many anxious months, a riddle I could not resolve. Perhaps the *gradation* of his copy rendered it not readily
perceptible; or, more possibly, I owed my security to the
masterly air of the copyist, who, disdaining the letter
(which in a painting is all the obtuse can see), gave but
the full spirit of his original for my individual contemplation and chagrin.

I have already more than once spoken of the disgust-
ing air of patronage which he assumed toward me, and of
his frequent officious interference with my will. This interference often took the ungracious character of advice;
advice not openly given, but hinted or insinuated. I received it with a repugnance which gained strength as I
grew in years. Yet, at this distant day, let me do him the
simple justice to acknowledge that I can recall no occasion when the suggestions of my rival were on the side of
those errors or follies so usual to his immature age and

seeming inexperience; that his moral sense, at least, if not his general talents and worldly wisdom, was far keener than my own; and that I might, to-day, have been a better and thus a happier man, had I less frequently rejected the counsels embodied in those meaning whispers which I then but too cordially hated and too bitterly despised.

As it was I at length grew restive in the extreme under his distasteful supervision, and daily resented more and more openly, what I considered his intolerable arrogance. I have said that, in the first years of our connection as schoolmates, my feelings in regard to him might have been easily ripened into friendship; but, in the latter months of my residence at the academy, although the intrusion of his ordinary manner had, beyond doubt, in some measure, abated, my sentiments, in nearly similar proportion, partook very much of positive hatred. Upon one occasion he saw this, I think, and afterward avoided, or made a show of avoiding me.

It was about the same period, if I remember aright, that, in an altercation of violence with him, in which he was more than usually thrown off his guard, and spoke and acted with an openness of demeanor rather foreign to his nature, I discovered, or fancied I discovered, in his accent, in his air, and general appearance, a something which first startled, and then deeply interested me, by bringing to mind dim visions of my earliest infancy—wild, confused, and thronging memories of a time when memory herself was yet unborn. I cannot better describe the sensation which oppressed me, than by saying that I could with difficulty shake off the belief of my having been acquainted with the being who stood before me, at some epoch very long ago—some point of the past even infinitely remote. The delusion, however, faded rapidly as it came; and I mention it at all but to define the day of the last conversation I there held with my singular namesake.

The huge old house, with its countless subdivisions, had several large chambers communicating with each other, where slept the greater number of the students. There were, however (as must necessarily happen in a building so awkwardly planned), many little nooks or recesses, the odds and ends of the structure; and these the economic ingenuity of Dr. Bransby had also fitted up as dormitories; although, being the merest closets, they were capable of accommodating but a single individual. One of these small apartments was occupied by Wilson.

One night, about the close of my fifth year at the school, and immediately after the altercation just mentioned, finding every one wrapped in sleep, I arose from bed, and, lamp in hand, stole through a wilderness of narrow passages, from my own bedroom to that of my rival. I had long been plotting one of those ill-natured pieces of practical wit at his expense in which I had hitherto been so uniformly unsuccessful. It was my intention, now, to put my scheme in operation and I resolved to make him feel the whole extent of the malice with which I was imbued. Having reached his closet, I noiselessly entered, leaving the lamp, with a shade over it, on the outside. I advanced a step and listened to the sound of his tranquil breathing. Assured of his being asleep, I returned, took the light, and with it again approached the bed. Close curtains were around it, which, in the prosecution of my plan, I slowly and quietly withdrew, when the bright rays fell vividly upon the sleeper, and my eyes at the same moment, upon his countenance. I looked;—and a numbness, an iciness of feeling instantly pervaded my frame. My breast heaved, my knees tottered, my whole spirit became possessed with an objectless yet intolerable horror. Gasping for breath, I lowered the lamp in still nearer proximity to the face. Were these—*these* the lineaments of William Wilson? I saw, indeed, that they were his, but I shook as if with a fit of the ague, in fancying they were not. What *was* there about them to confound me in this manner? I gazed;—while my brain reeled with a multitude of incoherent thoughts. Not thus he appeared—assuredly not *thus*—in the vivacity of his waking hours. The same name! the same contour of person! the same day of arrival at the academy! And then his dogged and meaningless imitation of my gait, my voice, my habits, and my manner! Was it, in truth, within the bounds of human possibility, that *what I now saw* was the result, merely, of the habitual practice of this sarcastic imitation? Awe-stricken, and with a creeping shudder, I extinguished the lamp, passed silently from the chamber, and left, at once, the halls of that old academy, never to enter them again.

After a lapse of some months, spent at home in mere idleness, I found myself a student at Eton. The brief interval had been sufficient to enfeeble my remembrance of the events at Dr. Bransby's, or at least to effect a material change in the nature of the feelings with which I remembered them. The truth—the tragedy—of the drama was no more. I could now find room to doubt the evidence of my senses; and seldom called up the subject at all but with wonder at the extent of human credulity, and a smile at the vivid force of the imagination which I hereditarily possessed. Neither was this species of skepticism likely to be diminished by the character of the life I led at Eton. The vortex of thoughtless folly into which I there so immediately and so recklessly plunged, washed away all but the froth of my past hours, ingulfed at once every solid or serious impression, and left to memory only the veriest levities of a former existence.

I do not wish, however, to trace the course of my miserable profligacy here—a profligacy which set at defiance the laws, while it eluded the vigilance of the institution. Three years of folly, passed without profit, had but given me rooted habits of vice, and added, in a somewhat unusual degree, to my bodily stature, when, after a week of soulless dissipation, I invited a small party of the most dissolute students to a secret carousal in my chambers. We met at a late hour of the night; for our debaucheries were to be faithfully protracted until morning. The wine flowed freely, and there were not wanting other and perhaps more dangerous seductions; so that the gray dawn had already faintly appeared in the east while our delirious extravagance was at its height. Madly flushed with cards and intoxication, I was in the act of insisting upon a toast of more than wonted profanity, when my attention was suddenly diverted by the violent, although partial, unclosing of the door of the apartment, and by the eager voice of a servant from without. He said that some person, apparently in great haste, demanded to speak with me in the hall.

Wildly excited with wine, the unexpected interruption rather delighted than surprised me. I staggered forward at once, and a few steps brought me to the vestibule of the building. In this low and small room there hung no lamp; and now no light at all was admitted, save that of the exceedingly feeble dawn which made its way through the semi-circular window. As I put my foot over the threshold, I became aware of the figure of a youth about my own height, and habited in a white kerseymere[10] morning frock, cut in the novel fashion of the one I myself wore at the moment. This the faint light enabled me to perceive; but the features of his face I could not distinguish. Upon my entering, he strode hurriedly up to me, and, seizing me by the arm with a gesture of petulant impatience, whispered the words "William Wilson" in my ear.

I grew perfectly sober in an instant.

There was that in the manner of the stranger, and in the tremulous shake of his uplifted finger, as he held it between my eyes and the light, which filled me with unqualified amazement; but it was not this which had so violently moved me. It was the pregnancy of solemn admonition in the singular, low, hissing utterance; and, above all, it was the character, the tone, *the key,* of those few, simple, and familiar, yet *whispered* syllables, which came with a thousand thronging memories of by-gone days, and struck upon my soul with the shock of a galvanic battery. Ere I could recover the use of my senses he was gone.

Although this event failed not of a vivid effect upon my disordered imagination, yet was it evanescent as vivid. For some weeks, indeed, I busied myself in earnest enquiry, or was wrapped in a cloud of morbid speculation. I did not pretend to disguise from my perception the identity of the singular individual who thus perse-

veringly interfered with my affairs, and harassed me
with his insinuated counsel. But who and what was this
Wilson?—and whence came he?—and what were his
purposes? Upon neither of these points could I be satisfied—merely ascertaining, in regard to him, that a sudden accident in his family had caused his removal from
Dr. Bransby's academy on the afternoon of the day in
which I myself had eloped. But in a brief period I ceased
to think upon the subject, my attention being all absorbed in a contemplated departure for Oxford. Thither
I soon went, the uncalculating vanity of my parents furnishing me with an outfit and annual establishment,
which would enable me to indulge at will in the luxury
already so dear to my heart—to vie in profuseness of ex-
penditure with the haughtiest heirs of the wealthiest
earldoms in Great Britain.

Excited by such appliances to vice, my constitutional
temperament broke forth with redoubled ardor, and I
spurned even the common restraints of decency in the
mad infatuation of my revels. But it were absurd to
pause in the detail of my extravagance. Let it suffice, that
among spendthrifts I out-Heroded Herod,[11] and that,
giving name to a multitude of novel follies, I added no
brief appendix to the long catalogue of vices then usual
in the most dissolute university of Europe.

It could hardly be credited, however, that I had, even
here, so utterly fallen from the gentlemanly estate, as to
seek acquaintance with the vilest arts of the gambler by
profession, and, having become an adept in his despica-
ble science, to practice it habitually as a means of increasing my already enormous income at the expense of
the weak-minded among my fellow-collegians. Such,

nevertheless, was the fact. And the very enormity of this offence against all manly and honorable sentiment proved, beyond doubt, the main if not the sole reason of the impunity with which it was committed. Who, indeed, among my most abandoned associates, would not rather have disputed the clearest evidence of his senses, than have suspected of such courses, the gay, the frank, the generous William Wilson—the noblest and most liberal commoner at Oxford—him whose follies (said his parasites) were but the follies of youth and unbridled fancy—whose errors but inimitable whim—whose darkest vice but a careless and dashing extravagance?

I had been now two years successfully busied in this way, when there came to the university a young *parvenu*[12] nobleman, Glendinning—rich, said report, as Herodes Atticus[13]—his riches, too, as easily acquired. I soon found him of weak intellect, and, of course, marked him as a fitting subject for my skill. I frequently engaged him in play, and contrived, with the gambler's usual art, to let him win considerable sums, the more effectually to entangle him in my snares. At length, my schemes being ripe, I met him (with the full intention that this meeting should be final and decisive) at the chambers of a fellow-commoner (Mr. Preston), equally intimate with both, but who, to do him justice, entertained not even a remote suspicion of my design. To give to this a better coloring, I had contrived to have assembled a party of some eight or ten, and was solicitously careful that the introduction of cards should appear accidental, and originate in the proposal of my contemplated dupe himself. To be brief upon a vile topic, none of the low finesse was omitted, so customary upon similar occasions, that it is a just matter for wonder how any are still found so besotted as to fall its victim.

We had protracted our sitting far into the night, and I had at length effected the manœuvre of getting Glendinning as my sole antagonist. The game, too, was my favorite *écarté*.[14] The rest of the company, interested in the extent of our play, had abandoned their own cards, and were standing around us as spectators. The *parvenu*, who had been induced by my artifices in the early part of the evening, to drink deeply, now shuffled, dealt, or played, with a wild nervousness of manner for which his intoxication, I thought, might partially, but could not altogether account. In a very short period he had become my debtor to a large amount, when, having taken a long draught of port, he did precisely what I had been coolly anticipating—he proposed to double our already extravagant stakes. With a well-feigned show of reluctance, and not until after my repeated refusal had seduced him into some angry words which gave a color of *pique* to my compliance, did I finally comply. The result, of course, did but prove how entirely the prey was in my toils: in less than an hour he had quadrupled his debt. For some time his countenance had been losing the florid tinge lent it by the wine; but now, to my astonishment, I perceived that it had grown to a pallor truly fearful. I say, to my astonishment. Glendinning had been represented to my eager inquiries as immeasurably wealthy; and the sums which he had as yet lost, although in themselves vast, could not, I supposed, very seriously annoy, much less so violently affect him. That he was overcome by the wine just swallowed, was the idea which most readily presented itself; and, rather with a view to the preserva-

tion of my own character in the eyes of my associates,
than from any less interested motive, I was about to insist, peremptorily, upon a discontinuance of the play,
when some expressions at my elbow from among the
company, and an ejaculation evincing utter despair on
the part of Glendinning, gave me to understand that I
had effected his total ruin under circumstances which,
rendering him an object for the pity of all, should have
protected him from the ill offices even of a fiend.

What now might have been my conduct it is difficult
to say. The pitiable condition of my dupe had thrown an
air of embarrassed gloom over all; and, for some moments, a profound silence was maintained, during which
I could not help feeling my cheeks tingle with the many
burning glances of scorn or reproach cast upon me by
the less abandoned of the party. I will even own that an
intolerable weight of anxiety was for a brief instant lifted
from my bosom by the sudden and extraordinary interruption which ensued. The wide, heavy folding doors of
the apartment were all at once thrown open, to their full
extent, with a vigorous and rushing impetuosity that extinguished, as if by magic, every candle in the room.
Their light, in dying, enabled us just to perceive that a
stranger had entered, about my own height, and closely
muffled in a cloak. The darkness, however, was not total;
and we could only *feel* that he was standing in our midst.
Before any one of us could recover from the extreme astonishment into which this rudeness had thrown all, we
heard the voice of the intruder.

"Gentlemen," he said, in a low, distinct, and never-to-
be-forgotten *whisper* which thrilled to the very marrow
of my bones, "gentlemen, I make an apology for this be-

havior because in thus behaving, I am fulfilling a duty. You are, beyond doubt, uninformed of the true character of the person who has to-night won at *écarté* a large sum of money from Lord Glendinning. I will therefore put you upon an expeditious and decisive plan of obtaining this very necessary information. Please to examine, at your leisure, the inner linings of the cuff of his left sleeve, and the several little packages which may be found in the somewhat capacious pockets of his embroidered morning wrapper."

While he spoke, so profound was the stillness that one might have heard a pin drop upon the floor. In ceasing, he departed at once, and as abruptly as he had entered. Can I—shall I describe my sensations? Must I say that I felt all the horrors of the damned? Most assuredly I had little time for reflection. Many hands roughly seized me upon the spot, and lights were immediately reprocured. A search ensued. In the lining of my sleeve were found all the court cards essential in *écarté,* and, in the pockets of my wrapper, a number of packs, fac-similes of those used at our sittings, with the single exception that mine were of the species called, technically, *arrondis;*[15] the honors being slightly convex at the ends, the lower cards slightly convex at the sides. In this disposition, the dupe who cuts, as customary, at the length of the pack, will invariably find that he cuts his antagonist an honor; while the gambler, cutting at the breadth, will, as certainly, cut nothing for his victim which may count in the records of the game.

Any burst of indignation upon this discovery would have affected me less than the silent contempt, or the sarcastic composure with which it was received.

"Mr. Wilson," said our host, stooping to remove from beneath his feet an exceedingly luxurious cloak of rare furs, "Mr. Wilson, this is your property." (The weather was cold; and, upon quitting my own room, I had thrown a cloak over my dressing wrapper, putting it off upon reaching the scene of play.) "I presume it is supererogatory to seek here (eyeing the folds of the garment with a bitter smile) for any farther evidence of your skill. Indeed, we have had enough. You will see the necessity, I hope, of quitting Oxford—at all events, of quitting instantly my chambers."

Abased, humbled to the dust as I then was, it is probable that I should have resented this galling language by immediate personal violence, had not my whole attention been at the moment arrested by a fact of the most startling character. The cloak which I had worn was of a rare description of fur; how rare, how extravagantly costly, I shall not venture to say. Its fashion, too, was of my own fantastic invention; for I was fastidious to an absurd degree of coxcombry, in matters of this frivolous nature. When, therefore, Mr. Preston reached me that which he had picked up upon the floor, and near the folding-doors of the apartment, it was with an astonishment nearly bordering upon terror, that I perceived my own already hanging on my arm (where I had no doubt unwittingly placed it), and that the one presented me was but its exact counterpart in every, in even the minutest possible particular. The singular being who had so disastrously exposed me, had been muffled, I remembered, in a cloak; and none had been worn at all by any of the members of our party, with the exception of myself. Retaining some presence of mind, I took the one offered me by Preston; placed it, unnoticed, over my own; left the apartment with a resolute scowl of defiance; and, next morning ere dawn of day, commenced a hurried journey from Oxford to the continent, in a perfect agony of horror and of shame.

I fled in vain. My evil destiny pursued me as if in exultation, and proved, indeed, that the exercise of its mysterious dominion had as yet only begun. Scarcely had I set foot in Paris, ere I had fresh evidence of the detestable interest taken by this Wilson in my concerns. Years flew, while I experienced no relief. Villain!—at Rome, with how untimely, yet with how spectral an officiousness, stepped he in between me and my ambition! at Vienna, too—at Berlin—and at Moscow! Where, in truth, had I *not* bitter cause to curse him within my heart? From his inscrutable tyranny did I at length flee, panic-stricken, as from a pestilence; and to the very ends of the earth *I fled in vain.*

And again, and again, in secret communion with my own spirit, would I demand the questions "Who is he?—whence came he?—and what are his objects?" But no answer was there found. And now I scrutinized, with a minute scrutiny, the forms, and the methods, and the leading traits of his impertinent supervision. But even here there was very little upon which to base a conjecture. It was noticeable, indeed, that, in no one of the multiplied instances in which he had of late crossed my path, had he so crossed it except to frustrate those schemes, or to disturb those actions, which, if fully carried out, might have resulted in bitter mischief. Poor justification this, in truth, for an authority so imperiously assumed! Poor indemnity for natural rights of self-agency so pertinaciously, so insultingly denied!

I had also been forced to notice that my tormentor, for a very long period of time (while scrupulously and with miraculous dexterity maintaining his whim of an identity of apparel with myself) had so contrived it, in the execution of his varied interference with my will, that I saw not, at any moment, the features of his face. Be Wilson what he might, *this*, at least, was but the veriest of affectation, or of folly. Could he, for an instant, have supposed that, in my admonisher at Eton—in the destroyer of my honor at Oxford,—in him who thwarted my ambition at Rome, my revenge at Paris, my passionate love at Naples, or what he falsely termed my avarice in Egypt,—that in this, my arch-enemy and evil genius, I could fail to recognize the William Wilson of my schoolboy days,—the namesake, the companion, the rival,— the hated and dreaded rival at Dr. Bransby's? Impossible!—But let me hasten to the last eventful scene of the drama.

Thus far I had succumbed supinely to this imperious domination. The sentiment of deep awe with which I habitually regarded the elevated character, the majestic wisdom, the apparent omnipresence and omnipotence of Wilson, added to a feeling of even terror, with which certain other traits in his nature and assumptions inspired me, had operated, hitherto, to impress me with an idea of my own utter weakness and helplessness, and to suggest an implicit, although bitterly reluctant submission to his arbitrary will. But, of late days, I had given myself up entirely to wine; and its maddening influence upon my hereditary temper rendered me more and more impatient of control. I began to murmur,—to hesitate,—to resist. And was it only fancy which induced me to believe that, with the increase of my own firmness, that of my tormentor underwent a proportional diminution? Be this as it may, I now began to feel the inspiration of a burning hope, and at length nurtured in my secret thoughts a stern and desperate resolution that I would submit no longer to be enslaved.

It was at Rome, during the Carnival of 18—, that I attended a masquerade in the palazzo of the Neapolitan Duke Di Broglio. I had indulged more freely than usual in the excesses of the wine-table; and now the suffocating atmosphere of the crowded rooms irritated me beyond endurance. The difficulty, too, of forcing my way through the mazes of the company contributed not a little to the ruffling of my temper; for I was anxiously seeking (let me not say with what unworthy motive) the young, the gay, the beautiful wife of the aged and doting Di Broglio. With a too unscrupulous confidence she had previously communicated to me the secret of the costume in which she would be habited, and now, having caught a glimpse of her person, I was hurrying to make my way into her presence. At this moment I felt a light hand placed upon my shoulder, and that ever-remembered, low, damnable *whisper* within my ear.

In an absolute frenzy of wrath, I turned at once upon him who had thus interrupted me, and seized him violently by the collar. He was attired, as I had expected, in a costume altogether similar to my own; wearing a Spanish cloak of blue velvet, begirt about the waist with a crimson belt sustaining a rapier. A mask of black silk entirely covered his face.

"Scoundrel!" I said, in a voice husky with rage, while every syllable I uttered seemed as new fuel to my fury; "scoundrel! impostor! accursed villain! you shall not— you *shall not* dog me unto death! Follow me, or I stab you where you stand!"—and I broke my way from the ballroom into a small antechamber adjoining, dragging him unresistingly with me as I went.

Upon entering, I thrust him furiously from me. He staggered against the wall, while I closed the door with an oath, and commanded him to draw. He hesitated but for an instant; then, with a slight sigh, drew in silence, and put himself upon his defence.

The contest was brief indeed. I was frantic with every species of wild excitement, and felt within my single arm the energy and power of a multitude. In a few seconds I forced him by sheer strength against the wainscotting, and thus, getting him at mercy, plunged my sword, with brute ferocity, repeatedly through and through his bosom.

At that instant some person tried the latch of the door. I hastened to prevent an intrusion, and then immediately returned to my dying antagonist. But what human language can adequately portray *that* astonishment, *that* horror which possessed me at the spectacle then presented to view? The brief moment in which I averted my eyes had been sufficient to produce, apparently, a material change in the arrangements at the upper or farther end of the room. A large mirror,—so at first it seemed to me in my confusion—now stood where none had been perceptible before; and as I stepped up to it in extremity of terror, mine own image, but with features all pale and dabbled in blood, advanced to meet me with a feeble and tottering gait.

Thus it appeared, I say, but was not. It was my antagonist—it was Wilson, who then stood before me in the agonies of his dissolution. His mask and cloak lay, where he had thrown them, upon the floor. Not a thread in all his raiment—not a line in all the marked and singular lineaments of his face which was not, even in the most absolute identity, *mine own!*

It was Wilson; but he spoke no longer in a whisper, and I could have fancied that I myself was speaking while he said:

"You have conquered, and I yield. Yet henceforward art thou also dead—dead to the World, to Heaven, and to Hope! In me didst thou exist—and, in my death, see by this image, which is thine own, how utterly thou hast murdered thyself."

POEMS

THE RAVEN[1]

Once upon a midnight dreary, while I pondered, weak
and weary,
Over many a quaint and curious volume of forgotten
lore—
While I nodded, nearly napping, suddenly there came
a tapping,
As of some one gently rapping, rapping at my chamber
door.
" 'Tis some visitor," I muttered, "tapping at my
chamber door—

　　　　　　　Only this and nothing more."

Ah, distinctly I remember it was in the bleak December,
And each separate dying ember wrought its ghost upon
the floor.
Eagerly I wished the morrow;—vainly I had sought to
borrow

From my books surcease[2] of sorrow—sorrow for the
　　lost Lenore—
For the rare and radiant maiden whom the angels
　　name Lenore—
　　　　　　　　Nameless here for evermore.

And the silken sad uncertain rustling of each purple
　　curtain
Thrilled me—filled me with fantastic terrors never felt
　　before;
So that now, to still the beating of my heart, I stood
　　repeating:
" 'Tis some visitor entreating entrance at my chamber
　　door—
Some late visitor entreating entrance at my chamber
　　door;
　　　　　　　　This it is and nothing more."

Presently my soul grew stronger; hesitating then no
　　longer,
"Sir," said I, "or Madam, truly your forgiveness I
　　implore;
But the fact is I was napping, and so gently you came
　　rapping,
And so faintly you came tapping, tapping at my
　　chamber door,
That I scarce was sure I heard you"—here I opened
　　wide the door;—
　　　　　　　　Darkness there and nothing more.

Deep into that darkness peering, long I stood there
　　wondering, fearing,

Doubting, dreaming dreams no mortals ever dared to
    dream before;
But the silence was unbroken, and the stillness gave no
    token,
And the only word there spoken was the whispered
    word, "Lenore!"
This I whispered, and an echo murmured back the
    word, "Lenore!"—
                     Merely this and nothing more.

Back into the chamber turning, all my soul within me
    burning,
Soon again I heard a tapping something louder than
    before.
"Surely," said I, "surely that is something at my window
    lattice;
Let me see, then, what thereat is, and this mystery
    explore—
Let my heart be still a moment, and this mystery explore;—
                 'Tis the wind and nothing more."

Open here I flung the shutter, when, with many a flirt
    and flutter,
In there stepped a stately Raven of the saintly days of
    yore.
Not the least obeisance made he; not a minute stopped
    or stayed he,
But, with mien of lord or lady, perched above my
    chamber door—
Perched upon a bust of Pallas[3] just above my chamber
    door—
                 Perched, and sat, and nothing more.

Then this ebony bird beguiling my sad fancy into smiling,
By the grave and stern decorum of the countenance it
  wore,
"Though thy crest be shorn and shaven, thou," I said,
  "art sure no craven,[4]
Ghastly grim and ancient Raven wandering from the
  Nightly shore—
Tell me what thy lordly name is on the Night's
  Plutonian[5] shore!"
                        Quoth the Raven, "Nevermore."

Much I marvelled this ungainly fowl to hear discourse
  so plainly,
Though its answer little meaning—little relevancy
  bore;
For we cannot help agreeing that no living human
  being
Ever yet was blessed with seeing bird above his
  chamber door—
Bird or beast upon the sculptured bust above his
  chamber door,
                        With such name as "Nevermore."

But the Raven, sitting lonely on that placid bust, spoke
  only
That one word, as if his soul in that one word he did
  outpour.
Nothing farther then he uttered; not a feather then he
  fluttered—
Till I scarcely more than muttered: "Other friends have
  flown before—

On the morrow *he* will leave me as my Hopes have
  flown before."

> Then the bird said, "Nevermore."

Startled at the stillness broken by reply so aptly spoken,
"Doubtless," said I, "what it utters is its only stock and
  store,
Caught from some unhappy master whom unmerciful
  Disaster
Followed fast and followed faster till his songs one
  burden bore—
Till the dirges of his Hope that melancholy burden
  bore

> Of 'Never—nevermore.' "

But the Raven still beguiling all my sad soul into smiling,
Straight I wheeled a cushioned seat in front of bird and
  bust and door;
Then, upon the velvet sinking, I betook myself to linking
Fancy unto fancy, thinking what this ominous bird of
  yore —
What this grim, ungainly, ghastly, gaunt, and ominous
  bird of yore

> Meant in croaking "Nevermore."

This I sat engaged in guessing, but no syllable
  expressing
To the fowl whose fiery eyes now burned into my
  bosom's core;
This and more I sat divining, with my head at ease
  reclining

On the cushion's velvet lining that the lamp-light
 gloated o'er,
But whose velvet violet lining with the lamp-light
 gloating[6] o'er
She shall press, ah, nevermore!

Then, methought, the air grew denser, perfumed from
 an unseen censer[7]
Swung by Seraphim whose foot-falls tinkled on the
 tufted floor.
"Wretch," I cried, "thy God hath lent thee—by these
 angels he hath sent thee
Respite—respite and nepenthe[8] from thy memories of
 Lenore!
Quaff, oh quaff this kind nepenthe and forget this lost
 Lenore!"
Quoth the Raven, "Nevermore."

"Prophet!" said I, "thing of evil!—prophet still, if bird
 or devil!—
Whether Tempter sent, or whether tempest tossed
 thee here ashore,
Desolate, yet all undaunted, on this desert land
 enchanted—
On this home by Horror haunted,—tell me truly, I
 implore—
Is there—*is* there balm in Gilead?[9]—tell me—tell me,
 I implore!"
Quoth the Raven, "Nevermore."

"Prophet!" said I, "thing of evil!—prophet still, if bird
 or devil!

By that heaven that bends above us—by that God we
    both adore—
Tell this soul with sorrow laden if, within the distant
    Aidenn,[10]
It shall clasp a sainted maiden whom the angels name
    Lenore—
Clasp a rare and radiant maiden whom the angels
    name Lenore."
                    Quoth the Raven, "Nevermore."

"Be that word our sign of parting, bird or fiend!" I
    shrieked, upstarting—
"Get thee back into the tempest and the Night's
    Plutonian shore!
Leave no black plume as a token of that lie thy soul
    hath spoken!
Leave my loneliness unbroken!—quit the bust above
    my door!
Take thy beak from out my heart, and take thy form
    from off my door!"
                    Quoth the Raven, "Nevermore."

And the Raven, never flitting, still is sitting, still is
    sitting
On the pallid bust of Pallas just above my chamber door;
And his eyes have all the seeming of a demon's that is
    dreaming,
And the lamp-light o'er him streaming throws his
    shadow on the floor;
And my soul from out that shadow that lies floating on
    the floor
                    Shall be lifted—nevermore!

LENORE[1]

Ah, broken is the golden bowl! the spirit flown forever!
Let the bell toll!—a saintly soul floats on the Stygian[2]
    river;
And, Guy De Vere,[3] hast *thou* no tear?—weep now or
    never more!
See on yon drear and rigid bier low lies thy love,
    Lenore!
Come! let the burial rite be read—the funeral song be
    sung!—
An anthem for the queenliest dead that ever died so
    young—
A dirge for her the doubly dead in that she died so young.

"Wretches! ye loved her for her wealth and hated her
    for her pride,
And when she fell in feeble health, ye blessed her—
    that she died!
How *shall* the ritual, then, be read?—the requiem how
    be sung
By you—by yours, the evil eye,—by yours, the
    slanderous tongue
That did to death the innocence that died, and died so
    young?"

Peccavimus;[4] but rave not thus! and let a Sabbath song
Go up to God so solemnly the dead may feel no wrong!
The sweet Lenore hath "gone before," with Hope, that
    flew beside,
Leaving thee wild for the dear child that should have
    been thy bride—

For her, the fair and *debonnaire*,[5] that now so lowly
  lies,
The life upon her yellow hair but not within her eyes—
The life still there, upon her hair—the death upon her
  eyes.

Avaunt! to-night my heart is light. No dirge will I
  upraise,
But waft the angel on her flight with a pœan of old
  days!
Let *no* bell toll!—lest her sweet soul, amid its hallowed
  mirth,
Should catch the note, as it doth float up from the
  damnèd Earth.
To friends above, from fiends below, the indignant
  ghost is riven—
From Hell unto a high estate far up within the
  Heaven—
From grief and groan, to a golden throne, beside the
  King of Heaven.

To Helen[1]

I saw thee once[2]—once only—years ago;
I must not say *how* many—but *not* many.
It was a July midnight; and from out
A full-orbed moon, that, like thine own soul, soaring,
Sought a precipitate pathway up through heaven,
There fell a silvery-silken veil of light,
With quietude, and sultriness, and slumber,
Upon the upturn'd faces of a thousand

Roses that grew in an enchanted garden,
Where no wind dared to stir, unless on tiptoe—
Fell on the upturn'd faces of these roses
That gave out, in return for the love-light,
Their odorous souls in an ecstatic death—
Fell on the upturn'd faces of these roses
That smiled and died in this parterre,[3] enchanted
By thee, and by the poetry of thy presence.

Clad all in white, upon a violet bank
I saw thee half reclining; while the moon
Fell on the upturn'd faces of the roses,
And on thine own, upturn'd—alas, in sorrow!

Was it not Fate that, on this July midnight—
Was it not Fate (whose name is also Sorrow),
That bade me pause before that garden-gate,
To breathe the incense of those slumbering roses?
No footsteps stirred; the hated world all slept,
Save only thee and me. (Oh, Heaven!—oh, God!
How my heart beats in coupling those two words!)
Save only thee and me. I paused—I looked—
And in an instant all things disappeared.
(Ah, bear in mind this garden was enchanted!)

The pearly lustre of the moon went out;
The mossy banks and the meandering paths,
The happy flowers and the repining trees,
Were seen no more: the very roses' odors
Died in the arms of the adoring airs.
All—all expired save thee—save less than thou:
Save only the divine light in thine eyes—

Save but the soul in thine uplifted eyes.
I saw but them—they were the world to me.
I saw but them—saw only them for hours—
Saw only them until the moon went down.
What wild heart-histories seemed to lie enwritten
Upon those crystalline, celestial spheres!
How dark a woe! yet how sublime a hope!
How silently serene a sea of pride!
How daring an ambition! yet how deep—
How fathomless a capacity for love!

But now, at length dear Dian[4] sank from sight,
Into a western couch of thunder-cloud;
And thou, a ghost, amid the entombing trees
Didst glide away. *Only thine eyes remained.*
They *would not* go—they never yet have gone.
Lighting my lonely pathway home that night,
They have not left me (as my hopes have) since.

They follow me—they lead me through the years.
They are my ministers—yet I their slave.
Their office is to illumine and enkindle—
My duty, *to be saved* by their bright light,
And purified in their electric fire,
And sanctified in their Elysian fire.[5]
They fill my soul with Beauty (which is Hope),
And are far up in heaven—the stars I kneel to
In the sad, silent watches of my night;
While even in the meridian glare of day
I see them still—two sweetly scintillant
Venuses, unextinguished by the sun!

ULALUME[1]

The skies they were ashen and sober;
    The leaves they were crisped and sere[2]—
    The leaves they were withering and sere;
It was night in the lonesome October
    Of my most immemorial year;
It was hard by the dim lake of Auber,[3]
    In the misty mid region of Weir[4]—
It was down by the dank tarn of Auber,
    In the ghoul-haunted woodland of Weir.

Here once, through an alley Titanic,
    Of cypress, I roamed with my Soul—
    Of cypress, with Psyche,[5] my Soul.
These were days when my heart was volcanic
    As the scoriac[6] rivers that roll—
    As the lavas that restlessly roll
Their sulphurous currents down Yaanek[7]
    In the ultimate climes of the pole—
That groan as they roll down Mount Yaanek
    In the realms of the boreal[8] pole.

Our talk had been serious and sober,
    But our thoughts they were palsied and sere—
    Our memories were treacherous and sere,—
For we knew not the month was October,
    And we marked not the night of the year
    (Ah, night of all nights in the year!)—
We noted not the dim lake of Auber
    (Though once we had journeyed down here)—

Remembered not the dank tarn of Auber,
    Nor the ghoul-haunted woodland of Weir.

And now, as the night was senescent
    And star-dials[9] pointed to morn—
    As the star-dials hinted of morn—
At the end of our path a liquescent
    And nebulous lustre was born,
Out of which a miraculous crescent
    Arose with a duplicate horn—
Astarte's[10] bediamonded crescent
    Distinct with its duplicate horn.

And I said: "She is warmer than Dian:
    She rolls through an ether of sighs—
    She revels in a region of sighs:
She has seen that the tears are not dry on
    These cheeks, where the worm never dies,
And has come past the stars of the Lion[11]
    To point us the path to the skies
    To the Lethean[12] peace of the skies—
Come up, in despite of the Lion,
    To shine on us with her bright eyes—
Come up through the lair of the Lion,
    With love in her luminous eyes."

But Psyche, uplifting her finger,
    Said: "Sadly this star I mistrust—
    Her pallor I strangely mistrust:—
Oh, hasten!—oh, let us not linger!
    Oh, fly!—let us fly!—for we must."

In terror she spoke, letting sink her
    Wings until they trailed in the dust—
In agony sobbed, letting sink her
    Plumes till they trailed in the dust—
    Till they sorrowfully trailed in the dust.

I replied: "This is nothing but dreaming:
    Let us on by this tremulous light!
    Let us bathe in this crystalline light!
Its Sibylic[13] splendor is beaming
    With Hope and in Beauty to-night! —
    See!—it flickers up the sky through the night!
Ah, we safely may trust to its gleaming,
    And be sure it will lead us aright—
We safely may trust to a gleaming,
    That cannot but guide us aright,
    Since it flickers up to Heaven through the night."

Thus I pacified Psyche and kissed her,
    And tempted her out of her gloom—
    And conquered her scruples and gloom;
And we passed to the end of the vista,
    But were stopped by the door of a tomb—
    By the door of a legended tomb;
And I said: "What is written, sweet sister,
    On the door of this legended tomb?"
    She replied: "Ulalume—Ulalume—
    'Tis the vault of thy lost Ulalume!"

Then my heart it grew ashen and sober
    As the leaves that were crisped and sere—
    As the leaves that were withering and sere,

And I cried: "It was surely October
   On *this* very night of last year
   That I journeyed—I journeyed down here—
   That I brought a dread burden down here—
   On this night of all nights in the year,
   Ah, what demon has tempted me here?
Well I know, now, this dim lake of Auber—
   This misty mid region of Weir—
Well I know, now, this dank tarn of Auber,
   This ghoul-haunted woodland of Weir."

THE BELLS[1]

I

Hear the sledges[2] with the bells—
    Silver bells!
What a world of merriment their melody foretells!
    How they tinkle, tinkle, tinkle,
      In the icy air of night!
    While the stars that oversprinkle
    All the heavens seems to twinkle
      With a crystalline delight;
    Keeping time, time, time,
    In a sort of Runic[3] rhyme,
To the tintinnabulation[4] that so musically wells
    From the bells, bells, bells, bells,
      Bells, bells, bells—
From the jingling and the tinkling of the bells.

II

Hear the mellow wedding bells,
Golden bells!
What a world of happiness their harmony foretells!
Through the balmy air of night
How they ring out their delight!
From the molten-golden notes,
And all in tune,
What a liquid ditty floats
To the turtle-dove that listens, while she gloats[5]
On the moon!
Oh, from out the sounding cells
What a gush of euphony voluminously wells!
How it swells!
How it dwells
On the Future! how it tells
Of the rapture that impels
To the swinging and the ringing
Of the bells, bells, bells,
Of the bells, bells, bells, bells,
Bells, bells, bells—
To the rhyming and the chiming of the bells!

III

Hear the loud alarum bells—
Brazen[6] bells!
What a tale of terror, now, their turbulency tells!
In the startled ear of night
How they scream out their affright!
Too much horrified to speak,
They can only shriek, shriek,
Out of tune,

In a clamorous appealing to the mercy of the fire,
In a mad expostulation with the deaf and frantic fire,
Leaping higher, higher, higher,
With a desperate desire,
And a resolute endeavor
Now—now to sit, or never,
By the side of the pale-faced moon.
Oh, the bells, bells, bells!
What a tale their terror tells
Of despair!
How they clang, and clash, and roar!
What a horror they outpour
On the bosom of the palpitating air!
Yet the ear it fully knows,
By the twanging,
And the clanging,
How the danger ebbs and flows;
Yet the ear distinctly tells,
In the jangling,
And the wrangling,
How the danger sinks and swells,
By the sinking or the swelling in the anger of the bells—
Of the bells—
Of the bells, bells, bells, bells,
Bells, bells, bells—
In the clamor and the clangor of the bells!

IV

Hear the tolling of the bells—
Iron bells!
What a world of solemn thought their melody compels!
In the silence of the night,

How we shiver with affright
At the melancholy menace of their tone!
For every sound that floats
From the rust within their throats
Is a groan.
And the people—ah, the people—
They that dwell up in the steeple,
All alone,
And who tolling, tolling, tolling,
In that muffled monotone,
Feel a glory in so rolling
On the human heart a stone—
They are neither man nor woman—
They are neither brute nor human—
They are Ghouls:
And their king it is who tolls;
And he rolls, rolls, rolls,
Rolls
A pæan[7] from the bells!
And his merry bosom swells
With the pæan of the bells!
And he dances, and he yells;
Keeping time, time, time,
In a sort of Runic rhyme,
To the pæan of the bells—
Of the bells:
Keeping time, time, time.
In a sort of Runic rhyme,
To the throbbing of the bells—
Of the bells, bells, bells—
To the sobbing of the bells;

Keeping time, time, time,
   As he knells,[8] knells, knells,
In a happy Runic rhyme,
   To the rolling of the bells—
Of the bells, bells, bells—
   To the tolling of the bells,
Of the bells, bells, bells, bells—
   Bells, bells, bells—
To the moaning and the groaning of the bells.

ANNABEL LEE[1]

It was many and many a year ago,
   In a kingdom by the sea,
That a maiden there lived whom you may know
   By the name of ANNABEL LEE;
And this maiden she lived with no other thought
   Than to love and be loved by me.

I was a child and *she* was a child,
   In this kingdom by the sea:
But we loved with a love that was more than love—
   I and my ANNABEL LEE;
With a love that the winged seraphs[2] of heaven
   Coveted her and me.

And this was the reason that, long ago,
   In this kingdom by the sea,
A wind blew out of a cloud, chilling
   My beautiful ANNABEL LEE;

So that her high-born kinsman came
    And bore her away from me,
To shut her up in a sepulchre[3]
    In this kingdom by the sea.

The angels, not half so happy in heaven,
    Went envying her and me—
Yes!—that was the reason (as all men know,
    In this kingdom by the sea)
That the wind came out of the cloud by night,
    Chilling and killing my ANNABEL LEE.

But our love it was stronger by far than the love
    Of those who were older than we—
    Of many far wiser than we—
And neither the angels in heaven above,
    Nor the demons down under the sea,
Can ever dissever my soul from the soul
    Of the beautiful ANNABEL LEE.

For the moon never beams, without bringing me
    dreams
    Of the beautiful ANNABEL LEE;
And the stars never rise, but I feel the bright eyes
    Of the beautiful ANNABEL LEE;
And so, all the night-tide, I lie down by the side
Of my darling—my darling—my life and my bride,
    In the sepulchre there by the sea,
    In her tomb by the sounding sea.

To ——————[1]

I heed not that my earthly lot
    Hath little of earth in it—
That years of love have been forgot
    In the hatred of a minute:—
I mourn not that the desolate
    Are happier, sweet, than I,
But that *you* sorrow for *my* fate
    Who am a passer by.

THE VALLEY OF UNREST[1]

Once it smiled a silent dell
Where the people did not dwell:
They had gone unto the wars,
Trusting to the mild-eyed stars,
Nightly from their azure towers,
To keep watch above the flowers,
In the midst of which all day
The red sunlight lazily lay.
Now each visitor shall confess
The sad valley's restlessness.
Nothing there is motionless—
Nothing save the airs that brood
Over the magic solitude.
Ah, by no wind are stirred those trees
That palpitate like the chill seas
Around the misty Hebrides![2]
Ah, by no wind those clouds are driven
That rustle through the unquiet Heaven

Uneasily, from morn till even,
Over the violets there that lie
In myriad types of the human eye—
Over the lilies there that wave
And weep above a nameless grave!
They wave:—from out their fragrant tops
Eternal dews come down in drops.
They weep:—from off their delicate stems
Perennial tears descend in gems.

THE CITY IN THE SEA[1]

Lo! Death has reared himself a throne
In a strange city lying alone
Far down within the dim West
Where the good and the bad and the worst and the
    best
Have gone to their eternal rest.
There shrines and palaces and towers
(Time-eaten towers that tremble not!)
Resemble nothing that is ours.
Around, by lifting winds forgot,
Resignedly beneath the sky
The melancholy waters lie.

No rays from the holy Heaven come down
On the long night-time of that town;
But light from out the lurid sea
Streams up the turrets silently—
Gleams up the pinnacles far and free—
Up domes—up spires—up kingly halls—

Up fanes—up Babylon-like[2] walls—
Up shadowy long-forgotten bowers
Of sculptured ivy and stone flowers—
Up many and many a marvellous shrine
Whose wreathéd friezes[3] intertwine
The viol, the violet, and the vine.
Resignedly beneath the sky
The melancholy waters lie.
So blend the turrets and shadows there
That all seem pendulous in air,
While from a proud tower in the town
Death looks gigantically down.

There open fanes and gaping graves
Yawn level with the luminous waves;
But not the riches there that lie
In each idol's diamond eye—
Not the gayly-jewelled dead
Tempt the waters from their bed;
For no ripples curl, alas!
Along that wilderness of glass—
No swellings tell that winds may be
Upon some far-off happier sea—
No heavings hint that winds have been
On seas less hideously serene.

But lo, a stir is in the air!
The wave—there is a movement there!
As if the towers had thrust aside,
In slightly sinking, the dull tide—
As if their tops had feebly given
A void within the filmy Heaven.

The waves have now a redder glow—
The hours are breathing faint and low—
And when, amid no earthly moans,
Down, down that town shall settle hence,
Hell, rising from a thousand thrones,
Shall do it reverence.

THE SLEEPER[1]

At midnight, in the month of June,
I stand beneath the mystic moon.
An opiate vapor, dewy, dim,
Exhales from out her golden rim,
And, softly dripping, drop by drop,
Upon the quiet mountain top,
Steals drowsily and musically
Into the universal valley.
The rosemary nods upon the grave;
The lily lolls upon the wave;
Wrapping the fog about its breast,
The ruin moulders into rest;
Looking like Lethe,[2] see! the lake
A conscious slumber seems to take,
And would not, for the world, awake.
All Beauty sleeps!—and lo! where lies
(Her casement open to the skies)
Irene, with her Destinies!

Oh, lady bright! can it be right—
This window open to the night?
The wanton airs, from the tree-top,

Laughingly through the lattice drop—
The bodiless airs, a wizard rout,
Flit through thy chamber in and out,
And wave the curtain canopy
So fitfully—so carefully—
Above the closed and fringéd lid
'Neath which thy slumb'ring soul lies hid,[3]
That, o'er the floor and down the wall,
Like ghosts the shadows rise and fall!
Oh, lady dear, hast thou no fear?
Why and what art thou dreaming here?
Sure thou art come o'er far-off seas,
A wonder to these garden trees!
Strange is thy pallor! strange thy dress!
Strange, above all, thy length of tress.[4]
And this all solemn silentness!

The lady sleeps! On, may her sleep,
Which is enduring, so be deep!
Heaven have her in its sacred keep!
This chamber changed for one more holy,
This bed for one more melancholy,
I pray to God that she may lie
Forever with unopened eye,
While the dim sheeted ghosts go by!

My love, she sleeps! Oh, may her sleep,
As it is lasting, so be deep!
Soft may the worms about her creep!
Far in the forest, dim and old,
For her may some tall vault unfold—
Some vault that oft hath flung its black

And winged panels fluttering back,
Triumphant, o'er the crested palls,
Of her grand family funerals—
Some sepulchre, remote, alone,
Against whose portal she hath thrown,
In childhood, many an idle stone—
Some tomb from out whose sounding door
She ne'er shall force an echo more,
Thrilling to think, poor child of sin!
It was the dead who groaned within.

A DREAM WITHIN A DREAM[1]

Take this kiss upon the brow!
And, in parting from you now,
Thus much let me avow—
You are not wrong, who deem
That my days have been a dream;
Yet if hope has flown away
In a night, or in a day,
In a vision, or in none,
Is it therefore the less *gone?*
All that we see or seem
Is but a dream within a dream.

I stand amid the roar
Of a surf-tormented shore.
And I hold within my hand
Grains of the golden sand—
How few! yet how they creep
Through my fingers to the deep,

While I weep—while I weep!
O God! can I not grasp
Them with a tighter clasp?
O God! can I not save
One from the pitiless wave?
Is *all* that we see or seem
But a dream within a dream?

DREAM-LAND[1]

By a route obscure and lonely,
Haunted by ill[2] angels only,
Where an Eidolon,[3] named NIGHT,
On a black throne reigns upright,
I have reached these lands but newly
From an ultimate dim Thule[4]—
From a wild weird clime that lieth, sublime.
          Out of SPACE—out of TIME.

Bottomless vales and boundless floods,
And chasms, and caves, and Titan woods,
With forms that no man can discover
For the dews that drip all over;
Mountains toppling evermore
Into seas without a shore;
Seas that restlessly aspire,
Surging, unto skies of fire;
Lakes that endlessly outspread
Their lone waters—lone and dead,—
Their still waters—still and chilly
With the snows of the lolling lily.

By the lakes that thus outspread
Their lone waters, lone and dead,—
Their sad waters, sad and chilly
With the snows of the lolling lily,—
By the mountains—near the river
Murmuring lowly, murmuring ever,—
By the gray woods,—by the swamp
Where the toad and the newt encamp,—
By the dismal tarns and pools
    Where dwell the Ghouls,—
By each spot the most unholy—
In each nook most melancholy,—
There the traveller meets aghast
Sheeted Memories of the Past—
Shrouded forms that start and sigh
As they pass the wanderer by—
White-robed forms of friends long given,
In agony, to the Earth—and Heaven.

For the heart whose woes are legion
'Tis a peaceful, soothing region—
For the spirit that walks in shadow
'Tis—oh, 'tis an Eldorado![5]
But the traveller, travelling through it,
May not—dare not openly view it;
Never its mysteries are exposed
To the weak human eye unclosed;
So wills its King, who hath forbid
The uplifting of the fringed lid;
And thus the sad Soul that here passes
Beholds it but through darkened glasses.[6]

By a route obscure and lonely,
Haunted by ill angels only,
Where an Eidolon, named Night,
On a black throne reigns upright,
I have wandered home but newly
From this ultimate dim Thule.

Dreams[1]

Oh! that my young life were a lasting dream!
My spirit not awakening, till the beam
Of an Eternity should bring the morrow.
Yes! though that long dream were of hopeless sorrow,
'Twere better than the cold reality
Of waking life, to him whose heart must be,
And hath been still, upon the lovely earth,
A chaos of deep passion, from his birth.
But should it be—that dream eternally
Continuing—as dreams have been to me
In my young boyhood—should it thus be given,
'Twere folly still to hope for higher Heaven.
For I have revelled when the sun was bright
I' the summer sky, in dreams of living light
And loveliness—have left my very heart
In climes of mine imagining, apart
From mine own home, with beings that have been
Of mine own thought—what more could I have seen?
'Twas once—and only once—and the wild hour
From my remembrance shall not pass—some power
Or spell had bound me—'twas the chilly wind

Came o'er me in the night, and left behind
Its image on my spirit—or the moon
Shone on my slumbers in her lofty noon
Too coldly—or the stars—howe'er it was
That dream was as that night-wind—let it pass.
I have been happy, though in a dream.
I have been happy—and I love the theme
Dreams! in their vivid coloring of life
As in that fleeting, shadowy, misty strife
Of semblance with reality which brings
To the delirious eye, more lovely things
Of Paradise and Love—and all my own!—
Than young Hope in his sunniest hour hath known.

SILENCE[1]

There are some qualities—some incorporate things,
    That have a double life, which thus is made
A type of that twin entity which springs
    From matter and light, evinced in solid and shade.
There is a twofold *Silence*—sea and shore—
    Body and soul. One dwells in lonely places,
    Newly with grass o'ergrown; some solemn graces,
Some human memories and tearful lore,
Render him terrorless; his name's "No More."
He is the corporate[2] Silence: dread him not!
    No power hath he of evil in himself;
But should some urgent fate (untimely lot!)
    Bring thee to meet his shadow (nameless elf,
That haunteth the lone regions where hath trod
No foot of man), commend thyself to God!

ELDORADO[1]

Gaily bedight,
  A gallant knight,
In sunshine and in shadow,
  Had journeyed long,
  Singing a song,
In search of Eldorado.

But he grew old—
  This knight so bold—
And o'er his heart a shadow
  Fell as he found
  No spot of ground
That looked like Eldorado.

And, as his strength
  Failed him at length,
He met a pilgrim shadow—
  "Shadow," said he,
  "Where can it be—
This land of Eldorado?"

"Over the Mountains
  Of the Moon,[2]
Down the Valley of the Shadow,[3]
  Ride, boldly ride,"
  The shade replied,—
"If you seek for Eldorado!"

ISRAFEL*[1]

In Heaven a spirit doth dwell
"Whose heart-strings are a lute";
None sing so wildly well
As the angel Israfel,
And the giddy stars (so legends tell)
Ceasing their hymns, attend the spell
    Of his voice, all mute.

Tottering above
    In her highest noon,
    The enamored moon
Blushes with love,
    While, to listen, the red levin[2]
    (With the rapid Pleiads,[3] even,
    Which were seven)
    Pauses in Heaven.

And they say (the starry choir
    And the other listening things)
That Israfeli's fire
Is owing to that lyre
    By which he sits and sings—
The trembling living wire
    Of those unusual strings.

But the skies that angel trod,
    Where deep thoughts are a duty—

---

* And the angel Israfel, whose heart-strings are a lute, and who has the sweetest voice of all God's creatures.—KORAN.

Where Love's a grown-up God[4]—
    Where the Houri[5] glances are
Imbued with all the beauty
    Which we worship in a star.

Therefore, thou art not wrong,
    Israfeli, who despisest
An unimpassioned song;
To thee the laurels belong,
    Best bard, because the wisest!
Merrily live, and long!

The ecstasies above
    With thy burning measures suit—
Thy grief, thy joy, thy hate, thy love,
    With the fervor of thy lute—
    Well may the stars be mute!

Yes, Heaven is thine; but this
    Is a world of sweets and sours;
    Our flowers are merely—flowers,
And the shadow of thy perfect bliss
    Is the sunshine of ours.

If I could dwell
Where Israfel
    Hath dwelt, and he where I,
He might not sing so wildly well
    A mortal melody,
While a bolder note than this might swell
    From my lyre within the sky.

FOR ANNIE[1]

Thank Heaven! the crisis—
    The danger is past,
And the lingering illness
    Is over at last—
And the fever called "Living"
    Is conquered at last.
Sadly I know
    I am shorn of my strength,
And no muscle I move
    As I lie at full length—
But no matter!—I feel
    I am better at length.

And I rest so composed,
    Now, in my bed,
That any beholder
    Might fancy me dead—
Might start at beholding me,
    Thinking me dead.
The moaning and groaning,
    The sighing and sobbing,
Are quieted now,
    With that horrible throbbing
At heart:—ah, that horrible,
    Horrible throbbing!
The sickness—the nausea—
    The pitiless pain—
Have ceased, with the fever
    That maddened my brain—

With the fever called "Living"
   That burned in my brain.

And oh! of all tortures
   That torture the worst
Has abated—the terrible
   Torture of thirst
For the naphthaline[2] river
   Of Passion accurst:—
I have drunk of a water
   That quenches all thirst:—

Of a water that flows,
   With a lullaby sound,
From a spring but a very few
   Feet under ground—
From a cavern not very far
   Down under ground.

And ah! let it never
   Be foolishly said
That my room it is gloomy
   And narrow my bed;
For man never slept
   In a different bed—
And, to *sleep*, you must slumber
   In just such a bed.

My tantalized[3] spirit
   Here blandly reposes,
Forgetting, or never

    Regretting, its roses—
Its old agitations
    Of myrtles and roses:

For now, while so quietly
    Lying, it fancies
A holier odor
    About it, of pansies—
A rosemary odor,
    Commingled with pansies—
With rue[4] and the beautiful
    Puritan pansies.

And so it lies happily,
    Bathing in many
A dream of the truth
    And the beauty of Annie—
Drowned in a bath
    Of the tresses of Annie.

She tenderly kissed me,
    She fondly caressed,
And then I fell gently
    To sleep on her breast—
Deeply to sleep
    From the heaven of her breast.

When the light was extinguished
    She covered me warm,
And she prayed to the angels
    To keep me from harm—

To the queen of the angels[5]
    To shield me from harm.

And I lie so composedly,
    Now in my bed,
(Knowing her love,)
    That you fancy me dead—
And I rest so contentedly,
    Now in my bed,
(With her love at my breast,)
    That you fancy me dead—
That you shudder to look at me,
    Thinking me dead:—

But my heart is brighter
    Than all of the many
Stars in the sky,
    For it sparkles with Annie—
It glows with the light
    Of the love of my Annie—
With the thought of the light
    Of the eyes of my Annie.

SONNET—TO SCIENCE[1]

Science! true daughter of Old Time thou art!
    Who alterest all things with thy peering eyes.
Why preyest thou thus upon the poet's heart,
    Vulture, whose wings are dull realities?
How should he love thee? or how deem thee wise?

Who wouldst not leave him in his wandering
To seek for treasure in the jewelled skies,
    Albeit he soared with an undaunted wing?
Hast thou not dragged Diana from her car?[2]
    And driven the Hamadryad[3] from the wood
To seek a shelter in some happier star?
    Hast thou not torn the Naiad[4] from her flood,
The Elfin from the green grass, and from me
The summer dream beneath the tamarind tree?

A DREAM[1]

In visions of the dark night
    I have dreamed of joy departed;
But a waking dream of life and light
    Hath left me broken-hearted.

Ah! what is not a dream by day
    To him whose eyes are cast
On things around him, with a ray
    Turned back upon the past?

That holy dream, that holy dream,
    While all the world were chiding,
Hath cheered me as a lovely beam
    A lonely spirit guiding.

What though that light, thro' storm and night,
    So trembled from afar—
What could there be more purely bright
    In Truth's day-star?[2]

To ———[1]

The bowers whereat, in dreams, I see
　　The wantonest singing birds,
Are lips—and all thy melody
　　Of lip-begotten words—

Thine eyes, in Heaven of heart enshrined
　　Then desolately fall,
O God! on my funereal mind
Like starlight on a pall—

Thy heart—*thy* heart!—I wake and sigh,
　　And sleep to dream till day
Of the truth that gold can never buy—
　　Of the baubles that it may.

ROMANCE[1]

Romance, who loves to nod and sing,
　　With drowsy head and folded wing,
Among the green leaves as they shake
Far down within some shadowy lake
　　To me a painted paroquet[2]
Hath been—a most familiar bird—
　　Taught me my alphabet to say,
To lisp my very earliest word
While in the wild wood I did lie,
A child—with a most knowing eye.

Of late, eternal Condor years
　　So shake the very Heaven on high
　　With tumult as they thunder by,

I have no time for idle cares
　　Through gazing on the unquiet sky.
And when an hour with calmer wings
Its down upon my spirit flings—
That little time with lyre and rhyme
　　To while away—forbidden things!
My heart would feel to be a crime
　　Unless it trembled with the strings.

Spirits of the Dead[1]

Thy soul shall find itself alone
'Mid dark thoughts of the gray tombstone—
Not one, of all the crowd, to pry
Into thine hour of secrecy.

Be silent in that solitude
　　Which is not loneliness, for then
The spirits of the dead who stood
　　In life before thee are again
In death around thee, and their will
Shall overshadow thee: be still.

The night, tho' clear, shall frown,
And the stars shall not look down
From their high thrones in the Heaven
With light like Hope to mortals given;
But their red orbs, without beam,
To thy weariness shall seem

As a burning and a fever
Which would cling to thee forever.

Now are thoughts thou shalt not banish—
Now are visions ne'er to vanish;
From thy spirit shall they pass
No more—like dew-drops from the grass.

The breeze—the breath of God—is still,
And the mist upon the hill
Shadowy—shadowy—yet unbroken,
Is a symbol and a token,—
How it hangs upon the trees,
A mystery of mysteries!

To Helen[1]

Helen, thy beauty is to me
   Like those Nicean[2] barks of yore,
That gently, o'er a perfumed sea,
   The weary, way-worn wanderer bore
   To his own native shore.

On desperate seas long wont to roam,
   Thy hyacinth hair, thy classic face,
Thy Naiad[3] airs have brought me home
   To the glory that was Greece
And the grandeur that was Rome.

Lo! in yon brilliant window-niche
   How statue-like I see thee stand!
   The agate[4] lamp within thy hand,
Ah! Psyche,[5] from the regions which
   Are Holy Land!

EVENING STAR[1]

'Twas noontide of summer,
    And midtime of night,
And stars, in their orbits,
    Shone pale, through the light
Of the brighter, cold moon,
    'Mid planets her slaves,
Herself in the Heavens,
    Her beam on the waves.

I gazed awhile
    On her cold smile;
Too cold—too cold for me—
    There passed, as a shroud,
    A fleecy cloud,
And I turned away to thee,
    Proud Evening Star,
    In thy glory afar
And dearer thy beam shall be;
    For joy to my heart
    Is the proud part
Thou bearest in Heaven at night,
    And more I admire
    Thy distant fire,
Than that colder, lowly light.

ALONE[1]

From childhood's hour I have not been
As others were—I have not seen
As others saw—I could not bring
My passions from a common spring.
From the same source I have not taken
My sorrow; I could not awaken
My heart to joy at the same tone;
And all I lov'd, *I* lov'd alone.
Then—in my childhood—in the dawn
Of a most stormy life—was drawn
From ev'ry depth of good and ill
The mystery which binds me still:
From the torrent, or the fountain,
From the red cliff of the mountain,
From the sun that 'round me roll'd
In its autumn tint of gold—
From the lightning in the sky
As it pass'd me flying by—
From the thunder and the storm,
And the cloud that took the form
(When the rest of Heaven was blue)
Of a demon in my view.

NOTES

<u>TALES</u>

The Tell-Tale Heart

1. **The Tell-Tale Heart:** Originally published in January 1843 in *The Pioneer* magazine; Poe revised the tale and published it again in *The Broadway Journal*, August 23, 1845.
2. **death watches:** A species of beetle, so called because their presence in walls (they can be heard gnawing on wood) is taken to be an omen of impending death.
3. **scantlings:** Small timbers supporting a floor.

The Cask of Amontillado

1. **The Cask of Amontillado:** This story was first published in *Godey's Lady's Book*, November 1846.
2. **a pipe of . . . Amontillado:** Amontillado is a Span-

ish sherry, which Poe possibly thought was Italian. Montresor imagines a pipe, or large cask, of amontillado to be a sufficient lure to get Fortunato to accompany him into his wine cellar.

3. **nitre:** Potassium nitrate, which covers walls of caverns in gray-white crystalline deposits and is used to make gunpowder.

4. *roquelaire:* A knee-length cape. Montresor, like Fortunato, is in costume for the carnival.

5. **Medoc:** A French red wine.

6. *Nemo me impune lacessit:* Latin: "No one provokes me with impunity."

7. **puncheons:** Large casks.

8. **De Grâve:** Another type of French red wine; Montresor is having a joke with himself about his plans for Fortunato.

9. *In pace requiescat!:* Latin: "May he rest in peace!" Montresor's revelation that he is telling this story fifty years later and his use of the Latin prayer suggests that he is telling it on his deathbed, perhaps to soothe a guilty conscience.

The Black Cat

1. **The Black Cat:** First published in the *United States Saturday Post,* August 19, 1843.

2. *baroques:* Extravagant or grotesque stories.

3. **Pluto:** Roman god of the underworld.

4. **Intemperance:** The excessive consumption of alcohol.

Ligeia

1. **Ligeia:** First published in the Baltimore *American Museum*, September 1838.

2. **Joseph Glanvill:** English clergyman and philosopher (1636–1680). Scholars have been unable to locate this passage in Glanvill's work.

3. *Ashtophet:* Poe is probably referring to the Phoenician goddess of fertility, Astarte.

4. **Delos:** Greek island presided over by the god Apollo and his sister, Artemis.

5. **"There is no exquisite beauty . . . without some strangeness in the proportion":** Poe is paraphrasing slightly from the essay "Of Beauty" by Francis Bacon, Lord Verulam, Viscount St. Albans. "There is no excellent beauty that hath not some strangeness in the proportion."

6. **Cleomenes:** Greek sculptor whose statue of the goddess Venus was supposedly inspired by a divine vision of Apollo.

7. **Nourjahad:** A reference to the novel *The History of Nourjahad* (1767), about a harem-keeping prince, by Frances Sheridan.

8. **Houri:** In Muslim mythology, the virgins who await men in heaven; "houri" literally refers to their dark eyes.

9. **Democritus:** Greek philosopher (c. 460–370 B.C.) known for his inquiries into the structure of matter, astronomy, and ethics. The saying "truth lies at the bottom of a well," meaning the truth is hidden, is attributed to Democritus.

10. **Leda:** Mother of Castor and Pollux, twins who were

fathered by Zeus. Castor and Pollux are also the names of two stars in the constellation Gemini.

11. **Lyra:** Constellation whose name means "the lyre" or "the harp." The large star in Lyra is Vega, the second brightest in the Northern Hemisphere. Lyra contains several binary star systems.

12. **Saturnian lead:** This is a reference to Ligeia's interest in alchemy, an occult science that was the precursor to chemistry. Alchemists tried to turn matter from one form to another, most famously lead into gold.

13. **Azrael:** Muslim angel of death.

The Masque of the Red Death

1. **The Masque of the Red Death:** Originally published in *Graham's Magazine*, May 1842.

2. **Avatar:** Originally a reference to the human incarnation of a Hindu god; here meaning its manifestation or sign.

3. **pest ban:** First visible signs of the disease.

4. **improvisatori:** Performers who improvise songs and poems.

5. **decora:** Plural of "decorum," here meaning the rules of style.

6. **"Hernani":** Controversial play by Victor Hugo that was greeted with rioting at its premiere in 1830.

7. **out-Heroded Herod:** Herod, ruler of Palestine, was known for his extravagance as well as his cruelty. This line alludes to William Shakespeare's *Hamlet*, where Hamlet utters the same words referring to bad actors.

8. **habiliments:** Garments.

9. **mummer:** A pantomime performer.

10. **thief in the night:** 1 Thessalonians 5:2–3 contains one of several references to the Lord returning like a "thief in the night": ". . . then sudden destruction cometh upon them . . . and they shall not escape."

The Fall of the House of Usher

1. **The Fall of the House of Usher:** Originally published in *Burton's Gentleman's Magazine*, September 1839.

2. **Son cœur est . . . —De Béranger:** "His heart is like a suspended lute; as soon as it is touched it resonates." These lines are derived from "Le Refus," a poem written in 1830 by Pierre-Jean de Béranger (1780–1857), a French poet and songwriter.

3. **direct line of descent:** The narrator is referring to the Ushers' habit of inbreeding.

4. *ennuyé:* Bored; suffering from ennui.

5. **affections of . . . cataleptical:** She has fits during which she becomes rigid, like a corpse.

6. **ideality:** A reference to the Romantic idea of a transcendent level of ideal or pure thought. Usher's ideality is corrupted by his line of study.

7. **Von Weber:** German Romantic composer Carl Maria von Weber (1786–1826).

8. **Fuseli:** Swiss-born painter Henry Fuseli (1741–1825), best known for his two paintings entitled *The Nightmare*.

9. **seraph spread a pinion:** A seraph is the highest-ranking order of angel in the Judeo-Christian hier-

archy, each possessing two or three pairs of pinions, or wings.

10. **Porphyrogene!:** Greek: "born in the purple." The color purple has long been associated with royalty, and so a porphyrogene is one born into royalty.

11. **Watson, Dr. Percival . . . See "Chemical Essays," vol. v:** Note added here by Poe to lend credibility to Usher's poem. Richard Watson (1737–1816) was a British theologian, who became the Bishop of Llandaff; Percival was probably a Dr. Thomas Percival (1740–1804), the author of *Medical Ethics* (1803); Lazzaro Spallanzani (1729–1799) was an Italian professor of natural history.

12. **We pored together . . . Campanella:** Jean-Baptiste-Louis Gresset (1709–1777), a French poet and dramatist, two of whose poems were "Vert-Vert" and "La Chartreuse;" "Belphegor," or "Belfagor arcidiavolo," by Niccolò Machiavelli (1469–1527), is a satirical novella about men and women; Emanuel Swedenborg (1688–1772) was a Swedish mystical philosopher; Ludvig Holberg (1684–1754) was a Danish historian and playwright; Flud, or Robert Fludd, was a practitioner of palm-reading, or chiromancy, as were Jean D'Indaginé and Marin Cureau de la Chambre, and all three wrote volumes under that title; Ludwig Tieck (1773–1853) was a German Romantic poet, dramatist, and fiction writer; Tomasso Campanella (1568–1639) was the author of the utopian *City of the Sun*.

13. ***Directorium* . . . *Œgipans*:** Nicolas Eymeric was the grand inquisitor of Aragon beginning in 1356; his *Directorium Inquisitorium* contained instructions for interrogating heretics. Pomponius Mela

was a Roman geographer who described a variety of strange creatures in faraway lands, including the goatlike Œgipans.

14. **Vigilæ . . . Maguntinæ:** "The Vigils of the Dead According to the Church of Mainz."

15. **donjon-keep:** A dungeon.

16. **"Mad Trist" of Sir Launcelot Canning:** Unlike Usher's other books, critics consider this one an invention of Poe's.

17. **doughty:** Resolute; fearless.

18. **alarumed:** Made an alarm or call to arms.

The Murders in the Rue Morgue

1. **The Murders in the Rue Morgue:** Originally published in *Graham's Magazine*, April 1841.

2. **What song . . . —Sir Thomas Browne:** From Browne's essay *Hydriotaphia, or Urn-Burial*.

3. **draughts:** Checkers.

4. **involute:** Intricate; involved.

5. *recherché:* Exotic or refined.

6. **whist:** A card game played with partners, similar to bridge.

7. **Hoyle:** Edmond Hoyle (1672–1769), author of *A Short Treatise on the Game of Whist*.

8. **phrenologists:** Believers in a pseudoscience, popular in the nineteenth century (Poe makes frequent reference to it), premised on the belief that the shape of the skull corresponds to aspects of a person's character.

9. *Théâtre des Variétés:* A theater that produces variety shows.

10. *quondam:* Latin: "former."

11. **Crébillon's tragedy:** Prosper Jolyot de Crébillon (1674–1762) was a French dramatist, author of *Xerxes* (1714).

12. **Pasquinaded:** To be publicly mocked. From the Piazza di Pasquino, a piazza in Rome where satirists posted lampoons of public figures.

13. *et id genus omne:* Latin: "and all that sort of thing."

14. *charlatânerie:* The act of perpetrating a fraud; charlatanism.

15. *rencontre:* Encounter, sometimes hostile.

16. **Dr. Nichols:** A reference to astronomer J. P. Nichol, author of *Views of the Architecture of the Heavens in a Series of Letters to a Lady* (1837).

17. **stereotomy:** The science of stonecutting.

18. **Epicurus:** Greek philosopher (341–270 B.C.) who taught that all matter is made up of atoms floating in space.

19. *Perdidit antiquum litera prima sonum:* Poe gives a quote from the Roman poet Ovid's *Fasti:* "The first letter has lost its original sound."

20. **Napoleons:** Twenty-franc gold coins.

21. *métal d'Alger:* A metal made in Algiers from a combination of lead, tin, and antimony.

22. *robe-de-chambre—pour mieux entendre la musique:* That is, calling for his robe so that he can understand the music better. Dupin is quoting a play by Molière, *Le bourgeois gentilhomme,* in which Jourdain, the eponymous bourgeois, believes that the trappings of nobility will give him the finer sensibilities of a nobleman. In the same way, Dupin says, the French police make a big show of their efficiency, although they have no real intelligence.

23. **Vidocq:** Eugène François Vidocq (1775–1857), Napoleon Bonaparte's minister of police, whom critics have speculated was an inspiration for Dupin.

24. **Truth is not always in a well:** A reference to the Greek philosopher Democritus' claim that "Truth lies at the bottom of a well."

25. *loge de concierge:* A doorkeeper's apartment.

26. *Je les ménageais:* French (idiomatic): "I handled them carefully" (or tactfully).

27. *outré:* Unusual, strange.

28. *a posteriori:* Latin: "after the fact"; drawn based on previous experience and empirical evidence.

29. *Maison de Santé:* Sanitarium, or insane asylum.

30. **Cuvier:** French naturalist Georges Cuvier (1769–1832), author of *The Animal Kingdom* (1817).

31. *au troisième:* French: "on the third floor."

32. **Neufchâtelish:** A reference to the supposedly uncultured people of the Neufchâtel region of France.

33. *Jardin des Plantes:* A botanical garden in Paris.

34. **Laverna:** The Roman goddess of impostors and frauds.

35. *'de nier . . . n'est pas.':* The French translates thus: "of denying what is, and explaining what is not," a line from Jean-Jacques Rousseau's *Julie ou la Nouvelle Héloise* (1760).

The Purloined Letter

1. **The Purloined Letter:** Originally published in *The Gift: A Christmas, New Year, and Birthday Present* (1845).

2. **Nil sapientiæ . . . —Seneca:** Latin: "Nothing is more

hateful to wisdom than too much cunning." Lucius Annaeus Seneca (Seneca the Younger, c. 4 B.C.–A.D. 65,) was a Roman dramatist, statesman, and Stoic philosopher.

3. **meerschaum:** A kind of pipe, named for the hard white clay material used to make the bowl.

4. *au troisième:* French: "on the third floor."

5. *au fait:* Well informed.

6. **Abernethy:** John Abernethy (1764–1831), a London-born physician known for his sense of humor as well as his medical expertise.

7. *escritoire:* A writing desk.

8. **Procrustean bed:** In Greek legend, Procrustes ("He who stretches") was a villainous host who fitted his guests to the bed he had for them, stretching them on a rack if they were too short for it and cutting off their legs if they were too long. He was killed by the hero Theseus.

9. **Rochefoucault . . . Campanella:** François, duc de la Rochefoucauld (1613–1680), French moralist and author; La Bougive: possibly a mistaken reference to Jean de la Bruyère (1645–1696), a French writer; Niccolò Machiavelli (1469–1527), Italian political philosopher; Tommaso Campanella (1568–1639), Dominican monk and author imprisoned for heresy.

10. *recherchés:* Exotic, strange, or elaborate.

11. *non distributio medii:* Latin: "undistributed middle," a logical fallacy that makes an illegitimate connection between the major premise and the minor premise of an argument. Example: All students wear blue jeans. My mother wears blue jeans. My mother is a student.

12. **'Il y a ... plus grand nombre':** Roughly, "It is safe to wager that every idea that is popular is a bit of stupidity, because it is suited to the opinion of the majority." Chamfort was the pen name of Sébastien-Roch Nicholas, an eighteenth-century French writer, known for his epigrams.

13. **"if a term ... 'honorable men' ":** Dupin is making a distinction between distinguished men in society and honorable men, just as *ambitus* (a circuit, revolution) is distinct from "ambition" and *religio* (duty) is distinct from "religion."

14. **Bryant:** Jacob Bryant (1715–1804), author of *A New System; or, an Analysis of Antient Mythology*.

15. **intrigant:** One who engages in secret plots or intrigues.

16. **vis inertiæ:** Latin: "power of inertia," or the tendency for a body to remain at rest or in motion unless some force is applied to it.

17. **facilis descensus Averni:** Latin: "The descent to Hades is easy," a line from Virgil's *Aeneid*.

18. **Catalani:** Italian opera singer Angelica Catalani (1780–1849).

19. **monstrum horrendum:** Latin: "horrendous monster," from Book III of the *Aeneid*; refers to the cyclops Polyphemus.

20. **Un dessein si ... digne de Thyeste:** "So malevolent a plan, if unworthy of Atreus, is yet worthy of Thyeste." From the play *Atrée et Thyeste* (1707), by Prosper Jolyot de Crébillon (1674–1762).

The Gold-Bug

1. **The Gold-Bug:** Originally published in two installments in the Philadelphia *Dollar Newspaper,* June 21 and June 28, 1843.

2. **What ho! . . . —*All in the* Wrong:** Despite Poe's attribution, these lines are not in Arthur Murphy's 1761 comedy *All in the Wrong.* Poe either got the lines from another source or made them up. They refer to the conventional wisdom that the bite from a tarantula causes a mania for dancing.

3. **Huguenot:** A group of Calvinist Protestants who were driven out of France and relocated in America, among other places.

4. **Fort Moultrie:** U.S. Army fort on Sullivan's Island near Charleston, South Carolina. Poe was stationed there from 1827 to 1828.

5. **Swammerdamm:** Dutch naturalist Jan Swammerdamm (1637–1680) pioneered use of the microscope.

6. **foolscap:** A long sheet of writing paper, originally named for its fool's cap watermark.

7. *scarabœus caput hominis:* Latin: "man's-head beetle."

8. **him 'noovers:** Or "his maneuvers."

9. **pissel:** Jupiter's pronunciation of "epistle," or letter.

10. *brusquerie:* An instance of being rude, or brusque.

11. *solus:* Latin: "alone."

12. *empressement:* Pressure.

13. **curvets and caracols:** Equestrian terms for a leap (curvet) or a capering turn (caracol).

14. **bi-chloride of mercury:** A substance used to pre-

vent deterioration of wood objects or museum pieces.

15. **Zaffre . . . *aqua regia*:** Legrand is referring to an alchemical process: Zaffre is oxidized cobalt, and aqua regia is a solvent made from hydrochloric and nitric acids.

16. **regulus:** Metallic sludge that sinks to the bottom of a furnace during smelting.

17. **caloric:** Heating element.

18. **Golconda:** Or Golkonda, an ancient city in India, near present-day Hyderabad, famed for its diamond mines.

Ms. Found in a Bottle

1. **Ms. Found in a Bottle**: Originally published as the winner of a contest sponsored by the *Baltimore Saturday Visiter*, October 19, 1833.

2. **Qui n'a plus . . . *Quinault—Atys*:** "He who has no more than a moment to live has nothing more to lie about," a line from Philippe Quinault's libretto for the opera *Atys* (1676), composed by Jean-Baptiste Lully.

3. **German moralists:** German writers of the eighteenth and nineteenth centuries, known for their rigorous moral and philosophical works.

4. **Pyrrhonism:** Skepticism; after Pyrrho, a Greek philosopher of the third century B.C.

5. ***ignes fatui*:** Latin: "foolish fire"; things that dazzle or deceive.

6. **Lachadive Islands:** Present-day Laccadive coral

atolls in the Arabian Sea, off the coast of the Malabar region of India.

7. **coir, jaggeree, ghee:** *Coir:* a fiber produced from the shells of coconuts; *jaggeree:* a sugar product made from palm sap; *ghee:* clarified butter, traditionally made from the milk of a water buffalo.

8. **crank:** Listing with unbalanced cargo and in danger of capsizing.

9. **grabs:** A variety of sailing ship used in the East India shipping trade.

10. **Malays:** People of Southeast Asia, particularly from the Malay Peninsula.

11. **simoon:** A strong, dry desert wind, here used to convey a powerful storm at sea.

12. **New Holland:** Former name of Australia.

13. **kraken:** Sea monster from Norse mythology, possibly based on the giant squid, which it resembles.

14. **East Indiaman:** A large merchant ship involved in the East India trade.

15. **press of sail:** The greatest amount of sail that a ship can carry safely.

16. **hove in stays:** A reference to a vessel as it tacks, that is, when the wind shifts from one side of the sails to the other.

17. **shifting-boards:** Removable partitions in the hold of a ship to keep cargo from shifting.

18. **ratlin-stuff:** Material for rope ladders.

19. **yawl:** A small utility boat for a ship.

20. **studding-sail:** A small sail used for extra thrust in good weather.

21. **top-gallant yard-arms:** The uppermost horizontal poles from which a ship's sails are hung.

22. **sibyls:** Female prophets of Greek and Roman legend.

23. **Balbec, and Tadmor, and Persepolis:** *Balbec:* also known as Baalbek, a city in current-day Lebanon; *Tadmor:* city in Syria, legendarily founded by King Solomon; *Persepolis:* capital of Persian kings, later looted by Alexander the Great.

24. **poop:** Enclosed superstructure of the stern of a ship.

A Descent into the Maelström

1. **A Descent into the Maelström:** Originally published in *Graham's Magazine*, May 1841.

2. **The ways of God . . . —*Joseph Glanvill:*** Poe is paraphrasing slightly a passage from Glanvill's *Essays on Several Important Subjects in Philosophy and Religion* (1676). The "well of Democritus" refers to the Greek philosopher's well-known claim that "truth lies at the bottom of a well."

3. **Lofoden:** Or Lofoten, a Norwegian island group.

4. ***Mare Tenebrarum:*** Latin: "sea of darkness," refers to the Atlantic Ocean, so called by al Idrisi, the "Nubian geographer" to whom the narrator refers.

5. **Jonas Ramus:** Jonas Danilssønn Ramus (1649–1718) was a Norwegian priest and historian. Ramus identified Scylla and Charybdis, the whirlpool and clashing rocks of the *Odyssey*, as the Maelström and its surrounding region.

6. **Norway mile:** Approximately 4.5 English miles.

7. **Sexagesima Sunday:** The second Sunday before the Christian season of Lent.

8. **Phlegethon:** A river of fire, and one of five rivers in the underworld of Greek myth.

9. **Ferroe Islands:** Faroe Islands located between Iceland and northern Scotland.

10. **Kircher:** Athanasius Kircher (1601–1680), a German Jesuit scientist and mathematician, claimed that the Maelström drew water in and expelled it into the Gulf of Bothnia through a network of tunnels.

11. **smack:** A small sailing ship for coastal fishing.

12. **Mussulmen:** Muslims.

13. **See Archimedes . . . lib. 2:** The storyteller is here referring to the observations of the Greek mathematician and scientist Archimedes. Poe used his exclamation "Eureka!" (I have found it!) as the title of his 1848 work of cosmological theory/prose poetry.

The Pit and the Pendulum

1. **The Pit and the Pendulum:** Originally published in *The Gift: A Christmas and New Year's Present* (1843).

2. **Impia tortorum longas . . . vita salusque patent:** Latin, translated roughly: "Here the furious mob, unsatisfied, / Long harbored hatred of innocent blood. / Now that the fatherland is saved, and the cave of death destroyed, / Wholesome life appears where grim death has been." The Jacobins were the radical group responsible for the Reign of Terror during the French Revolution.

3. **inquisitorial:** Reference to the Spanish Inquisition, a Catholic institution that for more than three centuries punished heretics and attempted to force the conversions of Jews and Muslims.

4. **galvanic battery:** A chemical generator of electricity.
5. ***auto-da-fés:*** French, literally "acts of faith"; refers to the ceremonies accompanying the public burning of heretics by the Inquisition.
6. **Toledo:** Spanish city that was headquarters of the Inquisition.
7. **most hideous of fates:** The narrator is referring to being buried alive.
8. **moral horrors:** Spiritual or mental, as opposed to physical, ordeals.
9. **surcingle:** A leather strap around a horse's midsection to hold a pack or saddle on its back.
10. **Ultima Thule:** The end of the world, or of all that's known.
11. **moiety:** A portion of something, usually approximately half.
12. **ague:** A fever marked by chills and sweating at regular intervals.
13. **General Lasalle:** Antoine, comte de Lasalle, a general in Napoleon's army who captured Toledo in 1808 and brought a temporary end to the Inquisition.

William Wilson

1. **William Wilson:** Originally published in *The Gift: A Christmas and New Year's Present for 1840*.
2. **What say of it? . . . —Chamberlain's *Pharronida*:** Despite Poe's attribution, these lines do not appear in William Chamberlayne's 1659 verse romance.
3. **Elagabalus:** Also Heliogabalus; a Roman emperor (218–222) known for his blasphemous religious ritu-

als and disregard for the proper management of the Roman government, who was murdered in an uprising by the Praetorian Guard.

4. *peine forte et dure:* French, literally: "strong and lasting pain"; a form of capital punishment in which the condemned is crushed under heavy weights.

5. **lustrum:** Five years.

6. *outré:* Unusual or strange.

7. *exergues* **of the Cartaginian medals:** Inscriptions on coins minted by the Carthaginian empire of North Africa.

8. **connings:** Learning by memorization.

9. ***Oh, le bon temps, que ce siècle de fer:*** "Oh, the good old days, that Iron Age!" The narrator is quoting the French satirist Voltaire.

10. **kerseymere:** Wool fabric with a twill weave.

11. **out-Heroded Herod:** Herod, ruler of Palestine, was known for his extravagance as well as his cruelty. This line alludes to William Shakespeare's *Hamlet*, where Hamlet utters the same words referring to bad actors.

12. *parvenu:* Suddenly wealthy.

13. **Herodes Atticus:** Wealthy Greek rhetorician (c. 101–177) who patronized learning and the arts in Athens.

14. *écarté:* A card game for two players.

15. *arrondis:* French: "rounded"; the narrator is acknowledging that he has shaved his cards in order to cheat.

POEMS

The Raven

1. **The Raven:** Originally published in January 1845 in several different periodicals, including the New York *Evening Mirror* and the *American Review*.
2. **surcease:** A cessation of or release from.
3. **Pallas:** Pallas Athena, the Greek goddess of wisdom and scholarship.
4. **shorn . . . craven:** Coward; the speaker is making reference to the medieval practice of shaving the heads of cowardly knights.
5. **Plutonian:** Referring to Pluto, god of the underworld, and his realm.
6. **gloated:** Here meaning glanced off of or reflected light onto.
7. **censer:** A vessel for burning incense.
8. **nepenthe:** In Greek mythology, a drug that causes forgetfulness.
9. **balm in Gilead:** A soothing ointment; refers to Jeremiah 8:22 in the Bible: "Is there no balm in Gilead?; is there no physician there?"
10. **Aidenn:** Poe's spelling of Eden, after the biblical paradise.

Lenore

1. **Lenore:** Originally published in *The Pioneer*, February 1843.
2. **Stygian:** Extremely dark or gloomy; the river Styx was the mythic border of the Greek underworld.
3. **Guy De Vere:** A conventional name, perhaps, for a

chivalric lover. De Vere was the family name of the
seventeenth Earl of Oxford, whom some speculate
was the actual author of William Shakespeare's plays.
4. *Peccavimus:* Latin: "We have sinned."
5. *debonnaire:* Of a good family or nature; from the
French *"de bon aire."*

To Helen

1. **To Helen:** Originally published in *Union Magazine*,
November 1848. Mrs. Sarah Helen Whitman was a
widow whose poem dedicated to Poe appeared in
the March 18, 1848, edition of the *Home Journal*.
2. **I saw thee once:** Poe had seen Mrs. Whitman in
Providence, Rhode Island, on one occasion in July
1845 as she stood in front of her house while he
walked past.
3. **parterre:** The lowest level of a garden, usually ter-
raced and landscaped.
4. **Dian:** The moon; a reference to Diana, the Roman
goddess of the moon.
5. **Elysian fire:** An allusion to the Elysian Fields, a
final resting place for the souls of the heroic and vir-
tuous in Greek mythology.

Ulalume

1. **Ulalume:** Originally published in the *American Review*, December 1847. Poe coined the name, from
the Latin *ulalare* (to wail) and *lumen* (light), to mean
something like "sorrow's light."
2. **sere:** Dried and withered.

3. **Auber:** Likely a reference to Daniel-François-Esprit Auber (1782-1871), a French composer of operas, whose works include 1839's *Le lac des fées* (The Lake of the Fairies), based on a German legend.

4. **Weir:** Likely a reference to Robert Walter Weir, a nineteenth-century landscape painter of the Hudson River School known for his misty, somewhat dark landscapes.

5. **Psyche:** Princess in Greek mythology whose marriage to Cupid results in her becoming immortal; more generally, she embodies the soul.

6. **scoriac:** Consisting of rough, cindery lava.

7. **Yaanek:** Perhaps a reference to Mount Erebus, the only active polar volcano, located in Antarctica.

8. **boreal:** Usually refers to the North Pole.

9. **star-dials:** Poe's imagined nighttime equivalent of sundials.

10. **Astarte's:** The Phoenician goddess of love and fertility.

11. **the stars of the Lion:** The constellation Leo.

12. **Lethean:** A reference to Lethe, the legendary river of forgetfulness in Hades.

13. **Sibylic:** Prophetic, after the female prophets of Greek and Roman legend.

The Bells

1. **The Bells:** First published in *Sartain's Union Magazine*, December 1849.

2. **sledges:** Heavy sleds, or sleighs.

3. **Runic rhyme:** Magic spell.

4. **tintinnabulation:** Onomatopoeic word for the sound of ringing bells.
5. **gloats:** Reflects light (an older meaning of the word, now obsolete).
6. **Brazen:** Made of brass; harsh-sounding.
7. **pæan:** A song or hymn of praise or tribute.
8. **knells:** Rings a bell for a death, funeral, or disaster.

Annabel Lee

1. **Annabel Lee:** Originally published in the *Richmond Examiner* in August 1849 and, after Poe's death in October of that year, in the *New York Daily Tribune* (October 9, 1849) and the *Southern Literary Messenger* (November 1849).
2. **seraphs:** The highest order of angels, with two or three pairs of wings.
3. **sepulchre:** A tomb or burial place.

To ———

1. **To ———:** Variant of "To M———," published in *Al Aaraaf, Tamerlane, and Minor Poems*, 1829.

The Valley of Unrest

1. **The Valley of Unrest:** Originally published as "The Valley Nis" in *Poems, by Edgar A. Poe. Second Edition* (1831). Poe published a revised version under the present title in the *Southern Literary Messenger*, February 1836.
2. **Hebrides:** Islands off the western coast of Scotland.

The City in the Sea

1. **The City in the Sea:** Originally published as "The Doomed City" in *Poems, by Edgar A. Poe. Second Edition* (1831), then as "The City of Sin" in the *Southern Literary Messenger* in August 1836, and "The City in the Sea" in *American Review* in April 1845.
2. **fanes . . . Babylon-like:** *Fanes:* temples; *Babylon-like*. refers to a city noted in the Bible for its immorality.
3. **wreathéd friezes:** A frieze is a sculpted ornamental band around walls or furniture; *wreathéd* suggests the Hanging Gardens of Babylon, one of the Seven Wonders of the Ancient World.

The Sleeper

1. **The Sleeper:** Originally published under the title "Irene" in *Poems, by Edgar A. Poe. Second Edition* (1831). The first version published under the present title appeared in the Philadelphia *Saturday Chronicle*, May 22, 1841.
2. **Lethe:** River of forgetfulness in the underworld of Greek mythology.
3. **soul lies hid:** A reference to the eye, with its "fringéd lid," being a window to the soul—the window in this case closed in death.
4. **length of tress:** A reference to the idea that the hair continues to grow after death.

A Dream Within a Dream

1. **A Dream Within a Dream:** A version of this poem originally appeared in *Tamerlane and Other Poems* and was published in its present form in the Boston newspaper *Flag of Our Union* on March 31, 1849.

Dream-Land

1. **Dream-Land:** This poem was originally published in *Graham's Magazine*, June 1844.
2. **ill:** In the sense of ill-willed or malicious.
3. **Eidolon:** A ghost or phantom.
4. **Thule:** Greek word for the farthest known point of land.
5. **Eldorado:** Mythical city of gold sought by the Spanish conquistadores in the New World.
6. **darkened glasses:** Partly closed eyes; suggests 1 Corinthians 13:12: "For now we see through a glass, darkly."

Dreams

1. **Dreams:** Originally published in *Tamerlane and Other Poems* (1827).

Silence

1. **Silence:** First published in the Philadelphia *Saturday Courier*, January 4, 1840. Originally titled "Sonnet—Silence," despite the fact that it has fifteen lines rather than the fourteen sonnets usually have.
2. **corporate:** Or corporeal, meaning "of the body."

Eldorado

1. **Eldorado:** Originally published in the Boston *Flag of Our Union*, April 21, 1849. El Dorado was a city of gold the Spanish conquerors of the New World believed lay in the western part of the continent. In Poe's time it connoted the gold rush underway in California.

2. **Mountains of the Moon:** Mountains in Africa, once thought to be the source of the Nile River; possibly the Ruwenzori Range that separates Uganda and the Congo. In literary terms they represent a place a fantastic distance away.

3. **Valley of the Shadow:** Possibly a reference to Psalm 23:4: "Yea, though I walk through the valley of the shadow of death. . . ."

Israfel

1. **Israfel:** Originally published in *Poems, by Edgar A. Poe. Second Edition* (1831).

2. **levin:** Lightning.

3. **Pleiads:** Or the Pleiades, a cluster of seven stars in the constellation Taurus who were sisters, according to Greek mythology.

4. **grown-up God:** As opposed to the cherubic Cupid of Roman mythology.

5. **Houri:** In Muslim mythology, one of the virgins who await men in heaven; "houri" literally refers to their dark eyes.

For Annie

1. **For Annie:** Originally published in the Boston *Flag of Our Union*, April 28, 1849. Poe apparently wrote it thinking of Annie Richmond, an acquaintance with whom he carried on a literary flirtation.
2. **naphthaline:** A flammable oil; "napthaline river" suggests one of the fiery rivers of Hades.
3. **tantalized:** Tortured with desire and left unsatisfied, a reference to the fate of Tantalus in Greek mythology, a king who was punished by the gods by spending all eternity just out of reach of a supply of fruit and water.
4. **rue:** An herb with bitter leaves, symbolic of regret.
5. **queen of the angels:** The Virgin Mary.

Sonnet—To Science

1. **Sonnet—To Science:** Originally published as the introductory poem to *Al Aaraaf, Tamerlane, and Minor Poems* (1829).
2. **Diana from her car:** Diana is the Roman goddess of the moon; her "car" is the chariot she rode across the sky.
3. **Hamadryad:** Wood nymph in Greek mythology.
4. **Naiad:** Water nymph in Greek mythology.

A Dream

1. **A Dream:** Originally published in *Tamerlane and Other Poems* (1827).
2. **day-star:** The sun. The poet is comparing the trem-

bling light of a faraway star with the brighter light of the sun.

To ——————

1. **To ——————:** Originally published in *Al Aaraaf, Tamerlane, and Minor Poems* (1829).

Romance

1. **Romance:** Originally published in *Al Aaraaf, Tamerlane, and Minor Poems* (1829).
2. **paroquet:** Parakeet.

Spirits of the Dead

1. **Spirits of the Dead:** Originally published in *Tamerlane and Other Poems* (1827).

To Helen

1. **To Helen:** Originally published in *Poems, by Edgar A. Poe. Second Edition* (1831). The Helen in question is Mrs. Helen Stannard, actually Jane Stith Stanard, the mother of a schoolmate of Poe's, whose death when Poe was a boy affected him greatly.
2. **Nicean:** A reference to Nicea, a city now known as Iznik in modern-day Turkey.
3. **Naiad:** Water nymph in Greek mythology.
4. **agate:** A semitranslucent chalcedony, usually with multicolored bands.
5. **Psyche:** Princess in Greek mythology whose mar-

riage to Cupid results in her becoming immortal; more generally, she embodies the soul.

Evening Star

1. **Evening Star:** Originally published in *Tamerlane and Other Poems* (1827). The evening star is actually Venus, named after the Roman goddess of love.

Alone

1. **Alone:** Unpublished and untitled in Poe's lifetime, it was written around 1829, and first published in *Scribner's Monthly Magazine*, September 1875.

INTERPRETIVE NOTES

Poe's Stories

Poe published nearly eighty short stories in magazines and newspapers in the 1830s and 1840s. He was one of the earliest, and one of the most prolific, American practitioners of the form. Many of his stories are satires on other writers or intellectual fads of his day and are largely unread by modern readers. The tales that have ensured his continued fame are those of horror, death and life after death, and madness. Such themes came naturally to Poe, who was prone to periods of deep melancholy and who had lost virtually everyone he loved in his life by the time of his own death at age forty. How much his unhappy life affected the content of his stories is a subject critics continue to debate.

Poe saw himself as an outsider throughout his life: in the family of a foster father who disinherited him; in the army, where he was never happy following orders; and in society, where he had flashes of literary success but usually was penniless. His stories are mostly about outsiders, too, people who are isolated by a terrible fate or by their own peculiar psychology. Almost always, the tales recognizably take place in the minds of their narrators, and so they really only seem to have one character. We know almost nothing about the old man in "The Tell-Tale Heart," for example, except that even his catatonic presence in the world drives the narrator to murderous madness. In "William Wilson," the narrator is shadowed throughout his life by his exact double in appearance, manner, and even name, so that William Wilson is both the protagonist and antagonist of the story.

Poe is also generally credited as the inventor of the detective story, although scholars have established that he was drawing on earlier sources when he created the character of the ratiocinative detective C. Auguste Dupin. Dupin, who has a genius for devising intellectual solutions to baffling mysteries, clearly inspired Arthur Conan Doyle when he created his own, more famous, intellectual detective, Sherlock Holmes. And writers, for television and movies as well as print, have been devising variations on this type of character ever since. Every year the Mystery Writers of America recognize Poe's central importance to the genre by giving out awards for excellence called the Edgars.

Poe's major stories, despite their differences in details of plot and setting, focus on some central themes: themes of murder and madness; of engulfment, confinement, and catastrophe; of mind over matter, in the form of doubles and life after death; and of puzzles and cryptography. These are by no means exclusive or definitive categories. Poe scholars have grouped and regrouped his stories into many different schemes over the years. But nearly every one of his tales can be considered in light of at least one of these themes.

Madness and Murder. "The Tell-Tale Heart," "The Cask of Amontillado," and "The Black Cat" are all narrated by murderers, and not very sympathetic ones. In "The Tell-Tale Heart" and "The Black Cat," the narrators might have gotten away with terrible crimes, but their guilty consciences overwhelm their attempts to appear normal. In "The Cask of Amontillado," the narrator did get away with murder; the story itself is his confession fifty years after the fact.

In "The Tell-Tale Heart," the narrator insists that he is not mad, then proceeds to tell a gruesome story of murdering the invalid old man he looks after and dismembering and hiding the body. He confesses to the crime because he can still hear the beating of the old man's heart under the floor where he hid it. In "The Black Cat," the narrator starts in similar fashion, proclaiming his sanity despite the incredible events he describes. Alcoholism led him to abuse his wife and the pet cat he felt a special attachment to; after he killed the cat in a fit of drunken spite, a similar-looking one came along, seeming to the narrator like a vengeful double of the first. He tried to kill the second cat and struck his wife dead with an ax when she got in the way. He, too, hid the evidence of his murderous act, but when he accidentally walled up the cat in the basement with his wife's body, the animal's cries gave him away.

Both of these stories have retained the power to shock in the matter-of-fact way the narrators confess to their crimes. Nameless and seemingly lacking any real motive or sense of remorse, they are perfect examples of what author Hannah Arendt, in a different context, referred to as "the banality of evil." The killer in "The Tell-Tale Heart" claims to love the old man—it's just that his vulture-like "pale blue eye" stares at him, chilling his blood. The drunken husband of "The Black Cat" attributes his terrible behavior to "perverseness," which has a ring of authenticity about it in terms of an alcoholic's self-loathing justification of his actions. In both cases the men seem to be lashing out murderously against a sense of being trapped in their own lives. They try to wall up the evidence of their discontent, but it still breaks through and exposes them.

"The Cask of Amontillado" is a variation on the same plot, with Montresor burying his nemesis, Fortunato, in the family catacombs where he keeps his wine. Killing him in this way also serves to hide evidence of Montresor's madness. At least he offers a motive that makes sense: he intends to avenge himself on Fortunato for a "thousand injuries" and one insult, though neither injuries nor insult are specified. We are never told what Fortunato's crimes against Montresor were, but it is hard to imagine that they rival Montresor's evil act of vengeance. Montresor is more successful as a murderer than the narrators of "The Tell-Tale Heart" and "The Black Cat," but the fact that he is telling the story to someone suggests that ultimately his crime could not stay hidden either.

In each of these stories Poe utilizes one of his favorite devices, the unreliable narrator. And his narrators—high-strung, opium addicted, frequently delusional or psychotic—are especially unreliable. Their insistence on their sanity tends to have the opposite effect of confirming their craziness. They are intent on justifying themselves and consequently are oblivious to the immorality of their behavior. Montresor in "The Cask of Amontillado," for example, and the narrator of "William Wilson" never seem to realize that they are actually the villains of the stories they tell.

Tales of Entrapment, Engulfment, Catastrophe. Some of Poe's most overtly fantastic adventure stories convey a sense of being trapped, engulfed, or otherwise overwhelmed by hostile natural forces. These tales are dreamlike or allegorical in that they seem to make the most sense when understood in symbolic terms. "Ms. Found in a Bottle" and "A Descent into the Maelström" are set at sea, but they are not really sea stories, in the sense of Robert Louis Stevenson's or Herman Melville's. Poe's interest in the sea is like that of Coleridge in "The Rime of the Ancient Mariner": as the setting for man to have an existential confrontation with the enormousness and the indifference of nature. In "Ms. Found in a Bottle," the author of the manuscript is the only survivor when his ship sinks in a hurricane. He writes from an enormous ghost ship that is being pulled along in the same storm, on which the decrepit crew does not acknowledge his presence. Himself a ghostly stowaway on the ship's doomed voyage, he can only watch as they are sucked into a whirlpool at the South Pole, pulled down to an uncertain fate.

"A Descent into the Maelström," with a description of the Norwegian coast at the beginning to help establish its authenticity, also features a giant whirlpool. Unlike the narrator of "Ms. Found in a Bottle," who apparently dies at the end of the story, the Norwegian fisherman sucked into the vortex in "Descent" is able to lash himself to a barrel and thus float to the surface rather than going down with the ship, as his brother does. The fisherman (who, in a slight variation on Poe's usual technique, tells his story to the narrator) relates how, when he was certain he was going to die, he could appreciate the beauty of the nighttime sky seen from the depths of the whirlpool. Still, the terror of his experience that night aged him, turning his hair completely white.

"The Masque of the Red Death" is another story of enclosure, set within the walled palace of a prince. The courtiers around the prince dance away their lives, arrogantly assuming that they are safe from the plague that ravages the world outside their quarantined luxury— except when the clock tolls the hour and the orchestra stops, reminding them of time's irresistible passing. The end of the story, when the courtiers are all felled simultaneously by the red death, is Poe at his most chilling. The specific symbolic intent of "The Masque of the Red Death" has been debated by critics, some of whom consider the story an antiaristocratic fable, while others take its theme to be more universal. Clearly, though, like "A Descent into the Maelström" and "Ms. Found in a Bottle," it offers a vision of man's helplessness against nature's capacity for annihilation.

Stories of Mind over Matter. The presence of doubles in characters' lives and the apparent possibility of life after death are recurrent themes in Poe's stories and verse. They seem to represent the mind's control over the physical laws of the universe. In "Ligeia" the title character is the narrator's deceased first wife, a student of the occult who wills her own return from beyond the grave. She takes possession of the narrator's second wife, Lady Rowena, through a glass of wine Rowena drinks. The narrator passes a harrowing night as Rowena dies and is reborn as Ligeia, with her long, black hair and otherworldly eyes. Curiously, the story ends there, leaving the reader to wonder what happened after the two lovers reunited.

In "The Fall of the House of Usher," considered by many critics to be Poe's best story, the lady who seems unable to live in the world is Madeline, twin sister to Roderick Usher. The last members of a family weakened by intermarriage, Roderick and Madeline look alike, and they are destined to die in each other's arms. They both suffer from unusual mental conditions: Madeline has spells of deathlike trances, and Roderick (like the narrator of "The Tell-Tale Heart") is oversensitive to the slightest sensory stimulus. Again, the processes of the mind are given a morbid physical expression—most notably in a poem by Roderick called "The Haunted Palace," in which he dramatizes the tormenting thoughts that haunt the palace of his mind: "Vast forms that move fantastically / To a discordant melody." (Poe first published "The Haunted Palace" separately from "The Fall of the House of Usher," in the *American Museum of Science, Literature, and the Arts*, April 1839.) The story climaxes with the deaths of the last two Ushers leading to the literal collapse of the family home, the haunted palace of inbred generations of the Usher family.

Poe was fascinated with the death of a beautiful woman as a literary device, but there's no sense of triumph or joy when Ligeia and Madeline return from the dead. Rather, those stories provoke terror over the double, that creature who should not exist but somehow does. The same theme is explored in "The Black Cat," with the mutilated Pluto and his ominous double, and, most fascinatingly, in "William Wilson." In that story the narrator describes his encounters with his doppelgänger, also named William Wilson (the narrator uses an alias to tell the story), who foils his schemes to cheat, seduce, and steal from gullible targets. The narrator, because he is the one telling the story, gets to be *the* William Wilson; nevertheless, it seems clear that the other Wilson is probably the more honorable person. Despite the fact that the narrator is a scoundrel, Poe successfully conveys chilling moments when he looks upon his twin and realizes with terror that he is not unique in the universe.

Stories of Detection and Ratiocination. After his gothic tales, Poe is best known for "inventing" the detective story, with "The Gold-Bug" and stories featuring the eccentric French detective C. Auguste Dupin, including "The Murders in the Rue Morgue" and "The Purloined Letter." There were intellectual detectives, and mysteries solved by rational means, in stories and novels before Poe's; but by focusing the story on the process by which the mystery is solved, and by giving the detective a companion to narrate his ingenious solutions, Poe established a format for detective stories that has been followed ever since. As he observed in a letter to his friend and fellow writer Philip Pendleton Cooke, his detective stories operate by a kind of literary sleight of hand that makes Dupin's deductions seem more impressive than they actually are: "In the 'Murders in the Rue Morgue', for instance, where is the ingenuity of unravelling a web which you yourself (the author) have woven for the express purpose of unravelling?"

The Dupin stories and "The Gold-Bug" show Poe at his most pedantic. Novelist D. H. Lawrence called these stories "mechanical tales" in which the "interest is scientific rather than artistic." "The Murders in the Rue Morgue" opens with the narrator, a friend of Dupin's, giving an extended introduction about the powers of the analytical mind, then describing the rare gift for analysis that Dupin possesses. For Dupin, men seem to have "windows in their bosoms"—that is, he can easily see the truth about them that lies beneath their superficial appearance. He gets most of the facts he needs to solve the Rue Morgue case from newspaper accounts of the incident. The unusual details described in the newspaper, combined with a cursory examination of the physical evidence, tell Dupin that the deaths were not murders at all, since the killer was not human but an escaped animal. In "The Purloined Letter," Dupin matches wits with a government minister who is also a thief and an extortionist. The police, as effective in this matter as they were in the Rue Morgue case, have searched the minister's home but are unable to find the sensitive letter he has stolen. Dupin astonishes them by producing the letter; and the rest of the story is his lengthy explanation of a fairly simple solution: the minister was hiding the letter in plain sight, in a card-rack hanging from the mantelpiece. Dupin's explanation of how he arrived at his solution by putting himself in the mind of his adversary anticipates the prominence that such "profiling" is given in criminal investigation today.

"The Gold-Bug" initially seems to be about another of Poe's obsessed, deranged protagonists. The amateur entomologist Legrand worries both his faithful slave, Jupiter, and the narrator, another nameless figure who, like Dupin's companion, is on hand to play the role of straight man to his brilliant friend. The golden scarab beetle that Legrand has found is ultimately incidental to the plot. It leads him to the surprising realization that he is in possession of a pirate's treasure map. He keeps Jupiter and the narrator literally in the dark until they actually find the gold; then, like Dupin, Legrand explains in excruciating detail how he solved the cryptogram that led them to the treasure. As in the Dupin stories, Legrand's puzzle solving seems less impressive if one remembers that Poe created the puzzles with the idea that his characters would solve them. But Poe was proud of his ability to decipher codes like the one in the story, and in another article on the subject invited readers to send in cryptograms of their own for him to solve.

Poe as a writer was fascinated with extreme states of consciousness, of the sorts experienced by dreamers and madmen. But he put great stock in the rational mind, as well. The narrators of "A Descent into the Maelström" and "The Pit and the Pendulum" are examples of Poe protagonists who use their wits to survive in extraordinary situations.

Poe's Poems

Poe considered himself a poet first and foremost. He wrote verse precociously, publishing his first collection, *Tamerlane and Other Poems,* when he was eighteen years old. By the time he was twenty-five, in fact, he had composed most of the poems he would ever write. In the 1830s and 1840s, Poe turned more to writing stories and reviews as a way to make ends meet. He did return to poetry in the last years of his life, when he wrote most of the poems that he is remembered for today—"The Raven," for example, was introduced to the public in 1845, and "The Bells" and "Annabel Lee" were rushed into print after his death in 1849.

Poe's poems are symbolic, rhythmic, otherworldly, and allusive. He strove for a "unity of effect," as he explained in his 1845 essay "The Philosophy of Composition"; he planned for "The Raven" to be short enough to read in one sitting and to combine a melancholy tone and language with a beautifully sad poetic subject, the loss of a beloved woman. Critics continue to argue about how serious Poe was regarding his methods in "The Philosophy of Composition"—some claim that the essay is actually one of his literary hoaxes. However he wrote "The Raven," though, it was undeniably the popular success he designed it to be. It was reprinted around the country, which brought Poe widespread fame but (because of the copyright laws of the day) little financial reward.

"A Dream Within a Dream." Dreams and dreamers are common in Poe's verse, as a glance at the titles of his poems makes plain: "The Sleeper," "A Dream Within a

Dream," "Dream-Land," "Dreams." Other poems, such as "The Valley of Unrest" and "The City in the Sea," while not expressly descriptions of dreams, are dreamlike in the symbolically charged fantasy landscapes they portray. Dreams were important to the Romantics for the visions they provided of other planes of existence or of a timeless mythic past, and Poe was more vision haunted than most. His embrace of the poet's role as visionary brings an intensity to his poems—the "unity of effect," without which they might seem artificial and dated.

Sleep is also linked with death in Poe's poems, and as such it leads naturally into his favorite poetic topic. "The Sleeper" is dead, and the narrator prays that nothing will disturb her eternal rest: "Soft may the worms about her creep!" "Dream-Land" is a nightmare vision of a land of death "Out of SPACE—Out of TIME." Poe's dreamland is not a pastoral scene but an apocalyptic landscape with "surging" seas, "skies of fire," and "lone and dead" lakes. Similarly, "The City in the Sea" takes as its subject the biblical story of God's destruction of Sodom and Gomorrah; as in a dream, the poem's vision of a sunken (or sinking) city, with a hellish light that seems to illuminate it from below, is simultaneously vivid and indefinite. The poem is haunting, but it defies clear description.

Poe's Romantic preoccupation with dreaming was, in a way, entirely conventional and in fitting with the style of the time. It is his use of the convention, his fervent search for the visionary experience to be found even in nightmares, that distinguishes his verse.

The Death of a Beautiful Woman. Poe rather famously wrote in "The Philosophy of Composition" that the death of a beautiful woman "is, unquestionably, the most poetical topic in the world"—that is to say (facetiously or not), it is the one that most readily creates the atmosphere of melancholy he thought was the most beautiful literary effect. It is not necessary to delve too deeply into his life story to appreciate why Poe would be drawn to death as a poetic subject; beginning with his mother when he was two years old, he lost a succession of women in his life. But Poe does not mourn those women in his poems, at least not directly. "Ulalume," "Lenore," and "Annabel Lee" are all examples of dead women as poetic subjects. The poems tell us nothing about what they were like as living women; their main importance for Poe is the musical quality of their names.

"Nevermore." Poe's famous late poems, "The Raven," "The Bells," "Ulalume," and "Annabel Lee," are almost experiments in their poetic effects, as he spelled out in "The Philosophy of Composition." Thematically, these poems are in keeping with his earlier works: They are about the death of a loved one and the subsequent escape, or the inability to escape, into a world of dream or fantasy. What most makes them remarkable are their rhyme schemes and rhythmic language. No other poet of early America paid such close attention to the musicality of the words he chose.

"The Raven" makes onomatopoeic use of the mournful long *o* sound in the name of the speaker's lost love, Lenore, the repeated phrase "nothing more," and, of course, in the raven's lone word. When the speaker first realizes that the bird will only say "nevermore," he is amused—but when melancholy overtakes him again, he torments himself by asking the raven questions that confirm his worst fears: nevermore will he be reunited with Lenore or find relief from his memories of her; nevermore will the bird stop reminding him of his grief.

"The Bells" is an even more radical experiment in sound poetry, particularly with its hypnotic repetition of the word "bells," at first a "tintinnabulation," but by the end building to a cacophony of sorrow. In describing four phases of life, each section of the poem is longer than the last; the final section, devoted to iron funeral bells, repeats "rolls," "time," "bells," "knells," overwhelming the rest of the poem as, to Poe's mind, the sorrows of death overwhelm life.

"The Bells," "Ulalume," and "Annabel Lee," all written after the death of Poe's wife, Virginia, are particularly poignant in light of that last great loss of the poet's life. Ulalume, like Lenore, is another name that suggests sorrow—Ulalume through its similarity to the word "ululate," meaning to keen with grief, and its rhyme with "tomb." Also similar to "The Raven" is the speaker's apparent desire to torture himself: Lost in thought, he wanders to the crypt of Ulalume, wondering, "what demon hath tempted me here?" But in the ballad "Annabel Lee," written in the last year of Poe's life at a time when he knew that his physical and psychological health was failing, he seems to look forward to a time when he would be free from sorrow. Unlike "The Raven," where the speaker is assured that he will not be reunited with Lenore in heaven, the speaker here proclaims that "neither the angels in Heaven above, / Nor the demons down under the sea, / Can ever dissever my soul from the soul / of the beautiful Annabel Lee." As the speakre lies down next to Annabel Lee in her "sepulchre there by the sea," we may imagine, after all, some end to Poe's lifelong torment.

CRITICAL EXCERPTS

Reminiscences and Critical Biographies

Griswold, Rufus Wilmot. New York *Tribune*, October 9, 1849. In *The Recognition of Edgar Allan Poe*, edited by Eric W. Carlson. Ann Arbor: University of Michigan Press, 1966.

Fellow New York journalist Griswold was Poe's literary executor and someone he considered a friend. Poe's literary reputation has never completely recovered from Griswold's obituary of Poe, published in the *New York Daily Tribune* the day of Poe's funeral and reprinted widely, and his 1850 memoir of the dead writer, both of which were extremely uncharitable in their assessment of Poe and in some cases helped to spread untrue smears against his character.

Edgar Allan Poe is dead. He died in Baltimore the day before yesterday. This announcement will startle many, *but few will be grieved by it*. The poet was well known personally or by reputation, in all this country; he had readers in England, and in several of the states of Continental Europe; *but he had few or no friends;* and the regrets for his death will be suggested principally by the consideration that in him literary art lost one of its most brilliant, but erratic, stars.

Moran, John J. *A Defense of Edgar Allan Poe: Life, Character, and Dying Declarations of the Poet.* Washington, D.C.: William F. Boogher, 1885.

As a resident physician at Washington Medical College in Baltimore, Moran was the doctor who attended Poe when he was brought in after being found unconscious in the street. He was present at Poe's death. Nearly forty years later, he took it upon himself to attempt to rectify some of the misinformation surrounding Poe's life and death—the widely held belief, for example, that he died from alcohol poisoning.

It was my sad duty as his physician to sit by his deathbed; to administer the cup of consolation; to moisten his parched lips; to wipe the cold death-dew from his brow; and to catch the last whispered articulations that fell from the lips of a being, the most remarkable, perhaps, this country has ever known. Let me entreat your thoughtful attention, therefore, to a plain, unvarnished story of a checkered life, and the strange and melancholy events that darkened the last hours of a dying genius. . . . I am persuaded that I should lend my feeble aid as a witness to the truth, and refute the foul accusations cast upon the memory of Poe, and repel the vile slanders respecting his death.

Quinn, Arthur Hobson. *Edgar Allan Poe: A Critical Biography*. New York: D. Appleton-Century, 1941. Reprint, Baltimore: Johns Hopkins University Press, 1998.

Quinn's biography of Poe is still considered the best biography of the poet. Quinn relied on research in the Poe family archives and tried scrupulously to avoid the untruths about Poe that had been perpetuated by both his enemies and his admirers.

Reams of print have dealt with the question of whether the sorrow of the poet was described objectively by Poe or whether he was dramatizing a real love. This controversy is really unnecessary. Poe's dread of the loss of Virginia, born of her recurring danger and nurtured by his devotion, had become a spiritual offspring, as concrete to him as the child he was denied could ever have been. In one sense, therefore, the poet was describing an emotional creation which had become objective to him, and the vivid reality of the poem is a consequence. But the primary inspiration was the abstract love of a beautiful woman—whether she was Helen, Eleonora, Lenore, or any other variant of the same name. Whether she was actually dead, or whether he feared her inevitable doom, is a detail.

Walsh, John Evangelist. *Midnight Dreary: The Mysterious Death of Edgar Allan Poe*. New Brunswick, N.J.: Rutgers University Press, 1998.

Walsh, who had previously won an Edgar Award in 1969 for his 1967 book *Poe the Detective: The Curious*

Circumstances Behind the Mystery of Marie Roget, investigates the greatest mystery of Poe's life: What happened to him in the week prior to his death on October 7, 1849. He provides a detailed account of the known record, debunks some of the persistent theories about Poe's death, and speculates plausibly about what he thinks actually happened.

> Earlier that morning, after a journey of some thirty hours by train and steamboat, he had reached Richmond from Philadelphia, where he stopped over on his way south from his home in New York. The latter part of the journey had not been pleasant, for he was still feeling the effects of another of his prolonged drinking bouts, this one in the Quaker City, and in fact the worst yet. So extreme had been his intoxication in Philadelphia, where he lingered for two weeks, that he'd experienced his first full-blown fit of *delirium tremens*, complete with visions.

Early Reviews and Responses

Baudelaire, Charles. Preface to *Nouvelles histoires extraordinaires par Edgar Poe*. 1857. In *The Recognition of Edgar Allan Poe*, edited by Eric W. Carlson. Ann Arbor: University of Michigan Press, 1966.

Baudelaire, one of the greatest of French poets, saw Poe as a soul mate based on their similar life experiences and artistic vision. Baudelaire's translations of Poe's poems and stories introduced him to French readers, who have generally held him in higher esteem than do his fellow Americans.

. . . we shall see that this author, product of a century fascinated with itself, child of a nation more infatuated with itself than any other, has clearly seen, has imperturbably affirmed the natural wickedness of man. There is in man, he says, a mysterious force which modern philosophy does not wish to take into consideration; nevertheless, without this nameless force, without this primordial bent, a host of human actions will remain unexplained, inexplicable. These actions are attractive only *because* they are bad or dangerous; they possess the fascination of the abyss. This primitive, irresistible force is natural Perversity, which makes man constantly and simultaneously a murderer and a suicide, an assassin and a hangman. . . .

Lawrence, D. H. "Edgar Allan Poe." In *Studies in Classic American Literature*. New York: T. Seltzer, 1923.

British novelist Lawrence argues that Poe wrote more as a scientist than an artist and that his only real literary subject was his own psychological torment.

Poe had a pretty bitter doom. Doomed to seethe down his soul in a great continuous convulsion of disintegration, and doomed to register the process. And then doomed to be abused for it, when he had performed some of the bitterest tasks of human experience, that can be asked of a man. Necessary tasks, too. For the human soul must suffer its own disintegration, *consciously*, if ever it is to survive.

But Poe is rather a scientist than an artist. He is reducing his own self as a scientist reduces a salt in a crucible. It is an almost chemical analysis of the soul and consciousness.

Huxley, Aldous. "Vulgarity in Literature." In *Music at Night and Other Essays*. London: Chatto & Windus, 1931; Garden City, N.Y.: Doubleday, Doran, 1931.

Huxley's criticism of the vulgarity that "spoils" Poe is specifically directed at his admirers who are not native speakers of English, especially the French.

Was Edgar Allan Poe a major poet? It would surely never occur to any English-speaking critic to say so. And yet, in France, from 1850 till the present time, the best poets of each generation—yes, and the best critics, too; for, like most excellent poets, Baudelaire, Mallarmé, Paul Valéry are also admirable critics— have gone out of their way to praise him. Only a year or two ago M. Valéry repeated the now traditional French encomium of Poe, and added at the same time a protest against the faintness of our English praise. We who are speakers of English and not English scholars, who were born into the language and from childhood have been pickled in its literature— we can only say, with all due respect, that Baudelaire, Mallarmé, and Valéry are wrong and that Poe is not one of our major poets. A taint of vulgarity spoils, for the English reader, all but two or three of his poems—the marvelous "City in the Sea" and "To Helen," for example, whose beauty and crystalline perfection make us realize, as we read them, what a very great artist perished on most of the occasions when Poe wrote verse.

Eliot, T. S. "From Poe to Valéry." In *The Recognition of Edgar Allan Poe*, edited by Eric W. Carlson. Ann Arbor: University of Michigan Press, 1966.

Like Huxley, Eliot, in this 1948 lecture at the Library of Congress, had little positive to say about Poe's writing; but by considering from the viewpoint of his French admirers, he was better able to appreciate Poe's significance.

Poe is indeed a stumbling block for the judicial critic. If we examine his work in detail, we seem to find in it nothing but slipshod writing, puerile thinking unsupported by wide reading or profound scholarship, haphazard experiments in various types of writing, chiefly under pressure of financial need, without perfection in any detail. This would not be just. But if, instead of regarding his work analytically, we take a distant view of it as a whole, we see a mass of unique shape and impressive size to which the eye constantly returns. . . . I can name positively certain poets whose work has influenced me, I can name others whose work, I am sure, has not; there may be still others of whose influence I am unaware, but whose influence I might be brought to acknowledge; but about Poe I shall never be sure.

Critical Response in the Mid-Twentieth Century

Auden, W. H. Introduction to *Edgar Allan Poe: Selected Prose and Poetry*, edited by W. H. Auden. New York: Rinehart, 1950.

British poet Auden's introduction to this collection of Poe's work was an important early indication of a change in the estimation of Poe within the English-speaking literary establishment.

Both these types of Poe story have had an extraordinary influence. His portraits of abnormal or self-destructive states contributed much to Dostoevski, his ratiocinating hero is the ancestor of Sherlock Holmes and his many successors, his tales of the future lead to H. G. Wells, his adventure stories to Jules Verne and Stevenson. It is not without interest that the development of such fiction in which the historical individual is missing should have coincided with the development of history as a science, with its own laws, and the appearance of the great nineteenth-century historians; further, that both these developments should accompany the industrialization and urbanization of social life in which the individual seems more and more the creation of historical forces while he himself feels less and less capable of affecting his life by any historical choice of his own.

Wilbur, Richard. "House of Poe." In *The Recognition of Edgar Allan Poe*, edited by Eric W. Carlson. Ann Arbor: University of Michigan Press, 1966.

The following appreciation of Poe by poet Wilbur, presented as the Library of Congress Anniversary Lecture in 1959, focuses on "Poe's fundamental subject": "the poetic soul . . . at war with the mundane physical world."

It is not really surprising that some critics should think Poe meaningless, or that others should suppose his meaning intelligible only to monsters. Poe was not a wide-open and perspicuous writer; indeed, he was a secretive writer both by temperament and conviction. He sprinkled his stories with sly references to himself and to his personal history. He gave his own birthday of January 19 to his character William Wilson; he bestowed his own height and color of eye on the captain of the phantom ship in *Ms. Found in a Bottle*; and the name of one of his heroes, Arthur Gordon Pym, is patently a version of his own. He was a maker and solver of puzzles, fascinated by codes, ciphers, anagrams, acrostics, hieroglyphics, and the Kabbala. He invented the detective story. He was fond of aliases; he delighted in accounts of swindles; he perpetrated the famous Balloon Hoax of 1844; and one of his most characteristic stories is entitled *Mystification*. A man so devoted to concealment and deception and unraveling and detection might be expected to have in his work what Poe himself called "undercurrents of meaning."

Moss, Sidney P. *Poe's Literary Battles: The Critic in the Context of His Literary Milieu*. Durham, N.C.: Duke University Press, 1963.

Moss's book focuses on Poe the critic, arguing that his opinions were formed in the crucible of the rivalries of wars of words among literary journalists of his day, conflicts to which Poe himself was a frequent contributor.

And having in general sound literary values, he condemned the prevailing notion that popularity and sales were measures of a book's worth by insisting there were standards of judgment other than those of the market place.

The efforts that Poe made to safeguard a tradition whose value it is impossible to exaggerate were absolutely necessary, but a less militant man would not have devoted a career to the task. Whatever his motives, for he was by no means entirely altruistic, his militancy is attested by the fact that for almost his entire career he single-handedly fought the two most powerful cliques in America—those in Boston and New York—which were determining that tradition. Whatever his motives, his devotedness to that tradition is attested by the fact that he persisted in his assaults (the lapses that occurred during his breakdown notwithstanding) despite the very real danger of ruin—a ruin to which he was finally reduced.

Hoffman, Daniel. *Poe Poe Poe Poe Poe Poe Poe*. Garden City, N.Y.: Doubleday, 1972.

Former U.S. poet laureate Hoffman's analysis emphasizes his personal response to Poe as a writer and a persona. His idiosyncratic writing and intuitive judgments lead him to unusual insights about Poe.

Typical of Edgarpoe. His art conceals while it reveals, reveals while it conceals. Nothing is further from his intention than to sing a simple song, or use the language of clear and common speech. These meters, rhymes, and redundancies, the portentous tone, the inflated diction, all, like the early references to musician and painter, put the actual experience at a poetic distance, impose upon it a new form, an expression completely different from that given to gross affairs like passions and hungers of the flesh, a language other than that in which this workaday world haggles over prices and orders breakfast. To explore his inward soulscape Edgarpoe had to take the vocables of the workday dialect and from such unpromising stuff create moods and meanings nc'cr attempted yet in prose or rhyme.

Critical Response in the 1980s and Beyond

Deas, Michael J. *The Portraits and Daguerreotypes of Edgar Allan Poe*. Charlottesville: University Press of Virginia, 1988.

Deas's unique take on Poe is to consider the writer's career in the context of the photographic portraits taken of him in his adult life.

The physical similarities between Poe and a character such as Usher have led at times to an unfortunate blurring of the distinction between life and art, with some readers attributing to Poe the same compulsions and maladies suffered by his fictional creations. The misapprehension is little dispelled by the author's most frequently reproduced portraits, the six daguerreotypes taken during the last eighteen months of his life—each of which depicts a worn and evidently troubled individual. The "Ultima Thule" daguerreotype typifies the matter: with its nocturnal tonality and saturnine gaze, the portrait suggests one of Poe's Gothic tales as readily as it does the sunlit daguerreotype studio in Providence where it was taken in the autumn of 1848. Moreover, later likenesses such as the "Ultima Thule" plate have provided a kind of visual credence to Rufus Griswold's defamatory description of Poe, and have been instrumental in shaping a popular image of the poet which, while perhaps satisfying the public demand for stereotypes of genius, appears to have little basis in fact.

Peeples, Scott. *Edgar Allan Poe Revisited*. New York: Twayne, 1998.

Peeples, in updating the Twayne's United States Authors series book on Poe, provides a readable critical overview that merges traditional scholarship with new approaches such as feminist criticism and New Historicism.

In considering Poe's posthumous reputation, we encounter yet another dichotomy: between the alcoholic madman and writer of immoral tales on the one hand and the devoted husband and son-in-law, the seeker of supernal beauty on the other. We might take another step back and posit a split between the shadowy pop culture icon alluded to in movies, songs, novels, and television shows and the body of work that inspires meticulous scholarly research—and endless debate, as we have seen. There are, of course, many Poes, not only because he was a kind of literary ventriloquist but because readers bring such a variety of expectations to his poems and tales. Still, Poe encourages us to think in terms not of multiplicity but of dichotomy: the self we know versus the self we don't know; everyday experience versus the reality of dreams and art; the mathematician versus the poet; the desire to reach a mass audience versus disdain for that same audience; the impulse for survival versus the impulse for self-destruction; faith in the transmigration of the soul versus fear of the "conqueror worm."

Vines, Lois Davis. "Poe in France." In *Poe Abroad: Influence, Reputation, Affinities*, edited by Lois Davis Vines. Iowa City: University of Iowa Press, 1999.

Poe Abroad is a global survey that provides ample proof of Poe's widespread popularity. In "Poe in France" Vines outlines the biographical similarities that led Charles Baudelaire to embrace Poe as a kindred spirit.

Baudelaire's "singular shock" when he first read Poe has become legend in literary history. He discovered in Poe's family history uncanny parallels with his own life and in Poe's work ideas he had already considered. Baudelaire's strong feelings of identity with Poe were based on a number of similarities. They both had lost their biological fathers at an early age and had to deal with surrogates, a stern stepfather in Baudelaire's case and a foster father in Poe's. As a consequence, their mothers played a major role in their lives, creating a source of both conflict and comfort. Although Poe had three mother figures— Elizabeth Arnold Poe (his biological mother whom he lost at age two), Frances Allan (his foster mother), and Maria Poe Clemm (his aunt and mother-in-law)—it was Clemm whom Baudelaire idolized. In the dedication to his first volume of Poe translations, he paid tribute to her: "I owe this public homage to a mother whose greatness and goodness honor the World of Letters as much as the marvelous creations of her son." Each writer sought his mother's approval and encouragement as he confronted a day-to-day existence that was resolutely hostile, or at least indifferent, to literary aspirations.

QUESTIONS FOR DISCUSSION

Poe is one of the most divisive figures in American literature. American writers have tended to think of him as "the jingle man," as Ralph Waldo Emerson called him, an occasionally ingenious but generally second-rate poet. European writers, on the other hand, are more likely to consider him one of America's greatest writers—the "finest of fine artists," as George Bernard Shaw put it. Which, if either, camp do you think is correct? How do you account for Poe's greater popularity outside his own country?

Using examples from at least two stories, discuss the importance of setting for Poe. Are there any stories where the setting can't be determined? How does the setting affect the characters' psychological states, and how do their psychological states affect the setting?

Consider the stories "The Tell-Tale Heart" and "The Masque of the Red Death" and the poems "The Raven" and "Dream-Land" in light of Poe's intention to create a "unity of effect" in his writing. Do you think he succeeds in these works? Why or why not?

As of this publication, nearly 200 film and television productions credit the works of Edgar Allan Poe as a direct source, and many more than that bear a marked influence in style and subject matter. Why has he had such an effect on popular entertainment? Identify three elements of Poe's stories that you believe have had an influence on horror and fantasy movies today.

Poe claimed in his essay "The Philosophy of Composition" that "the death . . . of a beautiful woman is unquestionably the most poetical topic in the world. . . ." Why do you think Poe believed this about the death of a woman, as opposed to an admired man or a child, or another topic entirely? Are the female characters in Poe's works fully developed compared to the male characters? Does the "poetical" effectiveness of the depiction of a woman's death depend on her being a convincing character?

Research the concept of the doppelgänger. What are some examples of doppelgängers in Poe's stories and/or poems? Why do you think this was a subject of particular interest to Poe?

Locate instances of humor in Poe's stories and poems. Do you think that he intended his tales of death, mourning, and horror to be taken completely seriously? What examples can you find to suggest that he might have been writing tongue in cheek?

Poe's C. Auguste Dupin is considered the first "armchair detective," so called because he figures out the solutions to mysteries mostly from the comfort of his own home. (Two other famous armchair detectives are Arthur Conan Doyle's Sherlock Holmes and Rex Stout's Nero Wolfe.) In "The Murders in the Rue Morgue" and "The Purloined Letter" is Dupin motivated to solve the mysteries by a desire to see justice done or by other considerations? How do his motives affect your response to him as a character?

SUGGESTIONS FOR THE
INTERESTED READER

If you enjoyed *Great Tales and Poems of Edgar Allan Poe*, you might also be interested in the following:

A Study in Scarlet, by Sir Arthur Conan Doyle. Doyle introduced the famous "consulting detective" Sherlock Holmes and his companion, John Watson, in this 1888 novel. Although Doyle readily admitted that Holmes and Watson were patterned after Poe's C. Auguste Dupin and his nameless sidekick, in *A Study in Scarlet* he has Holmes dismiss Dupin as a "very inferior fellow. . . . He had some analytical genius, no doubt; but he was by no means such a phenomenon as Poe appeared to imagine."

Lolita, by Vladimir Nabokov. Nabokov considered giving his notorious 1955 novel the title *The Kingdom by the Sea*, an allusion to Poe's "Annabel Lee," and has his narrator, Humbert Humbert, call his lost childhood sweetheart Annabel. Like many of Poe's narrators, Humbert, a pedophile and murderer, gives an unreliable, self-justifying account of his terrible behavior.

The Masque of the Red Death (VHS). Producer-director Roger Corman made seven popular movies based (somewhat loosely) on Poe's stories and poems during the 1960s, most of them featuring the actor Vincent Price. This 1964 movie is generally considered the best of them.

Low Life: Lures and Snares of Old New York, by Luc Sante. Poe, who lived in New York City for a time in the 1830s and 1840s, is only one of the many colorful personalities who pass through Sante's fascinating 1991 social history of the seedier aspects of life in the metropolis during the early nineteenth century.

The Pale Blue Eye, by Louis Bayard. In this 2006 novel Poe is an eccentric young West Point cadet who helps a detective solve a series of murders at the military college.